Jaspar's War

Jaspar's War

a novel

Cym Lowell

ROSEMARY
BEACH
PRESS

New York

Rosemary Beach Press
www.RosemaryBeachPress.com

ISBN: 978-0-9914913-0-8

Digital editions available.

ART DIRECTION: BLUE MOUNTAIN MARKETING
BOOK AND COVER DESIGN: JOHN LOTTE

Manufactured in the United States of America
First Edition

*F*OR MY DALE LYRANE

WHO SAVED ME, LOVES ME,

AND ENCOURAGES ME

WITH FAITH AND PRIDE.

SHE IS MY WARRIOR!

Jaspar's War

Chapter 1

Greenwich, Connecticut

"*POCK!*" The distinctive sound of a plastic bat driving a Wiffle ball into the outfield triggered shrieks from children as they ran and played. My ten-year-old daughter Chrissy dropped the bat and raced toward first base, actually a luminous orange Frisbee.

"Run, Chrissy," I shouted as she rounded first, heading toward second. Auburn ponytails, woven with my fingers, flew in her wake. Theo, my twelve-year-old son, played shortstop. Chrissy watched his face. "Go!" he telegraphed. I clasped my hands, hoping that she would not slide face first into base. Scratches and cuts were no deterrent when she was so focused.

It was Easter weekend, a time for relaxation and family in Greenwich, Connecticut. Neighbors, friends, and local dignitaries filled our park-like estate. We had room for a ball field where neighborhood kids could congregate. Private security personnel were out of sight.

It was an annual celebration of faith. Parents and grandparents sat all around, absorbing the beautiful sunshine and mild weather. They brought coolers of drinks, soda pop for the kids, beer and wine for the adults. It was my version of a neighborhood tailgate party. My dream of family and community had come true.

"Throw the ball," the other team yelled as the outfielder cocked his arm.

"Down, Chrissy!" Theo yelled.

Their father had taught her to ignore the ball and watch the coach.

"Your agility will always give you an edge," he said.

Small thin legs churned as the ball was launched. I cringed watching her dive. Dust flew from the infield side of the base. The second baseman caught it just as the little fingers touched safety, and the catcher's hand smacked her hip.

"Safe!" the father serving as umpire shouted, crossing out-stretched arms in exclamation.

I jumped for joy. Theo stood back, pride on his face. Chrissy brushed grass and dirt from her bottom, beaming at her brother. She gave me a thumbs up. No blood. I was relieved. Taunts from the other boys about coddling his sister only amused her proud big brother.

Neighborhood kids enjoyed the afternoon Wiffle ball game on the lawn between our pool and tennis courts. I organized the games just as I had played them as a child. My dad called it "scrub." As a player made an out, she would go to right field and the catcher moved up to bat in the prescribed rotation.

"Jaspar, when will Trevor get home?" my best friend Crystal Jamison asked about my husband. I took my seat, still reveling in the joy of observing my children care for each other. She sipped a glass of Sancerre, basking in the sun and relaxing in a rocking chair brought from the pool.

"Trevor is so good at teaching passing techniques," she said watching her own son. "Joshua will be a senior this year, so he needs to make a strong showing for college scouts. Trevor is his hero."

I remembered Trevor dropping back to pass on the sacred turf of Notre Dame Stadium in South Bend, then stepping forward to deliver his trademark bullet to a receiver streaking across the goal line to seal a national championship. The memory was so strong. I longed for him to be back at my side. Before departing, he told me of his fear that his fabled career on Wall Street had been a fraud. Our conversation had to be completed.

"*POCK!*" brought my attention back to the kids on the grass. They all raced to field the ball. Chrissy was on her way around third as the batter ran to first, the wobbly ball flying just over the head of Theo. He ran after it, looking over his shoulder at Chrissy racing toward the plate. Reaching the ball, he turned and launched a strike to the catcher, doing his best to nail her.

"Run Chrissy," I yelled rising again. She jumped on home base in triumph as the floating ball was caught too late.

"Batter up," Theo yelled as I returned to my seat.

"Trevor's on his way home from London," I answered my friend's question.

Crystal and I first met when we came to New York after college. Her husband Raymond played football with Trevor at Notre Dame. They were quite a team. A fleet, sure-handed receiver, Raymond caught the passes that Trevor threw. Trevor's career ended in a national championship game. Raymond came to New York drafted by the Jets. Trevor took an entry position on Wall Street. I dated Raymond early in college before I met Trevor or he began dating Crystal. She and I were kids just off campus coming to the big city. Neither of us had any real preparation for the strange new world. We found jobs in finance, me at the Federal Reserve on Wall Street and Crystal in a research office of a secretive private equity firm owned by an Indian tribe. Similarity of situation and background facilitated fast friendship. Her drawl from rural Georgia complimented my odd mixture of Australian Outback and Northern Indiana twang. As our husbands succeeded, we searched for a place where we could live in relative obscurity. Greenwich was perfect. Our children grew up together, like the extended family of my dreams.

"He's gone so much now," Crystal responded. "You seemed excited when he went down there. Almost as if he were answering a call to duty."

"He's been seeking European agreement for the president's stimulus plan."

Trevor took to Wall Street. He began as a runner for energy traders and became fascinated with learning to anticipate market movements. His skill expanded in a master's program at Columbia, propelling him to a position where he implemented a strategy to take advantage of an inconsistency in risk pricing. Successful exploitation brought us success.

Trevor's firm, Westbury Madison & Co., became *the* pre-eminent Wall Street investment bank, profiting whether the economy flourished or crashed due to what Trevor believed was his own strategy. When the financial world crashed, President Hamilton Henrichs asked him to lead the effort to resurrect the economy of America and the world as secretary of the Treasury, a position once held by Alexander Hamilton. The financial press criticized the appointment. "Wolf Hired to Rebuild Hen House?" asked headlines in the financial and popular press.

"I am proud of him," I answered, anxiously twisting the ever-present bangles at my left wrist. They were gifts I've treasured from my Indian friends. "He works hard and travels constantly trying to plug holes in the economic dam of the world."

Inside, far different feelings had germinated. Something was wrong. *What happened to you, Trevor?* He was distant, ignoring me in ways that I had never experienced. He seemed to avoid me. *Is he having an affair?* I wondered, fearing that a slowly ebbing sex life could be a marker of something more than job stress. *Have I become less desirable or is there something troubling in his new life in Washington that he cannot find words to tell me?*

"You seem distant, honey" I finally said as he was leaving days earlier. "Have I done something?"

"I know," he answered, with an unusual tone of resignation in his voice. "It's not you, sweetheart. Please don't think that. I'm sorry. I've discovered treachery that you may be able to understand better than me. I need your help," he blurted out, taking me in his arms with a grip that felt desperate.

"Is it something at Treasury?" I asked, relieved that his distance was due to business. But his distance troubled me. It was so unlike anything I had experienced in our life together.

"Yes, it's there and also in the White House. It's unbelievable," he answered in a voice that trembled as his hands shook. "I've been used by people I trusted. It began at the firm."

"At Westbury?"

"Yes. I've tried to piece the story together. We can discuss what to do when I return."

My relief soon gave way to fear. Trevor was afraid; I had never seen that in him. Was my intrepid hero cracking?

* * *

"HEY MOM, come pitch," Theo yelled as one player jumped into the pool. The scrub game was more fun with full teams in the field and at bat. The kids liked me to pitch because I threw softly. "Like a girl," Theo would say, happy that he could always whack my pitch. His friends tried to throw curves or fastballs with the plastic sphere with holes on one side. I learned from my dad how to pitch so the ball hung right in Theo's sweet spot. Of course, I did the same for all the kids; unfortunately I usually struck out as batter.

My father was a missionary. After my mother died when I was just three he raised me. For many years we lived in the Australian Outback. When it was time for college, we moved to South Bend, Indiana. I was the first member of my family to go to Notre Dame on a scholarship. Dad was proud. He lived long enough to express his pride. His greatest joy, he often said with breaking voice, was that I had grown as a woman of faith: "Your mother's heart would burst with thankfulness."

"Gotta go," I responded to Crystal, touching her shoulder and grabbing my mitt. Theo was the next batter. I picked up the ball as I marked my territory around the luminous strip of plastic that served as the pitcher's mound. Theo looked like pictures of my dad at the same age.

My son stepped to the plate, pointing the bat at me. "Gotcha, Mom!" he declared for the entire neighborhood to hear. I had to play the role. Glove on my knee, I leaned forward with the ball behind my back as if I were looking for a signal. I glanced at runners on base, then the batter.

"Strike the turkey out!" Crystal yelled.

"Yeah, yeah!" our friends echoed.

"Strike one!" the umpire shouted as Theo's bat slapped the back of his shoulder, so intense was the swing.

"Mom?" his lips mimed, looking at me.

"Strike two!"

The words roused cheers from parents ringing the field. Beer and wine had flowed long enough to produce a boisterous mood. Adults always lost in these games, so the prospect of me striking out the best of the kids triggered excitement.

I gripped the Wiffle ball, knowing where to place my fingers for an underhand throw. It could be a screwball, twisting into the right-handed batter, as I had done on the first strike then reversed for the second. Or, I could push the ball with my knuckles, and it would drop as he was getting ready to swing. Theo's focus was like his father's. He looked straight into my eyes, curious. I was jolted back to the moment. In throwing strikes, I had allowed my anxiety to overcome Theo's needs.

"POCK!" The sound rewarded me as the ball sailed over the head of the left fielder. Theo winked as he ran to first. It would be a home run. I had thrown his pitch. Maternal pride filled my soul.

"Yeah, Theo!" Chrissy yelled in a squeaky voice.

He also leapt on home plate in triumphant exclamation, ending the game. My boy led them all to the pool with Chrissy at his side.

* * *

AFTER THE GAME, Crystal and I organized the food brought by our friends and neighbors. Fathers and older boys unloaded tables from a rental company trailer in our driveway, arranging them in a horseshoe around the pool so we could eat and talk.

"Have you seen the kids?" I asked her when Theo and Chrissy seemed to have been absent for a long time.

"Oh, come on, calm down," Crystal responded. "What could happen here?"

We joined our neighbors at a tent erected on the ball field. One of our traditions was to have entertainment as the late afternoon set, so the children would not be so impatient for darkness and the fireworks. I had arranged with the local Mohegan tribe to have a troupe perform traditional dance routines of celebration. Crystal and I worked for many years with the tribe. Our project was developing job opportunities, which had evolved into a business of creating replicas of art, apparel, and pottery from their rich cultural heritage. Our work was gratifying and successful. Members of the troupe mingled in the crowd entertaining the kids. On stage, each child was outfitted with handmade costumes complete with colorful feathers and leather trim. Tribal artists applied face and body paints to duplicate markings from the proud history of the Mohegan people. We were all lost in the magic. It became difficult to separate child from tribal dancer.

"This is amazing?" Raymond declared, enjoying the collage of color and laughter. His career with the Jets ended suddenly when a vicious cross block broke his ribs and punctured his heart muscle. He became a youth counselor in the Greenwich school system, close to home and family.

I searched the faces of dancers and children trying to find Theo and Chrissy, ignoring the conversation surrounding me. I had not seen either since the game ended. Always in the midst of the children, they should be playing and laughing. I tried not to panic, but was failing. When the exhibition was at an end, darkness began to envelop the scene. "Crystal, they're not here!"

"Raymond, get the officers," she directed, taking my arm.

"No child has left the grounds," the head of security detail assured me, deploying his team to search. As the fireworks display began, the Greenwich police, as well as the Connecticut

State Police began checking cars, trucks, and the equipment of the Mohegan troupe. No one was allowed to leave. Backup security teams arrived as the dark sky was illuminated by a kaleidoscope of color.

I barely heard the increasingly anxious discussions of friends and security people. Chrissy did not like chaos and always curled up in my lap at such times. "Where are you, sweetheart?" I asked pacing back and forth.

Neighbors were herded onto the driveway as officers checked each person. Police cars with emergency lights blocked the entrance to our property. Flashlights illuminated fence lines as the search broadened.

"Who delivered the tables?" the senior security officer asked, trying to confirm all who had come and gone.

"I, I, I don't know," I stammered, my mind not able to focus on even a simple question.

"Where *are* they officer? They can't be hiding this long. They wouldn't run off. Who would take them?" I asked.

"Ma'am, we're trying to . . ."

"Mrs. Moran?" a man in a suit asked politely, interrupting the security officer's response. In the midst of the chaos, a dark sedan had been allowed to enter the driveway.

I was drifting into shock.

"Mrs. Moran, I need to speak to you," the man repeated gently taking my arm.

"Who are you?" the security officer asked.

"I am Peter McGuire with the FBI," he said, holding out identification. "What's going on here?" he asked, looking at dozens of flashlights sweeping grounds and trees. Neighbors stood by the garages. The Indian troupe clustered by their vehicles.

"My children have disappeared," I blurted out.

Crystal had called my priest, Father Michael O'Rourke. He was the priest in the rural Australia diocese of my childhood and my dad's best friend. When I got to Notre Dame, Father Michael was there as a youth pastor. "I am your guardian angel," he often declared. The image was an essential element of my faith. He had been present throughout my life. He came at the first hint of trouble or joy. Father Michael explained the situation as the security leader departed to check how the search was going.

Something passed over the FBI agent's face. "Mrs. Moran, is there someplace we could speak in private?"

"Let's go in the house," Crystal suggested as she and Raymond led us inside.

We stepped in the front door. The FBI officer motioned for Crystal and Raymond to sit on either side of me on a sofa.

"May I get you anything, Mrs. Moran," he asked.

"No, what is it?"

He knelt and took my hand. "Mrs. Moran, we regret to inform you that Secretary Moran's plane en route from London has apparently crashed into the ocean near Iceland. Search planes are on their way. It will take several hours. The conditions are horrendous in the remote area where the plane disappeared."

I barely heard the words. The rest of the evening was a blur. Friends took turns staying with me throughout the night. Father Michael was at my side when I awoke to the distinctive cathedral chime of my phone.

"Theo or Chrissy at last!" I said grabbing for a ray of hope. "They must have gone to a friend's house."

The chime continued. My mind cleared enough to sit up, hold Father's hand, and look at the phone.

"It's Trevor!" I blurted. His name was on the caller ID. My mind jumped to the conclusion that he was safe after all. "Thank God!"

"Honey, where are you?" I asked. *He'll take care of this.*

Long moments elapsed in silence as I pressed the phone to one ear then the other. "Trevor? Honey?"

"A text message will arrive momentarily," a mechanical voice enunciated slowly. It sounded as if the words were spoken from underwater. The connection terminated, leaving only a cold dial tone.

I looked at the phone.

"Jaspar, what is it?" Father asked, standing next to Crystal and Raymond. I looked up at each of them. Their eyes narrowed with questions. Anxiety blew through me like a chill Arctic wind.

"I . . . I don't know. The caller ID said 'Trevor Moran.' Then there was this scary voice." I startled when the chime for a text message sounded. My eyes riveted on the words:

> Your children are gone
> because you asked
> about something not
> your business.
>
> Your husband started
> to answer and is being
> digested by sharks.
>
> If what he believed
> becomes public, your
> children will also
> become ocean shit.
>
> Your silence is their
> only path to life.

Chapter 2

Six days later

HEARTACHE AND CONFUSION enveloped me. My dad would have known what to do. A few close friends and Father Michael provided emotional support as investigation of the crash, and Trevor's death, were initiated. Even with the ongoing investigation, and the knowledge from the FBI that the call and text message was traced back to the London area, there still was no word about Theo and Chrissy. "How could someone have his phone?" I kept asking. No one offered a meaningful response.

The remains of my life had the volatile elements of a media circus. The sitting secretary of the Treasury, a one-time football and Wall Street hero, was dead under suspicious circumstances. His plane was unrecoverable under miles of Arctic Ocean. Trevor's phone was taken before the flight, suggesting the crash had been planned. His children were missing, surely kidnapped. I left home only for a memorial service attended by the president, his Cabinet, and celebrities of the political and financial worlds.

What was Trevor trying to tell me? He was fearful, needing my help because of some treachery in Washington. I replayed every word of our conversation, read through files in his home study. No clues appeared.

My life was so full, then so empty. I was alone with grief and fear for my babies, living in a house under surveillance as if I were a suspect.

Sensational speculation became rampant. Cable news shows assembled teams of experts. "What's going on?" "Cover-up?"

11

"Moran Murdered to Silence Him?" all became popular headlines and trailers. I listened and read them all, trying to comprehend what had destroyed my life. That text had ordered me to be silent, but Trevor really told me nothing. There were only vague words about something he had learned that began at the firm and somehow involved the Treasury and White House. There was nothing specific. Files in his study contained only our own personal financial information. *What am I supposed to be silent about?*

Trevor's role on Wall Street, then at the Treasury, fueled belief that he was murdered to stop or facilitate the new stimulus program. The financial wizardry of Westbury Madison & Co. was linked to the economic collapse of the global economy. Most of our friends became distant as the media blitz gathered steam. Somehow, all the problems of the world related to my cherished and trusted husband. Words of support from colleagues did not quell the tornado of speculation.

Our financial records were seized by the FBI. They interrogated me about the text message. "What did you ask your husband?"

I could recall only the question of whether I had done something to push him away.

"Why did you ask that, Mrs. Moran?" the interrogator asked.

"He seemed distant. I was anxious," I answered.

"What did he tell you? The text said he answered some question of yours, about which you must be quiet or your children will become excrement."

"The note said *shit*! What are you people doing to find my children?"

"Please answer my question, Mrs. Moran."

"Trevor's only comment was, 'We can talk about it when I get home.'" I did not repeat his words about "fraud," "Treasury," or "White House." I knew nothing about the words. I had to be silent.

The interrogators went over and over the same things. Father Michael and faith were my bedrock in the continuing nightmare.

He came by several times a day. We prayed.

"What was going on, Trevor?" I asked and asked when alone, holding pictures of him and me throughout our happy lives. "What were you going to tell me when you came home, sweetheart? What happened to Theo and Chrissy? Are they dead, too? Why am I alone?" His confident, handsome face had no answer.

One morning, I wanted to hold my wedding rosary when Father Michael came to console me. It was safely stored in my mother's jewelry box, hidden away in a closet. Grasping the familiar beads, my fingers felt something strange.

"What is this?" I stammered lifting a small plastic device up to the light. "Westbury Madison & Co," was emblazoned on the royal blue surface.

"It's a memory stick," I realized, inspecting the device in the privacy of my closet. Trevor had reached out. The device had one of his trademark orange sticky notes. "Bearstrike," it said.

Of course, he would want the Chief to have this. I smiled at memories of our ties to the famous Native American investor. A stylized picture of the Chief often appeared in the financial press when stories were written of presumed triumphs of the shrewd investor. Since the tribe's finances were not public, its investment raids were shrouded in secrecy and ambiguity, a rich vein for press speculation. Comparisons were often made to the exploits of George Soros, Warren Buffett, and other such legends.

I knew him through his daughter Clemenca. She attended the nearby University of Chicago while I was at Notre Dame. We met working in outreach projects providing educational opportunity for disadvantaged people. Clemenca introduced me to her father on a visit to the tribal lands. I was entranced by his gentle manner and incisive mind, as well as his style of living in a physical world of his own creation. Years later, I introduced Trevor to the Chief, who became a trusted source of counsel. My friend Crystal worked for Chief's research office in Greenwich.

What did you leave? I wondered, turning the memory stick over and over in my fingers. My ever-present silver bangles clinked with the rhythm of my thoughts.

I went into Trevor's study so that I could pop the stick into the laptop. As I began reading the files, I felt warm for the first time since that horrible evening. It felt like Trevor and I were studying together once again. Anyone but me would find his notes accompanying the financial documents on the stick to be indecipherable.

I met Trevor at Notre Dame. I was tutor for the football team. He was smart enough, just not interested in schoolwork. My job at the time was to keep him eligible. I learned that he had a method of studying football. He made flash cards to memorize defensive formations and devise strategies that produced win after win. Coaches on both sides never understood his improvisations. "They are my keys," he explained, "which tell me what plays to call in the heat of a game."

In those early days, I was fascinated by trying to unlock the code of the ingenious system. It finally clicked. I could predict his play calling. I then organized study materials in the same manner, alternating the cards in the deck he always kept in his pocket. It became a code known only to us. His schoolwork soared along with gridiron triumph.

He used the same system as shorthand in business.

"What are you trying to tell me, sweetheart?" I mumbled reading a long series of notes on the screen. With fear and loneliness pushed to the back of my mind, I focused on deciphering his last words. I felt our deep bond in my soul as I studied what he had assembled. I could read his train of thought, but I struggled to connect it to the detailed financial records embedded in the stick. Even with my Federal Reserve training, comprehension would take time.

"Trevor?" I asked one day looking at the Leroy Neiman painting of him diving for the winning score of the Notre Dame championship. My emotional foundation was becoming faith and memories. The painting emitted a message as I looked and remembered, walking across the room to touch the vibrant colors. It was the play that ended his career. His shoulder was splintered in the third quarter. Television cameras caught the strangely dangling arm. He would not leave the game, even after defenders whacked and slammed the shattered bones. The world riveted on the gravely wounded player fighting to the last moment. Commentators expressed the amazement and admiration of millions of people watching the drama. At the goal line, the Fighting Irish trailed by five points. The clock expired as Trevor launched off strong legs with the ball snuggled in his healthy arm. The referee held hands aloft signaling the touchdown.

Trevor, propped up by Raymond, found me in the stands. "I love you," he mouthed, pointing to his heart with one hand and to me with the other. It was caught on tape and broadcast to the world.

My fingers touched the image of him looking at me. "You're communicating now, aren't you, sweetheart?" I said, closing my eyes and clasping my shaking hands to my heart.

Play with your heart; overcome your pain. Find our children. Win this game for us!

Chapter 3

"GOOD AFTERNOON, Jaspar, thank you for seeing me," said Jason Brontus, the U.S. Attorney for the Southern District of New York, as I showed him into our living room. It had been a place of enormous pride in earlier times. Crystal and I spent months studying home furnishing magazines and visiting showrooms from Fifth Avenue to the Champs Elysee when we bought our homes close together. Our friendship was sealed in the process of decorating. This once joyful, restful space had become my prison.

"Thank you for coming," I answered, happy to see a friendly face. He called moments after I touched Trevor's face in the painting and felt his message. *Is there some connection?* I wondered.

Jason was a professional friend of long standing. I had worked with the handsome Italian-American during my years at the Federal Reserve. He was with the Justice Department at the time, investigating financial crimes. I often provided technical expertise to explain transactional patterns of cases he was handling. Successful prosecutions fueled his meteoric rise. As the U.S. Attorney for Wall Street, Jason led the government's effort to police the American financial world, investigating and prosecuting executives as needed to maintain public faith in the integrity of the system. His name was synonymous with righteous vengeance.

As I lost touch with the financial world in favor of raising my children, Trevor provided similar technical input about transactional reality. He and Jason developed a respectful relationship, each providing off-the-record information to assist the other.

In the depths of fear and depression, I had not thought of Jason or criminal prosecution. Yet they were subjects emerging in the slowly dawning reality of my changed life.

"I am so sorry about Trevor and the children," he began.

He's nervous, I thought watching him perch on the edge of the couch where I invited him to sit. People usually relaxed in the comfort of the deep cushions while enjoying the view through expansive windows to the pool and manicured grounds.

"Can I get you something?" I asked.

"No thanks. Please sit," he answered, taking my hand and nodding toward the sofa close to his chair. He did not release his grip.

"Jason?" I said, sensing seriousness in his demeanor.

"I am so sorry and sad about the loss of Trevor. He was my colleague but your life," he said with a heavy voice, still holding my hand, clutching it actually. My jaws tensed trying to hold back the emotion that had been building in a torrent behind a cracking dam. "Is there anything I can do?"

"Thank you, Jason," I exclaimed, leaning into his broad shoulders as the dam breached. Grief finally racked my soul. I must have soaked his jacket with tears. He held me as if I were his sister. My father would have done the same, with patience for a broken heart.

"Theo and Chrissy?" I asked when my breathing resumed an almost normal cadence.

"Not a trace," he answered. "We have searched every conceivable avenue. They seem to have disappeared into thin air. I believe that someone is holding them. Their disappearance was carefully planned by skilled operatives."

I sat back, drying my face on the sleeve of the football jersey Trevor had presented to me on that day of triumph so long ago. I had given it to Theo, but retrieved it from his room on that worst day of my life hoping it would once again bring luck to a desperate situation. I hadn't taken it off since.

"Can I get you something," he asked, standing as I began to recover.

"No, please sit down. I'm OK. There must be no more hope. Is the search over?" I asked. "I've been expecting that. Please tell me what you know. I'm ready for the truth, whatever it may be."

"You're sure you want it straight?"

"Yes, please."

"It took a few days to find the wreckage of Trevor's plane. It was deep under the frigid waters of the Arctic Ocean. Search submarines finally reached the site. The plane had broken apart on impact. Investigators found debris scattered over a wide area, spread by high seas at the time of impact. Divers extracted the black box data recorder from the plane. They were also able to locate most of the critical engine parts, which have been brought to the surface by boats with winches," he continued.

"Trevor's body?" I asked, a small zone of hope remaining in my soul.

"I'm sorry, nothing identifiable was recovered. There are some body parts in DNA testing as we speak. I will let you know of the results."

My mind cringed at images of sharks and body parts. The strong, precious body of my hero broken and eaten, becoming the word in the message.

"You said he was lost, Jason." I chose my words carefully as I looked at the painting on the wall behind him.

He nodded.

"But if it is not confirmed by DNA testing or a body then he could have survived. Right?"

"Well, yes, but Jaspar, nothing could survive for more than a few moments in those conditions."

"What caused the crash?" I asked, beginning to suspect that his visit was for more than personal courtesy.

"The black box showed that the engines simply stopped, dooming all on board. It's strange, Jaspar. The engines appear to have been in perfect operating condition. They could fly tomorrow. The manufacturer brought a team of its own forensic mechanics to conduct the investigation. There were no fuel line or mechanical jams," he explained. "It's as if someone just turned the engines off mid-flight."

"Could it have been tampered with on the ground before take-off?" I asked, trying to understand how such a thing could happen to a U.S. government plane maintained for the country's leaders.

"That's unlikely, but it's being checked out," he answered. "It was a Pentagon jet parked at a high security military base outside London. Everything was secure from the time the plane arrived until it departed.

"I understand there was some urgency for Trevor to return. Official meetings were cancelled at the last moment. And he was coming to Greenwich, not Washington. Do you know anything about that?"

He's being clinical and looking for information, I thought. Brontus had been a trial lawyer with a prominent Manhattan law firm. His wife was a bond trader at Cantor Fitzgerald in the World Trade Center when the terrorists steered planes into the building. Pregnant for the first time with twins, she perished in the inferno. He lost interest in everything except trying to bring justice to the world. An active Tae-Kwon-Do black-belt, he was often described as menacing.

"No, the government security people just told us he would be home early," I finally answered. "If the plane did not malfunction, why did it crash?"

"Do you want my honest opinion?"

"Of course.

"I believe the crash was carefully planned, an intentional sabotage."

"In other words, you believe Trevor was murdered?"

"Yes, as preposterous as that may seem." His words reverberated through my consciousness. I had internalized that Trevor's apparently violent death and my missing children were somehow related. The press had been full of speculation.

"Why would someone want to kill him?"

"I have no idea, Jaspar," he continued. "There is no known gossip about Trevor, other than the usual jealousies of a man as rich and famous as your husband. He always seemed to walk on water. Everything he touched turned to gold."

"Then our world collapsed. He was murdered, and our children kidnapped, right?"

"Yes, I believe so. The text you received that night obviously indicates a connection between the events. It is like a ransom note, your children for your silence."

Jason paused.

"Did Trevor give you some information as that message seemed to indicate?"

Yes, he hid a memory stick in my rosaries. Should I answer? Trevor left it for me, and his friend Chief Bearstrike, not a prosecutor. The text demanded silence. Jason does know Chief, I thought recalling their introduction when Jason needed an independent, trustworthy evaluation of a financial threat to America.

"I don't have anything that I understand," I answered, honestly enough since I had not yet figured out the meaning of the information on the stick. I had given it to Crystal to deliver to Chief Bearstrike, as I believed Trevor intended.

"If you discover anything, please tell me. The political heat on this is intense," he responded. "It will get even hotter. We must find out what happened. A secure, top-level investigation has already begun. I will keep you informed."

"Of course," I answered. My researcher's instincts already understood what such an investigation would mean for me. *Our life and records will be turned inside out. I'll be a witness. There will have to be a public lynching of somebody. Who? Trevor's not here to defend himself, so he will be a convenient scapegoat? Me? The fate our children will be lost in the circus.* "What can I do?"

"Just cooperate. We'll make an official announcement of our conclusion about Trevor and the investigation in a few days. The president has asked for a briefing."

"Jason, please do not be delicate with me," I responded. "There are many questions swirling around all of this, and I'm in the middle like a target. Where will the investigation focus? The president will want to know what you think happened. He also has to make decisions. There is the economic crisis to be addressed. Choosing Trevor's successor. What will he say to the American people? He has said nothing really, other than respectful words at the memorial service."

"OK, you deserve simple candor," he responded, taking my hand again. "I will tell President Henrichs I believe Trevor was murdered and your children kidnapped. The reason must be to prevent something from becoming public. It must be something that Trevor knew or suspected. It must also relate to the current economic stimulus package rolling through Congress. We have to find out what that something is."

"What will the president say publicly? I'm not a politician, so I don't know. But if it were me, I would buy time to allow an investigation to proceed, get a better sense of what *is* going on," I said.

"I agree. The explanation could be something like 'some individual or group wanted to assure the silence of Secretary Moran. We do not yet know why, but we will stop at nothing to find out what happened and who is responsible. In the interim, I will appoint the most trustworthy financial expert in America to pick up where he left off.'"

"Who would that be?" I responded, thinking I knew the answer.

"Copper Starr."

I nodded, accepting confirmation of my instinctive thought. Starr had been Trevor's mentor at Westbury Madison & Co, and his predecessor at Treasury. I rose and walked to the windows. Sliding them open, I circled the pool and stood in the Wiffle ball field where I had last seen Theo and Chrissy.

I assumed Brontus followed, though I did not look around. My mind was far away.

"This is a mess," I began, choosing my words carefully. "There is already a firestorm of speculation in the press. Confirmation hearings for Secretary Starr will only fan those flames. He's a confidant of the president. The financial press has long speculated that he lobbied for the previous stimulus packages, benefiting him as he built Embank into the largest banking institution in the world. I can see the headlines: 'What's Going On?'

"It will be even worse than during Trevor's confirmation hearings," I continued, remembering the shrill criticism. "He was accused of the same thing."

"But Trevor's actions disproved those assertions," the U.S. Attorney responded, standing right behind me.

"Yes," I agreed, turning to look the man in the face, suddenly seeing the relationship of all that we had discussed.

"I'll get dragged into this, won't I?"

"I hope not. But if you do know anything, or have anything that could help with this investigation, it must be produced."

"You mean I could not be silent?" I answered, seeing the operative word of the message received from Trevor's phone as clear as the swaying trees on the edge of our property.

"Correct, you could not be silent in the face of official questions. But thank goodness you have nothing to provide," he answered, patting my shoulder. "I know you're scared and beside yourself with grief and fear. I understand how you feel, believe me. I wish there was something I could do beyond assuring you that the full resources of the federal government are investigating and will secure your personal safety right here. You can be sure of that."

As it protected Trevor and our innocent children?

Chapter 4

U.S. Attorney's Office, New York City
Two days later

JASON BRONTUS sipped from his ever-present coffee mug, longing for a cigar to help organize the confusion that engulfed him. Sitting around his personal conference table were the senior law enforcement officers of the United States, all reacting to the direction from President Henrichs to resolve the mysteries surrounding the death of Trevor Moran and the kidnapping of his children. Aside from the tragedy of the events, the resulting scandalous speculation delayed his economic stimulus plan, which was believed to be the key to his re-election.

"Thank you all for coming today. Among all the cases percolating in this office, the Moran affair takes the cake. It eclipses all the financial fraud and terrorism cases I've ever handled, even the internal spy cases where we had to protect national interests out of the public eye. There are several elements that need to be collectively addressed to make sure our approach in government is consistent. The president is obviously concerned about all of this," he added, looking at the White House chief of staff.

"It is my personal view that Secretary Moran was murdered," said Brontus. "Does anyone disagree with that?"

"The president requests that no such speculation be repeated publicly. There is already way too much of it in the press and all over the Web," the White House chief of staff responded.

"The elements of murder are perfectly clear," the CIA director added. "And it was an inside job at the supposedly secure airport in London. Kidnapping of the children provides confirmation. On the other hand, there is no evidence of foul play. The crash site debris is inconclusive on causation."

"I believe we are all in agreement," said Brontus. "Next, why would someone kill Moran?"

"Motive is clear enough, I think," began the FBI director. "The policies he was developing may have been popular in the market, but could have driven a stake into the heart of people with major bets on either continuing economic collapse or expansion. These are the type of people you prosecute if crimes are believed to have been committed. Such people might have been desperate enough to arrange the killing of a sitting U.S. Cabinet Secretary."

"And smart enough to do it in a manner that would be difficult to discover," the CIA director added.

"Or arrogant enough to believe they were beyond prosecution due to their own importance or connections," Brontus added. The White House official choked on that comment but said nothing.

"The next element," the FBI director continued, "is the kidnapping of the children without any known ransom demands other than the message to Mrs. Moran. It seems clear that they feared Moran may have left a trail of information. If these people would murder Moran, they would certainly kill his children."

"Or his wife?" Brontus asked.

"She is secure, I can personally assure you," the FBI director confirmed. "My best people are on site. Security is complete, including electronic monitors and 24/7 surveillance."

"All right," Brontus focused the discussion. "We will need to continue our investigations. First is the murder of Moran. Second is the kidnapping of his children. And third is to find out if there is an information trail. If so, it could lead to the parties responsible for the first two items. We will proceed on all fronts. The current responsibilities are for the FBI to protect Mrs. Moran and handle domestic matters, and the CIA to complete their part of the investigation and check out any international information sources. I will explore my U.S. financial world contacts for any leads. We can organize communications among us as usual."

"I need to report to the president," said the White House chief of staff. "He will insist on a detailed report. What shall I say?"

"Please advise President Henrichs that I, or Attorney General Sanaroff will personally report to him once we have made progress. There is nothing to report now beyond the mysteries being investigated in a cooperative manner. Answers will be forthcoming. Everyone needs to be patient," said Brontus.

"Understood," said the chief of staff. "As you all know, the media scrutiny of all of this is unrelenting. The president is ultimately responsible. If he wants to speak to the country, it will be to advise that the situation is under control as he also appoints a respected successor, which is expected to be Copper Starr."

There was a collective nodding of heads around the table.

What is the truth? Brontus wondered.

Chapter 5

JFK Airport, Long Island, New York
Five days later, on a Sunday morning

FATHER MICHAEL held my arm as we approached the Qantas ticket counter. We sat on a bench facing lines of people anxious to get on their way for long trips. Passersby were respectful, thinking that we were a priest and nun awaiting a flight to some distant mission.

When I arrived at the church that morning to teach my Sunday school class, the Secret Service escort left me with Father. They would be waiting at the end of the service. Father had a nun's habit for me. I changed quickly. Crystal cut my hair into a burr as she did her boys for the summer then arranged my headdress with black wimple and beads and removing any trace of makeup. She placed a rosary with a small puffy heart blending into the hard, round beads around my neck. It had Trevor's declaration upon his victory inscribed, *I Love You.* "The files are on a chip in there, if you need them. The stick is in the Chief's hands as Trevor wanted," she advised.

The discussion with Jason Brontus left me numb for several hours. When Father Michael arrived later, I knew that I could not sit meekly by enduring an investigation and media blitz that would ensnare me and assure the permanent loss of my children. I had to find my own game. My only asset was that the monsters who killed Trevor and took my babies were afraid of something in my possession that could wreck their plans. It must be what Trevor recorded in the stick.

If I disappear then Theo and Chrissy will be kept alive to ensure my silence.

I recalled the discussion with Father.

"I agree," he said. "If you disappear, your enemies will fear that you do, in fact, know something. They will hunt you down to make sure you are silenced. On the other hand, your absence will ensure life for your children. They are your leverage."

Within days he reported that arrangements had been made. I became apprehensive. "If I disappear now, it will only add fuel to the media fire," I objected, envisioning how the new twist would be played in the press. "Where did she go? To join her family after the scam? Where are they? What did they run away from?"

Father listened patiently to the questions. "Why do you care what anybody thinks, Jaspar?"

I had no answer.

"What would Trevor do if he were the survivor?"

"He would find a way to save our children."

"Yes, he would."

"You have two assets now. One is the memory stick," Father said taking my hand as if I were a penitent, which I was at that point. "The other is yourself."

"Me? What kind of asset is that?"

"You have heart and soul, my sister. You must take charge of your destiny, just as you always encouraged Trevor to do. If you must be a warrior, you are capable of being that or anything else. You just need time and coaching."

"Where will I get these things ?"

"I will put you in the hands of someone whom I have faith in and who you can trust. He will take you away. Bring just what you need for two days of travel plus a credit card and your cell phone," he directed. "No identification or passport."

"Who is it?" I asked when we were on our way. He responded by taking my hand. "Will you be in trouble for this?" I asked, fearful that he would somehow get connected to this cancer that had infected my life.

"Only you and I know, child," he answered with a gentle pat to my knee. "My lips are sealed and you will be beyond contact. I will return to the sanctuary before the Secret Service escort notices that you are not around to be taken home."

* * *

As WE SAT on the bench, I felt Father searching the crowd looking for someone. I did the same, diverting anxiety about my life and destination.

I noticed a man standing by a concrete post opposite the ticket counter. He seemed relaxed, resting with a foot braced on the wall. His skin was the color of coffee. Dark curls spilled over his ears and forehead, giving him the appearance of an impish child. A cup of Starbucks was in one hand with a muffin resting on its top. He seemed to break off a bite for himself, then drop a piece on the floor without a glance downward. His lips moved as morsels fell. No one was near him. *Who is he talking to?* I wondered. There appeared to be no Bluetooth or other device near his face.

He stood about my own height of five feet six inches. A soft leather jacket stretched across broad shoulders, covering a blue and white rugby shirt with lettering that I could not read. A tight waist tapered down to well-defined legs. The man had the quiet, confident bearing of a champion, like Trevor.

A worn bag lay at his feet on the concrete floor. Muffin bits fell into it. There was barely discernible movement. *What is it?* I wondered

A yellowish, brown head arose from the leather satchel. It looked up at the man, who seemed to nod in our direction. The dog twisted around, looking straight at me. It stood, coming to about the man's knees. She emerged and began walking toward me with her tongue hanging out, pausing to allow people to pass. Children stopped to pet and hug her as the man assured parents that the canine was friendly. He knelt as the youngsters drew their own crowd of onlookers. The dog accepted their affection, even rolling on its back for tummy rubs. The man's green eyes never deviated from my own. He and the dog seemed so natural with the children, patiently blending in as if they were all old friends.

Then the dog sat in front of me. A paw rose to touch my knee and she inched closer. She placed her head on my clenched hands. In her eyes, I saw the faces of my innocent children. Images of Chrissy and Theo flooded my consciousness. Pent-up emotions bubbled. Tears welled. Almost choking, I bit my lip trying to remain composed. Father clasped my hands and the dog's paw.

"Meet Alice," he said.

What! my mind screamed, head snapping around. "You know this dog?"

"Indirectly, yes."

"It belongs to that man?" I asked, looking up to see the curly headed man stepping toward us.

"Yes."

"And you know him as well?"

"The same as Alice. His name is Nulandi. They came to take you to a safe place in their homeland in Australia, where we once lived with your father. They will prepare you for the path to recover Chrissy and Theo," Father added.

"Australia?" I asked. Images of earlier life in the Outback flooded my mind, producing a sense of peacefulness. *Those were happy times.*

He nodded, patting my shoulder.

I leaned forward to caress Alice. She licked my arm. The warm touch was comforting.

"Mrs. Moran?"

I looked up into the face of the man who had been feeding Alice moments earlier. His voice was hoarse and gravely.

"I am Nulandi. Father here says that I need you as you need me."

I had no words. Touching the dog and looking to Father I must have seemed a trusting novice seeking divine guidance at an altar.

"This is your path, child," Father explained. His confirmation that my disappearance would preserve my babies' lives echoed in my mind. Images of their expectant, trusting faces had become my mainstay.

Alice leapt into my lap. Father recited a homily from my childhood. *I could see Trevor standing with Chrissy and Theo off in the distance. My dad stood just behind, touching Trevor's shoulder where grit had overcome physical weakness. Dad pointed at me with one finger and touching his heart with the other, as Trevor had so famously done.*

"Prepare me?" I asked. "What do you mean?"

The strong man knelt in front of me, opening the valise which contained a soft towel and water pouch for Alice. The dog slid off my lap, snuggling into travel mode. Zipping the bag, the curly-headed man sat on haunches gazing into me, offering his hands with palms up.

"Ma'am, I understand that war has been declared on you. Enemies murdered your husband, stole your children, and threatened certain death for them and yourself if you speak," he said. It felt like Trevor explaining strategic choices.

"And?"

"You have a choice. Stay here and passively let life evolve as it will."

"Or?"

"Put your oppressors on the defensive when you disappear, becoming a warrior on attack to find their weak spot."

Who is this man? Why is he here? I wondered looking at Father, who simply nodded.

"Warrior?" "Me?" I asked placing my hands in his still outstretched grasp. "I am a mother and housewife. How can I go on the attack?" I looked at Father who had used the same word to describe what I must become.

"Do you want to hold your children alive again?" he asked.

I nodded.

"Then, we can help. Alice and I are commandos. We can teach you to hunt, kill, extract information, live on nothing, deceive, and confuse. You will be the keystone of our team. Without you, it all falls down. You are the bait for these sharks."

My heart went cold, as did by ability to speak. Our eyes locked. I numbly nodded again.

"Then, you must learn to do what we do. Anything can and will happen where we are going."

"To get my children?"

"Precisely," he answered lifting me as if I were weightless.

"What do you see out there?" he asked, pointing out the window.

"Nothing."

"Is your life in this place where there is nothing?"

"No. It is with my children," I answered, "wherever they are."

"Look in Alice's eyes," her master said, unzipping the bag and lifting the dog's head. I knelt and looked closely. Her breath was warm, as her tongue touched my face. "What do you see there?"

"Bright light."

"What does it mean?"

"Readiness, confidence."

"Yes, which you will have."

Alice snuggled back into her bag. "Why are *you* doing this for *me*?" I asked.

"Do you remember Sister Ismerelda from the orphanage where your father served and you spent your childhood?"

The name triggered a flood of memories. She had been the Mother Superior at St. Benedicta's, where my dad and Father Michael served. In many ways, she had filled the void left by the death of my mother at such a young age.

"She is my sister. We were separated at birth. It is a story I will explain when there is time, not now. Father played a role in our finding each other. It saved my sister's life," he said touching his belly. "And it filled a void in mine. What you need is something I am destined to provide, as Father did for us."

I would later learn of another connection through Chief Bearstrike.

"It's God's path, child," Father said, handing my credit card and cell phone to the man. *Why does he want these?* I wondered.

Once again, I took Nulandi's hand to rise. Father turned to leave. I touched his shoulder. "Michael, thank you. We must both be safe," I said, accepting his embrace.

"I will be with you," he whispered. "It is God's will." The words rang in my mind, watching the only person I could truly trust walk away.

Why is God doing this to me? Is it a trial? Let's go!

Chapter 6

Over the Pacific

WE SAT in spacious first-class seats. Alice lay in the bag at Nulandi's feet without sound or movement.

"How is it possible?" I asked between Aboriginal stories that seemed to be inexhaustible in his repertoire. They began as we boarded, from the ticketing area at JFK to our plane, continuing whenever I was awake.

"She has been trained from birth to be my accomplice," he answered. "Alice is like a part of me."

Nulandi talked about his sister Ismerelda and my life in the Outback.

"How do you know about when I lived in Australia?" I asked.

"Your priest and my sister were together, remember? They stayed in touch, eventually reuniting Ismerelda and me. In your hour of need, you turned to him and he to her. I am also thorough in preparation. I've learned everything I can about you and will continue to do so. It is my nature and my job. Surprises are deadly in my business."

"You mean more than just my history, right?"

He assented with his eyes.

"Like can you trust me when the chips are down?" I asked, recalling Trevor's words about his linemen or colleagues in business.

"You understand."

I nodded. "Does the dog's name come from where we seem to be going, near Alice Springs?"

"Yes, she is the third of my dogs named Alice."

"You are part of each other, like in those stories?" I asked. His stories were about the bonding of man, beast, and nature, all inspired by a divinity I never understood. I always thought such belief to be pagan. As he spoke, it seemed natural, as if the rituals of my own church concealed a far simpler belief in a God of nature rather sunlit with hope.

When he was not talking, Nul looked out the window with hands clasped in his lap. He did not seem to sleep. I did for long periods, feeling safe for the first time since my life had been broken. We did not talk about the mess left behind. I often touched the rosary at my neck, with its tiny platinum heart and encryption. I found Nulandi's presence comforting, as if some semblance of Trevor and my father were alive in me.

He was often quiet as if in touch with something beyond himself. He had a tablet of drawing paper in his lap. "What are those lines?" I asked, as he drew intricate designs on page after page.

"It is my way of focusing."

"You can read them?"

"Sort of. As I draw, my mind parses what I know about your situation and what we need to do. I feel meaning, yes."

"You are feeling your way to a plan for me?"

"For us three, yes."

"It is in those lines?"

He nodded.

"Can you tell me?" I asked.

"First step is to get situated and begin."

"Begin what?"

"The path to your children."

"What is it?"

"Here," he answered, pointing to swirling, concentric lines on the tablet. "I understand your need for details. You are entering my world. It is different than anything you have known. Your instincts will evolve. Your children are safe for now," he said, tapping the epicenter where the circles converged.

"They are there?" I asked.

"I believe so."

"Your point is that layers surround them?"

"Exactly! You are perceptive, as your priest suggested," Nul responded. "There will be many layers of carefully designed camouflage to get through before we reach your children.

"We need to prepare. Be patient, observe, and learn to react. The training may seem odd to you, even brutal and heartless," he said, patting my arm in reassurance.

In those moments, I could not imagine the groundwork he was laying in me for the future.

"Is Alice OK?" I asked, giving up reconciling his words with my life experience. "She has not moved in hours."

Nul pushed the bag between my feet. I reached in, touching warm, coarse hair. Her licks were comforting. When I slept, my feet rested on her, like a foot warmer.

"What do you know about me?" I asked after a while.

"General details, provided by the priest. Background information about your husband assembled for me," he answered. "As we proceed, I will learn what I must about you in order to design our path." He turned to look at me directly. His eyes were kind, his demeanor confident.

"Our team will be just you, me, and Alice at least until our bait is taken. That is our first step. We will adapt from there. I must know you and you me, which will commence when we land. From that knowledge will emerge trust between us"

"What do you mean by *bait*?"

"We need to discover who holds your children. They are held to enforce your silence. When the enemies learn of your disappearance, they will search for you. We need for you to be the attraction that draws them to where we can engage on our terms."

"Do you think my children are alive in there?" I asked pointing to the epicenter of the drawing.

"Yes."

"How do you know?"

"I feel it."

"You trust your feelings?"

"Yes, it is how I survive. I always believed no one would take care of me."

His words did not immediately register on my consciousness. "So these circles are the layers through which we need to entice the people holding Theo and Chrissy?" I continued, drawing my finger across the circles.

"They will come for you. This time, they must make sure you will be silent for good."

"And my children?"

"When you are silenced their lives are just another risk for their mission. At that point, they serve no purpose and will be disposed of. The risk is that they are discovered or escape."

My fingers clutched my rosary, pulling it tight. I reached for his arm, which he allowed to rest in my lap. My heart calmed.

"I hope you come to learn that there are people who will care for you as you do them," I finally said. "Please tell me your story. Who are you? Father trusts you and I trust him. But I need to know you as you do me."

"I understand," he answered, taking a long sip of water from the large squeeze bottle he carried and refilled frequently. "I am an unwanted bastard who was trained to kill on command for almost thirty-five years beginning from before I had body hair."

The cold words reverberated in my soul. He said them simply, almost as if he were in a confessional. The expression and candor were disarming. I had never heard such words spoken as matters of simple fact and history. I looked into his eyes.

"You are a kind man. You love dogs and secure the safety of children—I saw you in the airport. How can this be?" I asked, tightening my grip on his strong forearm. He turned to face me, placing his fingers on top of mine.

"My mother was a native, called an aborigine by white people in my homeland. My father was a Swedish shepherd. In those times, state policy dictated that half-breed children be taken from their mother to protect the purity of the dominant race."

I had read of such policies. *He never knew a mother's love, like me. We are similar in that regard.*

"I was raised on an army base. I knew nothing except the job I was trained to do."

"To kill for that same state?" I asked.

He nodded, looking into my eyes. I saw an innocent little boy there. *An unwanted bastard? A mindless killer? Is this what I must become?*

"What does it feel like to kill?"

For the first time, he bowed his head. I lifted his chin. There were tears welling in his eyes.

"Nulandi, tell me, please."

"Nothing," he said. "I felt nothing for a long time, as if I were a machine doing a job. It was all I ever knew. Love was not an emotion within me. How could it be?

"Ismerelda found me. I did not know that I had a sister. She was dying from kidney disease. In the orphanage where she had been raised there was a record of when she had been brought in as a baby. There was a note that she had a twin brother. She was later sent to become a novice in a convent in the Philippines. The church wanted to remove such children to a different environment. She was trained, mature, and returned to the orphanage.

"It was the beginning of my life when my kidney gave her strength to do so much good," he said.

I wiped tears from his cheeks. "How did she find you?"

He looked up, biting his lip. "It was the Vietnamese family. I had taken them first to the orphanage."

Huh? I wondered, searching my memory of our talks for any clue about the people he spoke of with simple familiarity as if they were friends of mine as well. "Vietnamese family?"

"Oh," he stopped sensing the need to explain. "They are people I saved during the war there. They helped me. It cost the life of their father. I knew of the orphanage at St. Benedicta where we are going. I arranged for them to be taken from Vietnam on a military transport. The Sisters at St. Benedicta took them in. It was a safe place, a long distance from the homeland they had to leave.

"Several years later, I found a vineyard where they could work in Italy. Other Vietnamese joined them there. It was a special project for me. You will meet them," he said, tapping the concentric circles on his tablet, "if our plan works."

I nodded, hoping to see a connection. "Was your sister there when you delivered these people?"

"Yes," he answered. "But I did not know of her or that she had been brought there as a baby when I was taken to a different place. Apparently, she told them her story, as I am telling you now. She spoke of her dreams of a twin. When she got sick, there was no donor of her rare blood type. No family record existed to lead to a matching relative. Only the notation of a twin.

"The Vietnamese people remembered a similar story I must had told them about feelings of having a twin sibling. They contacted me, asking if I could come to the orphanage for a visit. When I arrived, there was a test. Our matching DNA confirmed our lifetime visions of one another." Nul's voice broke as he explained their reunion.

"That is wonderful. You were lost to each other and then found," I responded, touching his shoulder. Images of Theo and Chrissy filled my heart, bringing tears to my eyes. We both struggled to maintain composure.

"You mean that you were alone in life with dreams of one another?"

"Yes, and the dreams came true."

"Like the hope I have for my children?" I asked, feeling kinship with this quiet man.

"I hope so. The transplant of my kidney was successful. For the first time in my life, I felt love and kindness. My sister had obviously become a Christian. I joined her. I had served my time and resigned from the army. I had no identity in the outside world. I still do not," he explained, regaining his composure.

"How old are you now?" I asked, thinking he was too young to have served in Vietnam.

"I am 52. My life as a commando started at about age 12. I met the Vietnamese in 1972 when I was 16.

I nodded, patting his arm, perhaps understanding Father Michael's faith in the man.

"And now, what do you do?"

"I do what I was trained to do for hire. The money supports Sister's order and the convent that arose from the old orphanage. And the Vietnamese family in Italy. I travel the world using assumed names. It is easy with my history and network of people."

"What network?" I asked, trying to comprehend what was being communicated in words and emotion.

"During my time in the army I made many friends who now do what I do around the world. We often work together. I also saved many people from harm's way, getting them to places where they could survive in safety. They've become my extended family."

"You were trained to be a commando, but there was kindness in your soul that matured into giving life to the sister you never knew you had?"

"Yes, ma'am, that is me as I sit here next to you."

"Back there in the airport, you quoted Father Michael to say that you needed me as much as I need you."

His head bowed again. "Yes," he mumbled as I felt his heart race.

I unbuckled my seatbelt, taking the hulk of a man in my arms as I did my own children when they needed me. "Tell me, please."

"I . . . I . . . can only imagine the loss my mother felt when we were taken from her. We have no idea what happened to her. Or my father. There is no record. Maybe if I help you, I can in some way bond with them."

"Oh my God," I whispered in his ear, chanting a rosary of prayer for us both. *Never to know the love of a mother or a father, just institutions, taught to kill without mercy. What would that do to a child?*

"Thank you, sister."

"We need each other. I hope to teach you as you teach me," I said, not really knowing what he could learn from me. "What does your name mean?"

"The names of our people are symbolic. 'Nulandi' means faith. There is a legend of our people called 'Blue Fish and the Moon.' It is a story of two men. One was miserable seeing only the dark side of life. The other, Nulandi, saw light in life and was happy. When the miserable man died, he became a blue fish living for a time at the bottom of the sea until he was eaten by a bigger fish. Nulandi went into the sky to live with the Great Spirit, who turned him into a round and shining moon to turn the darkness of the night into silvery light.

"People on earth knew that when light fades, Nulandi the moon would grow again. Just as their spirits might die for a little while, then come to life and live forever."

I could not speak for several moments. *The moon spirit who provides light in the dark. Light for me?* I felt as if God were explaining to me why He delivered me to this odd man. I held Nul's hand, just looking at him.

"Like your namesake, do you see light in the dark of our mission?"

"It is my nature."

"For yourself or my children?"

"We are together."

His words echoed through my mind. The horrors of his life were beyond my comprehension. *What else is there about this man that will surface?*

"You said there is no record of your identity?"

"No official record. I do not exist in the world."

"May I call you Nul, which means faith to me. You have faith in our future, and so do I."

"I will call you Jas, three letters for each, meaning we are equal on this team."

"Alice must be senior as she has five letters in her name."

"Fair enough." The valise wiggled.

* * *

THE LONG FLIGHTS, with stops in Auckland and Sydney, came to an end in Alice Springs. *What awaits me out there?* I wondered looking out the window at the dry countryside. Pink parrots arose from the trees as we landed. Bright sunshine seemed to enhance their vibrant colors. Father Michael had given stuffies to Theo and Chrissy that looked identical.

An omen?

Chapter 7

Monte Carlo Casino

THE ELEGANT man stepped gracefully from his custom built red Ferrari.

"Good evening Monsieur Tremont," the liveried doorman said opening the door for the famous Formula One driver. A frequent visitor to the grand casino located across the yacht basin from his villa adjacent to the grounds of the Grimaldi family, Henré Tremont was a featured attraction. Whenever paparazzi reported his presence, fans flocked to the glorious gardens and fountains of historic Casino Square. There was no need to advertise though, especially when he was expected to win the Monaco Grand Prix to become the unquestioned racing star of all time.

Tremont surveyed the crowd as it surged forward. His dazzling smile graced popular magazines the world over. At five feet eight inches in height, and no more than one hundred fifty pounds in weight, he had the ideal size for a championship race driver. He brushed back his jet black hair with a casual pass of his hand. It curled around his ears and along the nape of his long neck. Bright grey eyes highlighted a rakishly handsome face, which always seemed to be in need of a shave. Dark hued, flawless skin beamed with vitality.

Fans touched his broad shoulders and held out pictures and programs, he headed toward the adjacent Hôtel de Paris talking and signing as he went. He moved like a leopard, the result, perhaps, of Olympic quality gymnastic routines. His consort for the evening stood amidst her own entourage. Amelia George had just arrived from a festival in Cannes where she received top honors for two movies nominated for Oscars in Hollywood. They were both hot topics for the media, which scurried for position to photograph the couple arriving together. Headlines would breathlessly declare more love in the offing for the icons.

The world-famous grand prix driver was inevitably compared to Sean Connery and Omar Sharif. He reveled in the attention with an enthusiasm that also fueled his determination to be champion.

As Henré reached for Amelia's hand, the crowds made way. The regal couple posed as flashes flared around them like spotting halos. He smiled, looking forward to a joyful evening with not a care for the trouble brewing in another identity that seemed to be more out of control than he was accustomed to allowing. "For tomorrow," he responded when briefed by the coterie of skilled experts about the continued stall in his quest to unleash a tsunami on the finances of the West.

"Time to go. I've missed you," she whispered.

* * *

Westerham, Kent, England

"Your parents will be along in a few days," the polite man said to Theo and Chrissy.

"Where are we?" Theo asked, a little groggy from awakening from seemed like a nap. It had lasted for several days. They sat at a table on a patio overlooking a lovely garden, full of flowers and trimmed hedges. A swimming pool shimmered from the lights turning on in early evening.

"You are in Greenwich, a short distance from your home. A situation arose where we needed to take steps to protect your family,"

"A situation? What kind of situation?" Chrissy asked.

"My name is Gordon Blair. I am a security officer. You are familiar, of course, with the work we do for your family since your father became a secretary."

"Yes, sir," Theo responded. "Your job is to protect us, though you are always behind the scenes in our lives."

"And many of your officers are good at video games and baseball," Chrissy added.

"Your father was on his way home from London when the party was underway. There was a threat. We brought you here from the party. Your parents are in Washington."

"Dad got home OK?" Theo asked.

"Yes. He is being debriefed for security purposes."

"At least you brought my clothes and my stuffy," Chrissy said clutching her teddy bear, and satisfied with the explanation. When they awoke in separate rooms, there was a drawer filled with their own clothes. The Native American costumes neatly folded on a dresser.

"When will mom and dad come to take us home?" Theo asked. Security arrangements were nothing new for the family. Even before Trevor's government service, their wealth required that precautions be taken. The same was true for most of his schoolmates in their neighborhood in Greenwich.

"In a few days. You have only been here a short time. Your father returned early in the morning then they went down to DC," Blair explained.

"How long did we sleep?" Theo asked. It felt as if he had slept for a long time, but he remembered nothing after putting on the handmade Indian costumes.

"Are my friends OK?" Chrissy wondered, clutching Phred as she reached for a glass of orange juice.

"They are all fine. We took everyone home and made sure they were comfortable. It was all very routine. Everyone understands the importance of your father's position."

Chapter 8

St. Benedicta, Alice Springs, New South Wales, Australia
A month later

"YOUR CHILDREN have disappeared from the face of the earth. All paths of inquiry have been exhausted, including my friends in military and intelligence research posts," Nul reported as we sat in a quiet corner of St. Benedicta, which had become a home for abused and abandoned women and children. Nul had provided funding for a complete remodeling of the stone buildings, including computers and electronic data systems that were used to provide life skills to residents.

Nul and Sister Ismerelda had prepared me for this discussion. After we arrived, Sister became my spiritual friend. There was so much need at St. Benedicta. I was soon immersed in caring for children and helping women become self-sufficient.

Nul loved to run and work out. I enjoyed learning his routines. At first, it felt like he was coaching me, as Sister did in her own way. Then he was absent for about ten days.

"He's on a race car team in Europe," she advised. "He loves to compete as a substitute driver, even for champions. He also touched sources for information about Chrissy and Theo."

Alice moved to my side. "Oh my God! Are you trying to tell me they're dead?" My heart pounded.

"Nothing of the sort. To the contrary," he answered, touching my knee with one hand and Alice with the other. "I am certain they are safe as we initially thought. Your absence will ensure that status quo, wherever they are being kept. Our goal is to find that place and return them to your arms. Our enemies obviously want to silence or kill you."

"How do you know?"

"While there is no word about your children in the public or intelligence worlds, there are rewards offered for you in my world."

"For me? Why?"

"The reason is surely to enforce the message you received at the beginning of this tragedy—maintain your silence. Your enemies want it to be permanent."

"By killing me."

"Yes."

"Then my children."

Nodding, he and Sister Ismerelda each laid a hand on my shoulders. I hugged Alice. My new family providing support. "Since they do not have you, or know where you are, the only leverage they have over you is the children," Nul explained.

"That is good news," Sister Ismerelda added. "It means your children are safe."

I just listened. Their confidence was reassuring.

"There is also movement in another direction that I suspect we will find to be connected to the murder and kidnapping," Nul continued. "The global economic mess is being attributed to a conspiracy, which is said to have been orchestrated by your husband before he went to the American Treasury. The name given to the conspiracy is 'West Mad,' a contraction of the name of his firm Westbury Madison & Co."

It took a moment to focus on the implications of his words. "That's absurd. Trevor could never have done any such thing. Why would he? He had everything already," I responded looking from one to the other, still holding Alice. Their faces were blank, measuring my reaction.

"Could he have been misled, or deceived, by someone he trusted?" Nul asked.

"I suppose so, yes. He was only human like the rest of us. Why do you ask?"

"Does the name Copper Starr mean anything to you?"

"Yes, he was the man who brought Trevor into that firm after graduate school. He also recommended Trevor to succeed him at Treasury. He was Trevor's hero and his friend," I responded. *Jason Brontus also talked about Copper.*

"His name and face are all over the financial press. Your American president is hailing him as the potential savior of the world's economic system. Starr is championing another round of economic stimulus, which some call a bailout for the banks that nearly broke the system with their greed," Nul added, picking up a remote control for a television that sat nearby.

"Is there news of my children?"

Ismerelda scooted close to me, putting an arm around my shoulders.

"Not yet."

"What is it then?" I asked, watching Nul insert a disk into the television's DVD player.

"A recording of a hearing at which this Mr. Starr appeared before some official committee of your government," he explained fast-forwarding through what looked like news commentary.

"Wait. Stop!" I shouted, seeing pictures of me on the screen, then Trevor, Theo, and Chrissy.

Nul rewound the frames. A famous news anchor was talking about Starr at the Senate hearings on the stimulus package. The pictures of us were in the background, as if we somehow provided context for the discussion.

"The hearing room is standing room only. As the world knows, the prior Treasury secretary died in a tragic plane crash, followed by the disappearance of his children, and then his wife. Specula-tion about the meaning of these events has been intense. Are they alive or dead, and, if alive, why did they disappear? Who took them?" the anchor intoned as the pictures of us streamed across the screen.

"U.S. Attorney Jason Brontus has stated that breaks in the case are imminent, though he provides no details," the commentator continued as a picture of Brontus appeared in the background.

A picture of the president appeared. "The global economy has been in a precipitous downward spiral. President Henrichs suffers the lowest popularity ratings in history. There is even speculation that he could pull an 'LBJ' and declare that he will not stand for re-election or accept a draft by his party. Rather, he would focus on doing his job without regard to re-election.

"The president's solution is a third round of stimulus spending to shock the U.S. economy back to life, creating jobs, confidence, and growth. Trevor Moran shepherded the plan through Congress prior to his death. A replacement Treasury secretary has not yet been nominated.

"The hearing today is hoped to spur the completion of the ratification of the stimulus plan in the Congress. The lead witness is Copper Starr, Chairman and Chief Executive Officer of EmBank, the world's largest bank measured by deposits. The colossus was built following his long tenure as secretary of the Treasury preceding Trevor Moran.

"The galleries are full reflecting the need for dramatic action to save an economy viewed by many to be about to fall off a cliff."

The picture shifted to the witness sitting at a table behind banks of microphones. "Doesn't Copper Starr look grand?" the anchor asked his fellow commentators. "He could be cast by Hollywood for roles requiring experience, dignity, and success. Look, he sits alone, no phalanx of lawyers and note takers. He knows what he's doing."

"Thank you Senator Douglass and colleagues," Starr began in a booming, confident voice. "There are two essential approaches to stabilize our economy and provide jobs for our people. At one end of the spectrum is a policy to allow weak institutions to fail in the vicissitudes of the free market. Without public support, this will surely happen on a broad scale. In my opinion, this will only prolong our economic wilderness.

"The other and more appropriate response is to prime the pumps of recovery with further injections of stimulus, via government takeover of bad loan portfolios. This will free banks to resume loan programs to fuel growth, jobs, and renewed economic expansion, all of which feed on each other," he stated with calm confidence.

The picture shifted back to the newscaster. "After stating his support of the president's proposal, Starr was asked about the mysteries surrounding Trevor Moran and his family." Another clip of us appeared on the screen.

"We all miss Trevor. He was a fine man and a skilled investment banker," Starr answered. "As you know Senator, Mr. Moran was my successor at Westbury Madison & Co. His death and the strange disappearance of his family haunt us all. There will be an explanation, which, I am certain, the U.S. Attorney will provide shortly. In the meantime, I am confident that Secretary Moran would have agreed with my assessment of need for the president's plan. We always thought alike."

Tears streamed down my cheeks as the newscaster returned to the table full of commentators for their pontifical assessment. Nul switched the television off.

"We are just old news," I finally blubbered. "Our fate is just a curiosity, now almost forgotten. Thank you for showing me these clips. It certainly puts our importance into perspective."

"Speculation is that this man wants to be head of the U.S. Treasury again. Why would he want that?" Nul asked.

"Maybe to help the nation in its hour of need?" I offered. "Why else?"

"It's not our concern, other than providing context for where our reality is," he began. "The American public may have moved on from the fate of you and your family, but our enemies have not. As I said, there are serious bounties offered for information that could lead to you."

"From the United States?"

"Not from the government, but from private sources, and in several countries. Our adversaries are obviously anxious to find you. Word on the street is, 'Big money for disappeared widow of former Treasury secretary. She must know something of value.' The amounts are enormous, in the tens of millions."

"Enough to endow our orphanage," Sister said, smiling as she patted my arm.

"What about my children? Are they hunted?" I asked, touching the cool skin of his arm.

"No."

"Because they are held?"

"Correct," Nul agreed. "Surely by the people offering bounty for you."

"Who are they?"

"No clues yet" he answered, speaking slowly, probably sill gauging my reaction. "I believe they are connected to your husband and this West Mad."

"Why do you think that?" I asked

"You believe your husband could not have orchestrated the economic collapse for his own benefit, right?"

"Of course!"

"Then why would the world jump to that conclusion?"

"Because he died in a strange manner and his family disappeared," I answered. "Or because it serves someone's interests and Trevor is not around to defend himself."

"Who would benefit from that, Jas?"

"Those who actually caused the collapse, I guess," I answered, the light starting to go off in my mind. "Oh, you're trying to explain that whoever caused the collapse knew that Trevor had discovered the truth and had begun to take steps to make it right." *That is what he was trying to tell me. What we would talk about on his return. And proof is on the stick. That's what I could not connect before I left.*

"That is why I think these events are all related," Nul

continued. His countenance reflected an understanding that the connections were being made in my mind. "In any event, when we find out who these people are, the path to your children will be direct. And I'm happy to report that we've begun to smoke them out."

"What have you done?"

"Do you ever remove those bracelets?" Nul asked without answering my question. "You touch and twist them so often, like now, when you are focused."

"These?" I asked, touching the silver bangles. "At least one is always on my wrist."

"You seem to touch them like a talisman of something."

"That's right, I do," I responded, pleased that he was watching me so closely. "They've been given to me over many years. The original came from Ismerelda, actually," I said looking at her, and rewarded with a smiling nod. "The symbol here is of the four directions of life," I added pointing to the crest.

"Each one has a symbolic meaning, given to me by the native people I love working with. My collection seems to grow. It feels like friends watching over me."

Nul nodded with a smile, touching the crest of each as he clasped them together. "We will need all the positive karma we can get, but Jas, it is time to put them away. They are jewelry. Where we are going, there will be room only for guile and weapons."

I was stunned.

"I will hold them for you," Sister Ismerelda offered.

My heart skipped a beat or two as I removed each in turn, kissing the symbol and handing them to Sister. "Nul, I am ready to move on. What have you done to prepare us?"

"Remember the credit card you provided to the priest?"

I nodded.

"We had a friend use it at an ATM machine. The area has been under intense surveillance in the interim," Nul explained. "It confirms our belief that you are a valuable prize."

"What will you do now?" I asked, seeing the focus in his eyes intensify. Alice even seemed to be paying more attention, lifting her head from my lap as if sensing change in the tone of conversation. I did not feel anxiety about Chrissy and Theo. Somehow, the situation felt under control. Nul's focus and attention were cathartic. *Why?*

"There is nothing that I alone can do, except listen to the chatter, see to your training, and continue dropping crumbs along the path I want our enemies to follow as they seek their prize," he answered, looking at me with a focus I had come to understand meant he had said all that he had to say. I wanted more information, but understood I would have to be patient.

Crumbs, I thought. *How funny, maybe the muffin bits I saw Nul drop to Alice just before we met at JFK were the beginning of that path. Another omen!*

* * *

THE PHYSICAL regimens laid out by Nul became grueling. My body seemed never to recover as the pace constantly accelerated. We drilled on routines he said would be elements of our first mission. If I asked where and when, he just put me back to the relentless grind.

I ran with kangaroos that lived in the bush near St. Benedicta. They seemed to mock me, even as distances became longer and longer. There were four of them, male and female, old and young, running with a zest for life. We ate and slept together, as nights were rarely spent under a roof.

"What role do they play in this process?" I often asked.

"Pacers. They pace you so I can measure your progress," Nul responded.

"How did you train them to be so domesticated?"

"Same as Alice, with love and care. They want to be loved, as do we all."

We did Pilates until my belly was like the river bed stones he taught me to throw with a leather sling. I learned to fight with my hands and feet using Tae Kwon Do. We parachuted from cliffs, swam in rivers and lakes. Alice always kept pace. And though I had been on my college swim team, the river by the orphanage was challenging. I had to force myself to swim a mile every few days.

The kangaroos hid when we practiced shooting but they seemed to enjoy watching us fight with knives. Their presence cheered me. My speed and skill grew. When I accidentally sliced Nul with a swipe delivered with such speed that he could not jump away fast enough, I could swear my roo friends hopped in delight. I knew that I was being trained for something on the horizon.

* * *

"Can you tell me your plan, yet?" I asked one evening around the fire. Alice sat with the kangaroos. Their names rolled off my tongue like they were my schoolmates. Onur the father, Yueci the mother, and their cubs Zeki and Cari.

"Are you ready?"

"For anything that will help rescue my children," I responded.

"Do you enjoy fishing?" he asked.

"Sure. I used to fish with my father long ago. He loved to make bait. We cleaned the fish and cooked them for dinners and sandwiches."

"Did you help make the lures, Jaspar?" Sister Ismerelda asked. It was the first time she had joined us in the bush.

"Yes, how did you know?" I asked. "It was one of my favorite chores as a child. Dad would secure a large hook in a vice on his workbench. My job was to wind the string. The binding had to be strong to hold the sharp hook as it lodged in the jaw of a fish when it bit. Then we could reel it in," I explained. I could see dad's shop and my little chair next to his. The smell of his chewing tobacco was lodged in my memory. "It was our thing."

"How did he design each lure?" Nul inquired. I looked from one to the other, comprehension slowly dawning as I thought about the metaphorical question.

"He began with a vision of what he wanted to catch. If it was bottom feeders, the lure had to be weighted and have reflective material to catch any sliver of light. Each type of fish required a unique design. Dad had hundreds of them, but he always made new ones. I was supposed to help him remember what did and did not work. We both forgot. It was part of the joy."

"What would attract the attention of those who hold your children?" Ismerelda continued.

"Me?" I answered.

"Why do you think that would be the case?"

"Because they need something from me? Is this why they kidnapped the children instead of killing them and me?"

"Yes, they fear something. Probably in that chip you carry around your neck," he continued, nodding at the locket held in my fingers as we spoke. I wondered if my friend Crystal had gotten the stick to Chief Bearstrike. *Will I ever find out?*

"You think my disappearance makes Theo and Chrissy valuable as lures to catch me?"

"No question in my mind," Nul said, "as you are the lure for their captors." As always, he was calm. He sat on a carpet of leaves under the trees, drinking water he had drawn from the stream. I sensed a plan in his mind, carefully thought out and tested. Sister's presence probably meant that a turning point was on the horizon.

"The need to permanently quiet you is surely the critical element of our enemies' plan. Ours will be to take advantage of that need for our own purposes, which we have already successfully commenced. They are on high alert."

"So, I am to be the lure on the hook to be cast?" I asked. "To get these sharks to rise from the depths of their hiding to feed on me?"

"Yes. You have been a good student. You will be attractive bait."

I listened as patiently as possible. It seemed all too incredible. Yet, I had faith in my new leader. My children and my life were in his hands, as Father Michael had told me. We were as safe as possible. Nul's facial expression seemed distant. *He's not telling me something.*

"Nul, is there something you need to tell me?" I asked.

His eyes seemed tense as he focused on me. "No, I was just envisioning a glimpse of the future."

The roos sat close by, jabbering and eating without a care in the world. It felt like watching my children play Wiffle ball back in Greenwich.

Alice stood and Nul leaned forward taking my hand. "Jas, being bait is the easy job. I have trained you to be more than that," he said extracting a dull pistol and a gleaming knife from his belt, handing them to me. We had practiced with them often. The weapons rested comfortably in my hands.

"I will also be a fisherman?"

"Yes, if they bite, then we can reel them in."

"I can do that."

"That is harder, but still only part of the process," Sister Ismerelda continued, leaning forward to speak barely above a whisper.

"I can cook them. Is that what you mean?" I asked, anxiety creeping up my spine.

"We will be reeling in people, not fish. Before you cook them, they must be dead," Nul said, looking over his shoulder where our friends with strong legs and short arms were playing.

My mind shrieked as the role of the roos suddenly became clear. Nul, Ismerelda, and Alice all seemed to nod. *They want me to kill them. Why?* I looked at the innocent family playing nearby as Alice meandered away. *I have never killed anything larger than an insect or a snake with Dad when we were fishing.*

The faces of Nul and Ismerelda were blank. *It's a test. They want to know if I can be trusted in whatever awaits us out there.* I felt my heartbeat skip. I heard Trevor's voice: "My strategy is as strong as its weakest link. There is no room for friendship. One mistake can scuttle an entire investment. This is business." *My mission is Theo and Chrissy.*

I bolted, holding gun and knife at the ready. "Losers," I yelled. Onur, Yueci, and their offspring sprinted after me in a chase game we had often played.

* * *

WHEN I PATTED the ground under which I laid the roos to rest, my fingers were coated with blood and dirt. My soul felt cold. Nul, Ismerelda, and Alice joined me with the light of the setting sun at their backs.

I felt a strange composure. I had killed innocent beings who trusted me. Nul's hands probed my shoulders, as Alice sat at my side.

"What do you feel?" he asked.

"I completed my job."

"Can you kill again?"

"Yes," I answered. "I understand that it may be my job to save my children. You are here to help me."

"Can you kill people you know?"

"If I must," I answered. "The roos loved and trusted me. Others may stand in our way in the future. Hopefully, it will include those who ordered my husband's murder and hold our children."

"What about us? Could you kill us," Nul asked, as I turned to look at Alice then him.

"If you stood between my children and me, yes," I answered.

Nul smiled, patting Alice.

Ismerelda picked up her belongings. Then stopped and knelt in front of me with hands on my knees. "You will enter a new world. God is with you. Your children are at the end of the road. Trust this man," she said looking up to her brother. "When your son and daughter are safely in your arms then you can moralize about what you have done."

I closed my eyes, clasping her hands. The words of her homily sealed my soul.

"May I say a few words?" a new voice said from the bush.

"Father Michael!" I reacted instantly and jumped to my feet. "I would recognize that voice anywhere, even out here," I said, his presence answered my questions about his safety.

"Yes, it's God's path," he said holding his arms out to me.

"It's casting time," Nul said, as I turned from Father's embrace. "Where?"

"On my lake, where chum in the water has the sharks circling."

Chapter 9

The Vatican, Rome, Italy
Three days later

I stood in St. Peter's Square, arm-in-arm with two women dressed as I was in the distinctive tan habits of Filipino Benedictine sisters. There were many of us in the crowded square. I looked into the late Sunday morning sky. Cloudless, crystalline blue hues illuminated the statues standing guard atop the roof lines of the Basilica. Bathed in bright sunshine, the saintly figures reminded me of Trevor and my children. I felt comfortable under the stone figures circling the courtyard, my cheering section.

"Lord, please protect my children. Give me heart and Nul vision to recover them," I whispered, eyes riveted on the figures above me, as my fingers touched my wrist where bangles would normally rest.

Nul, dressed in a nun's habit the same as me, was inside

preparing for the commencement of our journey. We strolled through the reverent crowd basking in the sunshine. Observers would assume us to be servants of our order rewarded with a visit to the Vatican. We walked with hands clasped, acknowledging greetings from the faithful. The Pope would soon be addressing the flock from his balcony.

We approached the ATM machine where my credit card had been used while we were still in the Outback. Intense searches of the area had followed, observed by Nul's faithful friends. They watched and reported what they saw, blending into the crowd but ready to respond. Several of them were dressed as sisters. They were Nul's Vietnamese friends who lived in Tuscany, owing their survival to him. I had not yet met any of them.

I inserted my credit card and punched in the PIN number. I leaned close to a glass portal where a security camera would record my face. It was important that there be a clear image, as opposed to the intentionally fuzzy picture left by my stand-in earlier. My hand withdrew Euros from the slot, folding the paper as I turned to walk toward the Basilica.

I wanted to step up on the base of a pillar to see if operatives of our enemy were converging on the machine, but I would not know who to look for even if I could deviate from my role. As I walked, other sisters joined me making a light brown wave of penitents entering the church with hands folded in prayer and thanksgiving.

In groups of three, we spread out around the massive marble columns supporting domes of the Vatican. Sister Ismerelda and another sister joined me sitting on a bench. Our faces were turned upward catching beams of indirect sunlight coming through windows so far above as to be portals to Heaven.

I recalled Nul's instructions. "Sit where your white face will be distinctive and keep your head up. If our enemy is searching, they will struggle to find you amidst all the sisters dressed alike. I want them to have a means of ultimately focusing on you then converging on the spot we've chosen."

"If so, the bait is swallowed?" I asked.

"Indeed," he agreed. Our plan was understood, rehearsed, and ready.

A congregation sat at the opposite end of the Basilica. Red and green robes of priests and bishops were resplendent in the beams of light from far above.

My fair, Anglo complexion was plainly distinguishable from the tawny pigmentation of my cohorts. About ten minutes remained before the end of the service. The crowd would hurry in our direction and into the courtyard to hear the Pope's address. It was at that point that the flow of people would be at its height, which was when Nul planned to take control.

"He's ready," Ismerelda whispered, nodding toward a sister standing calmly by a black and gold African elephantine pillar. It was Nul disguised in a habit. A tan headdress with a white linen wimple secured a black veil for a few of the nuns, including him but not me. The worn leather valise rested between his feet, as it had when I first saw him at JFK. It seemed like a lifetime ago. Nul's face hid in the shadows of the veil.

He moved his fingers. "They're coming," Sister said, reading the signals. My eyes scanned the crowd as I kept my head up high.

As the service ended, red-robed cardinals and bishops in green walked calmly by the fencing separating clergy from worshipers. Their pace was slow so they could bless each penitent standing with outstretched palms. Nul stepped away from the pillar as the crowd surged in our direction. I lost sight of him, careful to look up in prayerful worship, returning my gaze to the light above.

"*BOMB! BOMB!*" a voice echoed through the cavernous cathedral. Each word was magnified as it ricocheted off pillars and statutes.

People screamed in fear of being trapped in a place where they could be incinerated. Worshippers flowed around us like flood waters. Some fell, trampled by those surging from behind.

Official security swung into action. Shrieks of whistles from the Corpo della Gendarmeria, the Vatican police, added to the melee. They were soon inundated by the tide of fearful people running for jammed exits.

My heart raced as I looked to Sister Ismerelda. She nodded, returning to prayer. Pain coursed through me with knowledge that our actions were causing injury, perhaps death, to innocents in a place of worship. I knew that I had to steel myself to new reality.

"Bingo! You were spotted," Nul said as he joined us from behind, just loud enough to be heard through the roar of the crowd. "Change into these," he said, handing me clothes he drew from the bag slipped under the bench before he had yelled bomb. I smiled as the leather moved, knowing that Alice was ready for whatever was to come.

Sisters encircled me. I took off the habit and stood in my underwear with the rosary and locket around my neck. The sacrilege of being nearly naked in the house of God did not enter my mind. "Hurry," Nul said. "There's little time." I slipped into a masculine shirt and trousers. Sister removed the hood revealing my shaved head. Nul had decreed that my body be hairless like a stiletto. After a lifetime of caring for my long hair and complexion, needing only a dab of lotion and no make-up was liberating. It certainly provided visual confirmation of my new life as a member of a combat team.

"Perfect," Ismerelda proclaimed, pushing me away to stand just behind the column by our bench. One of the sisters rolled my habit, slipping it under her own.

The Swiss Guards and Vatican police tried to restore order as heavily armored bomb squad teams entered the cavernous building. Their equipment echoed like gunshots in a canyon. Machines designed to contain the explosion of bombs were like small tanks. Teams dispersed to search every corner, and then spread out for individual reconnaissance of items of interest. Any bag or parcel left behind as people fled was checked with scanners or deposited in the machines.

His plan is working like clockwork so far. I watched the thorough canvassing. Nul was amidst other sisters behind another pillar where he could see me and anyone who approached my position.

The leather valise was at my feet. It bounced slightly against my leg as a team turned in our direction. *What does Alice sense?* A bomb squad leader approached us with his gun drawn, and pointed to the bag.

Sister Ismerelda stepped forward. As her mouth moved, the officer looked at the sisters. A homily must have been spoken, as he bowed to accept the blessing. The sister at my side pushed the bag toward Ismerelda and the officer.

Looking up, the officer told us not to touch the bag. He walked among the sisters, lifting their habits with the barrel of his gun, checking for anything hidden beneath the folds, constantly looking back at the bag sitting on the open floor. Coming to the sisters with black veils, he lifted each veil, looking, we suspected, for a white face. As he looked at Nul, the officer grimaced at the sight of the ugly sister. The veil fell back into place, almost as affirmation that the face was not white. The officer did not seem to notice me almost hidden by the column.

"The bag, what's in it?" he asked in Italian having checked each sister.

"A guide dog for my blind sister here," Nul answered in a falsetto voice, pointing to one of the silent sisters who looked blind. "It could not be loose in the church. The boy over there is her handler," he continued, pointing to me in what seemed to be flawless Italian. The officer strained to see me through the people and columns. His attention was obviously focused on the bag.

"Open it!" he commanded, raising the pistol.

"The dog rests. I do not want to disturb her," Nul answered, leaning down with a protective hand over the bag.

The officer raised his weapon to strike Nul's hand. He hesitated as it occurred he was about to bludgeon a nun in the Vatican. Instead, he leaned forward to open the bag, then looked up as the sisters moved in around him.

"Back up," he commanded, still crouched but waving the gun in a circle and putting a whistle in his mouth to summon reinforcement. The sisters leaned in as the officer took a breath to sound an alarm.

"*KWACK!*"

Before I could react to Nul's sudden chop to the officer's neck, Ismerelda grasped my arm. Nul pulled the police officer behind a pillar. As he returned, the officer's gun was slipped into a pocket of sister's habit. She patted it.

Why doesn't Nul keep it?

We stood there for a few moments as if in prayer. Actually, Nul was waiting, gauging whether there was discernible reaction to the brief flurry of action. I stepped to his side, leaning to pick up the bag assuming we would be moving.

"Stand still," he whispered in an even voice. "They're checking every white face. Kneel and kiss my hand, then do the same with the others as you move away."

As I rose and stepped toward Ismerelda, a group of men moved rapidly toward us. I stepped among the tan habits, kneeling as if seeking absolution. The sisters huddled, blocking a sightline to me. The men were stopped by Nul.

"Parli Italiano?" asked an officer.

Nul shook his head.

"Anglais?"

Nul pressed thumb and forefinger together, indicating a minimal ability to communicate. The leader held out something. I could not see it, though I sensed apprehension in Ismerelda.

"Keep going," she said, nodding toward a magnificent sculpture of worshippers holding babies seeking Devine guidance. It rose above a draping waterfall made of gleaming red marble. A doorway was almost hidden under its arch. It offered shelter.

She's got the gun! I turned to step away. I wanted to stay to help if needed. Trouble was coming. Understanding my role, I stood under the mantel of stone, lustrous from hundreds of years of worshipping hands. The officers moved on.

"*BOMB, HERE!*" Nul screamed. Sisters scattered in all directions running for their lives. Whistles shrieked once again.

Nul took my arm as he came around from my blind side. "Let's go," he whispered with the valise in hand. We slipped through the door concealed in the marble. Stairs led upward at a steep angle, obviously not intended for tourists. Without handrails or light, the climb felt like a passage to a foreboding world. Nul led me by my hand, lifting and pulling as if we were hiking up a mountain. Pausing, he placed the bag on a step ahead, turned, and sat down.

"Are you OK?" he asked, still holding my hand. The stairwell was quiet, no sound from behind or ahead. I looked around. The sisters were not with us.

"They are doing their job as a diversion," he said, reading my thoughts. Their presence had been comforting as I entered a strange world where I was to be bait for sharks. Then to metamorphosize into a piranha to consume the beasts.

"The men down there were looking for a white woman in a habit," he said. "Our plan is working. Someone is on high alert for any sign of you. So far so good. They should now have your picture from the ATM and soon will be able to identify your image as a nun in this costume," he said touching his own. He held out his hand. I laid my forehead in it. "Ready for the next step?" His touch was calming.

"Let's go," I said. I lifted my head. "Game on!"

Chapter 10

WE EMERGED in the Vatican museum. Long lines of people waited to enter the Sistine Chapel. Mayhem in St. Peter's had not reached this level. People made way for the sister from far away and her young man. As we approached the Chapel, the reverence of faithful worshippers waiting to experience the majesty of Michelangelo was touching. Beautiful colors and the magnificent frescoes of the Chapel's ceiling were in sharp contrast to the chaos in the basilica below. *It won't last long.*

At the front of the line, Nul, as a sister, knelt in prayer. I did the same, unzipping the bag and pushing it open. I felt Alice stir.

"*CHAOS, GO!*" She leaped past me in an instant.

Her barking bellowed around us as she plunged into the crowd. Blood curdling growls echoed within the close rooms. People scurried, crouched, or pressed against walls making way for the seemingly rabid dog. Each bark was more gruesome than its predecessor, echoing off closed-in walls to make it sound like a canine herd. Nul had trained Alice to make the sounds on command. I learned that Australian dingoes normally bark only in swooshing noises, like a kind of howling, to give warning. Otherwise, they mostly communicate without noise. Alice was obviously different, in many ways.

Screams of fear arose from a sea of people searching for children and loved ones. They crowded toward exits. There was no place to move. Doors were locked. Whistles of distant security guards stoked the panic. Stampede was not possible in the close quarters.

"Now," Nul said, wanting me to lead him through the crowd.

As we stepped among frightened people, he paused to offer prayer and support. People reached out, obviously taking comfort in the calm demeanor of the sister and her friend. I could hear Alice in distant rooms, barks arising above whistles and commands of loudspeakers trying to restore order.

Our progress was slow. Nul directed people toward the exits, even coordinating with directions broadcast over loud speakers. His head remained alert, listening for sounds or menace. He held my arm as if for support. Actually, he restrained my natural instinct to run like the fearful people surrounding us.

Passing into a room filled with artifacts and no people, Nul twisted around the door jamb, pulling me against his chest. Strong arms encircled me as he watched ahead and listened in the direction from which we had come. He then switched places so my back was against the wall while he looked in the other direction. The barking got louder.

"Anything?" I asked.

"Nothing yet, but they'll be coming, probably reinforced and focused from what they experienced below," he answered. "Our enemies are sophisticated and will know that these events must be related, that all of this is tied to you. They obviously have the credit card data and will shortly have your picture from the ATM. At some higher level they will also be wondering what's going on. 'Why did she suddenly appear? Why at the Vatican? Where is she now? Who are these people?'"

"Our plan is in operation," I responded. A squeeze was his answer. It felt good to be pressed against the wall by this bull of a man. His body felt hot through the habit. He was alert, a man with a plan. I closed my eyes. *Do it again, please.*

Alice raced around a distant doorway, as if she knew just where we would be waiting. She looked like an Olympic runner crossing the finish line in triumph. Nul stepped back to accept the pressure of her paws to his legs and rubbed her head. I looked around as he tended to the dog, seeing no one.

We began moving again at a patient pace. In front of windows overlooking a pastoral garden, Nul extracted a rope from under his habit and tied it to bars across the window, apparently installed to keep people from falling if they leaned over to examine the beautiful landscape below.

"*CHAOS, GO!*" he repeated my earlier command. Alice charged off in a new direction, like a sheepdog herding its flock to safety.

"Arms around my neck!" Nul commanded, stepping over the bars and kicking through the glass panes, shielding his eyes from flying glass. I wrapped my arms around his neck. It did not occur to me that I could choke him with my urgent grip. He stepped off the ledge in free fall. My heart seemed to explode as I hugged the fearless man, trying to avoid looking at the ground several stories below.

We bounced on a ledge, dislodging tiles and statues as our momentum carried us over the edge. Nul held the rope as we rappelled down the stone wall. Out of the corner of my eye, I saw Alice leaping onto my shoulders.

"Oof!" I exhaled upon impact, landing on the man-nun. I did not have time nor space to wonder how he had managed to maneuver and absorb the blow of my fall. It was not something we had practiced.

Did I crush him?

Chapter 11

Pope's garden

Nul grasped me around my rib cage and lifted me as he rose. Setting me down on the ground, he commenced an inspection. I felt fingers and hands touch my body and head, like a trauma doctor at the scene of an accident. He nodded. "Feel OK?"

"I think so; nothing hurts," I answered looking at his face. It was cut and bleeding. His habit was torn. I noticed Alice patrolling around the walls of the garden.

"You are hurt," I said turning back to him, searching for something to clean the wounds. The garden was beautiful with blooming flowers, immaculately clipped hedges and flora that emitted a lilac smell. Its peacefulness belied the reality of our situation. I ripped the hem of his habit to provide a cloth.

"Hold still," I said, seeing that the cuts were not deep. I tried to be gentle in removing bits of stone and debris from the wounds. He did not make a sound. I could not do much about cuts in his scalp, though the bleeding seemed to be slowing. The hood and wimple were on the grass.

I sat back to look at him. I could see Alice in the corner of my eye. She stopped, then looked up toward the window from where we had jumped.

"She expects people to be coming after us from up there. Her instinct is to find an exit," Nul explained looking around the perimeter of the garden. "That's why her first move was to search around the walls." He touched my hand holding the sodden, bloody rag. "Thank you, I'm fine, nothing broken."

His hands returned to my hips, legs, and ankles. It felt like an inspection. "You're also unbroken," he confirmed, inspecting my face and scalp. He turned me to inspect my back.

"I feel fine, thanks to falling on you. How did you maneuver yourself under me anyway?"

"It's my dream to be there," the still bleeding man in a torn and dirty Philippine nun's robe said with a broad grin on his face.

What?! I looked into his face. *He's never even made the first pass at me.*

He laughed. "Gotcha. Thought I was flirting didn't you?"

"Nul, for goodness sake! We're being attacked and you're . . ." I began to protest when he took my hand in both of his.

"We are a team, Miss Jas," he said, watching Alice pace. She stopped to listen under steel doors at either end of the garden. They appeared to be barricades to the outside world. "A little humor helps ease the tension."

"Not for Alice," I said, understanding his point and trying to smile. "Are we trapped?"

"No, we're just waiting to see if the bait was taken. If so, our pursuers will appear. I also expect them to be looking from up there," he answered, peering up to the far above window.

"Then we go to the next step."

"Let's hope."

Alice listened by the far entrance then turned to look at us, panting. There was anxiety in her eyes. Over the weeks we had been together, I was amazed at the clear communication that came from the dog's motions and facial expression. She communicated in a universal language that I was beginning to understand. She and Nul read each other without sound. It was a strange new world for sure, though a place where I felt kinship and a sense of reality.

"You speak of *us*?"

"It is *us*, meaning Alice, you, and me," Nul answered. "As I said, we are the team. There are others on the edges, like our

Vietnamese friends back there in the habits. They are in front of us as well. But in treacherous situations, I prefer to work with the smallest team possible. When missions are hopeless, even experienced warriors sometimes protect themselves first, relegating *team* to a lower priority. It destroys teamwork.

"You are a brave woman. You have done what I asked without question. You are in fighting shape," he continued, pausing to look around the garden. There seemed to be noise filtering down from the broken window though I could not see anything when I turned to follow his focus upward.

"It's about time to move. I sense trouble coming."

"How will we find out who it is?" I asked.

"That will come. First, they need to be hooked. They will run like a fighting swordfish. We will patiently reel the line in to find out who they are."

"Understood. One step at a time."

"Jas, we have no way of knowing whether your children are alive. They could already be dead."

The words stung my heart. "I don't think you believe that," I croaked. "Why say such a thing?"

"If you want to bail out, do it now. It's not too late. I will get you to safety."

Fuck you! It's my children we're after.

"I'm here, part of the team. I'll go where you lead me and do my job," I answered, touching a finger to my mouth then wiping dried blood from his forehead. "Do you want to bail?"

"Fair enough. I never quit," he said patting my shoulder. "We're going into dark places where you will be exposed. It could cost your life without recovering the children."

"Understood," I answered. "It may take yours as well."

"That does not matter. I have been dead inside since I was a child," he said.

I started to object, but he motioned for me to be quiet.

"Also, the man you saw almost killed back there is likely only the beginning. Unless I am wrong, which is not often the case, the people who want to silence you will stop at nothing to assure that result."

"I thought he was dead, with just the flick of your wrist," I stammered, surprised that the officer had been spared.

"The man will be fine, just a severe headache when he is found. We kill when we must. That officer was just doing his job."

Nul man sat on the grass as if we were picnicking in a pastoral garden. Obviously, he was the product of a world of violence. It was his domain. Me? My grounding was in the church, it was the center of our family. As my life evolved to being a princess in a castle, my physical activity became Pilates and coaching high school swim teams. I wanted my body to be as taut as my life was soft. *And now?* I wondered sitting there. I don't think our eyes ever unlocked. *He's waiting*, I knew. *Go or no go?*

A cold image invaded my mind in response to his words. "The roos had to die to prove that my mission is stronger than my heart, right?" I asked. The chill in my words and belly had become an emotion that was oddly comforting. "That I'm ready to kill anybody or anything that gets in the way."

Our eyes remained locked. He did not speak, just touching his wounds and wiping blood on his tattered clothing.

"Consider me a lioness in search of my cubs. You've taught me what I need to be. I will not fail. Bait, killer, or whore, does not matter. If I fail, kill me."

"I promise you this, Jas," the warrior finally spoke. "If your children are alive, we will rescue them. If you get in my way, you will not live to see them."

"We are in agreement, sir," I answered holding my hands up in the gesture I had seen him and Ismerelda do as emotional bond. He grasped my hands, fingers interlaced, clenching in agreement. Alice licked our hands.

"OK, I must look beyond these walls to see if we're being pursued," Nul said as we arose from our brief respite in the beauty of what I later learned was the Pope's personal garden. It was the place from which Nul planned to launch our next step. Alice resumed pacing. I stretched, knowing that we would be moving again in short order.

Nul walked to the rope still dangling from the window three stories above and pulled himself up hand over hand. He climbed effortlessly, his strong body hidden under the long habit. His legs hung free until he needed to brace himself to look into the broken window. There was nothing. He turned to peer over the top of the wall. Broken glass was embedded to deter intruders, so he picked his way carefully. He rose until he could see the outside world.

My eyes diverted for a moment to check on Alice. Hearing distant gun shots, my head jerked back to Nul. He had fallen beneath the crest, holding onto crevices of the abutting walls. Stone fragments fell on him like rain. It took a moment before I realized that the rainfall was created by bullets fired from somewhere beyond the wall. He released his grip on the rope and repelled to the ground. His thumb was in the air as he landed.

"It worked! They're coming this way. They'll be swarming through the doors and over these walls."

"The plan?" I asked, recalling our rehearsal.

"Yes," he nodded, smiling. "Thankfully, we're surrounded by people desperate to get their hands on you."

"Join me, Nul," I said taking his hand. We knelt with his cold hand held in my anxious, sweaty fingers. "Heavenly Father looking over us, I pray for Your guidance and love. You have brought this man Nulandi and me together. We feel Your hands pushing us. We trust in You. If it is Your will, please give us the strength, courage, and patience to find Your path to Theo and Chrissy. Amen.'

"And to our true selves," Nul added, bending to touch his forehead to the grass, tapping his knuckles on the ground.

"*ALICE, READY!*" he barked as we stood. She sniffed at one gate then another, choosing the one in the bright sun facing east.

Nul stepped out of the habit. Picking up the valise he had thrown from the window, he twisted it inside out to make a backpack, stuffing the habit inside.

He removed a dowdy dress and a wig. He had chosen a costume to maintain his image as a stout black woman and mine as a young man.

"You know what to do," he barked, as sounds of a large team of armed attackers filtered over the walls and from the window above.

Follow Alice. Don't stop for anything.

I was being followed by assassins who could earn bounties by killing me. *On our game!*

Chapter 12

Nul tried the handle of the door. It was secure. Stepping back, he began pawing the ground like a raging bull in a ring about to attack. Unlike a bull, he understood that the matadors held stiletto swords behind their red capes.

"*AH-H-H-G!*" he grunted charging straight into the rusty door. It crashed forward with hinges shattering. Screams arose as the door crushed attackers preparing to blow it open. Their bodies caused the steel hulk to lay at an awkward slant. Nul stepped carefully, then plunged into a crowd of Swiss guards and Vatican police trying to get away from the crashing door with guns at their side.

"*BITE! BITE!*" Nul yelled in Italian

Alice barked ferociously as she charged into the largest group. Instinctively, they retreated even further. One of them screamed as Alice leaped at his face with open jaws.

I ran behind Alice as she released her victim, and then zoomed in a zigzag pattern around people, baby carriages, and wheelchairs.

Nul led us among throngs of people running toward a narrow lane lined with shops. Then through a labyrinth of streets laid out in medieval times to accommodate horses and carts. Local people pressed against walls making way for the raging canine. *WHRUF, WHARF!* Intensity of her barking was magnified by the closeness of the walls along the lane. I struggled to keep up. A broad piazza was visible ahead, opening to the Tiber River. We turned in a different direction.

Alice ran ten paces in front. I was in the middle, Nul at our back. Suddenly, she stopped as we came through a particularly narrow passage in a side street made of ancient cobblestones. Only pedestrians, motor scooters, and small animals could pass through. At the end, I could see a right angle turn. *A dead end?* I slowed my pace.

"REVERT! ALICE, REVERT!" Nul commanded. The dog reversed course and trotted toward us no longer barking. She seemed to be watching and listening for pursuers.

At the end of the lane there was a tiny open area with two doors almost hidden in the walls. Alice stood at the entrance. I followed Nul and then leaned against a wall, trying to catch my breath. "Where are we?"

"In a quiet place for a moment. We must change a little," he said, sweat pouring from his face. He opened the backpack, removed his dress and unrolled the habit, laying them on the bricks with the remaining contents of the backpack. Guns and cartridges blended into dark colors of the dress and habit. Nul picked up a web-like shoulder holster and strapped it in place.

Wow! I was unable to avoid staring at his chiseled body. He always seemed stocky. I had never seen him bare. *Hairless like me! I wonder why he insisted on this?* As he pulled the dress up from his ankles, guns were installed in holsters across his shoulders. A third Beretta was slipped into a pocket of the dress along with two knives after they were removed from sheaths.

"Your turn!" he commanded, adjusting the wig over his curly hair.

"For what?" I asked, wondering what he wanted me to do. There were no more clothes.

"Put your shoulders back," he responded, inspecting me. I was supposed to look like a teenage boy. *He seems anxious.* "Take the shirt off," he said "Your breasts must be flatter." With one of the knives, he cut a strip from the habit laying on the ground.

He held the strip of sodden cloth up as if measuring. Turning me from side to side, his examination was clinical. It seemed natural. He had to make sure I was ready for the next step. Nodding that the fit would be OK, he pulled the tan cloth tight as I swiveled then tied it in the back.

"Hope it doesn't hurt," he mumbled, turning me around again. "Flat enough, soldier," he declared approval with a slap on the shoulder.

I was just a little disappointed, feeling, I guess, that he should find me attractive. *Soldier! That's what I am, a soldier on a mission.* My sex appeal, like my former wealth, meant nothing.

"Flat bait?" I asked the man who I had come to trust, pirouetting as if on a Parisian runway.

Nul's face lit up with a broad smile and snort of humor. "You're great bait, for sure, and flat for now."

I am bait, I reminded myself, adjusting the binding to end a pinch under my arm. *The best lure ever!*

"I want you to look as boyish as possible in these bright colors. We want them to be confused. They know you're here, but surely they believe you are dressed like a nun. There'll be cameras. We'll make more scenes. Pictures will be compared. We want 'me to study whatever they can as we strike and disappear. They can waste time trying to find us while we prepare for the next step."

"But you need to remain in the shadows?"

"Yes, just a heavy old black woman, but ready to emerge with these," he answered patting guns under his arms. Some kind of dark chalk was extracted from another pocket of the dress, which he applied to my cheeks.

"*Voila!*" he said obviously happy with the results. "You appear to have a few days growth."

"How do *I* look?" he asked.

"Like my black mother," I laughed at the man in the matronly blue and green dress padded to show a belly and wide hips and conceal weapons. Tight cornrows were tied in the back of the grey wig cascading down his back. Dangly gold earrings completed the convincing identity of a stooped old woman. Makeup was applied to dry and darken his face. Nul's movements seemed natural, like an actor preparing for the stage.

What kind of man is this? I watched him stuff discarded clothes into the backpack. *He prays, kills, changes appearances like an actor, loves dogs, and cares about me.* I looked up at the bright sky far above the congested buildings. Clouds resembled caricatures of Theo and Chrissy playing ball. They were safe and waiting, I hoped.

"*ALICE, COME!*" She trotted back toward us, stretching her neck to accept a leash.

"Take my arm, I need your strength," Nul said in a voice that matched the old lady disguise. "When we emerge from this alley, go across the bridge. Stop at the last purse vendor where a little, stooped Vietnamese woman in a white sari will be holding a brown Louis Vuitton umbrella. She will sell you a purse with a zipper. Empty this into it," he directed picking up a light machine gun and clips still laying on remains of the habit, which he tied around them. "There is no more room in my padding. We may need these."

"When did you assemble all of this?" I asked astonished at the resourcefulness of what was occurring. Our escape had obviously been planned.

"I came prepared for whatever awaits us. Remember, we are our own resources. If my plan works, we will re-stock from the weapons, phones, and otherwise as our attackers fall. Each will lead to the next. Once our bait is swallowed, we just have to reel them in."

Alice began pawing, signaling that it was time to move on.

Nul held my shoulders and touched my forehead. "Sister Jas, you asked your God for help. He gave you me. I know it as certainly as I know that we must go. Take my arm and Alice's leash. I am now blind and helpless."

What's awaiting us?

Chapter 13

Bridge on the Tiber

AS A BLACK woman and her helper we walked through one of the doors in the wall. Nul twisted a lock with a key. *How did he have that?* A narrow passageway that must have existed from medieval times led to another door, which opened onto the piazza along the Tiber River.

Alice took the lead meandering along the water. For the entire world to see, she enjoyed the aromas of all the other dogs that preceded her. I held the arm of the stooped old lady, who actually watched Alice for guidance.

It looks normal, I thought surveying the busy stone walkway. Tourists, vendors, cats, dogs, baby strollers, and children made a collage of global peoples relaxing and enjoying the splendor of springtime in Rome. Music from street musicians and voices of troubadours completed a sense of peacefulness. As I walked, my heart chilled looking at each face. *Could this person be part of killing my Trevor and stealing Theo and Chrissy?*

We passed the ancient Vatican defensive castle prominent in the climactic scene of *The Da Vinci Code*. We crossed the river on a bridge where African men sold imitation designer leather goods, scarves, watches, and glittering jewelry. As Nul had planned, an oriental woman in white stood by a blanket and table loaded with purses and bags of all sorts and sizes bearing famous designer labels. She opened her hand toward a dark grey Louis Vuitton bag with a long shoulder strap. It was feminine in nature. Soft leather had been stitched with care for long life.

Alice drifted to the opposite side of the bridge where she could see in all directions. The black woman paid no attention. Apparently lost, Nul in disguise directed Alice with hand or paw signals passed back and forth in silent communication. Confirmation of all clear in the midst of milling people was confirmed by steady movement. From our practice, I knew that a lift of her knee as if marching meant trouble. She walked slowly, shuffling her feet.

The lady led me behind a blanket acting as a curtain to provide privacy for trying on clothes. I emptied the leather backpack into the bag. I put the Uzi machine gun, Nul's favorite tactical weapon, on top, as we had rehearsed. As I stepped out of the limited privacy of the blanket, Alice's paw rose in slow motion pointing in the direction from which we had come.

"Back behind," Nul said ambling to my side, nodding toward the blanket and accepting the grey bag. A stone railing overlooked the river. The Vietnamese lady joined us. Nul handed her the key he had used to open the door then walked back to join Alice. A wig was put on my head as we had practiced. It matched the hairstyle of my prior life in New York and Washington. Someone searching for me would have pictures from events or galas.

"We want whoever is watching to have an image of you to go with the credit card data. If you are seen in that way, your bait will have been ingested. Then we can set the hook," Nul had explained earlier.

"*ALICE, CLEAR OUT!*" I heard, holding my arms high so the lady could remove the corset. It felt good to be free.

It sounded as if Alice was running from one side of the bridge to the other, barking as if she were herding sheep. Pictures would show tourists scattering toward the railings as if on command, exposing dark clad men crouching in the middle of the bridge.

KAPOW! POP, POP, POP! KAPOW!

The sounds of close gunfire startled me as the lady adjusted my new hair. *My God! Is Nul shot or shooting?* Videos taken by tourists would show a stooped African woman crouching low on the bridge surveying the crowd, then putting the grey bag on the ground and cautiously extracting a small machine gun. The men in the middle drew weapons. They seemed confused as if looking for a target. The crouched woman must have been out of their line of sight. She shot each of the potential assailants square in the forehead with a single bullet from a weapon, later determined to be an Uzi.

It was silent as I parted the blanket shielding me from the actual scene, except for the familiar sound that day of distant sirens racing in our direction. Nul and Alice were going from body to body laying on the stone walkway in pools of blood. The Vietnamese lady held my arm. Nul looked at me, as he stuffed something in the bag. It seemed to be bits of the habit he had torn apart. *Dipped in blood?* I wondered.

"Wait," the lady commanded. In moments, Nul ambled to where we stood just in front of the curtain.

"Thank God!" I whispered instinctively throwing my arms around his neck. He pushed me back into the tiny enclosed area. A finger to his lips signaled silence, as he slipped out of the dress. The Vietnamese lady removed his wig and handed him jeans and a black shirt, then took the still smoking gun from his hand and put it in the grey bag. She handed Nul a much smaller automatic, then fit a leather cap on his head and gave us a thumbs up leaving the enclosure.

"OK?" Nul asked, holding out his hand, palm up.

I was astounded. He just killed a bunch of people who were probably looking for us. *What are you doing?* "Nul . . ." He cut me off by raising his hand.

"Are you OK?" he asked again, flattening his outstretched hand.

"Are you?" I asked, clasping the hand.

"We're good, partner. Let's go."

Dressed as a biker, Nul stepped back out to the bridge. In moments, he motioned for me to begin my stroll as we had rehearsed in the Outback for such an event. Police were coming from both ends. People stood by railings. Five men lay on the stones in blood puddles. Police and others arriving carefully stepped around the corpses. Everyone's attention was on the spectacle on the bridge. The dead men wore civilian clothes. Medics went from one to the other. *Excellent*, I thought walking slowly.

I paused on the side of the bridge where we had entered, being in no hurry. I strolled to the opposite side of the bridge, paused, then turned toward the end where Nul waited. It felt like I was on a Paris runway as an avant garde model. I wore teenage male clothes, flowing hair billowed in the breeze, and an unrestrained bosom bounced with every step. I felt eyes following me, hoping my image would find its way to our adversaries. They would certainly be scrutinizing the one-sided gunfight, which would become a feature on evening news shows around the world. I watched the flowing waters of the Tiber as I passed the bodies, blood, and mayhem from the collision of police, emergency vehicles, crowds of confused and scared people, and gawkers.

Leaning against a tree just past the end of the bridge over the Tiber was a classic motorcycle. It looked like the old English Triumph that had been my father's pride and joy in my youth. He tuned and polished it every Saturday. We then took a spin, rain or shine.

Nul stood behind the tree.

"Game on!" were my only words as Nul secured a helmet dangling from the handlebars around his head. He held the bike as I climbed on, Alice perched between us. I did not don a helmet. Rather, I made sure my wig stayed in place to flow like the mane of a horse in full flight as we took off. With a mighty kick, the machine roared to life emitting the deep belching sounds of my childhood. I put my arms around the biker's strong chest, as I had with my dad. I felt calm as we headed into traffic. *The plan is working.* My mind shifted to the next steps. We zoomed through traffic crowding narrow streets, even along sidewalks to avoid congested intersections. Nul maneuvered through alleys, as if in a familiar neighborhood, with the skill of an experienced race driver. *Did he do motorcycles?* The reality of where we were and who we hoped were after us faded in the thrill of the ride.

Coming out of a quiet alley, we weaved through traffic on the east side of the Tiber. I had walked the Spanish Steps with the sisters in preparation for this day. Anticipation of the ascension to come accelerated my pulse as we turned down the avenue leading to the famous Steps.

"Hold on!" Nul barked, twisting the throttle under his right hand and jamming the gearbox down several notches. The engine roared as the rear tire dug into the pavement. We raced forward through intersections, over walkways, and toward the Steps themselves. His muscles tensed under my grip. Alice's head had leaned out to catch the wind. The intrepid dog leaped to the ground racing ahead of the screaming bike before we embarked up the wide Steps. Crowds of people sat and walked along, with drinks and children in hand.

"*WHARFF-ARFF-RUFF!*" Startled crowds of relaxing people jolted upright. Their vision quickly shifted from barking dog to the roaring machine coming toward them.

I held on as the bike bounced, propelled by the powerful engine driving the rear wheel over each step as Nul lifted the front. My head rested on his shoulder, watching the often bemused faces as we flew by. I imagined how delighted Theo and Chrissy would be with this spectacle as the rocket rose, bearing right as the Steps wound around the base of the monolith.

Cresting, the bike slammed down on the paved street. Nul

turned sharply to the left behind the monument in front of the cathedral. Another Vietnamese woman awaited wearing biker clothes identical to Nul's. The engine never stopped. She held the belching cycle as Nul lifted me to the ground. We returned to the top of the Steps as the woman gunned the engine and raced down the road that led back into the melee at the bridge. Sirens screamed around us.

We peered down the picturesque Steps as people gathered in groups talking and pointing, following the path of the motorcycle down the hill. I fluffed the hair that had thankfully stayed in place. Nul held my arm this time hoping to attract a clear shot of me as I had appeared in pictures our enemies would have from the Internet or the news. A collage of pictures from the day would create an interesting story, which was our purpose. I hoped it would be heavily scrutinized, leading to the next step of our plan.

Nul still wore the helmet as we stood patiently. He pointed to the distance. I could see helicopters over the bridge. The ringing cadence of emergency signals amplified the blinking blue lights of police and flashing reds and yellows of emergency vehicles.

Nul seemed more focused on the Steps themselves. People huddled in groups pointing. *At us?* I hoped so.

"Were you the rider?" a man asked Nul, which seemed comically obvious.

"Yes."

"And you?" he asked me.

I nodded.

"Could I take your picture?" the man asked, lifting an expensive looking camera.

"Sure," Nul responded. We posed with the river and Vatican in the background. As we turned away, the landing above the Steps teemed with people trying to figure out what had just happened. Sirens came up the hill from the direction of the river and passed the motorcycle as it descended. Emergency vehicles screamed toward converging at the top of the Steps from the Piazza della

Repubblica square. Nul held my arm as we were greeted by a pha-lanx of Asian men and women in dress similar to our own.

"Alice, where is she?" I asked, suddenly aware that the dog was absent.

"She awaits," Nul said. "Be calm. So far, so good."

We walked with the group into the Hassler Hotel located at the top of the Steps. A liveried doorman welcomed us. The group entered the historic hotel and walked into a lovely sitting area with glittering gold framed mirrors and plush seating. There were refreshments and hors d'oeuvres awaiting us as if we were a tour group returning from a pilgrimage to the Vatican. An elegant man who seemed to have stepped out of a fashion magazine stood sev-eral steps to our side.

"Go with him," Nul said softly.

Chapter 14

U.S. Attorney's Office
New York City

"THERE IS more news of Jaspar Moran," said Brontus' chief of staff, knowing his boss would be delighted with this interruption. The office's high profile investigation into the still unexplained crash of Secretary Moran's plane had begun as a routine inquiry into tragic mechanical failure. Disappearance of Moran's children, then his wife, without a trace put the matter into more urgent perspective. The passage of time and disclosures about possible market manipulations by Moran's firm, Westbury Madison & Co., before and after his elevation to the Treasury post, vaulted it into the realm of constant media focus. Life of the Wall Street legend with a beautiful socialite wife assured media attention.

Continuing, global economic collapse fanned political flames demanding demonization of a guilty party.

Brontus could hardly be in public without questions being asked about West Mad, the iconic shorthand for the ever-expanding scandal. Speculation was rampant that Moran led a double life and was murdered to shut him up or avenge some double cross.

Even the White House sought answers to end suggestions it had somehow condoned scandalous trading conflicts of the infamous Trevor Moran. The firestorm was approaching Watergate intensity.

"Tell me!" Brontus responded, looking up from the piles of work on his conference room table. They had been alerted about the use of her credit card a week earlier. Investigators in his office and the Treasury were on high alert. Embassy people in Rome were in continuous contact with the local police and Italian security officials encouraging deeper digging into the first trace of information concerning the Moran family. While it was just one of many investigations under his jurisdiction, Brontus had taken personal interest in West Mad. He had worked with Jaspar Moran early in his career, unable now to conceive of the speculations that had come to define her. West Mad had even become a popular subject of crime show headlines. Commentators, with utter contempt dripping from shrill voices, questioned in almost every broadcast the failure of his office or the White House to make progress in the investigation. West Mad was a synonym for failure of the system to preserve and protect the economic health of America.

"Her credit card was used again, less than three hours ago, at the same machine close to the Vatican," the chief of staff began.

"What do we know?" Brontus asked, turning his chair to face the experienced senior lawyer who spearheaded the investigation. Brontus suspected that Moran may have been murdered out of some vendetta relating to West Mad. It had the feeling of a sophisticated terrorist attack carried out for a private purpose, not for some public demonstration. *Why such an act in the world of Wall Street financial manipulation?* The disappearance of Jaspar and her children, all without any proclamation or threats, added to the intrigue. The only communication had been the initial text message for her to remain silent.

"There is a clear picture of her face using the machine. She seems to be wearing a nun's habit. Finger prints were lifted from the machine, which was impounded by church security and inspected by Rome experts. They are Mrs. Moran's," he explained, handing Brontus a copy of the photograph.

"Sure looks like a habit. This is a new way for a famous person to disappear."

"The colors are of a Filipino order."

"Really?"

"There's more. A bunch of nuns dressed the same were in the middle of the riot in the Vatican."

Brontus stood and pointed to the picture in his hand. "This picture is connected to that?"

"Yes, according to our intelligence."

"But there's been no connection to Mrs. Moran or a bunch of nuns? Is there any information from local officials that she is in Rome dressed as a nun?" Brontus asked anxiously. The need to make progress in the spiraling case crowded everything else out of his consciousness.

"We haven't been able to generate any interest in the matter, even at our own embassy," the chief of staff continued. "But they're on high alert as we speak. Security at the Vatican is at an emergency level. Fire and bomb threats that caused riots and trampling of worshippers created shock waves for our Italian friends. There were even reports of a rabid dog biting people. One security officer was beaten."

"Killed?"

"No, just severely injured with a brutal blow to the neck. The man was hidden behind a pillar, probably part of an escape."

"Where does Jaspar fit in?"

"There is no way to know yet. But there are a series of connections. After the picture in your hand was snapped, the next connection was the discovery of her credit card in the Pope's personal garden. People were reported to have jumped into the garden from a window three stories above, outside the Sistine Chapel," the chief of staff continued. "One of them was dressed as a nun in the same kind of habit. Apparently, this happened after the bomb scare in St. Peter's. Witnesses reported these nuns in tan habits all over the place. When it began, they scattered."

"Nice camouflage," Brontus said, envisioning a scene where the objective was a smokescreen to conceal the real activity. "But what could *she* be doing there? In Rome, at the Vatican in the middle of chaos?" he asked, looking back and forth between picture and assistant.

"No answers, yet. There was also a fire scare and a rabid dog rampaging through crowds on the upper floor near the Sistine Chapel."

"But no actual bomb or fire, correct?"

"Affirmative. And no bites or injuries from the dog. Aside from the downed officer, the only injuries were people being trampled. No deaths, just twisted and broken limbs."

"Any sightings of these same nuns on the upper level?" Brontus asked.

"I asked that question," the deputy responded. "There was at least one of them who jumped from a window. They all had brown skin, did I mention that?"

"Any idea what the connection is?"

"Not yet. A young man was reported to be escorting a heavy looking sister before they jumped to the garden. That's where the Moran woman's credit card was found."

"But no more sightings of *her*?" Brontus asked, again holding up the picture and trying to envision the Jaspar he had known participating in such events. *What in the world is going on?* He tried to connect the events to the other mysteries of West Mad.

"No, not at the Vatican anyway," the chief began again. "Security teams collapsed on the garden and fired shots at a nun standing high up on a wall, apparently climbing a rope used to make the jump."

"Shots? Why?"

"Riots inside the Vatican had the responding officers on high alert. There were also some volunteers who joined the security forces. They might have been trigger happy."

"Shooting at a nun on Vatican grounds?" Brontus asked, shaking his head. "Wow! This is all very strange. I assume she escaped?"

"Reports are that the nun, apparently with the same skinny boy and dog escaped from the garden running right through security officers getting ready to attack. The dog bit one of them."

"Hold on," Brontus interrupted the explanation. "What about this boy?"

"We know nothing about him."

"Then find out."

"OK. There was a shootout on a bridge across the Tiber a little later. Five bodies were found. Some appear to be connected to Italian mobs based on tattoos discovered by cops at the scene." The deputy lifted pictures from the pile he had laid on the crowded desk, handing them to his boss. Crowds of people appeared in each photo. Brontus did not have time to look at faces of people in the grainy images.

"Finally, some motorcycle rider raced up the Spanish Steps crowded with tourists and lovers, with a dog clearing tourists out of the path. At the top . . ."

"Come on! This all sounds like a great plot for a crime show or a thriller. Is somebody suggesting that any of this could be connected to our missing woman?" Brontus asked, his eyes gleaming at the idea of the woman he had known being involved in such events. "I envisioned her holed up in some beautiful retreat in the

Swiss Alps protected by a phalanx of security as this weird drama played out. Now she appears to be on some kind of mission. Wait, I interrupted you. Is there more?" he asked looking at the photos.

Suddenly Brontus grunted and held a photo up to the bright overhead fluorescent light. "Well, I'll be damned! There's no doubt this is Jaspar standing at the top of those Steps. She looks like she's posing for fashion photographers with that motorcycle rider. And there's a dog. It looks military—not rabid. There are no nuns in this picture."

Brontus walked around the spacious room filled with bulging files stacked on every available space. He stepped carefully. "She's dressed like a boy. Could this be the boy from the Vatican?"

"I don't know. There's been no time for such detailed questions to be framed or answered."

"Good Lord!" the U.S. Attorney muttered. "In almost two months, there's been no trace of the woman or her children. It's as if they beamed to another planet. Now, suddenly, all of this happens at the Vatican. This story gets stranger by the hour. What in the world does it mean?"

"We have no answers, only questions. There's not even an Interpol record of her leaving the United States or entering Italy," the assistant added.

"What about eye witnesses? Any word yet?"

"Descriptions are inconsistent. Investigations have just started. A lot happened in a short period. It'll take some time to sort it out. These events, especially the melee in the Vatican and the bridge shootings, are a horrible black eye for the Rome tourist business, so our friends in Italian security are now on the job."

"Is that all?" Brontus asked

"Oh. I forgot to mention that the police found a cell phone laying in a gutter by the ATM machine. Initial reports identify it as registered to our Mrs. Moran. It's also being tested for finger prints. The only recent call was made to Alitalia. But no tickets have been purchased in her name on any known credit card."

Brontus continued walking around the room, tapping the back of each chair, straightening piles of paper. The man had a legendary temper, often ignited by perceived incompetence. Color rose in his neck. The chief anticipated direction or explosion or both.

"Have you been able to figure out those trades?" Brontus finally asked, changing direction. Background investigation of Moran revealed that he had amassed a vast fortune even after taking the helm at Treasury. He was betting against the official policies that he advised the president to implement to salvage the economy."

"No, sir," the deputy responded. "The largest trades were made over the month or so before his death. His assets were all in a blind trust, required for his confirmation."

"Who is the trustee?"

"The funds were held at EmBank, where Copper Starr is CEO."

"Was he trustee?" Brontus asked, surprised that the chairman and CEO of the bank would personally perform such a task.

"No, it is the bank's trust department," the assistant answered. "But surely Starr would have taken a personal interest. After all, they had been colleagues and friends for many years, including at Westbury Madison. Starr even recommended Moran for the Treasury job with his stroke with the president."

"Have you interviewed Mr. Starr to find out how such trades could have been made in a blind trust? It's too incredible to believe. Moran was a white knight, someone we all respected for so many reasons."

"Yes, Starr showed us the directions which had been signed by Moran at the time the blind trust was established. Mr. Starr said he strongly advised against the orders, but Moran insisted. He also required that the trades be implemented through secret Cayman Island accounts."

"The instructions were signed by Moran *before* his confirmation?"

"So our people say. The signature is apparently real."

Brontus nodded, resuming his pacing. "So, the U.S. Treasury Secretary has died in a suspicious plane crash under icebergs, as the president is about to launch another round of stimulus to resurrect a drowning economy. Moran's children appear to have been kidnapped. Then their mother vanishes into the night for months, appears in Rome with near riots and dead bodies following in the wake of what appear to be different groups of people. And now," he said, pounding a chair, "magically the wealth of a man universally respected zoomed into the stratosphere shorting the precise policies he insisted his government pursue. What the fuck is going on?"

The room became as quiet as a tomb. "Until now," Brontus continued, "I believed Moran was probably killed for some reason. What it could be, I had no idea. I wondered if it was some fraud that he was about to expose involving others. The apparent kidnapping of his children fits into such a scenario. When Jaspar disappeared, it got more complex. Then, nothing. I wondered if she might be having some affair. Or him? Or what? Now, . . . well now the mystery is deeper than ever," Brontus completed the soliloquy of thought, resuming the walk among files tacked on the floor. *Who could arrange to have a top security government plane sabotaged*, the respected crime solver wondered about the critical question still unanswered after months of examination. *Whoever it was had access.*

"I want you to freeze all of the Moran's accounts. They belong to the U.S. government," Brontus directed.

"Such actions could become public, sir."

"Who cares?" the boss answered. "Just make sure the funds are frozen. Better get a court order to be sure, which will surely be public. Serve it on Starr personally. I'll clear this with the president. These developments could be even more embarrassing to him than the mess that already exists if it all finds the light of day. I'll brief him."

"No problem with Starr. He showed us the transactions. He is fully cooperative."

A polite knock on the door brought the discussion to a close. "Mr. Brontus, excuse me," an assistant said politely, looking around the room for her boss, smiling when he was located. "Sir, it's time for you to depart for Oklahoma."

"What's out there?" the chief of staff asked.

"A meeting with Chief Westbrook Bearstrike," the U.S. Attorney responded. Mention of the name 'Bearstrike' brought silence to the room. Near-universal respect for the iconic Chief of the Cherokee Nation induced disconnect in the assistant's mind. *What could he have to do with West Mad?* It was acknowledged that no one had ever personally met him. And he was not known to have stepped off his remote reservation in anyone's memory.

"What's up with him?"

"I asked if he had an angle on the Moran situation. His answer baffled me."

Chapter 15

Aix en Provence, France

CARROOM . . . OOM . . . BAHRHOOM thundered the sleek red Ferrari as the driver worked the gearbox keeping its engine at maximum torque through the steep slopes and sharp turns of the Monte Carlo Grand Prix circuit. There were no fans, press, or trappings of the championship spectacle only days away. Built on the driver's sprawling estate in Provence, just outside Aix en Provence in south central France, it was a perfect replica of the famed Monaco course.

The driver competed against the clock to master the new

control system developed by his engineers to stabilize the vehicle. Its unique power plant produced enough thrust to propel a jet fighter on a mission at Mach-plus speeds. The private track allowed him to experiment with new strategies to be sprung on race day. The driver was determined to win the big one this time, his ultimate triumph. Racing under the name Henré Tremont, he had become a famously popular driver behind a carefully constructed façade of personality.

Bringing the sleek machine to a stop in the pits, he vaulted over the side with acrobatic grace from long years of physical conditioning. He unsnapped his helmet and smiled at his crew who responded with enthusiastic thumbs up.

Fatigue set in as he walked through the palazzo, an elegant replica of the Grand Casino built along the harbor of Monte Carlo. The magnificent edifice would render the glorious George V in Paris a place for budget-conscious tourists by comparison, just as he had intended. In his quest for extreme privacy, there had never been publicity about the estate. It was built in the fourteenth century as a retreat for the Popes of Avignon following the Crusades. His own ancestors traced directly to Saladin, the first Sultan of Egypt and Syria and conqueror of the European Crusaders. It was a fitting heritage for someone capable of causing financial collapse of the West while he became Formula 1 champion.

He was greeted by an unexpected arrival. "To what do I owe the honor of your presence, Sir Gordon?" asked the racer with the alias nom de plume of Henré Tremont. Sir Gordon was the recently retired head of the famed British intelligence service commonly known as MI5. He had organized sabotage of the plane scheduled to carry Secretary Moran back to the United States, as well as the kidnapping of the Moran children.

"A status report, Prince." Blair knew the man as Price Anwatol Alzjar.

"It must not be going well, or you would not be here. Tell me," he said, sitting on a silk brocade chair in the reception area outside his personal rooms. Thoughts of the evening were pushed aside for the moment.

"Unexpected events have occurred, but I believe the situation to be in hand," Blair began. "The children are safe and resting comfortably at my house near Oxford. My staff is accustomed to handling unusual visitors. Security is complete, I assure you. I personally attend to their awakening every few days in the event that we need them."

"They should never need to be awakened," Prince Anwatol snapped.

"As I said, the original plan calling for a short visit has been interrupted by unexpected developments. As you well know, such events are inevitable. It is our job to respond on the spot. As you know, the Moran woman has apparently surfaced in Rome. There are several indications of her presence, though they are ambiguous. News photos have been analyzed and indicate that the various images are indeed the woman."

"She is neutralized?"

"Not yet. Events have evolved in rapid succession. Don Navarro was forced to use his own resources as his usual intermediaries were unable to respond. The results have not been good," Blair began an explanation of the events at the Vatican.

"It sounds as if someone is playing a clever game of, how do you Brits call it? Ah yes, 'Hide the Ball.' The ball is the Moran woman. Must I remind you that we need to wrap this up so Mr. Starr can bring closure to the West Mad matter and the final U.S. stimulus injection can be implemented? There has been too much delay already. It was your security plan we were following when the woman somehow escaped."

"I understand, sir. These things happen. She will appear again shortly. Don Navarro is ready with the full force of his own and engaged personnel."

"The next report I expect will be of closure. Please bring the children here to my estate where they can be supervised by Dr.

Scheuer and his staff accustomed to addressing what will need to be done with them."

"As you wish," Blair responded with a slightly heavy heart. He was developing feelings of empathy for the children. "May I continue to look in upon them? A relationship will be important in the event I need to use them as lure for their mother."

"I trust that will not be necessary, but do what you must to be ready. It is time for this matter to be resolved."

"I understand," Sir Gordon responded, leaving for the car to take him to his private plane back to England. *Who is guiding this woman? Surely no Greenwich socialite could be doing these things on her own.*

Chapter 16

Apartment in Rome

"GET HIM, Theo!" I yelled at the top of my lungs clapping hands together in utter delight. Trevor sprinted between first and second base, taunting Theo or Chrissy to make a mistake. It was just us. We could have been anywhere. Trevor stopped just short of Theo's hand holding the firmly clasped white Wiffle ball. Theo's young arms stretched as far as they could to tag the runner out. The one-time collegiate champ reversed course racing past Chrissy before the ball got to her, sliding across the orange Frisbee serving as second base. When the ball arrived, she jumped on her father.

"You're outta here," she yelled in triumph, slapping the ball against his shoulder. Theo ran and jumped on top as well. They rolled around on green grass, laughing.

"Help me, Jaspar!" Trevor implored as he was pummeled.

I jumped as if springs were coiled in my legs and reached for the loves of my life. There was nothing. No Trevor. No Theo or Chrissy. No orange bases or white balls. Just grass. "Trevor? Theo and Chrissy? Where are you?" I wailed as my voice choked with emotion. Tears began spilling.

"*CRACK! KA-WHAM!*" exploded on either side of me, just like the crackling gunfire on the bridge. I searched the grass, fearing the worst. I did not look at myself. I felt fingers touching me. I leaned back, knowing that Trevor must be there after all. My heart swelled, tears slowed. I looked for the kids.

"Jas, it's OK," the deep voice said softly.

Darkness set in. Grass disappeared. It was cold. I began shivering as if I were naked in snow. My heart felt empty.

"Jas, talk to me," he said.

I heard the words. They seemed to come from someplace beyond the prism of my consciousness. I felt warmth on my legs, a touch to my cheek

"Trevor?" I whispered, feeling strong arms embrace me.

"No, it's me Nulandi. You were having a nightmare. You're safe."

When my eyes opened, the light was bright. My head throbbed. "Who was shot?" I asked, touching my arms and chest.

"Nobody. It was a dream."

I was silent for long moments trying to focus. "They were here, Nul," I said, turning to look at the man sitting on the edge of the bed. Suddenly, I was conscious of being exposed. I wore only a light top and panties. "What are you doing here?" I asked, trying to pull the sheet around my neck. It would not budge. Alice lay between my legs.

"You were screaming. I wanted to make sure you were all right."

"Trevor and the kids. It seemed so real. Like our former lives, fun and happy. Then it was all gone."

"I know," he said, beginning to move.

"No, no, don't go. I was just frightened. How long was I asleep?"

"It's been about six hours since I left you. It's almost nine in the evening," he answered tussling Alice and looking at me. His face was kind. He touched my forehead, tracing my hairline with out-stretched fingers. Instinctively, I closed my eyes. His touch was reassuring, especially after the dream. Gentle hands squared my shoulders. My back straightened in response.

"You played your part well today, just as we practiced," he said as if commenting on a sports performance. "You have good instincts. More importantly, you were calm in the face of attack and gunfire." I felt the thrill of achievement. I also felt connected to Nul in a way I had never exactly experienced. His fingers felt warm and chilling at the same time.

"As you trained me," I responded, searching his face. I had been exhausted when I lay down. He had been in constant action and motion. Yet, he remained as sharp as a razor, no fatigue evident.

"I obviously had excellent raw material to work from." His face grew more serious. "Jas, I need to explain what I have discovered."

"Where've you been?" Alice's warm body was comforting as I stroked her coarse fur.

"Why don't you get up and get dressed, then we can talk," he answered.

"No, tell me."

He stood and pulled a chair from across the room to sit by the bed. He got me a glass of water. Alice stayed still.

"Our plan worked. Sharks were circling, awaiting your arrival. They swarmed when you were cast in the water," he began. "As you rested, I went to the places where we made contact. On the bridge, lights were erected, so investigators could do their work. The bodies were still there. Police were everywhere. There were even Americans, meaning you must have been connected by secu-rity pictures, as we hoped."

"I thought you were right outside the door," I said, suddenly fearful that I had been alone.

"You were safe. Alice was with you and Anloc is in the next room. I had to do my work. I also had to have the blood samples from the bridge tested."

"Anloc?" I asked.

"You know, remember?"

"Oh yes, yes," I responded as my head cleared. "She's part of your Vietnamese Army." As we had prepared to implement Nul's plan, he explained the shadow team that would be with us. The leader was Anloc Tranh. I felt jealousy when he first mentioned the woman who was younger than me. Then he explained. Her grandfather had sacrificed his life for the safety of his family many years earlier in the Vietnam War. Nul had brought the family survivors to St. Benedicta in the Outback. It was a way station for their transition. In time, he took them to Tuscany near the hillside village of Radda where other family members had earlier been settled by Catholic missionaries. Nul arranged their escape from certain death when Vietnam collapsed in the 1970s. Farmers by tradition, the family found employment in the Tuscan wine country. As feelings of community and inclusion grew, Nul provided funds to acquire land. A vineyard emerged. Collective diligence earned acceptance in the rural community. Iconic blends garnered fame for their vineyard labels. The grateful extended family accepted Nul.

He often needed eyes and ears during his missions. As a small token of appreciation for their lives, the family provided whatever he needed. They had done so in Rome under the leadership of Anloc. Her mother was on the bridge and Anloc was in the Vatican and atop the Spanish Steps. She was the one who rode the step-climbing bike along the river and away from the crowds at the bridge.

"Is there any coffee?" I asked, beginning to awaken. Nul jumped up as if he had forgotten something. He returned with fruit and cups of coffee. It was not hot but helped me return to reality. "Tell me what you found out there."

He smiled and held his paper cup as if in a toast. "We certainly left a lot of trouble and scenes to be investigated in our wake, as I hoped. We executed our plan almost exactly as rehearsed in the Outback, at least until we got to the bridge. I did not expect those gunmen."

"Thank goodness you were prepared," I responded, images of the carnage returning to my mind. I stroked Alice as we spoke, recalling that in these months she was rarely gone when I was alone. If she sensed safety, as when Nul was present, she did her own thing. *The kids would love her.* I tried to focus on his words and not the images of Trevor and our children that lingered in my head.

"I visited each site. Police established cordons to keep the floods of tourists at bay during the investigation. As I walked amongst the crowds, I heard people ask if a movie were being shot, which was logical enough with all the activity and temporary lights.

"At the bridge, emergency vehicles stood by to remove the dead when the forensic work was complete. Detectives interviewed witnesses to learn what happened and obtain clues as to who might be responsible."

"Us?"

"Sure," he answered, scooting his chair close and patting my leg as I sipped the coffee, unconcerned about my minimal clothing. "I overheard some of the questions asked by the investigators. 'Where were you?' 'What did you see?' 'Did you take pictures?' 'Did you hear them speak?'

"I think they passed around a picture of you, probably from the ATM machine. I could not get close enough to be sure. It was of a woman judging by the comments."

"Did anybody recognize you?" I asked, surprised that he had been so bold, or reckless, to plunge back into the aftermath of our flight.

"No, I was just another brown-skinned biker walking around.

I was invisible wearing this," he answered pinching his jeans and a raggedy World Cup soccer shirt from the Italian victory over the French in 2006. He must have changed from the biker shirt.

"On the bridge, the bodies were covered with white sheets. Do you remember that I got blood samples from the ground by each before we left?"

"Vaguely, it was all a blur." He had mentioned blood samples before and it went right past me as I emerged from dream state.

"Well, I did."

"Is that important?" I asked, as Alice stood and hopped off the bed. She got a pat from Nul then walked through the open bedroom door. I assumed she would patrol the apartment.

"Everything OK?" a voice asked from the direction in which Alice had gone. I was startled. I didn't recognize the voice.

"Anloc. Come in. You two need to meet."

"Nul!" I objected. "I'm half-naked; give me a chance to . . ."

A small woman wearing biker clothes stood by the door, smiling at my discomfort. Her short hair had blonde streaks. Without make-up, her complexion was like Nul's. Her eyes seemed rounder than I would have anticipated for a Vietnamese.

She stepped forward with palm outstretched. "I am Anloc. I have heard so much about you, Jaspar. You did great today."

She paused. "Nulandi why don't you leave us alone?" she asked dismissing him. Nul left with a nod and a smile as he closed the door.

Chapter 17

"YOU LOOK ready to party," Nul declared when we finally emerged. It was nice to wear comfortable sports clothes rather than the habits and boy pants of the day. Anloc was wonderful company as I showered and dressed. Her talk was full of art and wine-making. For the first time in months, it was a pleasure to just be a girl meeting a new friend.

"Anloc says we're going up the road to the famous Harry's Bar," I responded, ready to keep relaxing. "I've read about it forever, but never been there."

"Indeed, it will be the safest place in Rome. Out in the open where no one would ever look for fugitives."

"Us?" I asked innocently.

"Yes, indeed. You are now a certified crook, sought by public and private authorities alike. Expect to see your face plastered everywhere," Anloc answered. "You will be a media sensation, intensifying the West Mad frenzy."

I nodded, knowing that my focus needed to be on our path not needless distraction from public media commentary.

"Jas, before we go, please sit. There are some things we need to address."

Anloc took a seat by Nul. I sat on a sofa across from them as the atmosphere returned to mission. *What is it now?* I wondered. Nul seemed to prepare me for the way forward one step at a time. My thoughts had proceeded no further than the role I played that day, other than wondering about my children and feeling their need for me. Anloc was no longer chatty girlfriend. She had the focus of a combat soldier.

"Next steps in our mission?" I asked, holding dog friend in my lap as if we were watching a movie.

"Yes, but I need to explain what has evolved to set the stage."

"And?" I asked, anxious to understand.

"Having successfully hooked our enemies, our focus needs to shift to reeling them into our lair. There are three elements of reality as we sit here," Nul began. It felt like times when I watched Trevor take charge.

"The first is the firestorm over what is called West Mad, which we discussed before. The heat continues to accelerate."

"It's a pile of shit!" I responded. "Where does that crap come from? Someone is leaking or coaching the press, right? Why are they doing that? Trevor is being lynched as scapegoat for the mess in the world. He cannot defend himself. Obviously, no one else is either," I vented with a voice accelerating with anger and frustration. Alice snuggled close as my composure began to evaporate. A different creature from the beast on attack in the Vatican. *My Trevor, never!*

"I have no answers for any of those questions, except they lead to my second point," Nul said. "I do not know who or what is behind West Mad. It is probably the same people who hired the goons we met on the bridge."

"And who murdered Trevor and stole my children."

"Yes, which connects to point number three. Identity of the men on the bridge provides the first clue on a path that just might lead to them and the murderer."

Alice groaned as I leaned forward, squeezing her between my torso and legs, anxious for Nul's punch line.

"At least some of the dead men were from a mafia group."

"How do you know?"

"From unique tattoos exposed around their shirt collars. One was visible and I checked the others as I gathered guns and phones plus the blood samples. Two of the five were from a family I know."

"How would you know such people?" I asked, sensing his familiar tone of voice.

Nul did not answer.

"Tell me. I understand the first two items, but this one is a complete mystery. Why would the Italian mafia be after me?"

"Jaspar, we don't have time now for details," Anloc picked up. "Suffice it to say that we have worked with these people. They are vicious."

"Their job was to kill me?"

"Yes."

"So what is *your* connection?" I asked, suddenly anxious as the cocoon I had lived in for months opened to a new reality. I was in play, a target for whoever was out there. Nul was quiet, calm but silent. Alice's face was turned into me. *Who is this woman?* I wondered looking at Anloc sitting in front of me in obvious control. *She's more than some Asian artist or winemaker living in Italy.*

Anloc leaned forward, crossing arms on her right knee resting atop its mate. Thin biceps were defined with strength. Her calm balanced my anxiety, with eyes holding my own. Not angry, not defensive. Confident. *She knows something*, I thought. *What is it?*

"Fair enough," she began. "You need to understand where we fit into this new information. Nulandi and I know this group from the bridge. We have worked for them," she said matter of factly.

"Doing what?"

"Killing." My heart beat slowed as images paraded in my mind, looking at the man I had come to trust. There was no surprise. He had so advised as an abstract matter; then I saw him in action in the Vatican. Violence was a pivotal element of where we were. Certainly my own murder of the innocent kangaroos had been part of an evolution, in me, not him. Any emotion about what had to be done on this path was in remission.

"Anybody?" I finally asked.

"Almost," Anloc answered.

"It's just business, like fixing computers?"

"Yes," she answered.

"What *are* you and Nul?" I asked, looking from one to the other. *What am I missing? Should I be jealous?*

"A team," Anloc answered.

"You are also an assassin?"

"Yes, it is what he trained me to be. Alice and I are his eyes and ears when he needs us," she added. "I also manage the business."

"And you worked for this mob?"

Nul nodded with a look of simple honesty on his face.

"Would you have killed Trevor or me?"

"Yes, for a price."

"To support these Vietnamese people?"

"Yes, and the orphanage. They are my family," Nul answered. My eyes closed. The word *family* beat in my heart. *I have no family! Trevor's dead, Theo and Chrissy stolen. West Mad spun. My world is gone.*

My eyes opened slowly. Nul and Anloc sat patiently. I felt something I could sense but not see or hear. *"Child, these people are here to help you put your family back together." Who is speaking to me?* I remember wondering. There was light above their heads. It seemed to fade as if a beacon had lit for a moment to show the way. I felt peaceful, ready.

"I respect that and have hope of finding mine," I said as my mind cleared. They still had not moved. Alice began stirring.

"We are here to help," Anloc answered, taking Nul's hand and reaching for mine. I clasped them feeling warmth. "Are you ready for what we have discovered?"

"Yes, please." Alice slid to the floor, her tail wagging as she circled looking up.

"As I said, we know all too well the family who the dead men worked for," Anloc began. "There are many groups loosely referred to as *mafia*, especially in Italy. Some groups are engaged in the usual types of criminal activity, such as kidnapping, vote selling, prostitution, and so on. This particular group originated in Castlemarina about 30 years ago. Its original capo, or capafami-glia," she said musically enunciating the cadence of the Italian syl-lables, "is a man named Luciano Navarro. His business graduated from such local stuff to financial enforcement. An example would be a bank with a sour loan to a debtor in default. The bank might ask Luciano for collection assistance. The debt would be repaid."

"And if it was not?" I asked, still trying to figure out the con-nection of the dead bodies on the bridge to me and us.

"Luciano's reputation is such that payment happens," Anloc responded.

"You mean people have been beaten up in the past?"

"No, daughters, mothers, or wives would be raped to start with. Burning or maiming was a second step, usually children or parents. The defaulting person had to be taught a gruesome les-son that would never be forgotten, also learned by other custom-ers. Not surprisingly, default is rare."

"Did *you* do these things?" I asked with horrific pictures in mind.

"Not those types of things," she answered. "The Navarro clan would use its own people for such chores."

"Then what *did* you do?" I asked, looking at Nul.

"I had a different role," he finally spoke up. "Old Luciano wanted to consolidate his power. I terminated several rival fami-lies in various parts of Italy and Corsica. I was paid well."

"Which we all benefitted from," Anloc added. "You will see when you come to our lands."

"Luciano must have been desperate to get you," she continued. "We have also learned that he contacted Nul after you used your credit card at the Vatican. When there was no contact, he obvi-ously sent his own men. He has never used them in public for fear of contaminating his ambition. Luciano is a financial and politi-cal pillar based in Siena. He is a careful man. His image is pristine. The reality is all beneath the surface. Our work has helped main-tain that façade."

The elements of where I was came into focus, as did understanding of why I had been delivered into Nul's hands. *Thank you, Lord,* I said in my mind looking up, sensing again the presence of someone or something I could not see. *Please give me strength to do what I must. Our path awaits.*

"What is most interesting is this," Anloc continued. "Navarro has ambition to be the next Prime Minister, like Silvio Berlusconi. Any taint of involvement in this West Mad mess would end those dreams. Accordingly, there is something here that made him desperate enough to engage his own men. Now two of them are dead. There will be a serious effort to hush it all up," she said pushing her hands toward the floor as if deflating a large ball.

"Why would *I* be of interest to *him*?" I asked

"I'm not sure but we'll find out," Nul answered.

"How?"

"It's our next step, one that we have not planned so it may not be smooth."

"Which is what?" I asked.

The explanation took a few minutes.

"I do need a few drinks at Harry's," I said when it was complete.

"Great, let's go," Nul said rising.

"Oh wait," I said, remembering the questions that had been in my mind since awakening. "Can I ask you about some other matters now that I understand the kind of people who are after me?"

Anloc nodded as Nul turned toward me.

"Father Michael is safe, right?"

"Yes, with Sister Ismerelda. Nothing has changed. He took a leave of absence to attend to a family emergency. No one has tried to reach him," Nul answered.

"Good. Do you know anything about my friend Crystal Jamison? You could not have met her. I've been worried. I left her with what our enemy wants to find and destroy," I said, clutching the locket.

"You mean the memory stick?"

I am sure shock spread across my face. "How do *you* know about *that?*" *Who else could know?* I wondered, fearful for the safety of my friend and her family. I had not thought of the danger when I entrusted the stick to Father Michael to give to her.

"I have not spoken to her or Father Michael, but the information was delivered as your husband directed to Chief Bearstrike," Nul answered.

"How do you know this?"

"Jas, it's a small world sometimes. I know the Chief. It is a long story for another day. Suffice to say for now that we speak in our own language. He asked me to tell you that someone named Brontus will be visiting at this home in Oklahoma," Nul added. "Is that important?"

Brontus? Brontus? I thought. *Who? Jason Brontus is the only one I know with that name. Why would he visit the Chief? What does it mean?* My mind spun, then relaxed as the new inputs fell into order.

Alice sat up with perked ears.

"It is good information?" Anloc responded to what was probably a peaceful look on my face.

"I just needed to know that Father Michael and Crystal were safe. If Chief and Mr. Brontus are now involved on our side, our team just got much stronger. I do want to understand your relationship to Chief. But right now, I'm ready for Harry's."

Alice headed for the door. Anloc picked up a bag. Nul already had his backpack. I did not ask where it had been or what was stored in it.

As I rose and looked up, I heard music. Sounds of distant trumpets came closer as the light reappeared. *It's the Amen chorus*, I thought hearing the lead in to my father's favorite song, the finale of Handel's *Messiah*. A choir was singing. My father always said it would be present when he met God. "*Your mother will also be waiting, sweetheart, so you must not be sad,*" he whispered on his death bed.

The *Hallelujah* chorus echoed in my head. *"Theo and Chrissy will be here with me, child, should you fail."* I looked from side-to-side. There was no one but Nul looking at me. His jaws were moving. He seemed to be under a waterfall, in a different world. *They are not there now?* The light faded as the final words were sung and my mind cleared.

"I win either way," I mumbled, feeling that my dad's vision was my own. I would succeed in the rescue, or join my children in Heaven.

"Jas, are you ok. I thought you were going to pass out."

"No, I'm ready. Let's go dance," I answered as Alice and Anloc returned with impatience written all over their faces.

"Shall I be a boy or girl?" I asked, ready either way. The path to my children felt secure. *They await.*

Chapter 18

Central Oklahoma
Two days later

A SLEEK Gulfstream jet looped over remote rocky hills. Early morning sunshine glistened from a fuselage bearing only hull numbers. It lined up for landing on a grassy strip carved from forest. When Jason Brontus confirmed his trip to the Cherokee reservation, Attorney General Sanaroff offered a government jet. Brontus declined, advising that Chief Westbrook Bearstrike insisted on his own plane.

"That seems strange, why?" the attorney general asked.

"I do not know for sure. I assume it's an element of the Chief's desire to be as anonymous to the world as possible," the U.S. Attorney answered. "I have spoken to him occasionally, but I have never met or even seen pictures of him in the last thirty years. He told me to bring the clothes on my back and that's all."

As the sheriff of Wall Street stepped off the ladder, he shielded his eyes to find his host. Bearstrike waited at the edge of the trees. *Amazing,* Brontus thought. Chief sat upon a beautiful golden stallion holding the reins of a second. It was a paint with a belly indicating a life of grazing.

The horseman waived. He appeared to be about seventy-five. Grey hair was in a braid hanging down over his shoulder and tied with a red cloth. A loose flannel shirt covered a thin torso. Jeans were secured with a rope at the waist. Bare feet hung free in the absence of a saddle.

Brontus returned the greeting as the plane lifted off. He also wore jeans with a blue sweatshirt and jogging shoes. There were no bags or communication devices of any kind. *He looks eager,* Chief thought as the forty-seven year-old attorney general approached with a cheerful, curious look on his face. Their contact in recent times had generally been initiated by Brontus seeking insight into financial fraud investigations. On a few occasions, there were complaints about investments made by Chief. In the case of West Mad, Brontus initiated the contact. Chief was asked about financial manipulations believed by the Justice Department to have taken place.

"It is a continuing terrorist attack. I will explain on my land," had been the unexpected response. From anyone else, Brontus would have ignored an opinion that was contrary to anything then known or considered. The comment demanded understanding even if the AG had declared the trip a dangerous waste of time. "Such a public statement by that man, or his fund, would be embarrassing to the president."

"Welcome, young man," Chief said leaping to the ground.

"Chief Bearstrike?" the city boy asked, surveying the weathered face of the most respected investor in the world.

"Thank you for coming. It is time we finally met."

"Thank you! We are really alone," Brontus responded, observing the rolling terrain covered by trees. Whispers of gentle breezes provided the only noise. While he had no expectations of what awaited him in this world, simple nature and a gentle man with horses would not have been in his vision. It was literally a distant planet from his life experience.

"Indeed we are. I'm looking forward to our time together. Ready to ride?"

"I haven't been on a horse since I was a boy," Brontus responded looking at the paint resembling the horse that Tonto rode in the *Lone Ranger* show of his youth.

"It's our only mode of transportation. There are no vehicles here. We will go slowly. Slivers here is as tame as an old dog. He knows the paths of my world by heart," Chief advised. He held the saddle as the U.S. Attorney struggled to get a foot in the stirrup to pull himself upright. When the operation was complete, Brontus patted the neck of the beast and adjusted to the saddle. "Where does his name come from?"

"He was sired by a champion. I explained to my granddaughter that he would follow in his father's footsteps. 'Like slivers of a tree?'" she responded. "The name stuck."

"What is *his* name?" Brontus asked, watching the agile man leap on the other horse with no apparent strain.

"Stone, meaning dependably strong. I bred him myself, like Slivers," Chief answered as Stone instinctively headed into the forest surrounding the landing strip. The grassy area made ideal grazing grounds for deer and buffalo roaming free without restraint of fences or predators other than those of nature. Chief lived in the middle of thousands of acres.

They rode in silence. Sounds of the forest provided a soothing symphony for the rider accustomed to chaotic city life. Chief rode in front, periodically circling back to check on his guest. *How can this simple man be the financial genius of the world?* Brontus wondered settling into the patient rhythm of Slivers and a world of birds, squirrels, and springtime Oklahoma. Eagles circled overhead, their shadows zooming across the land. *This is so peaceful*, he thought as travails of his normal world receded in his mind.

In time, a dirt path appeared. There were no tire tracks or evidence of motor vehicles. Riding up the hill, a dwelling came into focus. It was made of field stones and logs making it appear a part of the landscape.

"I built it myself long ago," Chief explained with pride as they settled on a cobblestone patio under a trellis of grapes and panoramic views of a stream, distant hills, and clear blue sky. "My daughter was young at the time," he continued, offering a cigar rolled in his own hands and a cup of red wine made from the grapes.

"A peace pipe?" Brontus asked.

"If we need one, sure," Bearstrike responded. "Wine and a smoke are a good way to get started. Even early in the morning as we get to know each other. So it is like a peace pipe. I hope we are on the same side with common understanding of the way forward to achieve our mutual interest."

Chief arranged coals in a fire set on a platform of stones on which Brontus rested his feet to relieve lower back strain and a sore butt from the long ride. Even in May, the fire was comforting. A few gentle puffs from Chief ignited a flame. He withdrew a stick and lit the smoke in Brontus' hand, smiling at the bemused look on the guest's face. Flying into the middle of a vast range of natural land, riding a horse for an hour alone with his own thoughts, sitting in another man's simple comfort with no one familiar or any communication was the means of transition Chief wanted for the task ahead. Brontus had to be drawn into a different world to internalize what he was to learn.

"Again, thank you for coming all this way, Mr. Brontus," Chief began.

"Call me 'Jason' please. The wine is excellent. Did you also make it?"

"I did, like everything else around us. I will show you how it is done if we have time."

"I would enjoy that, though I am not so handy. Will we have time?"

"You mean will you stay long enough?"

Brontus flicked ash from the cigar to answer in the affirmative.

"You are welcome to stay as long as you like. You will find everything you need in the cabin through the trees," Chief responded pointing toward the forest. No cabin was evident. "I think you will want to stay long enough to understand why I invited you to join me.

"And thank you for coming on such short notice. I know your time is in short supply. Your sure hand is desperately needed. My people and your world are in jeopardy because of the damaged state of the global economy. You asked if I had an angle on your investigations. I answered that the economic collapse was an element of a continuing terrorist attack."

"Those words are terrifying," Brontus responded. "I expected comment on whether the collapse was the result of simple market forces or something else."

Bearstrike nodded.

"The smoke is excellent," Brontus continued, understanding the need to ease into what could be a contentious discussion. "You made these also?"

"I was raised to live on the land, using what nature provides without modern day chemicals and processing," he said, pointing his cup to the trellis overhead. The cigars are from the grasses and weeds that your mother would have called 'greens' cured in the wine," explained the man equally comfortable working and living in the wilderness as he would be sitting in a Wall Street office surrounded by staff and elegance.

Brontus flipped ash into the smoldering fire admiring how Chief was able to keep it going with only slivers of wood and a few breaths. "Chief, may I ask a question?"

"Of course. I hope you ask many."

"Why did you invite me here? We have spoken occasionally. I've never heard of anyone actually meeting you." The U.S. Attorney had studied everything known about the famous investor. There was hardly anything to provide insight into the secretive man. Westbrook Bearstrike was referred to as the "voice of the winds" by the financial press. It was a tribute to his success and respect for his way of life.

As a young man, Chief had earned honors at the University of Chicago with a Ph.D. in international economics and applied mathematics. He interned and traveled in Europe. A Rhodes scholarship offer was declined so he could return to organize the Tribe's strained finances. His first success was getting its cattle business on a sound base. He then saw and exploited the opportunity for reservation gambling.

"I am a man of this place and our history. My life and world are here helping my people. Your ancestors ravaged us, stole our lands, and drove us to this wilderness. Most of us died on that journey. We were poor. Today, we are prosperous. There is a broad social net for all of my people with medical care, training, scholarships, and support. They are all family. My life has been to husband our resources for our life here."

"You refer to atrocities of long ago. You have accomplished so much. Why do you answer my question with that ugly history?"

Chief took a puff as if composing his thoughts. "I have brought you to a new and different place where you are helpless and have no means of communication. That was intentional. The reason I invited you requires an understanding of our history and where we sit with respect to the ongoing economic crisis."

"I am in a strange world for me; that's for sure. I am defenseless. You could take my scalp and feed the remains to the mountain lions I think I heard on the ride," Brontus responded, enjoying the wine and anxious to understand Chief's logic.

"They are there for sure, as are all other elements of the nature of this region. The atrocities of your people on mine are part of our legacy. Another part is deeply personal to me," the native explained. "When I was successful with our gambling operations, I was prosecuted for securities fraud at the instigation of politically influential competitors. They resented our guile in taking advantage of the treaty between our tribe and the United States. The indictment was struck down. I then decided to conduct our business in strict observance of the letter of the law of our tribe and your country that surrounds us. Our work would always be scrupulously clean and above board. As native people, we understood that we would be held to a higher standard. I have never again appeared in public or made any pronouncement of any kind."

"Your use of lawyers and accountants is legendary. I checked with IRS, Justice, and SEC. They all confirmed that you and your people cooperate fully with any inquiry, even when it is initiated by other countries. Just as you have to my questions over the years."

"That is our commitment, then and now. Our portfolio has flourished. Gambling produced wealth to be invested. We formed Trail Holdings as our investment fund. As you well know, many times that fund successfully attacked companies or governments of developing or developed nations. Our *Bear Strikes*, as they are bitterly described by the vanquished, often precipitated financial spiral of the targets and wealth for the tribe. Those who suffered loss often scream for investigation, declaring them to be victims." Indeed, when it was believed that Bearstrike had masterminded another raid on a currency or company, he would be depicted in the financial press by a drawing of an Indian Chief on a rampaging stallion wielding a tomahawk.

"When we or others have then investigated, the conclusion has been that you complied with all requirements," Brontus agreed. He had inevitably concluded that Chief was a clever, scrupulously compliant with the requirements of law and openly cooperative in spirit. It was through these investigations their paths had initially crossed.

"You still haven't answered my question. Why did you invite me now?"

"You'll see in a moment. May I refill?" Chief asked tipping a jug over the outstretched empty cup.

"This stuff is genuinely good. Do you sell it?"

"No, it's just for myself and my family when they visit." It was known that Chief had a daughter, Clemenca, who had initially followed in his footsteps, then married a lawyer in Dallas who became Trail Holdings' outside counsel and spokesman, Roy Hammer. Chief's wife had died in childbirth, and his daughter at a premature age after the birth of his granddaughter.

"Jason, you know me well from the times our paths have crossed," Bearstrike said. "The financial world is like hunting deer in the mountains. The bucks are instinctively cautious, following the same patterns to hide from natural predators. Sometimes, they come out into the open to mate or wade into a stream to drink. That is the time to be ready with bow and arrow. The same is true in global finance. Discrepancies occur between how investors bid up the value of something, say a currency, and actual underlying value. When I see those deviations occurring, I focus. If it continues, then I pounce. Instead of bows and arrows for meat, I use long and short financial instruments."

Brontus relaxed enjoying the explanation and feeling honored to be sitting in a place where apparently no outside white man had sat.

"I invited you here because the success of our tribe and its financial underpinnings are at risk from the terrorist attack that is continuing and threatening to cripple the economy of your country and the world. We may be remote out here, but we are nonetheless members of the global community. There is a cancer in our midst. You are about the only person in the world with balls enough to blow the whistle," Chief explained, pointing his smoking cigar at the U.S. Attorney for emphasis.

"My hope is that you will fly away understanding the fraud

that has been committed on the world and the danger at our doorstep."

"Chief, everyone in a position of responsibility in the world would laugh at your suggestion," Brontus responded. "How could any terrorist achieve such a feat of economic power?' would be their question."

"Understood. I have proof that I think you will find astonishing."

The words hung in the air as cigars were thrown into the embers and cups drained. Chief rose signaling time for a walk.

"Before we leave, may I pose an easy question?" Brontus asked. His host smiled and with a toast of an empty cup encouraged whatever was on the U.S. Attorney's mind.

"Where is your staff located? The holdings of the tribe must require research and administrative support."

"You are an observant man. Do you not see around here what I might need?" Chief responded with a smile and wave of his arm.

"Seriously, my team is located elsewhere on our lands. They come here as you have when we need to visit. Over the years, I have trained our people to analyze things in my manner. Our team is composed of bright, focused people whose insight is not tainted with conflicts of interest, deadlines, or other pressures beyond long-term results. They are motivated and diligent, having begun life in poverty and, often, broken homes. Through collective industry, they have created opportunities for themselves and their families to be as successful as they may aspire to be. We are supported by an extensive network of external colleagues who adhere to our code of ethics. Nonetheless, the core, the people who make all decisions, are members of our tribe."

"Amazing," the city man responded. "So you live here in peace able to focus on the financial world in your own independent manner."

"Precisely."

The mid-day sun heated the air as they walked along a path to a stream where horses grazed. Chief's words and implication were foreign to anything in his experience. *How can he prove something that the rest of the world would consider a joke? What if it is true? Who could be behind such treachery?*

"Chief, please tell me where you see terrorism. Surely, you are not just complaining about some soured investment, as your targets have often pointed at you as being responsible for their loses?"

"Fair enough," Chief responded, a broad smile crossing his face. He had not thought of that question. "We actually benefitted handsomely from the economic collapse. We anticipated what would happen on the way up and down, placing our bets accordingly, as I will explain in due course. But we were drops in the waterfall," he said, pointing to the stream gurgling a stone throw away under branches of huge oaks. The horses came close enjoying grasses along the water.

"Jason, you're familiar with the public perception of the causes of American housing bubble that burst in 2008 triggering the economic collapse."

"Please tell me your view of it. I need to understand why you believe terrorism is at the root."

"Very well. In America, a succession of Congresses and presidential administrations encouraged home ownership by providing mortgage subsidies. People with marginal or less ability to buy were encouraged to do so with little or no down payment," Chief explained.

"Agreed," Brontus responded.

"Mortgages were originated by companies rewarded for volume not quality. The paper was bundled into securities, wrapped in default insurance, and sold by Wall Street bankers to opaque offshore investors seeking higher returns than available from U.S. Treasuries. All pigs got fat at the trough," Bearstrike continued. Brontus nodded in agreement as they strolled along the creek. The trickling water provided a peaceful background for the intense discussion. Brontus thought he could see trout resting in the shadows feeding on the buffet of nourishment provided by the current.

"That is well known, as you said," the prosecutor responded as he removed his shoes to follow his host through the stream then up a winding path on a hillside with what appeared to be a stone neck arising from the crest. Brontus stepped gingerly in his bare feet. Chief walked normally.

"The terrorism, Chief, where is it?"

"Impatient fellow, aren't you?" the lead hiker responded reaching a rocky outcropping that offered panoramic vistas of the valley below. "This is my favorite spot."

Brontus did not need field glasses to see deer and antelope grazing by a lake. Cattle were on the horizon. Eagles circled overhead.

"This is beautiful Chief, nature at its most profound. There is nothing like this in New York City or New Jersey where I grew up."

"I'm glad you like it," Bearstrike answered. The table was being set for delivery of the main course.

"This bubble was an easy target for an old speculator like me," he continued, turning to see the horses following them.

"But our windfalls became too much. Something was wrong. It took me awhile to see that our trades were somehow being copied. A whale, with resources far beyond anything I could muster, raced at our side then charged ahead pulling us in its wake," Chief explained, handing each steed small apples that he carried in his pocket. "The market was driven up and then crippled when our buys turned to sells, reaping a windfall for us and the whale.

"The next step in this process was the two bank bailouts by your government intended to ignite recovery. I believed that each of them was a mistake. As an investor, it was obvious to me that vast sums of money were being poured into holes that would not stimulate the economy. Accordingly, I saw no basis to predict what would happen to place my bets, so I stayed on the sidelines, watching the bailouts, or stimuli, as your president called them, and studied the markets with fascination. I observed that this whale reaped additional windfalls with each round of stimulus. It felt like watching a gambler at a craps table push a pile of chips on the number with the highest odds. When it hit, he placed an even bigger pile on another number, winning again. If the process continued, the house would go bust. At some point, it becomes obvious that the game is fixed."

Brontus listened carefully as he stood on a rock, his chin resting on crossed arms atop the back of Slivers. He looked down at the smaller Stone standing by Chief.

"Something was quite wrong in the markets. I assumed at the time that whoever this whale was had access to details, like a gambler when the fix is in. Jason, have the bailouts been successful?"

"Obviously not. It appears that the U.S. is on the verge of returning to recession. Europe is even closer to the abyss. Lack of consumer demand in the West damages the export-driven economies of Asia."

"On that we agree. The situation is on the precipice of a catastrophe that is spreading like an aggressive, untreated cancer," Chief wrapped-up his explanation. "Now, to answer your question, the terrorism is in the attack on the global economic system by this whale, which must have access to the decision-making process of your and other governments of the world, who are rewarding those who attack our system. It is not mere Wall Street greed. It is terrorism." The loaded word hung in the air as both men patted the horses nudging Chief's pocket for more treats.

"Why do you say my government, Chief? It's yours as well," Brontus retorted.

"We are separate nations, Jason."

"Then why do you care?"

"Because the wealth of my tribe is tied to the economic system of the free world. If that world is being undermined by manipulation intended to destabilize the whole system, it is my responsibility to protect my people," Chief responded, as they headed back down the hill.

"Can you prove the implication of what you are saying?" the skeptical prosecutor asked. *He would not have me here saying these things unless he had proof. What could it be?*

"I have recently received actual trading records that explain the process used by this whale. It is poised to make the killing of all time if the next round of stimulus is pursued. I asked you here to show you those records."

"What is their source?"

"We need to get home," Chief responded looking over the vista. "Let's get you situated and feed our big friends and ourselves, then we can finish our discussion," he explained mounting Stone. Brontus followed.

Is this the reality of West Mad?

Chapter 19

As CHIEF assembled dinner, Brontus walked around the grounds. Slivers stopped along the gurgling stream. He seemed to have a destination. The intrigued prosecutor followed along enjoying the peacefulness of the late afternoon. The sounds of the forest seemed comforting, so different from Manhattan. Slivers slowed as if to walk with him.

"Where're you taking me old boy?"

The answer came via a twist of the head and rearing up of hind legs, followed by a trot. Brontus had to sprint to keep up. They came to a small clearing with a log cabin nestled in trees close to the stream. Jason entered. A shaving kit and clean clothes were laid out on the bed. They were all his size. The rooms were neat. The log walls had been finished to a gentle sheen. A large dining table by the kitchen was covered with piles of paper neatly organized. He thumbed the records. *For me?* It was best to let Chief take the lead in the process that was to be followed.

"There are no locks on the doors," Brontus said after checking front and back, as well as each of the windows. "Also no heat. Just a fireplace for the winter."

"*WHINNEY—WHINNNEY*" Slivers spoke, almost pawing the ground.

"Must be time to go, huh boy?" Brontus said rubbing the horse's face as the beast leaned into his new friend. It took a few tries, but the city boy finally settled on the steed's sloping back before he began cantering.

He could be taking me anywhere. Brontus had no idea where he was or how to get back to Chief's. They departed the stream and arrived at the cabin of Chief Bearstrike as the afternoon sun fell toward the horizon.

The meal was served on simple hand thrown ceramic plates and consumed near burning logs in the coolness of the early evening. As they dined, there was just enough moonlight to illuminate the creek and hills in the distance.

"Chief, I understand why you love this place. It is peaceful. Thank you for sharing it and your thoughts with me," Brontus began. "Slivers took me to a cabin way down the stream."

"It is for you. The horses know all. They are wonderful messengers. Old Slivers may show up to fetch you. Please remember to go with his flow. He is almost twenty years old, each year of which has been spent with me."

Chief filled their glasses with his own concoction of native herbs and stimulants, which tasted rather like beer. "You will sleep soundly," he said, poking the fire and sitting across from the U.S. Attorney, ready for the interrogation sure to come.

"Your explanation is interesting. If what you said came from anyone else, I would ignore it," Brontus began. "But I am prepared to invest whatever time it takes to get to the bottom of what you say. First, I need to make sure I understand what you have told me today."

"Good. Please proceed."

"Do you really think there is a terrorist attack in progress?"

"Jason, as you are painfully aware, some people in this world so hate Americans they flew airplanes into your most symbolic buildings in a strike against your culture and values. People who share this hatred of America, perhaps from oil-rich nations in other parts of the world, have vast sums of money at their disposal that could be used to manipulate American and global financial markets. If such people had access to internal government information, the attack could be devastating."

Brontus paused, obviously thinking. "I cannot argue with that point, scary as it is. You said that you recently obtained records of actual trades. May I take copies with me?"

"Not now. I asked that you come with nothing because I must be certain that we proceed in confidence. For now, the records must stay here. As we proceed, we can decide how to handle them."

"How did you get the information?"

"I cannot tell you just yet."

"But you will?"

"Yes."

"Your explanation of the bubble and economic collapse is all accurate. I am glad to know you made a bundle. You have not mentioned West Mad, which the world wants to believe explains what happened. To use your terms, Trevor Moran must have been the whale. Correct?"

"No, it is not him, as you will see.

"The flames of West Mad are fed by the continuing absence of Moran's wife and children," the prosecutor began again. "I worked with Jaspar Moran long ago. I even spoke to her before she disappeared. The pictures in the press of her in Rome and speculation about what is going on are quite amazing."

Chief sipped his drink and began to roll another of his cigars. He gestured to Brontus, who nodded.

"Frankly, I believe her disappearance is related to the note she received at the time of the plane crash. It said to be silent. Obviously, that means she knew something to be silent about," Brontus continued, lighting the smoke as he watched Chief fill their glasses once again. "Is that the information you will show me?"

"You will find the information to be quite interesting," Chief answered.

Brontus interpreted the answer to be in the affirmative. "Is it connected to West Mad?"

Chief accidentally bit off the nub of his cigar. "Yes," he finally answered, picking up bits of cigar and flipping them into the embers of the fire. "Moran drove his firm as the public face of the bubble as it grew. He was a famous icon, as college athlete and Wall Street guru. Then the crash came, and he went down to Washington. Two bailouts happened in short succession as markets kept falling. A bigger package was prepared. Then his plane crashed mysteriously into icy waters and his family disappeared," Chief recounted the situation. "There can be no question that West Mad is part and parcel of what awaits you. Jason, who could orchestrate all of those elements, if they are connected?"

"I had not thought of it in just that way, Chief," Brontus responded, picking up a fistful of wood chips to throw onto the fire. "These events commenced just after the tenure of Copper Starr as secretary of the Treasury."

"Moran was Starr's boy."

"Yes," Brontus confirmed.

"And Starr is now pushing another gigantic stimulus as secretary of the Treasury once again."

"Can you connect the dots, Chief?"

"Not exactly, but the records tell quite a story."

"Are they trading records?"

"Yes, as well as an explanation of what one person thought was going on."

"Jaspar Moran?"

"No."

"Her husband?"

"The information in hard copy is on the table in the cabin you have already discovered. You will find there everything you need, except communication capability."

"I now understand," Brontus responded. "You wanted me to come and study this information without distraction. If I agree to whatever terms you impose, I will then be able to use the information to proceed."

"Correct."

"And you will tell me the source of the records?"

"Let's cross that bridge when we get there."

"Who is the whale?" Brontus asked, assuming it to be the supposed terrorist.

"From the patterns of the trades that you will see, it appears to be the sovereign trust of the Queen of England."

Chapter 20

Sienna, Italy

"My job is to so engage your friend, so that he becomes fascinated with me, forgetting about you on your own mission?"

Nul and I sat on a bus nearing the end of the hour or so journey from Florence to Siena. At Harry's Bar with Anloc, we had a fine time. The piano player and singer were upbeat and engaging. It was the first wine I had tasted since the plane crash and kidnapping. Anloc and Nul danced, hands on hips gyrating around each other to the beat of popular songs. I did not participate for a long time. Finally, I joined in a celebration of success and engagement. We celebrated our tempering as a team in the flames of that day.

We knew it was just the beginning, but a successful commencement. Alice was outside with Nul's Vietnamese team, our army, on guard as always.

When we departed, Nul watched for a green laser flash indicating all clear from the top of the ancient Roman aqueduct a short block away. It separated normal street traffic from an expansive park.

A late night train took us to Florence. I had visited the beautiful Tuscan community with Trevor before we had children. It was magical. This time it was business. We dressed as Americans on holiday. There were no costumes or wigs, just casual clothing. It was a peaceful respite from Rome. We visited Il Duomo di Firenza, the famous leather school, shops, the statue of David in the Michelangelo Museum, strolled along the river, and relaxed at outdoor eateries. Had our discussions been overheard, he would have seemed a wealthy European of mixed race tempted by an American woman looking for a man with resources to provide refuge. "An observer might wonder from what?" Alice remained close by with Anloc and the others monitoring at various distances.

Our real purpose was to rehearse the role I was to play with the painter and actor Paulo Facti who we were to meet in Siena. He was locally famous. More importantly, he was patronized by Luciano Navarro, leader of the mafia family to which Nul believed the shooters on the bridge belonged. In Nul's assassination engagements with Navarro, he often used the acting skills of Facti to complete his assignment. Nul respected his work, though knew him to be greedy and on the prowl.

Facti would be surprised to see Nul appear with a woman, especially an American. Nul hoped that Facti would wonder what he was up to. The object was for Facti to become enchanted with me. If I was a client, it could mean more work. On the other hand, were I a romantic interest, he might view me as his own sexual target. Facti would not be dissuaded by Nul's presence. The painter could infringe on any relationship so long as he was under the protection of Navarro. If the boss took interest in a woman, the painter would be rewarded for finding a bedmate for the unusual tastes of the Don.

"Yes," Nul answered my question about my role. "I will leave you with Facti, though we will be around. You can summon Alice with the whistle." While in the Outback, Nul taught me to make a shrill whistle with thumb and forefinger compressing my tongue. I could do it even in stress. Alice was always close by when Nul was absent.

"We want Paulo to describe you to Navarro in glowing terms." If the shooters were, indeed, acting for Navarro, our hope was that the man would pounce on me as bait once again.

"I will go with the flow of Facti's questions as he tries to figure out what's going on," I confirmed. "He will be enchanted, I assure you." By this time, I had no illusions about what might be needed from me. The only anxiety was to successfully complete assigned roles. I would do anything to achieve the prize of recovering my children, one way or another.

"Good. I suspect he will want to photograph or draw you, probably the latter."

"I'll go with that flow as well?"

"Just remember that you are a woman seeking refuge and let nature take its course."

"Is this man Navarro familiar with your army?"

"No. He has his own people, as we experienced on the bridge. Ready soldier?" he asked patting my knee as we approached the bus stop. He looked into my eyes with the caution of a combat leader checking troops prior to embarking on a perilous mission.

I nodded. "Let's go."

* * *

"Welcome back to Siena, Mr. Nulandi," the ugly man greeted Nul. They embraced in the Italian tradition. The artist appeared to be in his mid-thirties. His shoulder-length hair seemed greasy, even dirty. He wore a shirt open to expose a hairy chest, accentuating a pudgy torso. His look was completed by a goatee that added to a rather slimy image on first impression. Nul had described him perfectly.

Their greetings were animated with the bumping of fists as if a championship game had just been won. The bus stopped at a crowded transit hub where people switched for rides home. In the congestion, it was impossible to hear their words.

I lingered inside for a few moments tending to my touristy bag. Nul had the valise over his shoulder. Alice was with Anloc for the moment. Weapons were mostly in other hands. Nul turned to point toward me. It was my signal. I stepped down. My skirt barely reached my knees as my long legs stretched to the street. In Florence, Anloc had helped me assemble the clothing I might need. Even without looking, I could feel heat of the painter's eyes focus from my toes to hair. The wig billowed in the wind as I paused at the doorway to look around. *Hungry man, as Nul anticipated. Good.*

"Paulo, I want you to meet my friend Janice Morgan from New York."

Facti stepped around Nul to embrace my hand in both of his. Chin hair tickled as he kissed me on each cheek.

"I am Paulo Facti," he announced in somewhat dramatic Italian-laced English. "Ms. Morgan you are too beautiful to be the client of this awful man, so you must be his lady friend, hey?"

"Paulo, have you no manners?" Nul scolded.

"C'mon, give me a break. I have never seen you with a woman," he responded picking up my light bag. He reached to lift Nul's from his shoulder. I had never seen the valise out of Nul's reach except in extreme danger. There was a message in his allowing the bag to be taken by Paulo, who seemed to measure what it contained by heft.

"No Alice today?"

"She's with a friend," Nul answered.

Does Facti know about the vineyards of the Vietnamese? I wondered.

"And no guns, I see," he said leaning against Nul. "She is a girlfriend."

I smiled demurely.

"Mrs. Morgan or Miss?" he asked, turning back to me. He put both bags in one hand and extended the other.

"Does it matter?" I responded, politely clasping his hand as we walked through narrow, winding streets draped with flags and colorful shops. "This is charming. I can't wait to go shopping."

"I am a wonderful guide," he said, as we headed down a flight of steep stone steps. Worn grooves reflected heavy usage over the millennia.

"This is the site of the Il Palio, the world's most famous horse race," Paulo explained. "Twice a year, horses with champion riders from each of the seventeen contradas, or neighborhoods, of Siena meet in this piazza to race," he continued. We walked around the gorgeous thirteenth-century Piazza del Campo, the town's symbolic and physical heart. "It dates from medieval times."

I stood in quiet amazement looking at the balconies of buildings surrounding the compact area where the race would be conducted. I pictured horses, riders, attendants, and a cheering crowd on bleachers and rooftops. "How could such a race happen in this confined area?" I asked, observing ancient buildings crowding the area paved with bricks. "The diameter of a race course is much too large, isn't it?"

"There are also thousands of spectators," Paulo added. "Tickets are extremely hard to find. I attend through a lady patron of aristocratic Siena lineage. She introduces me as her lover." I could feel Nul smiling, though his back was turned doing his own survey.

The painter spoke with animation even as he waived and spoke to people passing by, introducing me as a visiting friend from America. Paulo made no effort to include Nul in the conversations. He acted as if Nul were a servant, which seemed odd following their previous camaraderie upon meeting.

After we had completely circumvented the brick and cobblestone path, Paulo suggested a restaurant by the steps where we had started. The bar Il Palio was perfect. Inside the steep walls of surrounding buildings, remaining sunlight faded quickly. I retrieved a light sweater from my bag.

"You are not the normal type of person to be Mr. Nulandi's client, Mrs. Morgan," he declared after ordering a bottle of local wine, succulent grilled steak and the prized chianina bread served with local olive oil. I tried to remember the label of Anloc's family. The vineyard's name did not sound familiar, even after taking a taste and inspecting the label. "Very nice," I said, complimenting Paulo's selection.

"Nulandi came highly recommended," I answered Paulo's question between sips. The chilled, white Chianti was refreshing, an appropriate prelude for what I suspected would be coming.

"Mrs. Morgan is tracing her ancestors," Nul explained. "Her family came from this region long ago. Family lore has it that their lands in nearby Manteriggioni were stolen from her ancestors in long ago mafia wars."

"That's interesting. What is your family name? Maybe I know it. If not, I have friends," the painter responded, looking from Nul to me.

"We have it well in hand, Paulo, not to worry. I will be going there this evening," Nul responded.

"As you know, I have many contacts with extensive relationships everywhere. Just say the word, and they will be at your disposal."

"Thank you for allowing Mrs. Morgan to stay with you where I know she will be safe," Nul responded. "I will return in the morning. Perhaps we can meet here about eight."

"My home is yours, as always. I did not know my guest would be a bewitching American," Paulo said, patting my arm. "Mama mia! She will be as safe in my hands as yours, Mr. Nulandi."

The discussion over dinner was light as the men caught up. I was like a spectator, absorbing and preparing. We then crossed the Palio and walked through quiet streets in the early evening amidst breezes. Paulo's three-story townhouse appeared to be in a prosperous area. It had a studio on the first floor, kitchen and living area on the second, and bedrooms at the top. He showed me to a room with doors opening to a terrace. I laid my bag on the bed and stood on the balcony, surveying the peaceful community and far-off countryside. I could see the edge of a steep hill. Nul thought it could provide cover for escape if a ready exit was needed.

I could hear Nul taking his leave as I unpacked and freshened up. Although I had grown comfortable wearing no make-up, except for my disguises, I became adept at creating the image Nul required for the assignment.

"May I get you another glass of that lovely Chianti?" Paulo asked as I descended the stairs.

"Indeed," I answered, seeing that he had also primped. He wore a clean painting smock. He was ready to work. I accepted the glass, took some salted and peppered nuts from a dish and began looking at his work. Learning to appreciate art had been a joy of my prior life. Paulo's work was iconic. Sketches, completed paintings, and work in all stages of development hung from floor to ceiling. There were landscapes in the Tuscan tradition of red poppies, old villas, and meandering hillsides with grape trellises. A painting of a woman walking down the narrow circular walkway around the Palio festooned with red and black flags flying, where we had earlier walked, sat on an easel.

"Not bad, huh?" he asked leaning over the top of the unframed piece.

"Is it your sweetheart?"

"It could be you, the beautiful woman of my dreams," he answered.

"Well, I must say she does resemble me. Did you see a picture of me and do this?"

"How could that be? I just met you. Obviously, you were an inspiration even before our eyes met. It must be a sign, yes?"

"Of?"

"Well you know. A handsome Italian man and a beautiful American of Italian descent alone in Tuscany drinking wine and enjoying art. We are natural, don't you think?"

I smiled, refilling my glass and sampling the cheese and chorizo set on a small table. He did the same at my side as the inspection continued.

There were some nudes and a variety of character studies adoring the walls. The skill of composition and shading were breathtaking. I could imagine many of them hanging in my own home. Each would be a conversation piece, even providing thoughtful introspection. In some of the pictures I saw the faces of Chrissy and Theo. *Leave it, girl!*

"May I do you?" he asked as I returned to the moment. His hand rested on my hip.

I turned to look at him, noticing that he had replaced a blank canvas on the easel, about the size for a portrait. He held brushes in his other hand ready to reach for a palette that rested on a nearby table, a cheese cloth covering the paints.

"You mean to paint me or . . . ?" I asked, tilting my head toward the stairs.

"M-m-m-m, how about painting first. I could do your face, body, or the vibes that I feel from you. An abstraction of your feelings?"

"Maybe not so abstract, but yes."

"Do what you want," I said, pulling a stool to his side where lights would illuminate my face. "Clothes on or off?"

"Let's begin with your face." He worked with deft strokes,

measuring my features with fingers along the brushes as he peered at me from many angles. The wine and watching an artist at work were enjoyable. His touch was warm as he positioned my shoulders or unbuttoned my blouse. I stretched, with legs out and hands grasping the back of the stool. My shoes fell to the floor as I unbuttoned my blouse, imagining that Trevor was busily working away, and I needed his attention. Eyes closed deep in that imaginary world; my nipples felt erect. An almost forgotten hunger came alive. Paulo's eyes seemed riveted on my bare breasts as their covering fell to the floor.

"I thought . . ."

"You paint, I'm just getting comfortable. Watching you work turns me on."

"You and Nulandi are lovers?" he asked, working away.

"Certainly not."

"Good. Tell me, why are you using a man like him to find distant relatives in this area? There are others who are truly expert and loyal. I work for such a man. He might be interested in your search. He likes Americans. You must know what Nulandi is, right?" he asked. I did not answer.

"I am told that he is an effective and dependable man," I responded raising my legs toward the ceiling as if in a Pilate's class. Stretching to touch my toes, I turned on the stool as I unbuttoned my stiletto pants.

"He is that for sure. But his line of work involves eliminating, not finding, relatives."

"I am in good hands, Paulo," I responded, turning back to face him. I slipped the fabric down my legs, twirling the pants on my extended toes. Both feet turned in unison. The light cloth fell to the floor on top of the blouse. My face remained turned in his direction. The man's discomfort was obvious. His eyes were not on my face.

"A portrait, right?" I asked as demurely as possible, with thumbs inside the edge of my transparent, lace panties.

"Yes, as you wished."

"Keep your eyes on my face," I said, pivoting as my legs rose once again toward the lights. The clinging fabric encasing the object of Paulo's obvious lust slid off, flipped by one big toe.

"My face, Paulo. Paint my face, remember."

"What are you doing? I thought we would get to that later," he responded, looking up the stairway.

"A girl's got to get ready. I'm watching my own feast," I answered, eyeing the bulge in his pants.

Stretching again on the stool, my legs pirouetted in circles, spreading to the beat of the music that I had not noticed until that moment.

"There's no hair," he stammered, almost salivating. *Was this what Nul anticipated?* A smile crossed my face. In the Outback, Nul had insisted that my body be hairless. "Sleek like a deadly dagger," he had said.

"You like?" I asked, stroking myself.

"How do you expect me to paint?"

"You're an artist, right? I just want to make sure you're focused on my face."

"But I'm a man and—you're fucking gorgeous." He salivated as I spread my legs as far apart as possible, enjoying the stretching of midriff muscles.

"Do you like this?" I asked touching myself, spreading my labia just enough to feel how wet I had become. The image in my mind was Trevor. The reality of my situation was something entirely different. It was business.

He rubbed himself, placing the brushes in the brightly colored jar at his side as if in declaration, looking at me with covetous, almost pitiful eyes.

My tongue circled my lips.

Paulo came toward me unbuckling his belt.

"Let me," I said straightening and reaching for his hands, which fell to his side. Slipping off the stool, I knelt on the floor. I unhitched his pants and slid them down. He stood proudly in his shorts, his throbbing manhood seeking freedom. I stroked him. *Is he ready?*

"M-m-m-m."

The stiff member banged my cheek as I slid the shorts down.

"Please," he mumbled.

I took it in both hands. *Kinda small*, I thought thinking of Trevor. Massaging him softly, I tickled its head with my fingers, then my tongue. He viscerally shook with anticipation. I put my lips around him, biting gently. His knees weakened.

"*CRASH!*" The stool fell over as Paulo collapsed to the floor. I never let go of him, almost biting his rancid thing off.

"Don't stop," he moaned, as I knelt over him, wanting to find a palette knife to cut his throat. He was hard as a pipe. I slid on top, putting him in me. I imagined what a female rapist might do and pounded with all of the strength in my body. At the pit of my soul, it felt good.

"*AGG-G-HH-H*," he screamed in climax, going limp under me. I remembered the times I had no interest in sex and allowed Trevor to have his way. I let the painter lay there in obvious ecstasy.

"What the . . . ," he bellowed, as I drenched his face with a glass of water.

"Time to finish the portrait, big boy."

"But . . . ?" he objected in a satiated voice.

"Get up. That was just the first round. Is that all you've got?" I taunted, as if he were a competitor in an athletic event.

"I . . . ah, . . . are you serious?"

"Yes, finish," I responded sitting back on the stool, wetness slathered down my thighs. A smile of pride must have been plastered across my face.

* * *

ALSO NAKED, he was back into the painting in moments. The look in his eyes was of delight, as if he had just tasted something delicious and savored the thought of further indulgence.

"I understand that you have worked with Nulandi in his business?" I asked, enjoying the spectacle of the naked painter working away, his shriveled manhood looking like a frightened mouse.

"Indirectly, yes."

"Are you not then a bit hypocritical to be questioning my use of him?"

"Fair enough," he mumbled. His fingers switched brushes, palette touches, and canvas swipes in a graceful collage of motion. It was like watching a drummer in a rock band. I opened a new bottle of wine and filled both of our glasses, enjoying walking naked through his home. Years of intense swimming and athletics, and the training regimens in the Outback, were rewarded in those moments. It was not the fucking. No, it was the feeling of triumph in completing my mission. In those moments, I understood the joy Trevor felt in winning a financial battle or a game back at Notre Dame. I hoped to be winning my current assignment.

Paulo twisted to hide the picture as I passed.

"I want to surprise you," he explained. "Maybe create another kind of ambiance."

Twisting on the stool when I returned to the perch, I kept my legs together for the moment. I scanned the paintings high on the walls as he worked.

"Hold still, please," he repeated. I had stretched to see a nude close to the ceiling. It seemed odd. I could not quite make it out. "Paulo, is that picture over the high window of a man or some kind of animal?"

"You mean the reddish tinted one?"

"Yes."

"You have excellent eye sight," he answered as if mumbling to the floor. "I thought no one could see it. Anyway, it's just an experiment in colors."

"Isn't that a man baring his bottom with an odd grin on his turned face?" I asked. "An old man or what?"

"You are perceptive. It is one of my patrons who has rather odd taste, as many of them do," he answered, obviously wanting to change the subject. *The man is as hideous as Paulo.*

My eyes shifted to the nudes on the lower walls. They were either lovers or women who enjoyed displaying themselves with no hint of modesty.

"Come and see," he said after what seemed a short period and another glass of wine. He rose and took my hand to check out the product of his labor. "What do you think?"

"It's me," I said. It looked like an enhanced photograph. The detail was complete. He even caught the coquettishness of my having my way with him. "You are quite amazing, Paulo. It took only minutes." The image appeared to be that of a gorgeous movie star.

"Actually almost three hours, my lady," he responded, putting the brushes in a jar that smelled like turpentine and placing gauze over the paints. "Ah-h-h," he exhaled, stretching arms to the ceiling then to the floor to relieve the tension of his intense concentration. His hands rested on my shoulders, as we looked at my image.

"You look familiar," he whispered in a thoughtful voice. I listened patiently to see if anything would follow.

"Sure, probably from my fashion shots in glamour magazines," I responded as lightly as possible. He turned to wash his hands.

"Ready for more?" I asked, holding out my hands. The athlete in me was ready.

He stood and took my hands.

"I've just warmed up. You?" I asked, snuggling against him, checking to see if he was yet on the rise.

Good!

Chapter 21

Central Oklahoma

STONE AND SLIVERS knew the way to the cabin by the stream. Even in the dark, they followed its meandering course. It was well after midnight by the time they had finished their dinner and discussion. A forest alive with nighttime voices could have been a source of anxiety for the New York City prosecutor if there hadn't been just enough moonlight to provide comfort from the idea a mountain or bear might descend on him. Chief followed at a distance behind him. Each man was alone with his thoughts. They had far more in common than Brontus could ever have guessed.

The Queen of England? He kept thinking. He understood that Chief had wanted to talk about them, not his theory, until the records had been reviewed to frame the discussion.

How could the English crown be the agent of the economic collapse? It impacted her country just like the rest of the world. What mysteries await me in those records?

"It is all here, Jason," Chief explained standing in front of the kitchen table with piles of neatly organized paper. "I believe the story told in these files will explain why Moran was murdered, his children were kidnapped, and his wife has disappeared."

"Where is she?"

"Not for discussion today," Bearstrike answered, moving so that the table was between them.

Brontus suppressed his instinct to challenge and threaten him with the power of his office.

"There are several elements to the story in these papers. I have studied them carefully and organized the files, Chief began. "In this pile are West Mad reports of the crashing of the mortgage bubble and then the economy. I added a numeric code that keys to the next two stacks, which are trading records from the account of the queen during the same period."

"You organized these?"

"Correct. You may want to reorganize them to suit your own analysis. They are copies, so don't worry about messing up the order. Do with them as you see fit, so long as they remain in this room.

"The next stack is what I think are records of the blind trust established by Trevor Moran when he became secretary of the Treasury. As you well know, the purpose of such trusts is to remove the assets contained in it from the control of the government official. The trades are similar to those of the queen up to just before Moran's plane crashed."

Brontus looked from papers to the Chief. His weathered face had a vibrant glow. *Hope I look like that at 78,* the U.S. Attorney thought. *He is calm, like a professor instructing a student. What does he know? Why is he doing this?*

"What do you mean 'you think?' Are they or are they not?"

"Make up your own mind," Chief answered. "Frankly, I believe they are all phony, made to appear to be those of the queen and Moran. Again, you will have to decide for yourself."

"How did you get blind trust records?" Brontus asked, turning toward his host. "They should be private and confidential."

"Same comment."

"I know, 'not for today,' right?"

Bearstrike nodded as the prosecutor flipped through each pile.

"And the short stack over there, Chief?" Brontus asked, pointing to a small, paper clipped group of papers at the far edge of the table.

"I suggest you read those last. By the time you get there, you will have formulated your own picture."

Brontus picked a clipped set from the top of the stack. "They look like transcriptions," he said flipping through the pages he held in his hand. The focused prosecutor read a few lines, and then looked across the table, curiosity etched in his face.

"When you are done, including the last bunch, let's talk and choose our way forward. It will take you awhile."

"I'm here, Chief, until I understand what these papers and you have to say," Brontus responded, after replacing the last pile of papers. "Even the president is anxious to know."

"We can talk about all that. Meanwhile, everything you need should be in this cabin. If you want anything, just pick up that phone. It will be answered by an attendant and will be delivered in short order," Chief explained.

"From where?"

"The Tribal offices are a ways away, but they will send a helicopter."

"No other communication devices?"

"Correct."

"If I want or need them?"

"Again, Jason, we will get what you need. But first, study."

The U.S. Attorney walked around the table, touching each pile, and then looked around the cabin. "Do I need to put up Slivers?"

"No, he'll graze. The old boy is a fine sentinel, an over-sized guard dog. He has stomped many varmints and rattlesnakes."

Brontus looked in the refrigerator and cabinets. They were fully stocked. "How did you know that I love Scottish Ale?"

"We are resourceful."

"Will you have one with me before you leave?"

"I would enjoy that, thanks."

They filled their cups and walked to the nearby stream where Stone and Slivers grazed on the grassy banks. The men meandered on a broad berm of rock and sand.

"Chief, you knew Trevor Moran, correct?"

"Yes, we had interesting dialogues over the years. It began when he was just getting started in the investment business. Our fund has made many successful bets on insurance. Mr. Moran was working on a syndication of some risks. He learned that we had sold them to his client. He tried to get in contact with me for a while. All such contacts are screened. A member of our team was a big Notre Dame fan and asked me take the call to discuss the situation, which I almost never do. To be honest, I was curious about the skill of a former college football player who became a Wall Street legend. He should have asked why I had sold out, which I would not have answered. Instead, he asked about the viability of this particular type of business."

"And?" Brontus followed-up when there was no explanation.

"You mean, what did I tell him?"

"Yes, please. I'm trying to understand this dynamic."

"What dynamic?" Chief asked.

"Between you and Moran. The documents back there had to come from Moran in some manner, perhaps through his wife. I know you won't explain now. But you obviously had some relationship with Mr. Moran, which I do need to understand."

"OK, Jason," Bearstrike responded as they walked. He stopped under an apple tree. The crunching of hungry horses provided a patient cadence.

"I simply told him to stay away. 'I sold these for a reason,' I advised. 'Let someone else buy, then short it,' was my advice. He made a killing. An anonymous contribution was made at that time to one of our welfare funds. I am sure it came from Mr. Moran," Chief answered. "Thereafter, he called periodically with similar high level questions."

"Why did you talk to him? I understand, as you said, that you almost never talk to people outside the tribe other than with law enforcement people like me."

"To begin with, I knew his wife long before I met him."

"Jaspar?"

"Yes, she was in college at Notre Dame at the same time my daughter Clemenca was at the University of Chicago," Bearstrike responded.

"Where you also went?"

"Yes. They met working in an outreach program teaching English to children of immigrants to your country. Friendship grew and continued after school. Years later, she asked Clemenca to introduce Trevor to me. He was interesting and honest, unafraid to demonstrate his own ignorance. In this business, straight people are rare. It began with thoughtful questions about hypotheticals. He had clever insight. I gathered his job was to implement strategies of someone else. He never explained what or who. For the most part, I agreed with the direction of his questions."

"Did you invest alongside him?"

"No, I work alone."

"Did he ever ask you about home mortgage paper?"

"No, and I would have said nothing because I was so far into it myself, as we discussed earlier."

"If I am right that the papers I am about to dive into must have come from her, what is your connection? How did they get to you?" Brontus asked as they returned to the cabin with empty cups.

Chief swung up onto Stone. "I'll check in with you tomorrow. Take your time. There is a story to be discovered. If you need anything, use the phone."

"Hold on, Chief!" the prosecutor exclaimed, stepping forward and holding onto the rider's leg. Stone stopped as Bearstrike's heels pressed into his ribs.

"You know something about Mrs. Moran, don't you?"

"After your study, we can discuss your questions," Chief answered enjoying watching the New York City prosecutor try to control the horse.

"You want to see if I am on board with wherever you want to go before you get into detailed explanations, right?"

"Tomorrow, Jason."

"OK, one more question. Is there a connection between the Queen's Trust and Moran?"

"Their investments were parallel, too parallel. They had to have been made by the same hands. You'll see it in the records."

Brontus slowed, his thoughts far away. "You're serious aren't you? The Queen of England and Moran, who became the secretary of the Treasury, secretly invested together?" Brontus asked, as Slivers bumped him forward with a nudge to his back.

"City boy, you need to feed him. The oats are in the bucket on a shelf in the little barn behind the cabin. Slivers will show you," Chief smiled at the proud prosecutor stumbling like an awkward school boy. "To answer your question, you can see for yourself in the records."

"You must be joking. Is a new bubble growing?"

"Not in the sense you are asking. The economy is flat, but there is danger. The stimulus plan the president is championing would be a bonanza for the strategy followed by the queen's fund."

"Are you in it?"

Chief said nothing as Stone walked along.

"Is West Mad a charade of some kind?"

Stone paused and circled back. "Jason, you are heading in a sound direction, thinking and asking perceptive questions. As I keep saying, go study, then we can talk."

Did he just confirm that West Mad is some kind of charade? Brontus watched the stallion trot off into the woods. *If so, who could be directing it? Whoever it is must have the president's ear. Good Lord!*

Chapter 22

Siena, Italy
Next day

I STRADDLED the fat, sweaty man as he writhed beneath me claw-ing at my chest in passionate release. My body felt bathed in slime. I clasped his wet hair and jerked it out of his skull.

Shrieks of pain echoed in my ears.

"Where are my children?" I screamed into his ugly face, push-ing the bloody scalp to the side with one hand, and then pulling his head up by an ear. The heel of my other hand jammed into his lower jaw shattering teeth.

"Stop, stop! I do not know," the fat little man squealed as my fingers clasped his throat in rage and frustration. "He has them over there."

* * *

MY EYES opened slowly looking for Theo and Chrissy. The ceil-ing was barely illuminated in a soft pinkish yellow. *The sun must be rising*, I felt the warm rear end of Paulo resting against my knee. The dream remained close to my awakening consciousness. Images of the fat man dying in my hands swirled as I tried to grasp who it could be. *Oh, yes*, I connected. *The fat man in that picture high on the wall in the studio. Why would I dream about him?* I won-dered, turning to look at the naked man asleep at my side snoring softly.

The picture in my mind receded as I took inventory. My face felt pasty. My legs, belly, and breasts were damp. Images of us in bed crowded out those of the dream. Paulo was a torrid lover, over and over. He fell asleep between my legs. He was talented in ways that I had never known.

I hope I engaged him. I sat on the edge of the bed looking around the messy room. My fingers absent-mindedly touched my scalp. *Oops, no wig.* It lay between the pillows. With hair in hand, I tip-toed into the bathroom.

When I emerged from the shower, I saw Facti casually leaning against the sink smoking a cigarette.

"Was I?" he asked with a smirk on his face.

"You mean 'man enough'?" I smiled, remembering my taunt, then winked as I dried myself nonchalantly, as if we were a couple.

He smiled blowing a chest full of smoke toward the ceiling.

"Indeed, being painted by my Italian lover is intoxicating. An encore?" I asked, taking the butt from his mouth and throwing it in the toilet bowl. I extended my hand.

"There's no time now, silly girl," he said pointing to the clock on the wall. "We need to meet your friend at the restaurant. It's almost eight. We'll have tonight. Besides I need a rest. Nobody ever did me like that. You should have a medal."

"A fucking champion?"

Paulo just looked at me, as if trying to figure out what had come into his life.

"He can wait. This is more important."

"You slept too long, Janice. I'm ready to go. You get ready, and I'll make coffee." The painter turned his head from side to side looking at me. "I've seen you before haven't I?" he said.

"I can only say that we didn't meet before yesterday," I answered. "And we sure did meet."

* * *

WHEN I came down to the kitchen, I was hungry. All I could find were nuts and snacks left out in our haste the evening before. They were stale, but the only nutrients available. I ate slowly as I walked back to the gallery of Facti's work. The variety of its compositions was intriguing, as well as the range of subjects. Under different circumstances, his work could have been interesting to study. My focus went to the reddish depiction of the fat, bare-assed man. I pulled a ladder over to get a closer look. It was even more hideous at eye level. *What is the connection to Theo and Chrissy?* I tried to discern its importance in my dream. *Is my subconscious telling me something?*

The coffee was ready when I climbed down. My portrait was wet to the touch. *Trevor would have loved this. It would have hung in the center of his study.*

Pouring a cup, I noticed that we were a little late to meet Nul. *Be patient!* I reminded myself. *Let's see if I completed the assignment.* I thought of Alice whom I had not seen since we left Rome. I knew she was close by. I wanted to go to the window to look for my friend.

"Janice, you never answered my question about why you're using an assassin to find your lost relatives," Paulo said good naturedly as he descended the stairs.

Good, I thought. *He's thinking about things that don't add up.*

"Well?" he responded, putting his hands on my shoulders and kissing me on both cheeks. "You look even better in the morning sunlight. I can't wait for tonight. What will you do during the day?"

"I intend to enjoy the shops and take long walks as I imagine what I can do to you tonight."

"Here in Siena?"

"I assume so. Your friend may want me to visit some people depending on what he found last night. I know he had meetings arranged," I explained, wanting to ask why he was so concerned about where I might be.

"Let's go meet Nulandi and see what his plan is," Paulo said searching among clutter in a closet. He extracted a heavy looking bag. It must have been designed to hold recent work, so drying paint would not smudge. He confirmed that the picture of me would fit, and then he slid it in.

Why is he taking my portrait?

"I forgot a setting," he said, placing a blank canvas and his paints in another bag. I thought he did so to make his taking of my portrait a little less obvious.

* * *

Nul sat at a table enjoying his own coffee at the Bar Il Palio where we had parted the evening before. He sat calmly in the sunshine wearing tourist clothes: baggy shorts, a tent-like shirt, and shades that almost covered his face. The loose clothes would provide cover for weapons. The trusty valise hung on the back of a chair. Nul had connected the handles so it was a backpack. When he saw us coming, he folded his paper.

"I need to be off for a sitting. Meet at my place this evening?" he asked.

"You have my cell," Nul responded. "We will enjoy the beauties of Siena. We have a meeting in the late afternoon. It will be about an hour's drive. Just call and we can coordinate."

We both watched the painter move away at a rapid pace. He bounded up the stairs we had descended the evening before, disappearing into the morning crowd. I ordered juice, an omelet, and spicy sausage.

"Hungry girl," he observed. "How did it go?"

"He painted a picture of my face. He's carrying it in one of those bags."

"Interesting. Was it a portrait?"

"Yes, flattering indeed."

"And he's carrying it now. Very interesting," Nul said,

thinking. "He obviously wants to show it to someone."

"He was anxious about where I'd be today."

"Good. Looks like you got his attention. Let's see what happens. We need to connect with Anloc and Alice to confirm the means of covering our backs. Alice will be with her by now. Something like the bridge in Rome can happen at any time, so we need to be prepared."

"What do you anticipate?" I asked.

"Anything is possible. There could be nothing or more shooters. Facti may be a productive contact. We'll see." I could feel Nul's strategic mind arranging pieces on the board in his head.

"Are you OK?" he asked.

"I'm good. What's next?"

"You seem to have lit a fire under him," Nul said as we walked through streets that became less congested as we moved away from the Palio.

"I hope so," I began an explanation of what had transpired, including my dream and the painting of the fat man.

"Describe the man in the picture," Nul asked turning to look at me with a quizzical look on his face. I explained everything I could remember. "It sounds like Navarro himself. The picture and your dream may be prophetic."

"How so?" I asked.

"We are hoping to learn if there is connection between those men on the bridge in Rome and Navarro. My aboriginal people believe dreams to be subconscious projections. Your instincts may anticipate such a connection," he explained. I began looking for Alice around each corner. I missed her alert demeanor, fearless protection, and unconditional love. I knew she was close; I just wanted to see her. I had similar thoughts about Nul when he was not present, so dependent had I become on his physical prowess and focused determination.

"While you occupied Mr. Facti, I did some reconnoitering to plan a route if hasty retreat is necessary," he continued.

We met Anloc and Alice in a small parish church yard. Alice was happy to see me, though restrained while on duty. Anloc explained deployment of the team that would remain in the Siena area if we needed assistance. Nul described the exit strategy, hoping that problems would not arise between points of safe exit from Siena. "If they do, we will improvise as on the bridge."

"I have the same feeling I did in Rome," Anloc observed as we returned to the city center with Alice on a leash. "Something is coming our way."

To bite me!

* * *

Central Oklahoma

STONE GALLOPED at a steady pace. Sun barely reached above the horizon. Chief Bearstrike held a loose-fitting bridle in one hand. The other mimicked the wing of an eagle in air currents, rising and falling as he adjusted the angle of his hand. The bridle had no bit, as Chief could control Stone with knees and voice, but it provided something other than the horse's mane to hold onto.

He was deep in thought about Jaspar Moran. Remembering his own helpless anguish when his only granddaughter had once been missing and presumed dead, he empathized with the emotions she must be having. *Nulandi is impressed with her,* he thought, recalling their conversation before the prosecutor arrived. Stone's legs flew through the forest and over open land. *Brontus will need to know my connection to each of them once he's on board.*

They sauntered toward the cabin where the prosecutor was studying the records. Like everything else in his world, Bearstrike had built it from timber and rocks gathered from nearby forests and streams. Nestled beneath the branches of trees, it was hidden from view by ground or air.

Bearstrike leapt off Stone while still hundreds of yards from the cabin. The horse wandered to the stream where he could drink and wait in the shade. He knew to watch fish in calm pools to be pointed out if Chief wanted to catch a meal. There was no need to tether the stallion to a tree or otherwise impose restraint.

Before leaving his own space, Bearstrike had activated his computer screens to display in bright colors the results of the strategy he had devised after studying the same data Brontus was perusing. He bet against any further stimulus. Odds on his bets got longer as markets rose in anticipation of the president's program, resulting in redoubling of the bets. He walked between rustling trees with steps unnoticed by deer or rabbits.

Lights were ablaze, but no movement was discernible in the cabin. He moved closer to large windows facing east and west to catch rising and falling sunlight. *Amazing,* he thought upon spying the prosecutor at work. A chart had been drawn on a chalkboard that he must have found in a closet. Bearstrike marveled, squinting at slanting vertical lines tracing market activity up and down, including reaction to prior stimulus injections from the government. *Never thought of that interpretation,* he considered comparing his own analysis. *But we are drawing the same conclusions.*

Formerly neat piles of paper seemed to be scattered all round. Brontus walked from place to place, seemingly explaining something to an audience obviously within the space of his own active mind.

"He's occupied," Chief said, rejoining Stone who stood by the stream watching its inhabitants. Water burbled cascading over boulders then settling into pools to make a comfortable habitat for the trout. They provided sport and food for Bearstrike. He usually threw them back to fight another time when he fished. On this day, he would take a few to grill for the U.S. Attorney whenever he surfaced. *He will need to relax before downloading.* Chief knew well the intensity of a surprising discovery, especially when it pointed to the treachery of supposedly honorable leaders within the reviewer's own government.

Like a skilled bird dog pointing at a roost of pheasants, Stone focused Chief's sure hands as he drew bow and arrow from the quiver resting comfortably over his shoulder. He silently placed the first arrow in position watching trout from deeper pools rise to feast on bugs near the surface. As confident jaws opened to bite, deadly arrows were launched.

In his peaceful realm, Chief could not know that another bite was about to occur on the other side of the world.

Chapter 23

WE WALKED through an area of shaded walkways and streets closed off for an outdoor market. Brightly colored clothes and scarves adorned people happily shopping in the early afternoon. We fit into the mode of tourists with ease. Alice patiently led the way, pausing to accept hugs and pats from children and adoring adults.

Temporary shops attached to vans snaked through the venues. Many of the vendors were Gypsies. Nul visited as if he were one of them. "We're brothers as social outcasts," he said matter-of-factly. *An engaging and charming man*, I thought trying to reconcile his description of himself as a beast with the gentle man I had come to know and respect. *People respond to his simple humanity. I do, too.*

We stopped at a coffee shop. With drinks in hand, we found a quiet bench under trees with our backs to an old stone wall. A small band playing for tips at a distance on a piazza provided peaceful ambiance. It was an Italian scene of dreams.

"Siena has a fascinating history," Nul explained when we could finally hear each other. "It was a way point in the time of the Crusades for warriors coming from what is now France and Belgium. When the Christians were finally defeated in 1291, it played an important role in the opening of China by Marco Polo, movement of the papacy from Rome to Avignon in France, completion there of the New Testament, and eventual return of the Popes to Rome hundreds of years later," he explained with obvious knowledge and expertise. The relationship of these elements of history was a new perspective for me.

When the cups were deposited in a trash container, we resumed our walk along the cobblestone streets alive with busy people and colorful flags flying from windows above shops.

"Paulo's work is a clever mix of the styles of Italian masters, Impressionists, contemporary artists, and his own unique talent," Nul said as we meandered along, stopping to look in shop windows. I had never thought of evaluating the work of an artist, even with Trevor, in building our art collection. Every few minutes, I entered a shop as Nul drifted away, leaving Alice by the doorway. She would sit on her haunches awaiting me for the entire world to see. When he returned, having confirmed our safety, we resumed our stroll. Alice stopped to drink from bowls placed by shop doors.

"Paulo said he thought he had seen me before," I said explaining his questions.

"Pictures from the Steps have been published," Nul responded, mindful as always of people around us as he spoke. "And they've been compared to other photos, especially when you disappeared."

"Or your hunch is right, and this Mr. Navarro and his people are searching everywhere for those who escaped from his goons on the bridge. Only I was not disguised. Perhaps he has seen private or security camera pictures of me." This had been our plan.

"Let's hope so," he agreed.

As we walked along, Nul's eyes scanned streets, people, roofs, windows, alleys, and cars. "We're just tourists here to experience a famous city of antiquity," he had explained. At lunchtime, we stopped at a pizzeria that must have been close to a college, as there were students crowding the streets all around. They sat on curbs, window sills, or any open space, talking loudly and gobbling their pies.

Nul held my hand while ordering a margherita with thin crust and a bottle of Chianti. He slipped his arm around my shoulder as he carried the pizza in one hand. The embrace was reassuring. Anloc's prophetic comment rang in my ear. *Something is coming.*

Alice waited by a bench under a tree. Her demeanor indicated nothing amiss. In the distance, the picturesque view of the Tuscan countryside was breathtaking. *Just like a painting*, I pictured my children in the beautiful landscape.

Alice patrolled along the walls of the streets on either side of the little park where we sat, returning every few minutes. "Tell me about Alice," I asked as we ate and enjoyed the soothing Chianti.

"By now, you know she is on duty," Nul said.

"Always it seems," I agreed, "though she sits at my side when you are not around."

"She is bred for protection in whatever form is necessary," he explained. "This Alice is actually the third. As I completed jobs after leaving the Army, it became crystal clear that I needed a trustworthy companion. So, I began doing my own breeding. It was difficult getting wild dogs to breed in captivity. Training was even more challenging. I worked with many dogs to find that first partner."

"You are a patient man," I responded, still thinking of his seemingly disparate personality traits.

"That first Alice was a natural, far different than all the men and women I had served."

"How is that?"

"She never deviated from the task at hand. No conflict or ego. Just a job to be done."

"How long did she survive?"

"Only a few years. She lost her life in a shootout while guarding my back. Others said she jumped to take a bullet . . . intended for me," he said with a catch in his voice.

The sun warmed my shoulders as it illuminated the face of

the man who had become my protector. As we spoke, his eyes revealed a sensitive, inquisitive, keenly intelligent, and confident man who was willing to share himself as we passed time in the open. We waited to learn if anything would transpire in the hoped for meeting of Facti and Navarro.

Why is Nul doing all of this for me? I wondered as I had since our first meeting.

"Fortunately, there was a puppy I had been weaning who became Alice the second."

"What happened to her?"

"Run over by a truck I had been using as cover in an ambush," he answered, looking away to see the current Alice returning.

"And this one?" I asked as she sat between us facing the street.

"It took almost two years to breed and train her. The job requires special instincts," he said stroking the coarse fur of his friend. "I learned much from her predecessors. This one is truly precious. She will save us both before we're done."

"I hope not at the cost of hers," I added.

Nul touched the top of my wig, which was bathed in sunlight, as he stood to get gelati from a vendor singing a short walk away. "What will you have?" he asked, "raspberry or cactus flower?"

"Cactus flower? In Italy? Come on, you're pulling my leg," I smirked watching a grin spread across his handsome face. The scratches and cuts from our jump in Rome were healing, though they framed a rakish visage. "Bring me what I deserve."

He walked with the same easy stride as in Rome. Girls watched him almost bounce along. He seemed like a happy man with light in life and happy, as his name signified. *What is it?* I wondered as he returned with cones in both hands and a skip in his gait. One was yellow. The other seemed to be an almost blushing pink.

"It's a combination of Italian cream and strawberry," he said handing me a cone. "It matches the color in your cheeks."

"What happened to the cactus flower?"

"Just enjoy." Licking slowly, I savored its refreshing taste. He had lemon. "Sour like me," he said with eyes dancing in mirth. He touched my cone to his nose, leaving a pinkish smear, which he promptly removed with a flick of his tongue like a lizard snatching a fly.

The afternoon sun was hot, even under the shady tree with a breeze coming up the hillside from far below. The old city must have been laid out in a manner to facilitate such natural cooling. Alice hopped from the perch between us and resumed surveillance laps. As we finished our dessert, she trotted up the cobblestones to stand in front of us. Nul attached the leash. Comfortable that nothing of interest had yet appeared on our horizon, we resumed our stroll.

We continued our perusal of the town, awaiting the outcome of my time with Facti, hiking up the hill to the Ufficio Catechistico Diocesano, or Cathedral of Siena, with its iconic bell tower of colored bands of marble arranged in horizontal stripes. Sitting on stone steps, we watched people come and go. Alice sat in front. Children and some adults stopped to pet the apparently docile pet. She seemed to beg for attention or food, playing like a puppy as adoring fans became comfortable with her. Nul took a turn around the piazza and surrounding streets as I sat with Alice. I felt relaxed, anxiety draining from me amongst people on holiday.

When Nul returned, he released Alice and took my hand. "Let's go inside. We need to talk while it is quiet."

We entered the church and sat in an alcove of the huge cathedral basking in the sunshine that filtered through stained glass windows. We chose a pew behind a small altar, against a cool stone wall with an ancient tapestry depicting St. George and the dragon. Nul turned toward me, one hand on the pew and the other on my leg. "You have asked me a couple of questions in our time together. I always wanted to answer, but often there was not time for complete response or I was not ready. Now is a good time," he began.

For the first time all day, a tremor crept up my spine. *Bad news?* I put my hand on his. "Tell me, please."

"You asked why I was helping you. I answered that my sister asked me out of respect for Father Michael and your long ago connection to the orphanage."

I nodded again. *Let him talk*, a patient voice in my mind counseled as his demeanor became somber. He had never answered this question. As I learned how sensitive and caring he could be, I periodically tried to engage him. He was almost always quiet or changed the subject.

"You also wanted me to explain my relationship to Chief Bearstrike."

"Please. Are they related?"

"Yes, which I want to explain," he said, never averting his eyes from me. I tried to have no expression or response.

"But I must use plain language. On one of my assignments, I was hired to do some killings in East Texas. It's a long story. In the course of my work, I discovered that the people were honorable and needed to live to complete an important mission relating to the so-called 'Jewish Gold' of the Nazi Holocaust. Ultimately, there was a highly publicized shootout in Washington."

"Yes, yes, I remember," I broke my vow of silence recalling the stories about a gunfight on the steps of the U.S. Supreme Court. It had been sensational news for weeks. "You were there, at the Supreme Court?"

"Yes."

My mind reeled. *Wow!*

"I saved these people. When it was all over, I came to know them. One of the critical people was the granddaughter of Chief Bearstrike. His only living descendant. She had been kidnapped. As I said, it's a long story."

I squeezed his hand, sensing that there was a whole lot behind his simple words. *A kidnapped child? Is that the connection?*

"Chief was grateful that his family had been saved. Over time, he supported Ismerelda's orphanage and handled investment of its and my resources."

And the connection?

"When Father Michael asked her for assistance for you, it was obvious that you were connected to the stories all over the Western media. In death, your husband became a pariah. Ismerelda asked me if we could help. She knew you from before and honored Father Michael. Because he was such a famous Wall Street personality, I checked with Chief to ascertain whether this was something we should become involved in. He encouraged us saying your husband was honorable regardless of what the press was reporting. 'If there is any way you can help, please do so. I honor that man,'" he said.

Nul's hand squeezed my knee, as he leaned forward to touch by forehead. "Do you know Chief well?"

"My husband did. He is reclusive. I never met him."

"Chief and I developed a code from our native languages for communication back then. He used it to explain his relationship to your husband, as well as the records that came into his possession from your friend Crystal. Chief also advised you and Mr. Moran had your own code that you transcribed for his review."

I was as stupefied as I was when told of Trevor's death. I could not put the pieces together. It was too much at one time. I looked around the nearly empty church. Placing my hands on the pew, I rose, stepped around Nul, and went to the main altar. I knelt in prayer.

"So we are not alone on our journey," I said upon returning.

"Correct. It may be coincidence or destiny," he answered. I felt calm once again. "When I learned of these connections, I felt an urgency to help you."

Perhaps, there is destiny for me as well. "This code you and he developed is another connection. My husband and I had our own, as you said. Chief and Jason Brontus will be examining transcriptions that I made." *Amazing.* I felt comforted. I patted his hand, which was still on my knee.

"Is there another thing you wanted to talk about?" I asked, feeling that he needed encouragement.

He knelt in the narrow space between the pews, almost bowing his head. I touched waves of soft curls. His words and action during our time together had framed an entirely different person than the word *beast* he used to describe himself. His life was inconceivable; never to have known a mother or even his sister until well into life. *What would that be like? What would it do to a young boy taught to kill?* I had wondered so often, even earlier that day, as I watched him with Alice and the local kids relaxing in the eye of a tornado. I could feel emotion welling in him.

"Tell me, please," I whispered leaning close, putting my hands on his shoulders.

"I was trained to kill from a time when I was hardly out of swaddling cloth," he said softly word by word, trying to control the emotion that came from deep inside his soul, perhaps never articulated before. "As a young boy, I could do things that no grown man could accomplish. I matured as an angry, driven person. I never stopped to wonder why. Killing made me feel better." Once started, the words began flowing like a stream from a melting glacier followed by long moments of quiet.

"It's OK, Nul. Just say what you feel," I said as I did with my children in their moments of fear and anxiety.

"I struggle with my feelings. Even more trying to put those feelings into words."

The contrast of the meaning of his name, happy man, and this reality was jolting. Warm tears rolled down my knees as his body convulsed. Maternal instincts in me responded. It was all I could do to let him tell his story, not hug the battered child inside to my breast.

"It feels cold in me, like I am some kind of machine."

I clutched the slumping man who gripped my legs like a vice. His body shook. The tears felt like the glue of two lonely people needing bond.

"Nul, I understand. You are who you are. There was purpose in what happened to you," I responded, feeling that I was consoling

Theo. "The essence of my faith is resurrection and rebirth. What you have been defines you no more. You can be reborn," I said placing my hands on his head. "God will judge you on the basis of who you are, not what you did.

"I judge you based on my own experience. I see you partially in the eyes of Alice. She is a loving animal with precise training. I believe you are the same, with your heart and soul just emerging."

He looked up into my eyes.

What do you need from me, Nul?

"Sister said to help you. 'Your faith will emerge in that process, brother, I feel it,' she said to me." The vice around my leg tightened.

"Jas, will you with your great faith guide me to find my own? It is what I want and need. My life is meaningless without it," he said.

I wiped the tears from under his eyes. "I am here for you as you are for me, Nul. Let us both find our lives."

"Thank you," he said as long minutes passed. I sat back against the pew, comforted by the wetness of my legs from the tears, still glistening in his eyes. "I no longer want to be what I have been. What I will be, I do not know," he added, sitting again on the bench at my side.

My lips compressed holding him as if he were one of my lost children. *They must feel the same, if they feel.* I pushed the ugly thought away.

"Thank you, sister. Thank you for listening to me," he finally said in a child-like voice.

I just held him.

"It feels good to put words to feelings," he finally said. "There is just one more thing I need to tell you, then we must go."

"Please."

"My mother left a book with my things at the orphanage when the military took me. It was placed in a box. When I retired, sister still had it," he said looking up with red eyes as he sat in the pew.

"When I opened that box, well, I believe it was the first time in my life that I ever cried. There was a note in the book." He took deep breaths and spoke slowly. Crossing his legs in yoga position, with each foot atop the opposite knee, he turned to me, sitting with amazing balance on the narrow wooden seat. Breathing deeply, Nul composed himself.

"It spoke the simple words of a girl with a broken heart. They are inscribed in my soul—'My son, I will never know you. I suckled you just one time. You will grow up not experiencing my love, as I will not know yours. When you find your faith, please ask God to forgive me for what I did out of love for your father. He could not survive the wrath of my people. I may not either. I will pray to hold you again before I die. Whoever you become, your home is here in my heart. I love you, son, with all that I am. Please come home to me.'"

The words of loss hung in the heavy air of the church. I struggled to comprehend the feelings of abandonment and abuse of mother and son. I had a foundation of love. He had nothing.

When he finally spoke, it was with clear voice, relief in his eyes. "Jas, I am on my way home. Thank you for caring about me and giving me this chance to find my rebirth, as you call it," he said, taking my hands. "Now it's time to move on."

We walked out into the sunshine. Anloc awaited across the piazza. Nul took the leash and we walked toward the Palio. As we headed down a narrow lane after crossing the race course, Nul released Alice.

In the shade of a tree, I stopped to say a prayer. "Thank you, God. Thank you for bringing this man into my life. We have a common journey. Please give me the strength to do Your will," I whispered. Nul knelt beside me speaking softly in a tongue that I did not understand.

We intended to go to Paulo's flat. Alice went ahead to make sure the coast was clear. We walked silently in a circuitous route through the narrow, medieval streets. Nul held my arm. It was the same kind of grip when trouble had come in the Vatican to guide me up the back stairs to the Sistine Chapel. Now, his grip tightened as our pace slowed. His other hand crept to the small of his back. *What does he sense?* I wondered, knowing that he would not touch his gun unless readying for action.

"What is it?" I asked.

"Keep walking."

As I tried to discern the meaning of the change in his demeanor, Alice rounded a corner some fifty yards in front running at full tilt. "*YELP! YELP!*" she barked.

"Showtime!" Nul said pushing me toward a ceramics shop that he had pointed out earlier in the day, one of many potential escape routes. It was decorated with brightly colored urns, vases, and goblets. A small, gray-haired woman sat behind a lapidary table painting a pitcher.

What did Alice see?

Chapter 24

"PLEASE COME into my shop," the artist said rising to greet me. My name is Lucia Barone the owner of this shop." I inspected the beautiful pottery painted by the artist.

"May I show you something?"

"Could I see that vase over there," I said, stepping behind her, trying to peek through the open doorway. Nul seemed to be waiting. As I watched the street, then the lady, my mind checked-off Nul's instructions for the arrival of danger. "I cannot predict when or where attacks will come, but we have cast you as bait for the sharks. They will bite again. When that time comes, the weapon you have is your own guile. We are in no position to carry an armory of weapons. Make your instincts the instrument of survival."

I admired the beautiful ceramics while listening to Mrs. Barone explain her methods of mixing vibrant colors from local clays and minerals. The reds, blues, purples, yellows in innumerable combinations gleamed in bright overhead lights. I tried to listen patiently. Commotion from the street got louder. From the corner of my vision, I could see Nul talking to someone in agitated tones. *Alice?*

"What is out the rear door?" I asked Mrs. Barone. "Please call me Lucia," she responded showing me the area where she mixed the colorful glazes. I knew to look for an escape route for myself, or Nul and Alice, if needed. Urns filled with glazes were nestled in the corner of a small garden behind the shop. They were caked with color from so many combinations over an obviously long period of time. *I would love to purchase these and have them in my home*, I thought seeing an image of Chrissy, Theo, and Alice sitting by the hearth of an unknown place.

One of the urns contained utensils used to measure and mix ingredients. I picked one that looked like a garden trowel covered with sharp edges that were colored from dried glazes. It felt comfortable in my hand.

A fieldstone wall stood at the edge of the little yard at about chest height. I peered over to see what lay beyond, anticipating a sheer cliff. There was a rough path that looked like an old alley, though it was too narrow for vehicles. It also had a wall running along the outside probably providing a barrier to a cliff beyond.

"Where does this go?" I asked.

"Around to the street," the shop owner answered.

Really? I stepped through the gate. The path seemed to go behind old buildings constructed from hewn beams and bricks. I looked over the wall. The view was breathtaking like a painting of Tuscany. There was even a villa on a distant hill with lush green rows of grapevines basking in the sunshine and shade trees adorning a meandering driveway.

I followed the path as it wound around the curving hillside. A small opening was almost hidden in brick work. It was a narrow walkway that led in the direction of the street where we had been walking. I followed it, peeking around a corner. Men were running toward me. Looking the other way, my heart froze. Three men with drawn guns pressed Nul against a wall. Alice stood by his side, looking up at the muzzles obviously awaiting instruction. Nul shook his head, pointing to himself. *They're looking for me! He is feigning ignorance.*

One of the men kept looking in my direction. *At me?* His line of sight was to the men also coming with drawn guns. One was speaking into a phone as he ran.

Nul is surrounded! Do something!

Stepping onto the street, instincts from some place within me took hold. *Distract them!* I pulled my shirt down, pausing as on a Parisian runway. Twisting, I pushed my pants down making sure that all eyes were on me. Stepping out of the clothes, I had their attention. Alice's as well. Her tongue retracted as her eyes focused, looking around. *She understands.*

"*AYAAHAAH!*" I screamed running at the men pillorying Nul and waving the trowel. At a distance, it must have appeared to be a dagger.

The nearest gunman stepped back, stumbling. His instincts were confused by a naked woman running at him with a drawn weapon. He raised the gun.

Think about fucking me, you piece of shit! I thought, straightening my shoulders as if readying for a thrust. I looked into the eyes of Nul. They were cold and focused like a caged animal. He winked as his feet delivered a sharp kick to the interrogator's midriff.

"*AGH-H-H,*" the struck man groaned falling backward. In an instant, Nul grabbed the gun and smashed it into the man's head. Swiveling, he kicked the legs out from another attacker as Alice bit his throat. The third goon raised a weapon from Nul's blind side taking his eyes off me. Running at full tilt, I jumped over bodies and leaped as Nul had taught me. Landing on my left foot, I jammed the trowel into the assailant's neck, twisting with every ounce of strength in me. Nul turned to snap the man's neck amidst gushing spurts of blood.

BAM! BAM! BAM! came reports of approaching guns. Bullets zoomed past my ears as chaos churned. People in the narrow street ran toward the Palio taking cover wherever possible. Their screams added to a chorus of horror.

Nul grasped the gun of the last man to fall, handing it to me and pointing at the men running toward us. The attackers fired wildly.

"Come fuck me!" I screamed, rising and running at the attackers coming toward us. They paused, seeing dead comrades sprawled in the street, a man firing their weapons, and a naked vixen with bouncing breasts in full flight firing a stolen pistol. As they tried to pivot to run in the opposite direction, their heads exploded from our gunshots. It was the second time I had shot a gun to kill.

"Get their weapons, wallets, and bags," Nul yelled, as he scurried to pick up everything he could from the downed men. I could see Alice returning to get the backpack that Nul must have dropped by the door to the shop.

I went from body to body. With a tap to my shoulder, Nul pointed to the ceramics shop with a gun. He then fired shots into the air. Bystanders remained in cowering fright blocks away. Sounds of sirens reverberated off the stone walls of narrow streets.

How will we get out of this?

Chapter 25

Nul ENCASED my bare shoulders with his arm as he led us back into the shop. He dispatched Alice for a job along the path I had run. When we opened the door, Lucia stared with a look of incredulity and horror. I was nestled against Nul.

"Lucia, this is my husband," I explained. "They are after us."

She looked at us with curiosity, not fear in her eyes. "These men are local gangsters," she said.

Emergency equipment sounds and the wail of penetrating police sirens came from every direction. I turned to look at Nul, back to the lady, then down at myself. Blood soaked us both, providing a cover of sorts for my body. I touched each bloody spot, checking for wounds. The lady brought a towel, pointing to a sink in the rear of the shop where I could clean-up.

"Police?" she asked, pointing to her phone.

"No," Nul responded.

"Hospital?"

"No, we must get away," he explained in Italian.

"Police are coming," Lucia said, looking toward the window with rising sounds of commotion coming from the street.

"Yes."

"For you?"

"They will be looking for witnesses and survivors," Nul answered. "Please stand here for a moment as my wife dresses," he said escorting our new comrade to stand in the doorway, making no effort to clean himself.

"Oh, mio dio," she said looking out the door into the chaotic street. Bodies littered the place where tourists should have been browsing. Spilled blood seeped into ancient paving stones as it dried in the sunshine. Curious people edged in as emergency workers arrived. Local press stringers followed the sirens, snapping pictures. Helicopters approached.

"You survived this?" Lucia mumbled in horrified Italian.

I stepped to the back to wash myself and get dressed. Alice must have barked or otherwise gotten Lucia to open the door, trotting in with pieces of clothing I had discarded in my flight.

When I looked back to the front, the lady was patting Nul's face. *Huh? What happened?* Before I could speak, they were heading toward me. Nul held Lucia's arm. I realized that he had been slashed in the head. A gash crossed his brow and blood stains marred his face. She had tried to clean it. I stopped him long enough to give it another once over. The cut was deep and would continue bleeding for a while. His collection of wounds were becoming a laundry list.

"We did OK?" I asked. Nul patted the backpack into which he had placed the spoils of this fight.

"What's out back Lucia?" he asked turning to the shop owner and seeing sunshine out the door at the rear of the shop where Alice stood. I had not really looked at her. *My God*, I thought. Her mouth was also coated with blood dripping on the floor. The dog let me examine her jowls. I wiped the blood with a towel already soaked by cleaning Nul. Her gums were raw, but no serious injury. I washed my hands and face in a basin. In the mirror, I saw a woman who looked familiar, though with a new a cold set to her chin and a scowl. I winked. She winked back.

I went to the street to peek out the door again. *Amazing!* I thought seeing that Anloc and her friends had arrived. She saw me. I drew a finger across my throat and shook my fingers, meaning "we're leaving, create a disturbance."

"Let's go," Null yelled, trying to get my attention over the racket in the street. I turned to join him as the artist shut the door and put a "closed" sign in the window pane. She then followed Nul to the back.

"There is a working yard, then a path, and a wall along the edge of the hillside. There is a steep drop," Lucia finally answered Nul's question about the area behind the shop hidden from the street, as she had earlier explained to me.

"How far down?"

"A long way."

He stepped through the gate to the wall to see for himself, and then he surveyed the supplies in the yard. Alice was at his heel.

"That tarpaulin," he said pointing to a bundle of sheeting that must have been used to cover freshly turned clay pieces as they dried in the sunlight.

"Yes, I . . ."

"Can I buy it?" he asked, anxiously looking over her shoulder back into the shop. The sounds of police and emergency crews seeking to restore order wafted from the street. They would be checking the bodies of dead attackers as well as injured bystand- ers. They would not be searching for those who disappeared into the shop, not yet anyway.

"But it's filthy. I use it as a drop cloth," she protested.

"That's OK. How much?" Nul asked. The tarp had ropes strung through eyelets along the edges that were probably designed to secure it as a covering against winds from the valley.

"Take it," Lucia answered.

Nul pulled the ropes, tying them at the corners to test their strength. "Perfect!" he declared pressing one hundred Euros into her palm.

"It's too much."

"If anyone asks, tell them we jumped," he said taking my hand as we walked forward to the gate. My eyes must have widened as I looked at the tarp in his hands and the wall ahead.

He's going to jump!

I had earlier looked over the cliff. This leap would be far more dangerous than the one from the window at the Vatican. How would we survive it?

"Are you crazy?" I asked watching him slip the heavy backpack over his shoulders. My mouth must have hung open watching him adjust the straps. Strong shoulders tensed under the weight. "You can't jump with that. We'll drown for sure. Leave it," I said, exasperation dripping from my hoarse voice.

"It's OK. Put your arms and legs around me," he barked lifting my hands around his neck once again. He adjusted my legs around his waist. With his hands on my bottom, he pulled me into him as tightly as possible. It felt good. I could not have been on his back due to the valise-backpack.

"Alice," he commanded. She jumped between us as meat in a sandwich.

He lifted us to the wall making sure we were steady. The tarp draped over the wall. Holding onto it, Nul jumped up as if he were merely mounting a pommel horse in a gymnastic routine, not a wall facing a drop of hundreds of meters.

I gripped his waist with my legs, trying to provide some support for the backpack full of the attacker's guns and other paraphernalia.

"We did this before," I whispered hoping to add lightness to the certain death that awaited us.

"Piece a cake," he responded leaning around my shoulders to hold onto the tarp. I could feel him working the lines, twisting them around his arms then flapping the tarp in the air. The massage along my torso was almost relaxing. Over his shoulder, I could see Lucia, hands clasped in prayer.

"Hold on," he barked standing on his toes at the edge of the rock wall. *How many times will I hear those words?* I wondered. *Many more, I hope.*

"Look to the horizon Jaspar. Don't look down. We'll be fine."

Or road kill, I thought as we jumped into the abyss. My chin was locked onto his shoulder with my hands clasped under his arms. I imagined us being ground as grist in a mill by thousands of tires crushing life out of our bodies pulverized on the busy street far below.

The ropes scraped across our faces as we fell. There was a jerk as the parachute took hold in the air stream coming up the cliff. Nul's shoulders and laterals absorbed the shock. *"AGG!,"* he gasped. I felt the muscles of his entire body tense trying to hold the ropes as the g-force almost separated us from the parachute and each other. Alice seemed calm as Nul's strong hands tugged at the lines, first this way then the other. We became a glider, even rising a little in response to his motion in adapting to air currents.

"OK?" Nul screamed into the wind.

I held on for dear life. When I finally opened my eyes, the horizon provided a Tuscan panorama. I tried to determine if Nul was navigating or enslaved by the winds. Ignoring his command, I looked down. We had crossed the busy roadways and were soaring over the countryside. Strong arms pulled the ropes to guide our course to some destination I could not see. My legs remained locked around him. We twisted in the winds. There was a river in the distance to which Nul seemed to be heading.

Better to drown than be pulverized by tires, I thought with grim optimism.

As the minutes dragged on, I tried to imagine the strength required to hold the sheet for such a long time. The tension must have been intense, also weighed down by the valise on his back and dog between, at least doubling his body weight. His arms were strapped to the tarp.

"To water, be ready. Ball your legs," the pilot barked.

Obeying the command, my muscles felt like they were being stretched on a rack. I pulled my knees into his arm pits with the leverage of my fingers digging into his neck. I could hear his feet just brush tree tops.

"Let go!" Nul screamed.

"Oh, Heavenly Father . . ."

Chapter 26

Outside Siena

THE FREE FALL seemed to last an eternity. I hit the water butt first with outstretched legs slapping the water. The impact stung as if I had been whacked by a board. My body descended deep into the cold water. When I finally focused and tried to push myself upward, I became almost delirious. Determined not to drown, I reached upward with all of my remaining strength, gasping for unavailable breath. *"Don't die, rise to breathe, my daughter,"* I heard through the chaos in my drowning mind. There was hope in my life. My will to live was stronger than this adversity. My efforts to stay in shape and Nul's training served me well as my body responded to the command.

When I finally reached the surface, fresh air provided a welcome greeting. Exhausted, I thrashed in the water trying to stay afloat and looking for Nul. There was nothing but gentle ripples. I looked up into the sky to see if he might still be falling. The wall from which we had jumped seemed like a cloud so far away.

Where's the parachute?

"Nul?" I croaked swimming back and forth. Images of him drowning under the weight of the backpack were vivid in my mind as I saw no sign of him.

Can I do this without him?

"Yo!"

I twisted to see him rise above the surface like a Pacific whale arching over on his back and crashing back into the water. He swam as if there were no care in the world, coming to me with a certainty of where I waited.

"Are you OK?" he asked. I touched his face with appreciation for what he had done. The blood on his face had been cleansed by the water.

"Can you swim farther?"

"How far?" I asked.

He pointed to Alice who had found the nearest point of land. I had not seen her after I let go. She paddled at a brisk pace. No problem, I nodded.

"You go. I'll gather up the rigging." It was only then I saw he still held the parachute in his hand and the backpack was still firmly attached to his shoulders.

How could he have come back to the surface with those anchors?

I had barely touched the shore when Nul caught up with a large ball of plastic and rope. He held it like an over-sized exercise ball under his arm and led us into a grove of olive trees. "We need to keep moving. They will come looking for us," he said. "I want to get to a place by the river where we can see in all directions. Then we can rest."

Alice led the way. When we reached an opening in the fruit trees, Nul spread the tarp he dragged behind us. I thought he wanted to eliminate any trace of our path, but he intended the opposite, hoping that the smoothed ground would attract attention. He wanted to be followed.

Without saying a word, he took off his clothes and hung them on low branches of the trees. He turned his back, so I would not be embarrassed by him standing naked watching me remove my own sodden clothes.

"*HA—HA—H—HA—HO!*" I laughed for the first time in months. Nul turned his head with genuine surprise written all over his face.

"After all we've been through, do you really think I care whether you watch me hang up my clothes?" Indeed, the smile on his face was endearing, almost fatherly, in terms of kindness and caring. *How charming*, I thought. And from a warrior. I made a show of it, which he watched with interest. *Good.*

With clothes and backpack hung to dry, we sat on the wet plastic. Nul was deep in thought. I stretched my arms and legs watching his brows furrow.

"That was kind of fun, don't you think?" he asked, as if we'd been on a roller coaster in an amusement park.

"Fun? I don't think so. Thrilling, yes, which seems to keep happening to us."

"For sure," he said touching my shoulder and biceps. "You are a strong woman, Jas. In both body and spirit. I admire you. There is no whimper in you. A job to be done, you do it. Kangaroos, men, friend, or foe. Thank you! We have an uphill struggle in front of us. So far, we have progressed just fine. I hope it continues."

His touch felt soothing. The gentle prodding was tender and caring.

"OK, soldier," he continued. "Here we are. Mission accomplished for now. Whoever has chomped on our bait will be coming. If we can hold on when that bite comes, we may have our string. My backpack hanging over there is full of wallets, guns, and communication devices from our shootout on the street up there. The phones will be dead from the water, but I may be able to extract data from the chips when we get to a place where I can work. The stuff from the bridge will also have been analyzed by Anloc and her team."

"Soldier? Me?"

"Indeed, you have earned your stripes. You are a fighter in a war in which we face an enemy with deep resources. You have something that is vitally important to resist relentless attack."

"I must win this war Nul," I said leaning back not thinking that I was naked in front of a man I cared about deeply. He was in the same condition, resting on a plastic sheet in a natural setting by a waterway in Tuscany. It could have been an idyllic scene for a story. Instead, it was my life.

"That is your secret weapon, girl. You will not be denied," he continued looking me over in the sunlight, filtered by dense leaves. "You are also a beautiful woman."

"You are beautiful, too," I answered admiring his taut body. The strength required to pilot a dirty tarpaulin as if it were a glider was doubtlessly beyond anything I could imagine, even after a lifetime with a college football player who had been attentive to his physical condition.

"Please listen to me," he said, rising to cup my face in rough, strong hands. "This mission has now taken on a life of its own. It will traverse terrain that we cannot even begin to predict. We will be together reacting and adjusting as necessary to achieve our objective. We are warriors in extremis."

His forefinger touched my forehead, traced down my nose to my chin, then my shoulders, He touched my nipples one after the other. I just looked into his eyes, which were riveted on mine. I felt neither shame nor sensuality.

His finger touched my hip bones, then my knee caps.

"You are dependable, Jas," he finally spoke. "We now sit here naked. An hour ago we were in combat. An hour from now we may be searching for food, sound asleep, or in harm's way. If it's cool, perhaps we might lay in each other's arms to keep warm."

I thought of sleeping with Paulo. *Should I say something? No, that was just a step in the process. It was necessary to advance the ball. Like killing the kangaroos or attackers on the street. He would certainly have done the same to advance our ball.*

"Are you trying to say we're not going to have sex?" I asked. "Trying to let me down gently?"

He merely smiled.

"Listen, I would kill you if necessary to save my children, and I expect you to do the same. You tell me what I need to do, whatever it is. I will do it. That is our deal."

"Agreed," he said as our hands grasped.

"OK, leader, we have the bad guys where we want them, right?" I asked.

"Indeed, our fishing worked. You are obviously tasty bait. My assessment of Paulo turned out to be correct. He sold us out."

The sun set as we relaxed, a slight chill in the air. Our clothes were dry enough. "You need to rest," the commander of our squad directed. I did not object.

"Where's Alice?" I asked, retrieving my clothes and making a pillow of sodden shoes.

"In the time we've been talking and relaxing, she's gone in both directions. Here she comes."

I turned and watched my friend trotting toward us from the opposite direction from which we had come.

"Has she found something?"

"Up stream, yes," Nul answered.

"What?"

"She believes there is no danger. Could be campers or others who could help us."

"How?"

"We need transportation and communication devices."

I looked in that direction. It was dark. I could only make out trees and the stream. "What about the Army? Can they help us?"

"Not now. No one can help us now, not even them. Besides, they would just get in our way, and probably get themselves and us killed. These people are after us, and we need to simply slip away," he responded. "An opening for us will arise. We need to be patient, keep moving, and prepare for the next attack.

"How could anybody find us here?" I asked, mystified at how we could be followed.

"I do not expect people to come, just an opportunity to move forward. Alice may have found something."

"His confidence was comforting, as always."

"Correct," Nul agreed. "I need to go upstream, and you need

to stay here with Alice guarding my back. If anyone comes after us, Alice will get you to me."

"What do you think will be coming?"

"Nothing that we can't handle. Please watch with Alice," he said, disappearing into the night.

Alice snuggled into me and I held tightly in my tired arms, like Chrissy with a stuffie.

Chapter 27

Central Oklahoma

"THESE TRADING records tell the tale don't they?" the U.S. Attorney asked, standing with Bearstrike at the fire pit watching the trout filets roast. He had ridden over to Chief's cabin on Slivers.

"I make the charcoal myself, including a natural accelerant," Chief explained the almost instantaneous eruption of fire when a match had been thrown into the randomly shaped briquettes.

Brontus seemed to be exhausted from a long day cooped up with mounds of data. A cup of Bearstrike's wine and discussion about the beautiful scenery viewed on the ride fueled a resurgence of energy. The city boy was obviously proud of navigating the unmarked path to Chief's cabin. *Brontus has become a member of our team here*, Bearstrike thought, smiling to himself with the knowledge that Slivers knew the way.

"I studied the pile of records," Brontus explained when ready to return to business. "I can see the outline of what could be a terrorist attack, which seems to be confirmed by Moran's notes that someone must have transcribed. The originals look like gibberish."

"They were for sure," Bearstrike responded checking the fish to make sure they did not burn. "We need to talk about that."

"And a lot more, Chief. I have a lot of questions including the ones you have evaded answering. The records don't reveal who, what, or why. You offered to provide answers so I would understand who is attacking our system, causing the collapse, and why. And then there is Mrs. Moran and the queen. We've just opened the lid on a giant can of worms," Brontus said.

Chief lifted dinner from the fire. The delectable aroma of the fish marinated in natural herbs induced hunger. "Let's eat. Our discussion will be better on a contented appetite." Bearstrike placed the filets on plates resting on an ancient hand-carved table at the edge of the porch. Vibrant reds and yellows of the sun setting in the west framed mountains in the distance, bathing the forests with a blanket of beauty.

"Let's begin with what I have found and its implications," Chief said when they had consumed the fish and cornbread baked over the same fire. He filled cups as they sat back in chairs fashioned from tree branches.

"I have scrutinized every line of the data you have read, digitized it for my own use, determined what I think it means, and acted upon it at my own risk," Chief began. "The trading pattern revealed is one I know well. I did largely the same on a smaller scale as compared to what some groups poured into the markets," he added, offering a round of smokes. "But before I explain what I have found and done, I want to hear your thoughts. I need to make sure we are on the same path."

"You believe this trading strategy caused the financial crisis?" Brontus began.

"Yes," Chief responded. "The patterns in these documents also reflect the approach I believe will be used for further attack. Another round of bailout most definitely will ignite another financial collapse."

"OK, Chief, I think I understand," the U.S. Attorney answered, trying to put it all in an order he could explain in Washington. He drained the cup then walked to the fire pit where a pot of coffee brewed. "Let me draw a picture," he continued, taking a stick from the embers and pushing chairs back to make space, as Bearstrike removed the dishes. Brontus smoothed the dirt then began drawing lines. He walked around the chart in the dust, erasing here and there, redrawing, and pausing to survey his work all the while puffing on his cigar.

When it was done, the prosecutor circled as if rehearsing his explanation. Satisfied, he turned to face Bearstrike returning from the kitchen. The investor stopped next to his guest.

Just like on the board in the cabin, Chief thought, admiring the work. *Like a skilled trial lawyer, using a visual image to prove his case.* "Tell me what you have drawn, young man."

They stood together to see the creation from the same angle. Brontus pointed with the stick to the left hand line.

FIGURE 1

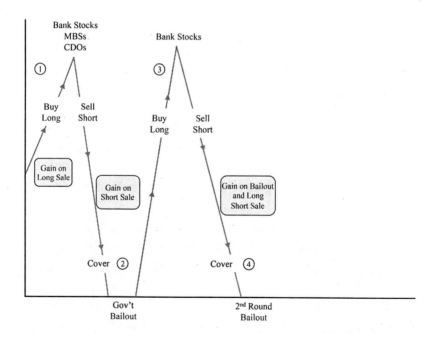

"The first upward line reflects the bubble that began with the mortgage-backed securities and sub-prime lending. Westbury Madison created the units and marketed them to push this market advance. It held much of the paper in its own inventory, selling periodically to produce the first level of profit which I have marked with a *1* in a circle. Correct?"

"You're smarter than you look, white man," Chief responded, chewing the cold end of his cigar and spitting into the fire. "The buying was done on a massive scale by Westbury hedge funds. The profit taking at *1* on your chart happened within a period of years. Investors were attracted by reported gains and stayed in the game, which is why the curve continued its upward arc. They bid the bubble up, setting the stage to profit when the rising rocket sputtered, right here," Chief continued, pointing to the top of the first ascending peak.

"These profits were then deployed to take short positions, selling stocks and securities not actually owned. When the market crashed under the massive sell pressure, cover was achieved by purchase at depressed prices producing profit *2* right here," the prosecutor continued, circling the *2* drawn in the dirt. "In other words, Westbury touted its hedge funds in the rising market as it bet against the rise for its own accounts."

"Precisely! However, there may not be a securities fraud issue here. An investment bank's schemes and strategies do not have to be congruent," Bearstrike said.

"I'm not so sure about that view, Chief, but I understand what you're saying. Whether the risks to the public were explained will have to be evaluated. If not, a raft of Federal crimes could have been committed," Brontus said. Referring back to the chart again, Brontus pointed out that as the contra bets succeeded, economic collapse followed as the banks incurred losses on the mortgage portfolios and became insolvent. "But for Westbury, the short strategy produced the windfall at *2*," he said.

"Correct again, in terms of the windfall," the Chief responded.

"What you have drawn is the strategy that I also followed, cautiously taking gains at each step. I did the trading in my own way, not through Westbury. Now, you will ask, is Westbury the terrorist? I believe it was a front for the real party of interest."

"The English queen?"

"So the files indicate."

"You don't seem convinced."

"No, it makes no sense," Bearstrike answered.

"Why?"

"The amounts were too massive. The resources behind these plays had to be in the range of trillions. Not even big banks could do that. The question is where did it come from? The answer will, I believe, identify the terrorists."

"And who murdered Moran and kidnapped his children."

"Precisely," Bearstrike answered. "The Queen's Sovereign Trust is plainly inadequate for this, though the records you have reviewed indicate that it was the source."

The prosecutor scowled with mind engaged. "So you're saying we must find some group with access to vast capital?"

"Yes, and wanting to destroy the system in the process."

"Who?"

"I have an idea, nothing more."

Brontus scowled, thinking through what Chief, voice of the wind in this crisis, was suggesting. "OK. Let's just call them the terrorists," the prosecutor suggested, returning focus to his dust chart.

"Now, when the banks were insolvent and stocks at essentially zero levels down here at 2, Westbury began again buying those same stocks with the profits generated by phases 1 and 2."

"They also had access to the billions of bailout money provided by your government," Bearstrike added. "The stocks were so cheap and the world so scared that huge positions could be acquired for relatively nominal amounts."

"By the terrorists?"

"Well, yes, and others like myself."

The prosecutor paused as if composing his next question for a witness.

"And these terrorists are a very real danger to your Western way of life. They intend to destroy it as they did the banking system before the bailout, which largely ended up in their pockets," Bearstrike added.

"Fair enough, let's use the term terrorists with the understanding it also includes good guys, like your tribe."

"Agreed."

"So, we can assume that the terrorists had effective control of some or all of the banks at the bottom before the next upward line began when the Fed disbursed the bailout money leading to *3*," Brontus continued. "In essence, the government thought it was rehabilitating failed banks to resume lending and restart the capitalist engine?" he asked, watching Chief spit into the fire. "You waste nothing, do you, Chief, not even the tobacco in the cigar butt?"

"Correct on both points. You should try chewing. It's therapeutic."

"Says Bearstrike the medicine man." The prosecutor's butt was on the carved table, where it had added another burn mark to the collage of such scars. Picking it up, he inspected the soaked, cold, herbal concoction. Flipping it in the air like popcorn, Brontus caught it in his open mouth. After chewing for a moment, he spit it into the fire. *Splat!* He actually enjoyed the taste and the green benefit of no waste.

Bearstrike smiled. "You could be an honorary Cherokee, white boy."

"And my kids would get their education funding?"

"A good topic to address when we have solved these mysteries," he answered, offering his hand to confirm a bond with a thumbs up, laughs, and good-natured slaps on the back. The horses looked around at the commotion.

"So, the government's largesse really benefitted the *terrorists*?" Brontus asked.

"Yes, the plans were not all bad. Misdirected, but not evil. It was a response by the same central bankers who allowed the bubble to grow. They were victims of the limits of their own perception and experience. Like a surgeon asked to cure sore muscles. He'll use a scalpel—it's all he knows. Markets were happy with the bailouts, so the trend line turned up here with restored confidence toward your *3*," Bearstrike answered. "Banks were happy. They had free capital to resume their evil ways, focused, as always, on their own short-term, best interest to sell whatever people were stupid enough to buy. Perhaps more importantly, the terrorists were happy. The bailout stuffed their accounts for the next attack."

"Then the process started again," Brontus responded pointing to *3* and *4*.

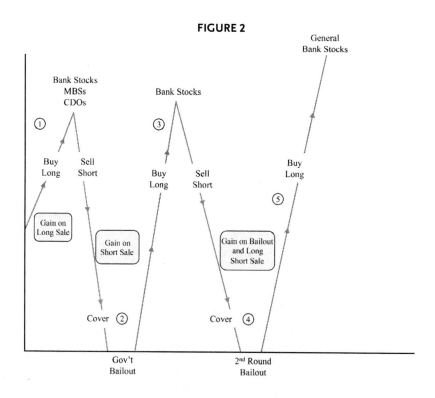

FIGURE 2

"Except for one thing. You have drawn two peaks and valleys," Bearstrike added, touching *1*, *2*, *3*, and *4*. "I believe a massive tornado is forming to inflate what is intended to be terminal to collapse the entire system." He took the stick and drew a circled *5*, followed by a bigger peak. "This is what I believe our terrorists are anticipating from the next, even bigger stimulus package that your president is demanding."

"You mean that the profits from *1* to *4* plus the next stimulus will be used to create your tsunami?" Brontus asked when Chief drew the third ascending trajectory.

"Precisely."

"Are you placing your investments to reap this new windfall as well?" Brontus asked. *How do I convince the president and Cabinet to stop this stimulus fiasco?* He watched Bearstrike tap the stick on the mountain to the right of *5*.

"No, I am placing my bets against that strategy."

The experienced prosecutor had to stop, his train of thought rejected. "You are betting that stimulus does not occur?"

"Correct. I'm doing it to discover the identity of the terrorists. It is obviously not Trevor Moran. He's dead. Or Westbury Madison, which is under investigation with its funds frozen."

"If there is another stimulus you could lose a bundle," the hard-nosed U.S. Attorney advised.

Chief nodded as sounds of the evening amplified their silence. "Could be, but I doubt it. The truth will come out. That is why we are here. I expect to make a windfall at the expense of the terrorists. If we do, my tribe will have to find some worthy public purpose for its gains. We already have more capital than we can spend for the benefit of our people, no matter how broadly we define the diaspora. We would likely expand our support to native peoples of all types within this country, then to other impoverished peoples. That is our mission."

"But your opinion is that if the heroin of more stimulus is dropped into the system, we will have this next attack followed by complete collapse?" Brontus asked for confirmation.

"Precisely, right here at circle 6," Chief confirmed, taking the stick and completing the chart. "Our system is then vulnerable to anything, like Germany's hyperinflation debacle in 1920."

"Chief, what we have drawn here is a scenario of intentional destruction, right?"

"Yes, in my opinion."

"We are in agreement. I need to study the files and your analysis further. I must then convince the president of this dust scenario and convince him to drop his demand for stimulus," the prosecutor said.

The U.S. Attorney walked round and round the chart as if sizing-up a feared adversary. Slivers walked in his direction, nodding his head and stomping his feet. Brontus stroked the horse's chin bones and tussled the mane between his eyes.

FIGURE 3

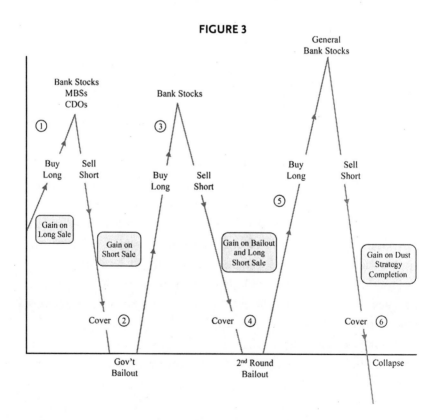

"OK, Chief," he finally said while sitting on the edge of the burning coals where he could look Chief straight on. "Moran was killed and his prominent firm destroyed. His children were kidnapped. Then his wife disappeared. You have his records and translated explanations you seem to acknowledge came from her. You suggested that the terrorist was the Queen of England, then you said that was not possible. If you are satisfied we are on the same team, will you please explain all of this so we can develop a plan of counter-attack?"

Bearstrike nodded, crossing his legs with a refreshed cup in his hand. "Will do. May I make a statement, ask a question, and then frame a proposal?"

"Please."

"As I will explain, Mrs. Moran is in the company of a friend," Chief said. "Frankly, they are leaving a trail of corpses behind as reflected in a wire service story of a few hours ago. Whether this means they are leading the bad guys into an ambush or something else remains to be seen. That is the statement. Is your government their adversary?"

"Mrs. Moran is leaving corpses?" Brontus asked, too stunned to react immediately.

Chief nodded.

"No, of course my government knows nothing of her whereabouts. I'm sure of it. We have no idea where she is or what she's doing," Brontus finally responded, doubt echoing in his voice. "At least not to my knowledge. What is the proposal?"

"I think you need a large cup of my wine before I make my proposal, which concerns the relationship between Moran's murder, Mrs. Moran's trail of death, the Queen of England, and your White House," the skilled investor said, handing over a wire-service story featuring a nude woman running at the camera with a dagger in hand and a headline of "Aphrodite Attacks."

Chapter 28

Outside Siena

NUL MOVED along the riverbank. It was too dark to see tracks that Alice may have made for guidance. She would walk in the water, on stones, or leaves so no marks would remain. He did the same. Wet clothing was ignored. Much of his life had been spent in operations on the ground adapting to whatever conditions existed. His normal process would be to secure his team, reconnoiter to see if they were in safe or hostile territory, then forage for food, clothing, cover or whatever else was needed. They had beached in a remote flood plain of the river. While there were no houses, farms, or barns close by, Alice had found something.

What happened in Siena? he wondered, picking his way through dense riverbank foliage that rose to shoulder level. All sorts of *flotsam and jetsam* lodged in branches, everything from plastic bags to snake skins. Dry conditions indicated no recent flooding.

I thought we had cleanly escaped Rome. Yet we were found in Siena? It must be Paulo, he thought with a smile walking along without a weapon other than a piece of driftwood. It was long enough to be a walking stick and sufficiently balanced to use both ends against multiple adversaries. He had left the backpack hanging in the tree to dry not expecting to need a weapon.

It could only be Don Navarro. Paulo reported us to Navarro. Nul knew both men. The mafia don was a patron of Paulo's work. Their relationship began when Facti got involved in a local drug scandal involving bribery and blackmail of city officials. It had been done without Navarro's knowledge or approval. The don engaged Nul to cleanse the mess while protecting the government people. They became indebted to Navarro when he took over the operation.

"The artist is worth saving," the don had instructed. The rest were disposed of by Nul without public or police notice. In the process, Nul came to acknowledge the painter, who provided an education in art appreciation. In the current context, Nul had suspected a connection to Navarro from the tattoos of the dead men on the bridge in Rome. It was what brought them to Siena, where it was confirmed. *Our bait may have succeeded,* he thought, pushing through the dense brush with no more sound than was made by the wind.

What did Alice find? he wondered, moving forward one step at a time.

If it is Navarro, why would he be involved in this West Mad? he paused to listen for sounds of people or activity. He heard nothing and resumed the slow trek along the riverbank. The night was illuminated by twinkling stars. Dense trees hid far away city lights. Sounds of the night and the rippling water were peaceful.

He knelt on rocks. After he read the note from his mother, he learned the rosary. "Hail Mary, full of grace. . . . Heavenly Father, I have sinned my whole life. I never confessed. I do now for all those people I dispatched from this world. This woman Jas seems to be on a path of your making. I will deliver her children as my sister asked," he whispered, bowing his head to the stones and tapping them with his knuckles. "Is this your plan for me as well, Lord?" Nul felt peace settle upon him. "Thank you, Lord."

About five hundred yards upstream, he encountered an enclave. A fire in the midst of a circle of vans had burned down to glowing embers. There was no sound. With stick in hand, Nul approached silently. He saw that there were men asleep near the once burning flame. Bottles of home-brewed potato liquor lay around. There was candlelight in each of the six vans, but no sign of movement. He tried each door peering inside. *Women and children, also asleep.*

Checking the trucks, he found neatly-stacked merchandise bins. *Merchants awaiting their next bazaar?* he guessed. *Perhaps we chatted with them today in Siena.*

At the edge of the clearing, a ragged old truck was stuffed full of boxes of fruit and vegetables smelling a bit too ripe. There was no one inside or lying nearby. *This will do!*

Nul put the transmission in neutral and pushed it a hundred yards away. When he was far enough removed, he switched license plates with one of the other vans. He searched around the sleeping men to see if he could find a cell phone. *I need to touch base with Anloc.* There was nothing to be snatched without disturbance.

Now what? he wondered, driving the van to what appeared to be the road to Siena. When he reached a cluster of ramshackle shops near a bridge across the river, he parked behind the buildings in a clump of trees where a trash dumpster provided cover. He dumped the fruit and vegetables. When it was done, Nul slumped against the truck. It had been a long, exhausting day. *I need rest.* He looked for a place to lay down, then reconsidered.

I've taken too long and Jaspar will be frightened when it all sinks in. I must get back. Fighting exhaustion, his pace accelerated as he retraced prior steps along the river.

* * *

THEO AND CHRISSY were in the clutches of a monster preparing to eat them like monkey meat on a stick. The room was bright. Bound to poles with jeering crowds all around, their heads hung as if in sleep. Salivating creatures brushed them with some kind of marinade. Firewood lay at their feet. A torch was close by.

"*NO!*" Alice pressed against me preventing movement. Her neck leaned over my mouth to muffle sound. She climbed on top of me. Strong paws reached around me with a vice grip. *It's OK. Relax!* was the cadence of communication.

"Theo, Chrissy?" I murmured, reaching into the darkness to

touch the souls I had just seen. "I love you. Where are you? I want you here with me," I whispered as Alice's hug tightened sensing that I was at the edge of hysteria. Though just a dog, she had experienced countless missions. Men and women often break under such strain. She had been trained to sense emotional instability and then clutch the damaged person even at the sacrifice of her own life.

I cried out in helpless release of pent-up emotion that had grown in me during the many weeks since their kidnapping. "Will I ever get them back Alice?" I whispered as calm began to return. She whimpered in my ear. In moments, my anxiety settled. Alice sat back on her haunches.

"You silly dog," I said touching a finger to her nose. She panted patiently, tongue draping from an open mouth. I lay back holding out my arms. Alice snuggled in facing the opposite direction from where Nul had gone. *Watching our back*, I knew.

"Who is this man of yours, Alice?" I asked. She had the capacity to create chaos and kill with vicious jaws, but she just lay quietly doing her job and accepting my embrace. "You do not know, do you? He is all you have ever known. He seems calm, never excited. Sister said I could trust him. You do." Alice looked into my eyes. Her even panting was warm on my face, which she slowly licked. Her paw patted my leg.

Does she feel like a child substitute? I wondered. *Dear Lord, please hold my babies safe until we can save them.* I slowly sank back into slumber.

In time, I rose again in a different frame of mind. "Where is Nul? Why did he not come back? Has he abandoned me?"

Alice was on guard, her back to me. She turned to face me with calm eyes, her head moving back and forth trying to understand. She perched her paws on my legs as if to answer "it's OK." I held them then jumped up clutching myself. Walking toward the river, I bumped into trees and underbrush in the darkness scratching and cutting my bare skin. I did not think to put on the clothing that had been my bedding.

I'm alone in this place in the middle of the night! my mind screamed. Submerged tension erupted again. The dream of lost children, awakening nearly naked in a strange, dark place after being attacked and killing to escape was overwhelming. Being without the sturdy man who had become my lifeline triggered an emotional meltdown.

My pace accelerated as I tore through the brush.

* * *

NUL RACED along the riverbank as fast as he could while keeping a low profile. He was bent at the waist, shoulders hunched, and head up picking a path through trees and overgrown underbrush, pausing periodically to listen. Hearing only the sounds of the river night, he resumed.

I am on a path, Lord, I can feel it, he thought, stopping by a huge tree. *Please give me strength.* The hardened, secret veteran of almost every war of the last thirty years said a silent prayer.

Helicopters emerged from the distance. Nul did not see the green and red wingtip lights hidden by the dense foliage of the river. They came from both directions. Instructions to the pilots were simple. "They jumped. Find their bodies or blow them away." The Italian army choppers were equipped with electronic and body heat scanners. Gatling guns could eviscerate anything in their path once triggers were electronically activated and barrels trained on targets.

Running in combat pose, Nul hurdled brush and skirted trees with sure feet. A voice was carried on the breeze. His ears perked. Fleeting sounds came from down river. *The Gypsy camp? Wrong direction.* Not a soul had been encountered coming toward the camp. *Who could it be?* He assumed it must be voices from the camp carried in roundabout winds beneath the hills and over the water. *I wonder if they discovered the missing van?* He accelerated, running at water's edge no longer concerned about tracks.

Is it Jaspar? Has someone come for her? he thought as recognition dawned. At about the same time, his ears picked up the familiar sounds of approaching choppers.

Attack helicopters. Coming from both directions! How could this . . . ? He realized that the enemy would be searching for body heat. *Jas and I are in the open. Stupid dumbass! You should have thought of this.*

* * *

MY HEAD slammed into a low tree limb. I barely paused racing ahead. "Help!" I screamed, staggered momentarily then resuming my pace.

Alice stepped in front sensing my freight. I ran past her.

I groaned, tripping over a rock hidden in the dark, producing another gash to my forehead. Blood and perspiration blurred what vision I had as my pace accelerated.

Alice bound in front determined not to be thwarted again. "Alice, what...?" I started to say tripping over the strong dog and falling forward on the rocks along the shore.

I heard sounds in the sky that resonated like one of Theo's action video games. Alice's ears perked as she pressed me to the ground. The night stars were magnificent. As the sound in the sky got louder I tried to look up to find its source.

WHOMP! came the sound of a heavy weight crashing on me, followed by *WHOOSH!* as the impact forced air from my lungs. A hand clamped over my mouth. I felt Alice at my feet.

"Shut up, Jas!" Nul whispered, pinning me to the ground. I heard and saw nothing, I only felt the hot, anxious body holding me completely still. "We have only moments to hide from what's coming."

"Jump in the water and swim about half way out. Then dive and hold your breath as long as possible. I will wait a moment then be right behind you to replenish your air with my own." I dove into the water and held my breath. It was easier than trying to reach the surface of the river earlier in the day.

The next thing I felt was Nul's hands on my neck. He held my head and pressed his lips against mine. His tongue opened my lips. Opening wide, I exhaled through my nose as fresh air was blown into my chest. We both went limp for what seemed an eternity with Nul's hand firmly holding my own. It was dark so I could not see blood from our cuts drifting in the current. Alice was under my legs, somehow holding my foot with her mouth. I had no time to wonder how she could have known to submerge to hold me in place.

* * *

NUL'S GRASP and lift signaled time to rise. We came up and looked around.

"Oh crap!" he exclaimed in a soft voice, twisting his head back up stream from where he had come to intercept me. "The camp," he said. "It'll be what the sensors lock onto." I did not know what he was talking about.

"The people up there in the camp will be caught in a firestorm. I'll explain later, hurry," he said leading me out of the water heading in the direction from which he had come. "Be ready to jump back into the water if the choppers turn our way."

"Alice, water ready!"

* * *

THEN WE heard belches of airborne guns blazing trails of death and destruction. Tracers illuminated splitting trees, exploding gas tanks, people running for cover. Nothing could survive the sudden onslaught of machine guns. I watched and listened as Nul led us into the river. We swam upstream ready to descend if the airborne machines turned in our direction.

Heat emanating from the camp must have dissipated. As we

watched, the aerial murderers set down. Mercenaries dressed in what appeared to me to be full battle dress searched the site with bright spotlights and hand-held devices.

"I walked through there," Nul whispered. We stood in water that came to my chin. "Mostly women and children. We probably saw them in Siena at the bazaar. Helicopters must have been searching for body heat, oblivious to the presence of anyone other than us. Onboard sensors must have locked onto the body heat of those poor sleeping souls. It is not an area where humans would be expected to be present unless on the run."

"Now, they're looking for us?"

"Not yet. The attackers will be taking DNA samples from each body, as we did, plus pictures for identification. We have some time for our next step."

"Will police come?"

"No," he responded, watching the men moving toward their helicopters. Only a few gunshots had been fired on the ground. The onboard guns must have done their job efficiently. "By morning, bodies of children, mothers, and fathers will be incinerated and the ash interred in landfills. Hulks of trucks will be removed and bulldozers will clear the site. Vegetation or flood will return the area to its natural state."

"It could have been us?"

"Yes, or your children if we fail."

Chapter 29

Central Oklahoma

THE IMAGE of a rampaging vixen seemed to leap off the page in the prosecutor's hands. "Aphrodite Attacks" read the wire service headline of the shootout in Siena. The picture of a nude woman in furious flight with weapon in hand attracted global attention to a rapidly escalating story. There was as yet no connection to the West Mad stories from America.

"Damn fine body on this warrior," he said with a gleam in his eye and a whistle on his lips. "Chief, is it time to relax and talk about women? Or are you into battle porn?"

"I gave it to you for a reason, but not those. Does she look familiar? Look closely."

"No."

"What if I told you my friend advised of an assault on them in Siena, and I found the story?"

"Seriously?"

"Read it again."

"Am I supposed to know her?"

"Yes."

Brontus took the page to a light. Reading carefully, he traced the face with an index finger. Consternation spread across his face as he looked back at Bearstrike, who nodded in affirmation.

"Holy shit, it looks somewhat like Jaspar Moran with no hair," he concluded. "I've known her for many years. I certainly never guessed she had a body like this," Brontus explained, walking round and round the fire pit. Lifting one of Chief's smokes, he sat back down and picked up a stick from the fire.

"Is it her?"

"Yes."

"Was she fighting or running?"

"I only know what's in the story and confirmation from my friend that they survived."

"Why was she naked?"

"I have no idea. It does not appear that her clothes were burned off. Whatever the reason, I'm sure it's interesting," Bearstrike answered.

"I gather that this event just happened."

"Within a few hours."

"Who are the dead men?"

"I don't know that either."

"Hold on Chief, I'm confused," Brontus protested, stepping to the table where a decanter labeled "Bear's Strike" sat. "Maybe a fill up will help clear it up. You, too?" He topped both cups taking his time before resuming his post by the embers that seemed to glow incessantly.

"We went from reviewing records and your framing of relationships, to Jaspar Moran engaged in a gunfight on a public street in Tuscany. What the hell is going on here?"

"It keeps getting more bizarre doesn't it?"

"Indeed. In all my years of prosecuting financial and other crimes this may be the strangest and most dangerous case yet. Please connect the dots for me."

"Mrs. Moran believes the children are being held to enforce her silence. Probably because the kidnappers fear that her husband assembled records that could lead to them, which is why he was murdered. She is being cast as bait hoping to reveal a path to their captors."

"And the fear is validated by the files I read in the cabin?"

"Precisely."

"Are you in contact with her?"

"Indirectly, yes. The man who is shepherding her is someone I know and trust. We are in touch."

"This is your friend?"

"Yes."

"How do you communicate?"

"He is an Australian Aborigine and converted his native language into a drumbeat. I adapted it with our language to make a code. We communicate on phones or audio devices with those vocal beats. It is an efficient system, facilitating constant communication when we need it, like now."

"Smoke signals?"

"In a way, but we are always too far apart."

"Who is he?"

"My friend."

"You will not tell me?"

"He has no identity as far as the world is concerned. It is a long and painful story that is not relevant in our mission."

"Which is?"

"As I said, to learn who is holding the children. That is the key to unlocking the other mysteries."

"Why is she risking the children's safety by disappearing and becoming this bait?"

"To the contrary. Her passive silence would be their death sentence once the terrorists' goal is achieved, which will occur once the stimulus is released, precipitating the final collapse in your dust chart. At that point, the children serve no purpose. That is the risk. She would then simply be awaiting their corpses."

"OK, let me see if I have this in the right order," Brontus said patiently. "Mrs. Moran is with your no-name Aborigine friend in Tuscany. She has been dangled in such a way as to be recognized. Contact has been made with some group resulting in a gun battle leaving dead bodies in the street. Even bad guys would not randomly shoot into a bunch of tourists unless their target was there. So we can assume that the baiting strategy succeeded."

"Agreed."

"Well, that's progress. The story says there were no guns found at the site and the killers escaped. Do you think your man picked them up?"

"I'm sure of it. They'll provide valuable intelligence."

"Any idea where they went? The story says they jumped off some cliff."

"No, but knowing my friend I am sure he will lay low, reconnoiter, then re-engage on his terms. There will be more action."

"One man, alone, against an armed gang?"

"Not totally alone. Mrs. Moran obviously has become a serious asset in the quest."

"And a dog. The story says a vicious dog was also involved?"

"Yes, again. My friend's friend."

"Chief, this would make a great movie. Your premise is that the economic health of the world is under attack. Its only defense is an Aborigine, a society woman, and a dog?" the prosecutor responded raising his cup in salute.

"The world is in good hands. You and I are also on the team."

Brontus could only smile and shake his head admiring the obvious confidence of the Chief.

"Is this Siena situation related to the similar shootout in Rome several days ago? The story didn't connect them, it just says it's the second public gunfight in Italy within a few days."

"Yes. Same result in both cases."

"Any idea who is behind it all? The kidnappers I mean."

"The terrorists, as we have been using the term," Bearstrike responded, pleased that the prosecutor seemed to be coming on board.

"Who is also directing these attacks?"

"I am sure of it. While I have no idea about the situation on the ground in Italy, I do have a line on someone connected to what I believe to be the U.S. side of the plot," Bearstrike answered.

"This relates to your proposal?"

"Yes."

"Before we get to that, sir, I have a personal question to ask you to be sure I'm grounded in where you fit into this puzzle."

"Shoot."

"Why are you doing this? You know this Aborigine. There must be more. You would not go to all of this trouble and risk unless there were some hook to drag you into what is obviously a stinking, dangerous mess."

"Fair questions. There are two reasons. The financial security of my tribe is at risk from the conspiracy that has become so clear to me. It also threatens our collective security, meaning all countries with inner-connected economic lives."

"Understandable, what is the second reason?"

Bearstrike paused, debating in his mind whether to explain the actual reality. "Jason, we are now in this together so there needs to be no ambiguity on either side," the Chief began. "As circumstances around the crash of Trevor Moran's plane became known, and the West Mad business erupted, I sensed that something was very wrong. I respected Mr. Moran, and no matter how hard I tried, I could not put the pieces of this evolving puzzle together."

Brontus nodded in agreement.

"There is only one person in the world I trust enough to begin working on what was then such an amorphous inquiry. I asked my friend to be prepared to undertake a new project. 'There is a skunk in this woodpile, and it's not Trevor Moran,' I said. I also explained that I had received documents he intended for me, which you have just reviewed.

"How did they get to me? They were on a memory stick. Mrs. Moran entrusted it to one of my colleagues, who she introduced to me long ago. My friend also advised that a Catholic priest had contacted his sister about arranging for Jaspar's extraction," Chief explained.

"Very interesting. Like pieces of the puzzle began coming together," the entranced prosecutor responded.

"So far so good, but there is a long path in front of us. At least, we are beginning to see the real landscape to continue adjusting our plan of attack."

"Chief, please explain how you came to meet this friend you describe with such confidence and respect. Your words and manner are endearingly personal. I need to know the connection, as it may become critical for me and my president as well," Brontus asked with a mind opening to new vistas of thought and emotional connection.

Bearstrike opened his hands to accept the clasp of his new partner, leaning forward to lock eyes.

He's shaking, Brontus thought, feeling emotion rise in the outwardly calm leader with tears welling in his eyes.

"I owe my friend a debt which could never be repaid with treasure or my life. Only with honor," Chief responded. "You know that I do have a family?"

"No, I wasn't aware of that."

"Yes, I had a daughter. Her name was Clemenca. She died several years ago. Her daughter, my granddaughter, was kidnapped. It ended with the shootout on the Supreme Court steps. I'm sure you remember it."

"Of course, but I didn't know you were involved."

"Only in an aspect that never became public. The Aborigine, as you call him, was hired to do a series of killings. In the end, he says he began to find his humanity. He facilitated their escape. But for his acts, which could have cost his own life, I would have no descendants," Chief explained, pausing to let emotions settle.

"As I came to know him, my respect deepened. I began investing his money as I do my own, which I never do outside the tribe. The man uses his wealth to benefit others, a story for another day. For some years now, we have worked together on several matters. He works on the ground using his expertise. I do my side here. We are a team that is as efficient as it is unknown to the world. Except for my family and his, you are the only outsider who knows anything of this relationship."

"Amazing," Brontus reacted with the sincerity of a man who had experienced his own personal tragedy in the loss of his wife and family. "Someday, I would like to understand the details."

"Yes, for another day," Chief agreed.

"One more question?" Brontus asked.

Chief nodded.

"You speak of your friend and Jaspar Moran in familiar terms. Do you also know her? You said you worked with her husband."

"Jaspar attended Notre Dame. My daughter, Clemenca attended the University of Chicago, as I did myself. They met in college. Jaspar visited her on this reservation. Year later, she introduced Trevor to me. He wanted me to have these records."

"Got it!" Brontus responded. "So fortunate for us all. Can your man preserve the life of Jaspar through these attacks? I will need her as a witness if I have to prove your theory."

"You can be assured that he will care for her the best way he can that is consistent with her role as bait. But her focus is to recover the children. She cares not about her life, your investigation, or the imminent economic collapse caused by your president."

"I can arrange a military extraction."

"No, please don't even think down that line. Events on the ground are moving too fast. They've hooked someone. If my friend needed assistance, he would ask."

The men were quiet, digesting what seemed to be an emerging common cause. Moonlight bathed the remote domain in luminous luster.

Bearstrike refilled cups and prepared a plate of sliced vegetables, hummus, and pita. It was consumed in silence.

"You got me here with a suggestion that the terrorist was the Queen of England. That was your bait," the U.S. Attorney began again. "Now, you say it's not, and hint that it's someone close to the president. Please answer my questions and frame your proposal, which I assume is the way forward."

Lifting his cigar from stones of the fire pit at his feet, Brontus settled in with fresh enthusiasm fueled by hope that the fog surrounding the mysteries of the Morans would be lifted. Nothing in his long career had been as frustrating as the inability to get his arms around the Moran case. Each step brought a new level of intrigue. At the very least, investigations needed to be undertaken and completed. President Henrichs expected answers. His economic recovery plan was on hold in the winds of West Mad.

"Let's begin with the records I reviewed," the prosecutor suggested, assuming his accustomed posture as inquisitor. "They come from the Westbury Madison files, so they are hearsay and useless to us in the absence of . . ."

"Yes, yes, I know that, of course I do. Mrs. Moran is a clever woman. She anticipated this. She has authentication that will stand up in any court, even if she is not present," Chief responded.

"What is it?"

"Declarations from her husband who made copies from his own records and wrote explanations, which she has translated."

"OK, that's not an issue for today. We know the source of the records, location and mission of Mrs. Moran, her team, and your theory of a conspiracy to destroy the capitalist economic system." The prosecutor tried summing up what he was beginning to understand. "Now, let's focus on the identity of the terrorist that you say is not the Queen of England."

"As you know from Moran's notes, the critical accounts are in the name of the Queen's Sovereign Trust. I am confident its presence is a subterfuge. By the end of each reporting period there was a netting of positions in those accounts," Bearstrike explained.

"So the reports would not alert her advisors?"

"Precisely, though some of them may have been involved. We'll see in due course. I suspect the real party of interest is someone who would be political dynamite in your country. This man is close to your president and has access to pools of capital to move world markets as in your dust diagram. Disclosure of the name would create chaos in the popular and political press. It would be resisted at the highest levels of your government, perhaps even for national security reasons. The same may be true of co-conspirators in other countries. What you have drawn in the dust would require collaboration on a variety of fronts."

"I appreciate your caveats, sir. Who is it?" Brontus responded. "Is there something you want in return for an identity?"

"How about three attack helicopters complete with fuel, armaments, and crew for combat operations on call in central Italy?"

"*WHAT!*" Brontus croaked, choking on the cigar smoke in his throat.

Bearstrike stepped to the prosecutor's side, straightening and patting his back. "Are you OK?"

Brontus gagged for several minutes. When he tried to speak, his voice was a falsetto squeaking of strained vocal cords. Bearstrike pumped some water from the well located just off the patio. The prosecutor coughed up phlegm stuck in his chest, holding his hand up pleading for time to clear himself.

"Thank you," he finally spoke, throwing his dead stub into the fire pit. He drank slowly, obviously deep in thought. "You know I have no authority to authorize that request. But if you say she is in danger, I guarantee she will be protected."

"I was only kidding, Jason. There is no such need, at least not yet," Bearstrike said, unfolding a piece of paper from his pocket. "I believe the connection to Moran, on these shores anyway, is Copper Starr."

"That's not possible. He was secretary of the Treasury before Moran and has been reappointed to fill the vacancy. He is a pillar of the Street, a man rich beyond reproach. And a lifelong friend of President Henrichs," Brontus protested, squeezing the arm of Bearstrike. "You must be kidding about this as well. It's not funny. I would be laughed out of office if I suggested such a preposterous hypothesis."

"Read this," Bearstrike said, offering clipped pages.

"What's this, more pictures?"

"Just read."

"It's a string of e-mails to Trevor Moran at his Westbury address," Brontus advised, reading down the pages of messages.

"The messages to Moran are signed 'Bannack' or just 'B.' Moran addresses his to 'BM.' Any idea who that is?"

"Have you read the transcriptions of Moran's notes back in the cabin?" Bearstrike asked.

"Yes, maybe too quickly, why?"

"In the last one, Mrs. Moran made a glossary of terms. Those words and initials are how Copper Starr referred to himself."

"You gotta explain that Chief. I obviously failed to read carefully enough at the end. I wouldn't have believed it in any event."

"Starr was raised in Montana as an orphan living with foster families. Bannack was the place of the original Montana gold rush long ago. Apparently, Starr's nickname as a kid was 'Bannack' meaning that he had dreams of gold."

"He certainly achieved that."

"Maybe it also explains why he would get involved in this conspiracy," Bearstrike added.

"OK, I'll accept that explanation for now. The messages seem to involve a back-and-forth about a direction from Bannack that the 'Windsor Accounts' be cleared early. What do you suppose 'Windsor Accounts' means?" the thoughtful prosecutor asked. "Is it 'Windsor' as in the House of Windsor of the Queen of England?"

"I believe so. We'll have to find out," Bearstrike answered. "In those e-mails, you see three-digit references to account numbers. Those numbers tie to the accounts and movements at about the same time as your point 2 on the dirt chart. The amounts moved are mammoth. The numbers tie to accounts of the Sovereign Trust."

"So what if Starr directed Westbury and Moran what to do, perhaps the accounts were his own or, he had authority to do so?" Brontus asked, trying to see potholes in the road being laid out for him.

"I have checked the public filings that Starr made. He was still Treasury secretary at the time. There is nothing even approaching the magnitude of these accounts," Chief explained. "So at the very least, there is disclosure failure if the accounts were his own, which I doubt."

"That would be a crime. If he was acting for the queen while U.S. Treasury chief, it would be a horrendous conflict of interest. In any event, how does Starr fit into your theory?"

"Starr was a Wall Street baron before he became Treasury secretary."

"Indeed, as Chairman of Westbury Madison before Moran," Brontus added. "Are you suggesting that Moran may have been a dupe, trusting his former boss until he made a discovery?"

"The economic collapse began on Starr's watch. He recommended Moran to the president to oversee dispensing the stimulus funds traced in your dust chart. Moran was murdered. We know from his notes that he smelled a rat. An all-out hunt is on for his wife by some group, obviously to seal her away with any records that may have been created," Chief explained. "Since Starr could not have financed such an attack on his own, he may have been the interface with others with such capital. It is that group that I believe to be the terrorists. My friend and Mrs. Moran have obviously attracted the attention of this cabal."

"If you are right, and Starr is involved with a terrorist group for his own benefit, then many of the senior people who made the policy decisions generating the bubble and its collapse may also be involved, right up to the president."

Bearstrike nodded, patting the clenched fist that held his arm. "Please don't break it, Jason."

"Oh, sorry. What you say seems farfetched. On the other hand, I understand the connections you make and respect your judgment. I will take this forward. What is your proposal?"

"Jason, you now know everything I do. I trust you as well. There are two sides to this mystery. One is Mrs. Moran and her children. The other is the sabotage intended by the terrorists. My mission is to thwart this attack. When you go back to Washington, please find out if the U.S. government is in any way involved in what is going on in central Italy. You do not have to champion my theory. Just ask questions and be patient to see what surfaces. Be especially careful with the president concerning the reality of Mrs. Moran, my friend, and their mission. He may be involved or at least complicit for his old friend. I will focus on my strategy and stay in touch with my friend. If we need your extraction offer, I'll let you know."

"Why would someone like Starr get involved in such a thing?" Brontus asked, noticing Stone and Slivers appearing.

"Greed or self-righteousness, maybe even insecurity. Those are the usual culprits of megalomania," Bearstrike answered.

Brontus paused with images of the daunting path ahead. "In our discussions, you have always spoken of *your* government referring to the United States and its allies. Tonight, you began referring to our system and our adversaries. Why are you using the collective *ours?*"

"Son, we are all in this together. My tribe is an independent nation. We fought wars for that independence. Then your predecessors marched us out here, away from our homeland. We have our distinct culture. But we need to be integrated with our neighbors. In our time together, I feel that you and I are cooperating in an area that is vital to both our nations. In this regard, we are *us* in a collective sense."

"I accept your proposal."

"Good. Working as a team, I suggest that we proceed on three fronts. My man and Mrs. Moran are fighting on the ground in Italy, the results of which we now seem to see in the press on a daily basis. You will visit with the president and ask his approval to confront Copper Starr. And I will make contact with the Queen's Sovereign Trust. If my belief in a terrorist attack is correct there would have to be a coordination of many elements to have achieved the success already accomplished. It is encouraging that we are proceeding on several fronts. Once we hit pay dirt down one path, it will doubtlessly have consequences on others," Bearstrike proposed.

"Agreed," the U.S. Attorney responded extending his hand to seal the plan.

The horses traversed the dark forest illuminated just enough with moonlight not to frighten the exhausted prosecutor.

"*O-s-da a-da-ne-di*, son," Chief said when the horses delivered them to the landing strip. "Good spirits be with you in your journey."

"Thank you, Chief, from our country."

What will he experience in the White House? Bearstrike wondered, galloping through the peaceful trees amidst the hooting of owls and occasional cries of wolves and mountain lions harmonizing with melodies of the winds.

What is Nulandi doing?

Chapter 30

Siena, Italy
Next day

"I AM AFRAID, Nul," I said, reaching for him as we sat in the van he stole from the Gypsy camp.

"I feel so strange. We're running like criminals doing things I could never have imagined. When I slept at the river, I dreamed of my children. Monsters were attacking them. I was helpless to do anything. When I awoke, Alice held me."

"She was protecting you," he answered, enveloping me with

one arm while maintaining surveillance in the mirrors of the street ahead and behind us. We could see Facti's home and studio. Alice prowled the streets.

"I know. Then I went crazy almost getting us shot apart."

"Forget about it. We are on our way to slay these monsters. Our running is preserving your children's lives, not endangering them. We've come through these battles with more to come. The caliber of weapons and nature of the attacks are escalating. The guns on those choppers were military grade, not local police machines. Whoever is pursuing us has government access to get such equipment deployed," he answered patting my shoulder. "And to massacre innocent people in that camp. They will never be accounted for, just plowed under to cleanse the site. Like dust in the wind."

In moments of calm, the reality of my acts surfaced. Killing, sex to intrigue a stranger, triggering violence to innocent people, and whatever may be necessary in the future. *What have I become?* I wondered, nestling into a safe spot in the dirty truck that smelled like a vegetable stand.

"You are a brave and strong warrior, I know you're scared. So am I. It's natural. The important thing is our plan has succeeded so far."

"You? Scared? How funny! You're Samson fighting Philistines and outsmarting the enemy no matter the odds."

"Fear germinates focus. I take nothing for granted. The enemy is arrogant and less motivated regardless of the resources that may be available. I always have the edge. Besides, I have an army behind me."

"You do?"

"Sure, a team of Amazons . . . Jas and Alice!" he said, tracing with his free hand the veins on my chest, up my neck and across my rather taut jaw. His finger stopped at my chin, tapping gently. He looked into my eyes with the barest glimmer of illumination from the moon and distant street lights.

I held onto his finger.

"What will you and your army do here?"

"Find out who that monster is."

"With what?" I smiled, a sense of humor overcoming fear. "This?" I asked raising the digit.

"Indeed, we have all we need," he answered, grasping my hands in his and holding them even higher. Besides, we're in the safest place to find our next step up the ladder, which Paulo will provide if he hasn't run away with his reward money for identifying us. Our enemy will not think to look for us back here."

"What will success with him bring?" I asked. "More danger?"

"For sure and ever escalating until the climax."

"Like good sex."

"Well yes, hadn't thought of it that way, but yes," he smiled, touching my nose in the dark. "We need to pump Paulo for his connection to those able to bring these attacks down on us." I pulled the clenched fists to my heart, saying a prayer for the safety of my babies. In that moment, I felt confident, focused, and prepared, like Nul.

Pushing fingers away, I looked into his eyes. "My children. Can we save them?"

"Yes, we are in a race with that monster," he answered, pausing with what felt like an urge to move on. "We are on their path. I feel it. Our success so far could not have occurred without your participation," he said, focusing again on me as he scanned the street in both directions.

"I am sure you feel guilt about what we have done. It is an honorable feeling. In any such campaign, there are steps that have to be taken. Some are vicious and impact innocent people, even taking their lives."

"Like the Gypsies and people on the street in Siena?"

"Exactly. Our job is to complete the mission. When you have the children back in your arms then you will have time to relax and moralize about what you or I have done to get there. I have had a lifetime of those feelings and can assure you that in the lap of success the process is meaningless in your heart. Our job is to do what has to be done then move on. Don't look back."

"More dust in the wind?"

He squeezed my hands in confirmation, providing a sense of achievement to replace the guilt.

"Who do you think sent the helicopters and the gunmen?" I asked.

"I suspect it may be my old employer Navarro," Nul answered, straining to look toward Paulo's home. I did as well. Alice moved into the street from the sidewalk in front of the home.

"Paulo must be present," Nul explained. Alice's sudden movement into the open indicated that all was clear. "Are you ready to see if our painter friend can be helpful?"

"Thank you, Lord," I whispered walking toward Facti's house. It was still hours to sunrise.

* * *

"PAULO. . . . Paulo, wake up," Nul demanded, lifting the feet of the man who lay flat on his back with arms sprawled and snoring loudly. His arms were bound with a makeshift rope constructed from dirty clothes that had laid scattered around the messy studio. There was no reaction from the inert body. Odors of alcohol, pot, and stale body functions left no doubt as to activities imbibed with the woman at his side. We had disabled electrical and phone connections before sneaking in via an extracted windowpane.

Securing the painter to the bed frame, Nul repeated the procedure on his stirring lover. She was bare under the sheet that still covered some of Facti's sweaty body.

"What are you doing?" she gurgled in Italian, trying to push Nul's hands away as he stuffed underwear hanging from the headboard into her mouth. Facti thrashed trying to find the source of disturbance and restraint. His bloodshot eyes struggled to focus.

CRACK! The impact of Nul's palm smashing into the side of Facti's face produced the grotesque sounds of a broken jaw and shattered teeth. Straddling the artist, Nul lifted Paulo's face by jerking his ears. Blood oozed onto the bedding. "You ratted me out, you son of a bitch," he said, pulling the bloody face close to his own.

"Nulandi . . . I, ah . . . thought you were taken care of," he groaned, his eyes seeming to focus.

"You've made three mistakes, asshole," Nul answered, shaking the shocked man. "First, you sold me out; probably with your painting of my woman. Then you led a squad of killers to us."

"I didn't, I . . ."

"Save your breath. You're the only one who knew where we were. The third was assuming that we could be put away. You are stupid and careless. I saved your sorry ass several times, even made peace for you with Navarro and gave you money to get started again. I took pity on you. I thought we were friends. Why did you do this? Who did you tell Navarro?"

"I didn't," he protested, bucking against his rider and the bindings. "What are you going to do to me?"

"How much did you get paid?"

"Nothing, yet. He promised a million Euros. I can live on that for a long time," Facti answered, trying to lick blood from around his mouth.

"Who?"

"I don't know. I just heard from a police officer that a big reward was being offered for somebody who looked like you and a white woman. There was a picture of her," he answered. "So I made the painting. In a few hours, it was confirmed to be Janice," he continued calming a bit as if the explanation would lead to release. "That's all I know. Please don't hit me again. Will you let me up to piss?"

Facti looked around Nul to me with a look of incredulity.

What is he thinking? That I would help him because of the other night?

Moans came from the woman indicating a similar need.

Nul left the room to access Paulo's computer, cell phone, or anything else that would identify a communication path. "Here, use this if either of them makes a move," he said, returning to hand me two large butcher knives from the kitchen.

My mind wandered back to the dream of the monster preparing to roast Theo and Chrissy. Their faces were curious, not frightened.

They're looking for me.

The scene was as clear as if they were tied to the bed waiting for me to remove their bindings.

I looked at Facti. His eyes pled. "Help me Janice. We . . ."

"Shut up," I answered swiping a sharp blade across his face, "or I'll jam a rag down your throat."

The barely conscious woman's stomach gurgled with sounds of distress.

Nul searched through the apartment. A cell phone was on a messy desk. Under papers, he found a tablet computer. He looked through each drawer to see if there was anything else that could be of assistance. A gun would have been helpful. Instead, he found a box of firecrackers on a closet floor. He placed them in the middle of the studio to implement the plan we had discussed.

The woman's clothes were in the bathroom. Her purse contained a cell phone and wallet buried in a mess of papers and makeup. He set the wallet inside the bag with the firecrackers, wanting to make sure that there would be no easily obtained identification of her. Our hope was that everyone would assume it was me.

Turning to Facti's phone, there was no security code protection. There had been a flurry of recent calls, most to the same local number. Nul fiddled with the phone's memory until he could access deleted voicemails. A focused frustration spread across his face as he put the phone in his pocket.

He did not recognize the voice. Must not be Navarro.

Facti squirmed under the weight of Nul sitting on his chest once again. "You lied Paulo. Who were you talking to?" he demanded clutching the painter's hair.

Facti shook his head violently trying in vain to get away, even striking the woman's shoulder. *"AG-G-GH,"* he screamed as Nul ripped hair from scalp.

"Who?" Nul repeated, holding the bleeding mess over the woman's face. She gagged, the underwear Nul jammed in her mouth preventing a retching reaction to the dripping on her helpless face.

Facti's eyes were glassy, lapsing into unconsciousness. *WHACK! WHACK!* Slapping revived him.

"Who?" Nul asked again, clutching another shock of hair.

Facti shook his head, pleading to be let alone. Maintaining the grip, Nul pulled him toward the girl. I knelt on the bed. Grabbing her hair, I twisted her toward Facti.

"Is she Navarro's?"

The painter continued shaking his head. As Nul nodded toward me, the woman choked, unable to control her retching. I pulled the panties from her mouth tugging her to the edge of the bed. She puked. The stench was awful.

I knelt on her lower back, grasping her hair to pull her head toward the ceiling. "Do *you* work for Navarro?" Nul asked sliding off the bed and coming around to face her, straddling the mess on the floor.

"No-o-o-o," she choked. 'Please let me go!"

"Hold her tight," he said, inspecting her arms, then down her butt and legs looking for the needle marks of a whore. Perhaps she was the prize for ratting us out.

"Turn her over." I sat on the pillows and pulled as Nul pushed her wet body.

"There," he said touching her flesh above the hips which bore the telltale tracks. "As I thought, just a street slut. Not one of

Navarro's," he answered with the ring of experience. "Plug her up again. We'll have to take the next step."

Nul checked the front and back windows. There was nothing unusual as the sun began peeking over the Tuscan hillside sending beams of light through the congested buildings of the medieval city. I could not see Alice but knew she was making sure we were not disturbed.

"We have a few minutes," he said upon returning. "I need to make a call."

* * *

THE WHINES of my captives suddenly stopped as Facti strained to hear words from the other room. Nul was mimicking the painter's speech pattern, causing Facti to writhe like he was covered with hungry fire ants. He obviously understood what was being said into his own phone, probably even anticipating the consequences.

Nul returned and again straddled the man. A swift chop to the neck produced unconsciousness. The woman was untied, allowing her to use the toilet. I supervised grasping the tether around her neck.

"Will you please let me go?" she spoke in broken English taking the gag from her mouth as I stood over her.

"Up to him," I answered nodding toward Nul.

"I have done nothing," she pleaded. "I was paid to be with him."

"By Navarro?"

"No, some police official. Said he'd kill me if I didn't do what he said. Everybody fucks me. I . . ."

"Be quiet," I said, stuffing her mouth full again.

When she was done, Nul sat her in a chair facing the front door, securing a small painting between bare legs. A blanket was placed over her lap with the exposed ridge of the frame looking like a gun barrel. She was secured tightly. He used a hammer and nails from the workshop to prevent the chair from moving or tilting.

I admired the handiwork knowing the plan but not how the trap would be staged. Facti was secured at her side in the same manner, with rags jammed in his mouth, though still slumped in his stupor. I tore a pillowcase into strips and tied them around their mouths and eyes. They would make no sound or movement.

Nul turned away from the captives, putting finger to lips. He pointed to me and back to his mouth with a cross of his hands, then pointing to his ears and at me again. *Don't speak, just listen.*

"We will take the bus to Florence and get away. We must return to Rome," he said, putting the tablet, phone, and purse into our trusty backpack. After the Gypsy camp attack, Nul had run back to our campsite by the river to recover the valise he had hung in a tree to dry.

He took the two knives from me and found a roll of framing wire in the studio. He rigged the wire to gas jets on the stove through picture hooks on the walls exposed once paintings were removed, and on to the front door. A pot was placed on a table by the door and the wiring connected. He wadded up paper and rags from the studio, then poured paint thinner over the pyre. The captives whined and struggled. I wiped all surfaces clean even though we wore latex gloves.

As we closed the rear door, Alice sauntered around the corner of the building.

* * *

"What happened on your call?" I asked as we stood against the walls of an alley. The van was parked a few short blocks away.

"It was Paulo's phone. The emails did not look interesting, but I had to look. There were many recent calls to and from the same local number. I called that number to see what would happen."

"And?"

"First, there was silence, then a question. 'Paulo, why are you calling this number? I told you never to call here again!'

"In Paulo's voice, I responded. 'I remember, but the man and woman who you are hunting must have escaped because they are in my flat. They are searching for something and have guns,' I answered. The phone went dead."

"Was it Navarro?"

"No, I suspect it's a local police official. That would tie this together. But he would be working for someone. We'll have to find out who to take the next step up our ladder."

"Who will be coming?"

"Not sure. Alice, watch!" Nul commanded. She resumed patrol crouched along the wall on the opposite side of the street. "From where I stand, I can see Facti's doorway. You face the other way to see if anyone is coming from the direction of the Palio. It won't be long, probably more locals. We'll see," he said, eyes focused down the street toward the wired door.

"Anyone coming the other way?" he asked moments later, as I focused up the street. Dawn broke on the horizon.

"Yes, some tourists and two old women with a girl holding their hands. They entered the Palio away from us. Looks like two grand-mothers out for an early breakfast with their young granddaugh-ter," I explained. "Oh, and a car just parked at the end of the street. It's a small dark sedan. Three men are getting out. They look like cops. Two are walking ahead and one behind. They have guns out!"

"Police?"

"No official uniforms or car. The one in back is talking into a radio or big telephone."

That makes five, Nul thought, observing two men coming toward him also preparing for action. "Jas, stay here and watch. Take my shoes. When I put the last man down, go see if there is a key in the ignition of the sedan. If so, move it to the curb of a side street facing away from the Palio. Then drive our van and park it a few blocks further away. Be sure to leave keys in the sedan but take the van keys. Then stand along the street in the shadows where you can see Facti's house.

He traded places with me to see the group coming from the car. As they passed our alleyway, he stepped out in bare feet holding the knives in each hand. Alice appeared around the corner behind the figures coming from the other direction.

How did she know?

* * *

"HEY, LUIGI," Nul said falling in behind the trailing man. The others were almost to Facti's. "Hey you, I said!" he repeated in Italian. The man turned to be greeted by knives swiping across his throat. Hands rose to protect himself way too late. Nul collected a compact Uzi before it fell to the ground.

BAM! BAM! CRACK! BOOM! POP! came from the door of Facti's flat as one of the men approached and kicked in the door. *KAWOOSH, POP!* followed as firecrackers ignited the paint thinner. A ball of flame met the in-rushing goons. Attackers on the street from both sides crouched pointing guns as they searched for the source of the apparent attack. Nul knelt on the street. As the explosion of fireworks stopped, the ball of flame settled. The first two attackers entered the flat. In a moment, the sound of automatic weapons reverberated from inside. The men were probably surprised by the bound couple sitting inside the entryway amidst flames with apparent guns in hand.

Nul slipped behind the next man on the street thrusting knives into his kidneys on each side. When the remaining man turned in response to the dying man's groan, Alice bit into his leg as he was dispatched with a single burst from the Uzi.

I could see the men inside running around then jumping toward the door trying to escape raging flames. They must not have noticed Nul entering from the rear. Another short burst was barely heard above sounds of the inferno. Nul was illuminated by spreading flames. He ignored the danger to pat down the dead men. Radios, cell phones, wallets, and weapons went into the painter's case he had earlier filled with Facti's computer, belongings, and the woman's purse. The contents would be added to the backpack full of similar souvenirs from the earlier dead men. Alice checked out the flat looking for any life.

Nul disappeared from view, probably turning gas jets in the stove to full open. He stepped out carefully closing the door. There were three bodies in the street. He leaned by each corpse checking for pulse as would an attending physician or first responder. He added their guns and communication devices to the case.

When he was done, Nul stood calmly looking at curious people gathering several blocks away from the shooting and the spreading fire. He extracted from his pocket the phone he had initially used to contact the person who sent these killers. He called the local emergency number. "Please send ambulances," he said, providing the address of the flat. He signaled for people in both directions to stand back.

Good man, I thought. He just killed five more men, stolen everything he wanted from their bodies, made sure they were dead, and was talking on the phone as if he were directing response and care for the injured.

He made no effort to conceal his face as he walked toward me, sliding into the crowd that was mesmerized by the flames. I had moved the car and van, then joined others gawking at the scene from a safe distance close to the Palio. There were not yet any emergency sirens to be heard.

At that moment, windows of the flat blew out as the released gas ignited. Flames shot out from the openings as ambulance sirens screamed their way to the chaotic street. People clung to the walls of buildings on either side of the street or hurried away.

Nul suddenly turned. Alice was running flat out toward me barking in alarm.

What is she doing? I wondered looking for Nul. Alice ran past him without pausing. Following her path, I saw men dressed like gangsters searching through the crowd as Nul started moving toward them.

Looking for us! I spotted a black man and white woman holding hands as they scurried away from the commotion. Like fishermen with a bite on their lines, the assassins drew guns and attached silencers. Nul extracted the Uzi. The men fell with only two shots. The couple would never know how close they had come to a different paradise than the one they expected.

Fire spread to surrounding buildings. Nul took my arm. He stopped to take pictures of the chaos with the phone he had been using, dropping it into the open bag of one of the onlookers. Fire trucks tried to get into the crowded street, sirens wailing.

We approached the sedan. Without a word spoken, Nul opened the rear door and placed the painter's case in the back seat. He sorted its contents, throwing the bag, including the Uzi, into the corner as I sat and looked forward. The remainder was tied with a cleaning rag that had been in the bag.

He drove the car around the edge of the medieval city, parking in an area near the school where Facti had taught. An open-air market laced through the streets like a giant snake. Merchants were erecting awnings and display racks, which folded neatly out from the sides of vans or small trucks parked for the day. No doubt like the people who had been machine gunned by helicopters at the river camp.

"Let's do some shopping," Nul said, stepping out of the vehicle and taking my hand as we began inspecting the wares of the Gypsy merchants.

I wonder if they miss the people from the river? "What happened back there?" I asked, striding to keep up.

"We can discuss it in a bit. For now, we need to buy some clothes," he answered, walking along the corridor between the street sellers. People crowded about us searching for bargains, apparently unaware of the shootout and fire on the other side of the Palio.

Spotting what he was looking for in racks displaying a variety of shawls and garments for Islamic women, Nul headed toward it. He selected a tan scarf and placed it over my head, crossing the ends and pulling them to cover my nose. He nodded in satisfaction then selected a greenish jacket made of thin material with long sleeves and dark green floral patterns. Holding it up to my shoulders, he again smiled with approval and chose dark tan slacks and black slippers.

"Go put these on," he directed, "and bring back your clothes."

I expected him to be waiting when I reappeared. He was not visible, even after I waited for what seemed an eternity.

What if he's gone?

Heading back toward the sedan, I was grasped by a strong hand. Jumping in fright, I turned expecting to face a pickpocket or killer. It was a Muslim woman in a long black abaya with a veil across her face.

"It's me," he whispered.

"Oh, Good Lord!" I responded, almost slumping in relief.

"The disguise worked. You stood right by me and didn't realize it was me," he said.

"Where is the stuff?" I asked, wondering about the weapons and phones he had wrapped up in Facti's cloth. He patted his skirt.

We walked away. "Where are we going, ma'am?" I asked.

"Ready for a few days of peace?" he asked, explaining that we needed to spend a few days at the location of his Vietnamese friends. "I need to examine our souvenirs from these attackers and try to assemble the information that will be revealed to plan our next step. You can also use some down time. Anloc is looking forward to showing you her world."

We walked to where I had parked the van. As Nul drove into rural Tuscany, I dozed off, imagining sending a communication to Theo and Chrissy and their smiling response. "She's coming." They were happy.

The peacefulness of the dream was shattered by the hideous

image of Facti's painting hung close to the ceiling in his studio. The reddish depiction of a fat, bare-assed man seemed to hover over my children. I awoke with a start.

"What is it?" Nul asked. "A nightmare?"

"I am just imagining the way forward. My children need me," I answered.

What is the connection of that obscenity of a painting to my babies?

Chapter 31

Aix en Provence, France

"Who asked that question?" Sir Gordon Blair responded after the customer relations officer had relayed the strange inquiry.

"He gave the name of Westbrook Bearstrike," she responded reading from notes taken from a transcription of a message left for the managing director of the Sovereign Trust. Most inquiries were easily handled. But this one was so odd that notification to the leader was imperative.

There was no immediate response from Blair. "Tell me the question again."

"He asked why there was so much volatility in the investment by the Trust in Westbury Madison funds."

The line was silent for many more seconds.

"Sir Gordon, are you there?"

"Do you have a recording? I want to hear the actual words, not a summary."

"Yes, sir."

"Play it for me."

"Hello, my name is Westbrook Bearstrike. W-E-S-T-B-R-O-O-K B-E-A-R-S-T-R-I-K-E. I am an investor in Aqua Prime managed by Westbury Madison. I see that the Sovereign Trust is also an investor. I would like to discuss with your manager the extreme movements in your investments, which have caused huge losses as positions are liquidated or placed to fill your orders. From my study of the trades, I fear they are unauthorized, like the *London Whale* writ large. I was a client of Trevor Moran before he went to the U.S. Treasury. I have requested explanation of this volatility from West Mad, but have gotten stonewalled. It is consumed in the West Mad scandal. You can reach me at . . ."

No one could see those trades, Blair thought, watching the Formula 1 prototype of his real employer race around the private track nestled in the rolling hills of Provence. Sir Gordon was skilled in the ways of the world of intelligence. He had served as director of the famed British spy and intelligence unit, MI5. Upon retirement, the queen had such faith in his impeccable integrity to ask that he manage the Trust. Adopting the lavish lifestyle of upper crust London rendered his finances a shambles. A promise of unimaginable wealth came from the man in the race car, payable upon successful implementation of the global strategy. Payoff was within sight. Blair's responsibility in the plot was to be chief of operations. He monitored all elements of the operation, which were carefully siloed, so each element was segregated from the others. The Trust was utilized as the outward face of their intrusions into global security markets. Only the obsessed man in the cockpit and Blair knew all the connections.

Prior to the message from London, his anxiety had skyrocketed following a report from the Siena police chief. The chief had been confident that Mrs. Moran and her accomplice had been cornered. But they escaped again, killing all attackers.

How can this be possible? Are they somehow succoring my people into ambush? What do they know?

Those fears were taken to a new level by the call from the Trust officer.

Those words advertise inside knowledge and a relationship to Moran.

Damnable man must have copied the records and gotten them to his wife, as he threatened, before we could get him out of the way. The bloody bastard. We were so close to payday. Just one last U.S. stimulus injection to be completed, and they would be home free, his wealth assured.

"You do not need to respond to this call," Blair directed the officer. "Delete the voice mail, erase the transcript, and keep no record of it." He made a mental note to confirm that the steps were completed, short-circuiting the security systems in place to prevent such acts.

Tranquility of the setting had been blemished by the ever-expanding mess on his doorstep. It was bad enough that the Moran woman had been missing for months. In her absence, the West Mad fiasco had taken root in the financial press and caused so much heat that the cowardice of the American president had delayed the stimulus. Now, reappearance of the woman in Rome, followed by successful escape from their hired thugs, police, and the Italian army, was alarming. His worst fear had been of actual data falling into the hands of a sophisticated analyst—someone like Chief Bearstrike—as trading patterns could be exposed.

How could he be involved?

Sir Gordon wondered if he needed to distract the Prince from race preparation. He walked to the area where the Moran children had been brought. He was to meet with Alzjar's personal physician who was monitoring their condition and medications. The Monte Carlo Grand Prix was just days away, and his employer was determined to win at any cost.

Chapter 32

"GOOD EVENING, Prince," Gordon Blair greeted the racer hours later after checking on the progress of the children, with whom he developed an interesting relationship while overseeing their detention.

"What?" the tired man grunted in response. "Why are you here? I thought you would be attending to next steps now that we are done with the Moran woman. Starr and our Washington people need to get that bailout money freed-up. I expect there to be no more delays or problems."

"Unfortunately, sir, the trap set in Siena did not work," Sir Gordon responded.

Prince Anwatol Alzjar plopped awkwardly into a brocade chair copied from the Louis XIV originals at Versailles. "What happened? I thought we had an overwhelming force trapping them in a place from which they could not escape."

"We did. Our informant told us the exact location. We had supposedly reliable, local SWAT team men encircling them. There was no time to get our own people on site. We only had moments to make the arrangements."

"And?"

"They escaped. All but one of our team was killed. The coward just ran away and knows nothing. Several of the bodies showed marks of being bitten by a vicious dog," Blair explained, handing over a copy of the local paper with pictures of the graphic scene. "A few tourists were also killed in the crossfire."

Alzjar's fatigue disappeared. He read the stories, especially the description of Aphrodite. "What the hell is going on, Gordon? This damnable woman is like mercury. She slips away every time. How can this be? And killing all these men? It's not possible. She must be supported by a transparent army as none of our people have seen or reported anything other than this mysterious black woman or man apparently always at her side."

"We don't know. The local SWAT team apparently had some black man seen with the Moran woman cornered. Then the dog started attacking as a woman, identified as Mrs. Moran, stripped naked and ran toward our team with a knife. She succeeded in distracting them and the tables turned."

"And then what happened?"

"There was a shootout. Nobody seems to know for sure how our men ended up on the street, but they did. Witnesses report that the black man picked up all guns, identification, and phones, then ran off. They apparently escaped through a ceramics shop. An artist reported that they jumped off a cliff. They must have rigged some type of parachute and landed in an uninhabited area," Blair reported, cringing at the incredulity in Prince Anwatal Alzjar's face.

"Don Navarro had the good sense to request the Italian army to dispatch search teams to an area where it appeared they had fled. A bunch of people were discovered. The helicopters blew them away. It turned out to be a camp of Gypsies. In the remains, there was no indication of Mrs. Moran or her friend."

"They just disappeared again, like phantoms?"

"So far, yes sir. We have doubled the reward for information that would lead us to them and flooded the area with our people and the local police."

"Fuck! I pay you a fortune to take care of these matters. In just a few days, there are, what, thirty or more bodies? That bitch could bring us all down if she has any data and it gets into the wrong hands."

"It's just a matter of time, sir. The last thing the Italians want is global press stories about murders in Tuscany with some iconic heroine, like 'Aphrodite.'

"Connection of this fugitive woman and the murder of her husband have amplified the West Mad story on front pages around the world. It has also delayed our stimulus money," Sir Gordon added.

"I want it ended. Kill the woman and her Africans, and then destroy any data she may have. Do you hear me?"

"I do. We may have to use the children," Blair responded, containing his frustration behind the façade of a tactician.

"Do whatever you have to. But put an end to it. We are so close to the payday of the century."

Alzjar was the leader of the group, a master at living in the shadows of the world. He was descended from Lebanese merchants who provided financing for growth of the Ottoman Empire. When it appeared the Empire's fortunes were waning, they switched sides and attacked the Turks with the infamous Lawrence of Arabia during World War I. They assisted in the liberation of the Middle East from occupation by infidels. In subsequent generations, members of the family accumulated mountainous financial resources. By U.S. and some European standards, the family wealth would be viewed as arising from illegitimate means. On the other hand, it was quite real.

Alzjar had been raised in opulence with private tutors and schooling. For college, he attended the University of California at Berkley. A brilliant student and a handsome young man from another realm, he fit into a social life unlike anything he had known in the cloistered palaces of his youth. In his admission application, Alzjar presented himself as an orphan living with other homeless children in a madrasa in Riyadh. It made a heartwrenching picture for liberal admission committees who provided the young man with a full scholarship and housing allowances. On campus, he lived in dorms consistent with the persona of the application.

An American campus lifestyle came naturally. Arabic good looks and skill on the soccer field yielded an active social life. Boys admired his athletic talent and easy camaraderie, as girls enjoyed his charm. Alzjar studied accounting and economics. He became sufficiently American in his quest for independence with his own sources of money.

Upon graduation, he found a job as an entry-level financial analyst for a famous currency trader and speculator in New York. Merrill Simon was a fanatic for the study of detail. His staff prepared charts and graphs, showing the movement of a laundry list of arcane subjects interesting only to such sophisticated speculators. Simon looked for deviations from historic patterns. When a spread was discovered that was contrary to conventional wisdom, it would be tracked. If persistence were found, a team would be assigned to develop a model to project scenarios of the future. The investor would then begin acquiring positions. Since Simon bet against the wisdom of the herd, he was often able to acquire major positions at minimal cost.

Typically, the bets were dry holes, because the deviation disappeared, or others saw the same phenomenon. Occasionally, the spread expanded as a bubble developed. Alzjar observed Mr. Simon's patience as bloated and over-confident investors pumped air into the balloon. When it broke, Simon reaped a fortune as markets crashed, with all the experts pointing fingers at the stupidity of their governments for failing to police the markets to prevent economic atrocity.

The Prince learned quickly, even taking small positions of his own. After a few years, he went to Princeton to study mathematics and statistical analysis in a Ph.D. program.

Returning to his homeland, he guided family investments with contrarian instincts honed to a fine edge. Alzjar also established a separate account, independent of his family, where he was not constrained by conservative religious and investment philosophy or family accountability. He remained an investor of Merrill Simon, deciphering each of his positions based on the scant information made available even to Simon's investors. When he thought Simon to be in error, the Prince bet against him. His secret personal account had long since eclipsed the family fortune.

In class reunions of Berkeley and Princeton, Alzjar was eulogized in memory, it having been reported that he perished on a trek in the African jungle to commune with mountain gorillas.

Blair sat still as the Prince processed the unexpected information. *He will erupt if I mention the inquiry from Chief Bearstrike.*

"Use the damned children in any manner necessary to carry out my orders. Do not fail again," he said with a finality reflecting confidence that his will would be done.

"I need the last tranche of my bailout money to initiate the political phase of our plans," Alzjar continued. *Once we get this round, we can lay low with a war chest to finance democrats or republicans. Our resources will outstrip trial lawyers or anybody else in America. We will be on the path to eventually take control of the political processes of the West,* Alzjar thought as fatigue from a long day of racing began to take hold.

"Even if anything did leak, it could ultimately only lead to the actual counter-party, the Queen of England," Sir Gordon responded with a smile. "That would make great headlines around the world. I can see it now: 'Queen Behind Financial Collapse.' It would be a colossal embarrassment to the Crown, and would bring back to the front pages of newspapers around the world the slimy stories of the royals—from Edward's abdicating the throne and cavorting with the Nazis, to Prince Charles and Lady Diana's loveless marriage, to the sexual shenanigans and toe-sucking photos of Duchess Fergie, and other embarrassing stories of the royals of Windsor."

"Just take care of Mrs. Moran. Use the children, increase the reward, and do whatever it takes. The Italian generals are available again to do an op for us. We must wash our hands of her."

"Will do, sir."

"Please leave me with that peaceful thought. I have a race to run," the Prince said with a wave of his hand as the lady of the evening held the door.

What will I do about Chief Bearstrike? Sir Gordon wondered admiring the woman who awaited the Prince.

Chapter 33

The White House, Washington D.C.
A day later

"WHAT CONCOCTION of peyote and Indian bullshit did you smoke on that reservation Mr. Brontus?" President Henrichs spit out as the U.S. Attorney of Wall Street explained the conclusions reached with Chief Bearstrike.

The meeting had been arranged by Attorney General Sanaroff, who began with a recitation that the discussion was subject to attorney-client privilege with himself representing the president. This surprised Brontus as it suggested his own boss felt that Henrichs had potential culpability.

"Nothing but the simple honesty of two men who you can trust, sir—Chief Bearstrike and me. He is concerned enough about the conspiracy he believes to be underway to have initiated contact. I now agree with him."

The Situation Room was elegant, bright, and uncommonly empty. Henrichs sat upright across the gleaming mahogany table from Brontus. The AG was at the end, physically and emotionally distant.

"I studied a room full of documents that I could defend in court. My message today is reflected by these two items, sir," he added, handing the president a copy of his dust chart and the email exchange between Moran and 'Bannack' or 'BM.'

Henrichs traced the peaks and valleys of the chart with a finger tapping on the circled numbers. Brontus had added dates on each peak and valley to make the colorful graphic readily understandable. Henrichs looked at Brontus as he thumped each point. Words were not exchanged. In the silence the burp of a mouse would have sounded like a lion's roar in the jungle.

"The suggestion is that my third round of stimulus would produce this crash?" he asked holding up the chart with his finger on the last downward crashing line.

"Yes, sir."

"Do you believe that?"

"I have no opinion on that part of it, sir. I am a prosecutor not a market analyst. On the other hand, the elements linked together by Chief Bearstrike are sufficient for me to believe that a terrorist plot against our economic system may exist. It needs to be investigated."

"What is this?" the president asked holding up the other item.

"Emails, sir. Please read them."

The president studied each page carefully. His reddened face from his initial outburst faded as he read and reread the papers. "Moran was still on Wall Street during this period," he finally spoke. "Who do you think 'BM' or 'Bannack' is?"

"Chief believes it could be Copper Starr," Brontus responded preparing to repeat Chief's explanation of Montana's history.

"Those are the names and initials Copper has used since our high school days," Henrichs responded, returning the papers. The president was silent for a few moments. "You know he is a lifelong friend?"

Brontus nodded, as the AG's face contorted having already lost its color.

"Aside from serving twice as my Treasury secretary, he has been a major contributor to campaigns throughout my political career. Westbury Madison manages my personal blind trusts."

"Yes, sir, I know all of that."

"If there were any truth in the suggestion that Copper is somehow involved in this conspiracy, it is likely that my own funds are invested to make me a beneficiary of it. If so, it would be a political fiasco."

"That is why I began with a recitation of privilege, Mr. President," the AG added.

The president's chin rested atop upright fingers forming a pyramid. A reputation for integrity and persistence as solid as the granite mountains of his home state had grown throughout a long career as governor of Montana and several terms in the U.S. Senate prior to ascension to the White House.

"The scenario you paint sounds like a James Bond movie. The world is awash in economic decay, which the existing institutions of government can neither comprehend nor stop," the president continued.

Wheels in the presidential mind spun in a frenzy of conflict. He was infamous for his ability to maintain outward calm in the midst of chaos. He had been elected by a wide majority of the American electorate seeking thoughtful leadership. During the campaign, each candidate from the established parties imploded on the public stage, including his predecessor in the White House. Henrichs had been a career naval officer. Upon retiring from active duty as an aircraft carrier captain, he became a blogger. His comments attracted a popular following. As Congress struggled in its long effort to reform failed economic policies, he applied his experience in managing the behemoths of the sea to frame policy prescriptions. Initially, he campaigned for a candidate he thought had promise. As opposed to normal politicians swinging like greased weathervanes in the breeze, Henrichs was a breath of fresh air. He spoke with a bluntness possible only from someone having no interest in elective office. He was then swept to victory as an independent.

"Abe?" the president asked the AG who was studying his verbatim notes with his head down.

"Yes, sir?"

"This is not a situation where I will tolerate any pretense of your or any lawyer's privilege. These matters will be investigated completely, and the results made public at an appropriate time. Chips will fall where may. If I end up a gold miner back home in the Bitterroot Mountains, maybe bringing Bannack back to life, I will do so with my head held high."

"Sir, as chief lawyer for your administration, I must . . ." Sanaroff began, standing to address the president as if the man were a babe in the manger.

"Abe, I understand. Please leave us, and leave your notes where they are."

"Sir?"

"Now, Abe."

Once the door was closed, calm spread across the president's face as if the conflict in his mind was resolved. "Thank you for bringing this to my attention at the earliest possible date. The stakes are enormous. It took balls of the first order to come directly to me under the circumstances. You have vindicated my faith in your being the most trustworthy prosecutor in the world. That is why I appointed you."

"We have only just begun this process, sir."

"I understand. I've never had the honor of meeting Chief Bearstrike, but his reputation speaks for itself. I look forward to doing so, though I guess I'll have to go to him, which I will be happy to do offline."

"We can arrange that, sir. Chief would be honored," Brontus responded.

"I asked Mr. Sanaroff to leave because I have no idea where his loyalties lie in this situation. My initial reaction was also for his benefit.

"As you know, my stimulus program is stymied by the continuing West Mad investigation, including the current media frenzy concerning Mrs. Moran. There is even speculation that these shootouts in Italy could somehow be connected to her disappearance. The press is having a field day with that picture from Siena. Aphrodite indeed."

Brontus smiled in agreement. The photo was indeed riveting and captured the rage of the world in a time of economic chaos and failed leadership.

"If your scenario were to find its way into the press, the current mess would become a firestorm of the first order. It would be my Watergate, perhaps even leading to impeachment. We would be pilloried as incompetent, stupid, and dishonest. I would become the fool of history," the president continued, "making Richard Nixon and Bill Clinton look like choir boys."

"I understand all of that, sir, as does Chief Bearstrike."

"Very well. Time is of the essence. Please explain the inter-relationships that you and the Chief believe to be evolving. We can then define our strategy," he continued, sitting back in his chair to sip from the ever-present cup of coffee. He had been given the cup as a young boatswain's mate in commemoration of becoming a petty officer third class. It was the beginning of a long career. An enlisted sailor, followed by college on the G.I. bill, years as fighter pilot, command of carriers, he loved the discipline of war preparation and successful implementation. He had often been nominated for promotion to admiral. He declined wanting to remain in operational command. The cup's original markings with a gold eagle, royal blue crossed anchors, and a red third-class stripe were long obscured by stains of thousands of gallons of coffee and his habit of washing it only in hot water. "It's like my mom's cast iron skillet, cured in fire, not soap," he often explained.

As the composed prosecutor explained everything he knew, including the progress of Mrs. Moran and Chief's friend, the president listened intently, thumping the dust chart on the table.

"Your explanation is entirely logical, I had not thought of a terrorist attack that reaps windfalls from my stimulus injections," the president responded. "That would explain why these policies have failed. The world continues in a recessionary spiral. Trevor Moran came into government as a public service to try to win that battle. I deeply respected him. The crash of his plane and his death, the disappearance of his children and wife are bright red flags. No one has answers. Copper Starr has retaken Trevor's post at his own insistence and is pressing for the third stimulus package. The fact that West Mad has delayed the process may be a good thing.

"My instinct has been to change course. On a carrier, we would turn into the wind to launch a strike. I am ready to do that. I just do not know who or where to strike. Nobody does."

"Your fighters are launched, sir."

The president's face lit up with humor. "An Aborigine, a socialite, a Wall Street prosecutor, an Indian chief, and a dog are the warriors to defend the world from economic disaster, and to protect me from impeachment and humiliation?"

"With you as the leader, our team is complete," Brontus responded. "Jaspar and friend, as Bearstrike calls him, are close to identifying the terrorists from the ground, as we are from here."

"The next step is for you to speak to Copper. I assume you will do this?"

"Yes, sir. It needs to be done in an official capacity."

"I understand and will stand back while you do your job. I will see to security and intelligence, and be on alert to respond to whatever happens, including rescues as needed in Italy. Correct?" Henrichs responded.

Brontus nodded, touching his coffee cup to the president's outstretched mug.

"Please delegate everything else on your docket. Proceed with the smallest team possible. I will say nothing to Copper or anyone else other than my own Secret Service team."

"Agreed, sir. There is one question I must confirm. Is the U.S. government in any way chasing Mrs. Moran in Italy?"

The president's eyes bore into the prosecutor reflecting

surprise and curiosity as he lifted the secure phone always at hand. The call was answered immediately.

Setting down the receiver, the president turned back to Brontus. "The CIA director said his people are following what is going on but advises that it has nothing to do with U.S. interests. I think our intelligence services do not see the connections you have explained, so the answer to your question is 'no.' Anything else?"

"Let's turn into the wind."

"And please arrange for me to meet with the Chief."

That will be interesting!

Chapter 34

Aix en Provence, France

THE BOY screamed trying to protect himself. The beast was reaching for him. A cauldron of boiling gruel awaited. Saliva dripped from the beast's jaws and blackened teeth. Light came only from the fire.

"Wake up, wake up, son. It's just a dream," the nurse implored.

Thrashing of the helpless young body eased as eyes opened. The matronly woman took his pulse. A huge man with grisly features stood behind her with chart in hand and stethoscope around his neck.

"Where am I?" Theo Moran asked. Passage of time was a mirage. "Where is Chrissy? Are my Mom and Dad here yet?"

The nurse stood back as the man with a purplish, pock-marked face and frizzy white hair touched the cold instrument to the boy's neck, causing him to lurch again.

"Hey!" Theo exploded. "Who are you?" he asked, trying to rise only to be restrained by IV drips in his arm and straps at his wrists. "Where are they?"

"You had an accident, son. You were brought here," the doctor explained reaching to touch the boy's shoulder. "They are just down the hall."

Theo's comprehension was sluggish. He had been awakened every day for exercise and medical checks. It all ran together.

"Where is Mr. Blair?" Theo asked, having come to enjoy his time with the Englishman who seemed to visit every day. He taught them to play cricket on the grass.

"Where are we?"

"In a hospital close to your home." The facility was indeed part of an acute care hospital complete with surgeons and a pharmacy, but a long way from Greenwich, Connecticut.

"Why am I strapped in?"

"The straps are just a precaution. Remember, you had an accident."

"I did?" he responded. It was all so confused in his mind.

"If you have nightmares, you could disturb these drips in your arms. Here, you are free to get up," the doctor answered, removing the straps and withdrawing the drips. As Theo stretched, an attendant brought in a tray of water and snacks.

"The bathroom is over here," the nurse instructed opening a door that was wide enough to accommodate a wheelchair.

"Oh good," he responded, stumbling a little.

"Can I see my parents now?" he asked upon return.

"If you are really ready, I will get them now," the doctor advised.

"Oh, good."

"Please drink this," the doctor added handing Theo a small cup.

"What is that noise?" the patient asked lying back down. "It sounds like Formula 1 engines. My Dad loves racing. I go with him. I didn't know there was a speedway in Greenwich."

"You are just hearing sounds from the busy street. When you finish the protein drink, I will bring in your family." Theo smiled as the drugs took effect.

They were in a chalet nestled in a wooded ravine. In the period when the Papacy reigned in Avignon, it had been a retreat for clerics some seven hundred years earlier. Pools, spas, and gardens provided elegant peacefulness. It had a spectacular wine cellar where the precious wines of Chateauneuf de Pape aged.

Rooms in the wine cellar had been outfitted as a hospital capable of handling any type of trauma or surgery. Doctors and nurses were located within close helicopter distance, paid to be available round-the-clock. The original purpose of the facilities was to treat injuries from crashes at the adjoining track.

Theo and Chrissy were in separate rooms connected by precise instruments monitoring bodily functions. Upon arrival, they had been examined and then drugged. They were allowed to awaken for exercise and food together. There was no opportunity for escape. Even the outdoor pools and grounds to which they had access were sealed. Security had been designed to allow clerics to enjoy their pleasures secreted from public view.

Consciousness once again ebbed away before Theo could organize his next thought.

"You will not need to do this much longer," the doctor advised as the nurse reconnected straps and drips.

Chapter 35

Radda, Italy

WHEN WE left the chaos of the bazaar in Siena, Nul and I returned to the bus station, wearing our robes. When we boarded, I felt the contempt from other passengers that Muslim women must feel in reaction to the head-to-toe garment with just a small visual portal.

I was asleep on Nul's shoulder when we stopped at the village of Radda located atop a picturesque hillside that I had seen from Siena during our jump from the cliff. Anloc awaited and escorted us around a corner, then up steep stairs. As we climbed, the view of vineyards stretching to the horizon was breathtaking.

She showed us into a room filled with the aroma of steaming vegetables. Oriental and Western people sat around a table in animated conversation. "Please meet my family and our friends," she explained.

"Our army?" I asked, producing a chorus of smiles. Nul stood in the background. Anloc introduced her mother Phoung, whose age I could not even guess. Her adolescent sons Nguyen and Lanh greeted me with enthusiasm. Features and skin tone of the family were a collage. Anloc was darker with high cheekbones and coarse hair. The boys were much lighter with almost olive coloring and wavy hair hanging to their shoulders. I said nothing, though sensing their amusement. A weathered man introduced himself as the vineyard manager, as well as to a young Italian man of about twenty-five training as a winemaker. They bantered in a collage of Italian, Vietnamese, and English.

Nul took my arm and showed me to a room and closed the door. "I need to go to another place to examine what we have collected," he explained, patting the heavy backpack that had accompanied us at each stop. "I need to find the next rung up the ladder. It may take all day or more. Whoever it was I spoke to on Facti's phone responded with immediate force. It is moving now. Our next step will come shortly. When I am done, it will be time to go again. Please relax with Anloc and our family. It is a fascinating place. Our vineyard is close by. Its name is *La Namviette*. Alice will stay with you."

"Do what you must," I responded. "I enjoy Anloc and look forward to talking and meeting family and friends." *Is it hers, his, or theirs?* I frankly felt dispirited at being abandoned and wondered what kind of situation I had been brought into.

Our family? Our vineyard? Who is our? Does he mean himself and Anloc? What about me?

* * *

"Anloc," I exclaimed. "I can't believe it!"

After lunch, we walked around the small village located about ninety minutes from Siena. It was a short walk to her workshop. Anloc's jewelry was an expensive line carried at stores like Louis Vuitton. In the chaos of our initial meeting in Rome, I had made no such connection of her name and the exquisite creations.

"It's gorgeous," I exclaimed with admiration. "You make these?" I lifted a bracelet from a worktable covered with pieces of silver and gold, a tray of jewels, small torch, and tools. It radiated sparkling hues when held up to the bright sunlight. In my prior life, Trevor spoiled me with jewelry for our many social functions.

"I learned at the finest schools in Florence and Milan. I then worked for a time in Florence. This one will complete the set for a movie star's entrance to the Oscars in Hollywood. She expects to win this year."

"Who?"

"Amelia George, who just won in Cannes and is all over the tabloids with pictures of her lover, the famous race driver Henré Tremont."

"She is elegant," I agreed. "I haven't read much of that kind of stuff recently, but it all sounds familiar. What is the movie?"

"30,000 Camels," about a woman who has to rescue her family from an impossible mess. Sort of like you, Jas. Maybe she will play you in a movie about this mission someday."

"Amazing! Where do you find the time?"

She smiled, reflecting pride of accomplishment.

"The training must have been expensive," I added admiring the jewels, wondering how it could be achieved by a family that seemed to be vineyard workers.

"Another gift of our Mr. Nulandi," Phoung answered, walking through the front door. She bowed in honor. She then reached for my hand.

"Mother wants to take you to our winery a few kilometers away. It is not open to the public."

Our? I wondered again walking down the hillside on the edge of the road used only by locals and lost tourists.

"I was not yet born when my family first met Mr. Nulandi," Anloc began answering my question about their origins. She referred to him with affection. "My mother and other relatives have told me the story. She has learned to speak Italian, but her English is probably about the same as your Vietnamese." Phoung smiled, bowing her head. "Her name honors the mythical Phoenix of their culture."

"Please tell me the story," I asked.

"He saved our lives. I understand he has done the same for you," Phoung began with Anloc translating as we processed arm-in-arm. Rows of grapevines provided peaceful ambiance.

"My husband was a fisherman during the war between your country and the Viet Cong. His name was Tran. He was older than me. I was almost fourteen when we married," she explained. I guessed her age to be about eighty observing the enthusiastic spring in her step.

"My mother must care about you, Jaspar," Anloc added as she translated. "She never talks about these details, even with family."

"We had a small boat in an area called Chu Lai in what was then the northern part of South Vietnam. My mother and two brothers worked on the boat. Those boys now live in Australia. We were poor. Our boat blended into the landscape of the river way of life. We had no electronics. Tran worked for the American soldiers transporting men up and down the river. It paid much better than fishing. They always came on board with heavy bags."

"You mean like Nul carries?" I asked, recalling the backpack strapped over his shoulder as he departed.

"Yes, yes," she responded. "The men were on missions with heavy guns." We walked slowly up a hillside toward a picturesque villa and barn-like buildings in the distance. Dry earth and rocks crumbled under our feet.

"The men came on board in the night. We dropped them at designated places. Then we waited, almost always hearing explosions and gunfire. They usually returned with prisoners, wounded comrades, but most often dead bodies. I was always scared," Phoung explained, dabbing at tears in her eyes as we walked, huddling together.

Anloc led us off the road and into groomed vineyards. The grass was much easier to walk on than the dusty road.

"On one mission, there was a dark-skinned man who spoke a strange language. He and Tran communicated in a way no one else could understand. It was Mr. Nulandi. When this mission was done, there were many wounded and dead. There were also three captives covered with blankets who fought to get free. There was blood all over.

"When we reached the place for the soldiers to disembark, no one waited. The officer demanded to be taken down river to a harbor. Tran protested knowing that enemy patrols were danger-ous. The officer drew a gun. Mr. Nulandi demanded that the mis-sion proceed in a different direction.

"A confrontation occurred with loud, angry words. 'The fuckin' slopes know way too much. We have to croak 'me and sink the boat,' the officer said," Anloc translated as we walked into the picturesque center of the winery. It seemed ancient though in excellent condition. The men from lunch were working with oth-ers repairing tractors and rakes.

Anloc led us into the main building. As I looked around the massive structure, my eyes must have widened in amazement. There were huge wooden vats with what appeared to be mon-strous screws at the bottom to crush the grapes. Open troughs carried the mash to other vats, obviously used for fermentation. Wooden barrels much taller than me were lined up to be filled. "They will age in the cellars for years," Anloc explained. I had not tasted wine since the night at Harry's Bar in Rome on our first day in combat. I was ready to try the family vintage. We walked out a side door and into the sunshine. Phoung led us to a table with chairs set in the shade of large trees in a courtyard.

"Mother," Anloc said in Vietnamese then shifted to English. She put hands to her mouth. "I never heard this part of the story," she explained as we sat down.

"What happened?" I asked.

"Mr. Nulandi picked the officer up by his shoulders and slammed him into the mast of the boat. 'That will not be done!'" As Anloc translated, Phoung mimicked with fists flying as if it were happening all over again. She began shrieking and punching the villain in her memory. I did not understand her words. They were angry. Tears spilled down her cheeks as Anloc reached out to hug her.

"Mr. Nulandi instructed us to proceed down river," she began again as Phoung calmed down. "We were met by a flotilla of American gun boats. We had no radio and so could not hear or respond to the hailing. Suddenly, machine guns opened on us, killing my Tran, several of the soldiers, and wounding me.

"Mr. Nulandi took the helm. He stopped the engine and found a shirt to use as a white flag. With a flashlight, he sent messages via some code. I later learned the message involved an American baseball player. 'We are Mickey Mantle's people.' The shooting stopped. We were boarded by a large group of soldiers with big guns. They pushed us into a corner of the deck and tended to the dead and dying. Mr. Nulandi helped lift the wounded and the dead. When they were gone, he steered us behind one of the American boats speaking on a radio they had given him. He arranged for a ship to pick us up."

Anloc had a glow about her repeating the story of Nul. I had never thought of his age, though he would have to be in his late fifties or early sixties to have been in Vietnam. He looked much younger. *Or was he just a boy?* I wondered, recalling Nul's explanation that he was killing when he had no man hair on his body.

Phoung seemed exhausted. Anloc stepped away, returning shortly with a tray of grapes, cheese, bread, and a carafe of wine. As we relaxed, a more peaceful countenance returned to the face of Phoung.

"When the Americans departed, it was just my family and Mr. Nulandi. He steered our boat to a quiet place on the river. He spoke none of our language, nor we his. Hand signals and patience were used to explain that my husband was dead. 'You must trust me to get you to a place far away, where you will be safe. OK?' he said. I knew there was no real choice.

"Mr. Nulandi then explained that burial must be in the water. I said 'no,' but he insisted. They wrapped Tran in an old sail, secured it with weights, said a prayer, and sent him into the water.

"Nulandi's faith was all that separated us from the same fate," Anloc repeated clutching Phoung as tears spilled down the old woman's creviced cheeks. As if some dam had breached, she bent into Anloc's arms crying and reaching for me. On my knees, I shared their embrace. Convulsions spoke of despair from deep inside her soul. A storm of words soon erupted.

"Mother says that Mr. Nulandi did what he said. He saved us. We would have been killed. He took us to a strange ship with people speaking funny words, like him," Anloc explained, her own voice breaking. "He brought us to his home in Australia, then to this place."

Phoung held my hands.

"Mother loves Mr. Nulandi. We all do. He visits us every year or so and stays as long as he can. My sons work in this winery with the others from lunch," Anloc explained with pride, nodding to where the men were working. The emotions of the women broke over me like waves on a beautiful sandy beach.

Our collective embrace continued for long moments. On my knees, it felt like being initiated into a new sisterhood.

"Why to this place in Tuscany?" I finally asked.

"Mr. Nulandi had to get us a long way away. He had a friend who lived here. We later learned that he was an Italian commando like Mr. Nulandi. They had done missions together. Mr. Nulandi also saved that man on many occasions. He offered us sanctuary. He is our other savior. This was his family's winery and vineyard."

"Is he still alive?" I asked.

"Yes, he is the winemaker. You will meet him later in the day I am sure. His name is Alfredo." I sat back to look at Anloc. *What is it?* her eyes asked as if anticipating that I had questions.

"You talk about this beautiful winery in the possessive 'ours.' Do you own it?"

"Our family does, yes," she answered with an almost angelic look. "We bought it from Alfredo."

"Who is 'we'?"

"Mr. Nulandi really."

"You have never heard this story?" I asked.

"Nothing after the burial of Phoung's husband," Anloc answered. Her hand nestled in Phoung's. So intensely was Phoung trying to understand my questions that her knuckles had turned white.

"Why did she explain it now?"

"Tears spilled from Anloc's eyes. Phoung erupted with words she wanted to be understood, looking from me to Anloc and back. When the words were translated, Phoung reacted with quiet words of understanding.

"Because Nulandi asked her to tell you everything. 'Answer any question,' he said. 'Jas is my salvation," Anloc repeated almost choking on the words. "He needs that, Jas, he is broken inside. Please offer him a path."

"You speak as if you are part of him," I responded trying to absorb the emotion of the woman. "Are you in love with him?"

Chapter 36

Piazza della Repubblica, Rome

"Do you have a Bearcat 376J scanner in stock?" the customer asked the geeky young man standing behind the counter of the electronics store on Piazza della Repubblica, just off the Via Veneto in Rome.

"We do, Sister. It is sophisticated equipment," he responded politely to the nun wearing the habit of a Filipino sister of the Order of St. Benedicta. It was Anloc's son Lanh, speaking in the high pitch of his mother. Nul was dressed the same waiting nearby. On the way into the city, they had stopped at a clerical supply store to acquire habits to match those worn by Jaspar and the Army at the Vatican.

"Oh yes, thank you, my son, for your concern. I know this equipment. It has been part of my training in the Vatican. It will be helpful in my homeland when I return. Please bring an unopened box."

Nul had specified the exact specifications of the machine. He waited at the plaza walking along the shops reviewing the strategy evolving in his mind. *It's dangerous to Anloc and our family, even more to Jas,* he thought, going over each step in the anticipated progression.

After departing the meal in Radda, he initially went to Anloc's workshop. He separated the contents of his bag taken from corpses in Siena into piles of personal effects, weapons, and cell phones or other communications devices, as Anloc had done with the items from Rome, stored in the workshop. He began looking for identities in the personal effects. There was an assortment of wallets, address and appointment books, keys, money, and junk. Money went into an envelope and junk into a bag he retrieved from a drawer. Identifying information was clipped together, including passports, driver's licenses, credit cards, and so on. *These people are all dead, so I have time to use them,* he knew. Each scrap of paper was searched for passwords for the devices knowing that most people wrote them down. Once he had a man's name, it was easy enough to search on Google. The investigative expertise developed over the years made assembly of the inputs and recovered data an efficient process. What he learned was recorded on post-it notes affixed to respective phones and cards. The key was having a place to start, which had been the intended purpose of harvesting the belongings from the corpses.

One item stood out. It was the number he had called resulting in the attack at Paulo's, belonging to one Giuseppe Madano in Siena. Nul suspected this man to have sent the killers. He was the chief of police in Siena.

As he completed his cataloguing and research, Nul checked his encrypted website. There was a note from Chief Bearstrike using their code: "Two promising candidates." Nul smiled at the indication of progress being made in America.

The second contact to Madano needed to be initiated.

I can't use the phones here. If I turn them on, I could betray our location. They went to Siena.

Walking as close as possible to the fire barriers protecting the ruins of Paulo's flat and the nearby buildings, they observed police patrols preventing looters from scavenging the site. Nul took a phone out of the bag and entered the number he had called that had resulted in the attack and inferno.

"Hello," a gruff male voice answered in Italian. Nul recognized it from the prior call. "Who is this?"

"It is Angelo Bellini," Nul answered, looking at his note on the phone.

"Who the hell is this really?" the cautious man answered, knowing that the name on the Caller ID was one of his men killed in response to that last call.

"We spoke before. I offered the woman you want. You fumbled that chance. The girls you sent were useless. I'll give you another opportunity when I call back," Nul said disconnecting the call, envisioning how he would draw the man into the open and continue his climb up the baited path to their pursuer. Anticipating this next step, he and Lanh took a train to Rome.

In the electronics store, Lanh as a nun extracted the unit from its wrappings to confirm the specs. Satisfied, payment was made with a credit card taken from the corpse of another of the attackers, providing a driver's license to confirm the identity. The clerk compared names on card and license, his mind focused on what a sister in some strange habit would do with equipment designed to search encrypted voice or data transfers.

"What will you do with the scanner, sister?" he asked, not able to look her in the eye as the head cover kept face in shadow.

"I need to monitor the area around our convent at home. We have experienced trouble. One of my sisters is being hunted. We need to protect her," Lanh answered. Walking away he was careful to keep his head tilted down.

"Oh!" the clerk blurted recalling the gunfire in and around the Vatican as the sister departed. "Oh, yeah! There were pictures of nuns in habits like those." Normally, he paid no attention to stories concerning the church. This was different.

Could that nun have been involved in the mess in St. Peter's?

The bounty for information was enormous.

The curious young man checked to make sure green lights of security cameras were illuminated. *Great, I have pictures.* Only then did he realize that a male name was on the credit card receipt. "Huh?"

When Lanh joined Nul on the bench at the designated spot by the cinema museum, the assassin had already called the police chief for the third time.

"What are you offering now?" Madano asked politely. His employer had directed that he do anything necessary to identify the caller assumed to be the woman or man always seen with Jaspar Moran. Tracing equipment monitored the chief's phone the moment he answered.

"The same as before. It seems strange for a police chief like you in Siena to be looking for some American woman who is not a fugitive, Mr. Giuseppe Madano."

The line became silent as if it were muted. The man was probably surprised to be called by name. *Perfect*, Nul thought. *Take your time. I hope you are tracing.*

"What is your offer?" Modano finally asked.

"The woman Jaspar Moran for one million Euros in twenties. Have it in a red canvas bag. I'll meet you at my present location at precisely this time in two days. You have my location, correct?"

"Hold on." Another silence elapsed for several moments. Nul moved to the spot he had in mind for the meeting.

"In Rome?"

"Yes."

"At Repubblica on the piazza just in front of the theatre, right?"

"Correct."

"How can I be sure I will get her?"

"We will stage the handoff, so you can observe the woman before dropping the money," Nul answered. "You will be met by a Vietnamese man wearing a 'Sonic the Hedgehog' sweatshirt."

"Where exactly shall we meet?" Madano asked.

"At the place where I'm standing at this time 5:45 p.m., two days from now," Nul answered, taking his time.

"Yes, I see you. But it is very crowded."

"Mr. Madano, you need to handle this yourself. If you fail this time, you will be killed by your own employer."

Chapter 37

Radda, Italy

RATHER THAN answering my question about her love for Nul, Anloc led me back into the vineyards. We walked among rows of grapes surrounding the winery. My anxiety built as we walked in silence.

"I do love Mr. Nulandi," she finally responded, "as do my mother and my sons. We are a family. We want you to feel the same. There is obviously something special between you and him."

The words seemed almost accusatory. Like at the river after our jump when Nul departed, I felt alone. *Alice?* I wondered, having not seen her since we stepped off the bus in Radda. As we had walked toward the winery, she ran through the vineyards. "Looking for rabbits," Anloc explained. "She knows this as one of her homes. She came up here when you arrived." In moments, the faithful beast was at my side.

"I certainly depend on him," I answered defensively. Alice

sniffed around roots of the vines. Hair on the back of her neck and ears stood up, reflecting that she was on duty. *Protecting me from rabid rabbits?* I wondered, comforted to see her. "I trust him. He has saved me from certain death many times these days. That is special to me, for sure," I responded, turning to face her. She took my hand leading me toward a bench under a pergola covered with blooming, fragrant flowers.

"I believe you and he are in need of what the other has to provide," Anloc began as we sat. "Your need is obvious. His is not. That is why he is undertaking this project in addition to the request from his sister."

"He said that to me as well. He tried to explain that to me in quiet times when we've been together. I didn't understand what he meant. Maybe I'm too focused on my own needs."

Anloc's eyes narrowed. "Do you have a better idea now?"

"Surely it's not sex. He's never shown interest in me in that way," I responded not sure whether they were words of pride or regret. My emotions were confused. I only wanted to hold my children. At any price. Nul's guidance was my only chance. I was at his mercy. And that of Anloc and the Army.

"No, not that."

"Have you?" I asked, knowing that there was a dynamic between them as well that was ambiguous, which she had side-stepped.

Anloc laughed, slowly at first then in bellows. "You now know the story of Mr. Nulandi and my family. He saved us and got us all started here. My mother offered me to him as his bride in tribute to her honor and gratitude. She said I would make him a wonderful wife, bear his children, and give him a life of peace and happiness. I said 'no.' She was upset. Eventually, I did marry someone of my choice. He was a local boy who worked for Alfredo at the winery. We had our boys. He died several years ago in a tractor accident. There has been no one else and probably never will be. But Mr. Nulandi . . ."

"Offered you in marriage?"

"It was her culture, an honor for me as well. As I was about to explain, Mr. Nulandi was humbled. He said I deserved better than him, as he would bring me only fear and uncertainty."

"Why did he say that?" I asked, hardly comprehending the proposal, declination, or presence of honor.

"You understand who Mr. Nulandi is, what he has done all his life?"

I nodded, rubbing Alice who sat against my leg. "When he prepared me in Australia for what we are now doing, he also expressed hope that our mission would assist him in finding his faith. Almost like being reborn, we Christians would say."

"Correct. He is complex. I have known him my entire life. When the woman I refer to as my mother made the proposal, she knew nothing of him except what he did for her family. His explanation was that the world was full of people who want to kill him. If it were known that he had a wife and children, it was only a matter of time until they would be murdered or worse."

"How would you describe him today?" I asked, knowing that I was still missing something fundamental in her words.

The small woman bit her lip as both hands brushed through her curly black hair. She absentmindedly tied it in a bun high on the back of her head then reached down to stroke Alice. Our hands touched. When she looked up and into my eyes, tears welled until they overflowed.

"This man has been here every year or so since I have memory," she began again. "He has told me what he can. I have searched everyplace trying to learn more about him. The records of his birth and removal from his mother are non-existent. His military service is top secret. The only records were at the orphanage in Australia."

"Do you know Sister Ismerelda?"

"Yes, I met her there. We had not heard from him for almost two years. Mother remembered the orphanage near Alice Springs where they had initially been taken by Mr. Nulandi. I spoke to the Sister. She said that conversation was possible only in person. I went to Australia. She explained her relationship to Mr. Nulandi and his support of the orphanage," Anloc explained, as if stepping carefully through a minefield. "He came while I was there. When I returned, I began helping with his financial affairs."

I tried to put the pieces together. "Money? Why would you . . . ?"

"Honey, look," Anloc answered, leaning forward to take my hands in her own. "He is highly paid for his work as an assassin. Payments are made to secret accounts in Switzerland, and then transferred through various companies and trusts coming to rest at a place that cannot be traced."

"He is gentle as a man and brutal in his work," I responded. Anloc squeezed my hand in response.

"The funds are managed in America by another kind of aborigine who is successful at investing. Mr. Nulandi supports the orphanage and missions for Aboriginal people. The only person who knows the origins of the funding is Sister Ismerelda."

"Other than you?"

"Yes, other than me. The other area of special interest is the rights of his people. He financed lawsuits that have been brought there to recover ancestral lands," Anloc explained with a glow.

I leaned forward to hug Alice who sat patiently, then looked up to the kind and soft eyes of my new friend. As I watched, they reflected the bright light of the late afternoon sun. A deep hazel brown gleamed. There were a few freckles across the bridge of her nose, stretching across high cheekbones. Her eyes were less slanted and more relaxed than Phoung. I noticed this earlier, but did not have time to think about it.

She took my hands, touching them to her face. "You must have many questions. I will answer everything that I can."

She is in love with him, I thought, sensing competition. For some reason, fear was palpable in my soul. *Not again!* my heart wailed, feeling a crushing fear of losing the man I had come to depend upon.

First Trevor, then Theo and Chrissy, now Nul?

"You look sad, Jaspar, what is it?"

"You are in love with him aren't you?"

"I will do anything for him, as will the rest of our family. We all love and depend upon him, as you do," she answered, still holding my hands. "We all share that common bond."

"A moment ago, you said there was honor for both sides in his declining the marriage offer. I don't understand that either. Something is missing. You say you love him but don't sleep with him."

"Correct," she acknowledged. "And neither do you, yet, I guess."

My confusion seemed to be buried under ever expanding layers of ambiguity.

"You are close and forming your own bond," Anloc added, with lightness in her tone that amplified the absence of a means for me to connect colliding emotions.

"Do you approve?"

"He is my father."

I was speechless, just holding her hands and feeling the warmth of Alice. The chirping of birds and far off sounds of machinery in the vineyards provided cadence as my mind and heart tried to process the information and conflicting emotions. I could only mouth the word *father?*

"He brought my mother and brothers from Vietnam to the orphanage, as mother said. After a few weeks, he arranged for them to come here for new life. He asked if they could take a baby. He was in the army then. His girlfriend was Vietnamese, born in Australia. She died in childbirth. Mother knew nothing of this actual background. She assumed it was the baby of strangers, rescued from Vietnam like her own family. Accordingly, I was raised as her own child. That is why she offered me in marriage, ignorant of our actual relationship, which only he knew."

"And that is why he trusts you completely."

She nodded, struggling with her own emotions.

"Will he be angry with you for telling me?"

"No. As mother said, he wants you to know everything. You need to know the truth. There is yet a long road in front of you both, and for all of us. I feel your children and happiness are at the end of that road. You will never need to doubt my dad or me, or my sons and our family. We are your family. You have been adopted by us, as was I.

"Will you have us?"

Chapter **38**

New York City

THE BLACK SUV pulled close to the curb on 69th Street on the west side of Park Avenue. Similar vehicles rested at each of the other corners around the block and along the park. Following their discussion with President Henrichs, Jason Brontus and Attorney General Abram Sanaroff flew directly to a private airfield in New Jersey. They were met by a team of FBI agents.

Six men in suits approached the doorman. He was surprised to see businessmen arrive a couple of hours before sunrise. An officer stayed with the obviously nervous man to make sure that no alert was given to Copper Starr, who occupied the two top floors of the prestigious fourteen-story residential building at 690 Park. Agents from the vehicles walked casually along the streets ready to move at a moment's notice. While no trouble was expected, the team was prepared.

With the passkey reluctantly provided by the doorman, Brontus, Sanaroff, a senior FBI investigator, and three agents entered the carved mahogany door located a few steps across a marble foyer from the elevator. The private security guard was jolted awake. As with the doorman, a trailing agent remained to prevent any warning to the man of the house.

Brontus turned on lights as he walked through the spectacular flat with pristine vistas of the city. Central Park and the river stretched to the west and Wall Street to the south. The palatial suite had been featured in cultural living and society magazines as a home of "beautiful people." Starr's wife Heather adorned the spreads with the beauty and poise of a popular Broadway star. Secretary Starr was legendary as an early riser who ran the reservoir or the Ellipse in Washington with younger members of his team.

"Who turned the lights on?" he asked calmly stepping down the circular staircase taken from a Normandy castle and restored to its original elegance. "A suitable entrance way don't you think?" he asked with his usual flair.

"We did, Copper," Sanaroff responded, stepping into the light at the bottom of the stairs.

Starr was dressed to go jogging with sneakers in hand. Surprise was not evident in his face as he made his way around the steps without holding onto the gilded handrails.

"Gentlemen, greetings. To what do I owe this honor?" the financier asked, extending his hand. "You have gone to a lot of trouble to see me off on a run. Did you subdue my security?" he asked with the confidence of a man in control.

"Not at all. They were happy to stand aside and keep our men company while we came to pay respects," Sanaroff began, addressing the man who had once been his client when the AG was senior partner of the whitest of the white-shoe downtown law firms, Honey, Jones & Cabot. "We need your help, Copper."

"My door is open anytime. You needn't have broken in. May I get you a drink or make some coffee?" the titan asked. "My boys will be waiting downstairs. They know to wait until I show up."

"I hope we will not be long," the U.S. Attorney said, moving into the living room where they could visit in greater comfort.

"What is it?" Starr asked, when he joined them with a tray of Perrier, squeezing a lime into his bottle without allowing a drop to fall errantly to the walnut flooring or Turkish carpet. He sensed nervousness in the visitors as he concealed his own anxiety.

Markets are turning against my bets. For the first few weeks, I thought it was due to the delay of the president's stimulus package. But something else is occurring. Now this. What am I missing?

"We have reason to believe there is a terrorist conspiracy underway that is intended to destroy America," Sanaroff began.

"Have you been drinking already, Abe?" Starr responded, contempt dripping from his voice.

"No, we are quite serious or we would not be here before sunrise," Brontus added, placing a copy of his dust scenario graphic on the coffee table, as he had with the president. It had become his means of explanation to each person drawn into the investigation.

"What's this?" Starr asked imperiously, picking up the single sheet of paper. Tracing its lines with his index finger, he tapped each of the circled numbers nodding until he got to the last line that dropped straight down.

"It is a picture of a series of steps that we believe reflects a sophisticated terrorist plot, as the attorney general said," Brontus picked up the line of thought.

This looks like the bets I have made. "These peaks and valleys are what happened in the markets since the president commenced his stimulus programs," Starr commented. "It is highly simplified. But accurate except for this last line. The markets are down, but nothing near this collapse."

"The plunging line is what is believed to be the intention of the terrorists," Brontus responded.

"Terrorists? What terrorists?"

"That's why we are here, Mr. Secretary. We need your help."

"Where did this chart come from? It is actually an interesting summary," Starr said. "The Federal Reserve?"

"I developed it with Westbrook Bearstrike," the U.S. Attorney answered leaning forward.

"*The* Chief Bearstrike?"

"Yes."

"Did he come to your office?" Starr asked with a smirk on his face.

"I went to the reservation."

"Of course, he never travels. And no one is known to ever have gone to his world. At least not in our lifetime."

"He is in Washington as we speak. At the White House."

Color drained from Starr's face.

"I originally drew this chart in the dust at the Chief's home. He summoned me to explain the plot he believes to be unfolding. Another stimulus payment would be the coup de grace."

"Like your point 6 here?" Starr confirmed.

"Exactly."

"So what do you want from me. I know nothing of a terrorist plot."

"We have reason to believe that this dust scenario is a strategy executed at your direction by Trevor Moran before he joined the government," Sanaroff picked up the discussion.

"What reason?"

"Moran's records from Westbury and his explanation of them. He downloaded all of it before his murder."

"So what? I had no connection with anything Trevor was doing. I was leading the Treasury. If he had some secret plan, I certainly wasn't privy to it."

"Please read this email," Brontus said, handing a copy of the email containing Starr's direction while secretary of Treasury to Moran to execute a trade with the Queen's Sovereign Trust.

"As I keep saying, so what?" Starr responded, after reading the brief note. He had no memory of it. "This could have been falsified by anyone. It's hearsay, and you know it."

"We can prove it's authentic," Brontus answered.

Starr took a sip of his drink, watching the eyes of the men he had known and worked with for many years.

What do they actually know?

He searched through his mind for anything that could explain why they were present. When he had been at Treasury, he had been frustrated by the failure of that administration to embrace his proposed means of addressing the economic decline of America. He was as certain his theory would work as he was that the Fed's policy of unending stimulus would lead to collapse. Upon return to private life, as chairman of Embank, which soon became the largest commercial bank in the world, faith in his theory escalated. He was approached by a British friend of long standing about monetizing the theory using largely monies to be provided from English sources. They would bet against the U.S. policies. He was intrigued and committed his own funds, which made up a tiny portion of the whole. The investments were multiplied with ever-increasing English investments added to the gains at each point on Brontus's chart.

"Have you cleared your presence here with Hamilton?" Starr asked, meaning the President. "You know that I can fry your asses over the impertinence of your invading my space?"

"The only thing you're going to cook is yourself, Mr. Secretary, so climb off the high horse," Brontus responded, leaning forward, just inches from Starr's casually crossed knee with hands resting on top like the roof of a cathedral. "We're here to give you a chance to save yourself, as requested by the president.

"We gather that Gordon Blair is a friend of yours," Brontus continued. "He is director of the Queen's Trust."

"Never heard of him."

"Your email mentioned him. Besides, you have spoken to him many times over the past few years, including when you were at Treasury."

"Not so," Starr shot back.

"We have the actual phone company records. He called you on

several different numbers, which have been traced to you. Recent calls have been for extended periods of time."

"Do I need to call my lawyer?"

"You're free to do whatever you want. We're just here hoping to clear-up some questions," Brontus answered, his demeanor shifting from curious questioner to suspicious prosecutor.

"Did you authorize the murder of Trevor Moran?" Sanaroff asked.

"I'm not saying anything until my lawyer gets here," Starr answered, rising from the sofa, spilling the mineral water. "What do you want from me?" Starr asked, sitting back down without making any calls.

"Just answer our questions. As Jason said, we came here to clear you in private, get any help you could provide, and move on," Sanaroff explained again. "Had our intentions been otherwise, we would have arranged a perp walk from your office. Would you prefer that? Then we could have our discussion after the press is full of pictures and questions. Jason and I would be interviewed and respond with 'no comment.' You would be thoroughly trashed. We prefer to head that off, if possible. So does your friend, the president."

"He knows about this?"

I talked to him last night. He said nothing.

"Yes."

Starr listened, his face flushing with color.

He's thinking way too much for an innocent man.

Two of the FBI suits who had been waiting below entered the room in response to an electronic signal sent by Brontus.

"The murder of Moran?" Brontus repeated.

"I don't know anything about it."

"Who would want him murdered?"

"Why do you say murdered? His plane crashed. Unfortunate, yes. But there has never been any mention of murder," Starr answered.

"You are literally right, no body or DNA has been found. The plane crashed in arctic conditions. Bearstrike thinks whoever is behind this terrorist plot wanted him out of the way. Any idea why that would be the case?"

"Same answer," Starr repeated, leaning back on the sofa and crossing his legs again, holding his knee more tightly.

I did tell Blair that Moran was asking too many questions.

"What about the kidnapping of his children? Those deeds and the murder are capital Federal offenses because Moran was a Cabinet officer," Brontus added.

"I have no idea."

"Back to that email, Mr. Secretary," the prosecutor said, shifting gears. Sensing the man's mind racing to get in front of the avalanche of new information, Brontus hoped to catch Starr between thoughts. "It was extracted from the Westbury Madison files, as we said. Its authenticity can and has been proven. We need to see if there have been other contacts between Blair and yourself and anyone beyond Blair. Accordingly, please let these experts have access to your computers and files," Brontus continued, tilting his head toward the agents standing off to the side. "Then we can be on our way."

"Incidentally, we have a subpoena ready, including for your trading records at Embank," Sanaroff added. "We want to see if they reflect the pattern on that chart, as do the Westbury records already traced by the Chief."

"That is not possible!" the frightened man responded. *Damn, those records will be clear about what I have done. I never thought any of this would see the light of day. Part of a terrorist plot? Gordon Blair and the Queen of England? What am I missing?*

"We can impound your computers and any communication devices, Sir. I also have in my pocket a warrant for your arrest," Brontus added.

"You can't take anything from me," Starr responded.

"Very well, here is the warrant for your home, office, cars, and anyplace else under your control," Brontus answered, pulling the folded sheaf of papers from his suit coat pocket. "We will be happy to proceed if that is what you want. We have a large team outside, including experts to examine your home, storage, and vehicles, impound records, or whatever."

"It's your choice, Copper. You can cooperate or not," the AG added.

There was silence for long moments. The men stared at each other, minds in overdrive.

"The computers, sir?" Brontus repeated. "Will you provide them to us now?"

I was so careful to leave no trail. How could I have been so dumb to send that one e-mail? If I call my lawyer, he will counsel, stonewall. That will bury me in infamy and humiliation.

"While you're thinking, let us tell you what we know," Brontus continued. "Moran's records include his wife's transcription of his explanatory notes. They had a special code, all of which was delivered to Chief Bearstrike. He personally examined them, confirming what he had concluded from watching the results of his own trading patterns. Let's call it the dust scenario."

Starr clasped his knee tightly but could not control trembling fingers.

Sonofabitch is poised, Sanaroff thought, watching Brontus undermine the confidence of the financial titan point-by-point.

"While we and Chief Bearstrike are working this side of the ocean, Mrs. Moran is on the trail of whoever is behind all of this. I am sure you've seen the press reports from Rome and Siena of Aphrodite," the prosecutor continued. "While she works the ground over there, we are focusing on the money trail. It has to involve far more than your and the queen's funds. The amounts committed are vastly beyond those resources."

While images of the naked woman with knife in hand were emblazoned in Starr's consciousness, his focus was elsewhere. *These guys are not going away or backing down.*

"Look, Copper," Sanaroff said, after allowing Starr time to reflect. "We are ready to indict you for murder, kidnapping, mail fraud, and a long list of other offenses."

God Almighty, what have I done? I just wanted to prove that I was right and everybody else wrong. It got out of hand. I was blind. All I cared about was vindication of my original plan. But, if there is no more stimulus, then I will be destroyed. I bet everything. Good God! Who else could be involved? I trusted Blair. Terrorists? Bulls and bears—and I'm a stupid pig.

"Your records and computers, sir?" Brontus asked again

"Can I have time to think about it, talk to my wife?" Starr answered. *And my lawyers.*

"Time is of the essence. We will proceed with or without your cooperation," Brontus answered, looking at the FBI men. "Gentlemen, you may start your search. You are to obtain all financial, computer, and other records in this space. As we discussed, I mean everything, including removing the computers and file cabinets. Search every drawer, nook, and cranny. Mr. Starr is to touch nothing."

"My wife is still asleep," the accused protested.

"You may wake her. One of the officers will be with you from now on at each step. Our patience is running out," Brontus said, motioning the officers to proceed. "Copper Starr, you are under arrest. You have the right to remain silent . . ."

"Hold on, Jason. I don't want to be arrested by my country," Starr interrupted. "Let's make a deal. I will tell you everything I know, provided the crime I am charged with will involve financial excess, not murder, treason, or anything else that accuses me of being something other than a pig and stupid, of which I now see that I am guilty."

"We can make no deal until you tell and show us everything. However, we can promise you that the outlines of what you propose are acceptable. There will likely be prison time to be served and fines to be paid," Sanaroff responded.

Starr nodded with hands between his knees staring at the floor.

"If we ever discover that there is anybody else at a senior level that you have not identified, Copper, there will be no deal, and I will embarrass you, break you, and make sure you spend the rest of your life in prison. Do you understand that?" Brontus continued. "And the Moran children, they must be recovered unharmed."

"I don't know anything of them, I swear," Starr responded, head sinking as he spoke.

"Tell us what you do know," Brontus directed. "Hold on. Before you say any more, we need to record this."

"That's fine. If you have the equipment, please get it set up," Starr responded, standing to listen to noises from above. "Heather, is that you?" he asked.

"Yes," a sleepy woman wearing a bathrobe said from the top of the stairs. "The noise woke me. Who are these people? It's not even five. Copper, what's going on?"

"May I?" he asked, nodding toward the stairs, indicating a desire to walk up to escort her down. Brontus walked a few steps behind.

"They're here to confront you, aren't they?" she asked, after introductions had been made. "Have you done something wrong?"

"I did not think so. They are here to ask some questions," he answered, returning to the sofa. She sat in a chair behind Brontus and Sanaroff. Another FBI agent arrived with sound and film equipment. Mrs. Starr sat still, not understanding what was going on. Her ignorance of her husband's activities was similar to his about what lay behind Sir Gordon Blair.

"May I relieve myself before we continue," Starr asked, knowing that there would be several minutes before the equipment would be ready. "My bathroom is in my study, where my safe is located as well. I will be happy to show it to you."

"Of course, we would like to see it before we proceed. We'll come with you," Brontus responded.

Starr walked down a richly paneled hallway to his study. When the lights were turned on, they illuminated a floor covered with Turkish rugs in calming sky blue with light pink and yellow floral designs. Mahogany paneling accented a reddish-purple desk made from some exotic wood by a skilled craftsman. Walls were festooned with pictures and honors including Starr with presidents and famous athletes. The most colorful showed Starr with Ernie Banks at Wrigley Field, with the red and blue Cubs circle emblem in the background. Both men were far past playing condition, though they stood arm in arm.

"You must be a Cubs fan," Brontus said.

"All my life," he answered, opening the bathroom door. "Began as a boy in Montana. Local minor league players in the farm system coached us at the work camp." Brontus stood aside with the open door, admiring an array of guns and hunting knives behind the desk. He touched each one in turn.

"This is an impressive collection, Mr. Secretary," the prosecutor complimented the collector.

"Also something from my youth in Montana. I grew up with guns and take comfort in having them close by."

"They're not loaded, I assume," Sanaroff said standing away from the weaponry.

"Of course not, Abe."

"Where is the safe?" Brontus asked, seeing no indications of an enclosure that could conceal more than routine financial records and jewelry.

"The safe is behind this wall," Starr said, pressing a button under the sheath of a long Bowie knife that appeared to be ancient. The knife rose, exposing a tumbler that Starr twisted back and forth until a distinctive electronic sound indicated the retraction of safety locking bars.

Brontus was fascinated by the hinging of the wall. The entire span opened to reveal a vault as in a bank. "Everything is here," he said as Brontus, Sanaroff, and one of the FBI officers entered the secure space with bright lights and polished steel. The remaining officer stood by Starr, motioning for him to also enter, as his wife closed the door to the bathroom. The officer took a step backward, away from the vault.

Watching the officer, Starr grasped the heavy door and leaned against the wall of weapons. He pulled the door toward him, blocking the vision of the FBI man still stepping toward the door. In the closed space, Starr lifted a 9mm automatic pistol with attached silencer from its perch. His finger flipped the safety, knowing that the chamber was ready for action.

Pausing for an instant with closed eyes, the man whose fortune was in a mess and reputation about to be in ruins raised the weapon. The vault door swung open. Surprised, Starr's focus slipped as the FBI agent reached for his arm to push the gun toward the floor.

KA-BAM!

A thud was heard from behind the bathroom door.

"Copper!" Heather Starr screamed.

Chapter 39

Siena, Italy

BY THE TIME Nul and Lanh returned to Siena, it was approaching midnight. They walked around Paulo's burned-out flat hoping to find the white van parked by Jaspar before the attack. They did not know the exact location. Deserted streets provided no clues.

Where would she put it? Nul wondered, knowing that it would be in a close, dark place. It was spotted at the end of a dead-end street. Keys were under the mat. License plates of an old Fiat van were switched.

As they turned onto the road to Radda, Nul knew the aged

vehicle would need tuning for the work ahead. His hobby had long been auto racing. In Alice Springs, he had a stable of fast cars, including an old Formula 1 Ferrari racer that he loved to tinker with and enter in local contests. He could have won championships. Chief Bearstrike acquired an interest in a Formula 1 team on his behalf. Initially, Nul worked in the pits. He became qualified to race, largely testing cars and not competing in Grand Prix races to win. That was the task of other drivers. Since his identity had to remain secret, Nul was content to measure himself against the best in practice racing, like a scout team in American football.

The van would need to perform in a similar manner.

* * *

Radda, Italy

I SLEPT FITFULLY. Sensing movement, Alice rose from the bed. Anloc had escorted us to a remote corner of the space above her shop.

"Are you awake?" Nul whispered, tiptoeing into the room.

"Sort of. I keep having nightmares about my children. They are pitiful and crying for me." Alice slid aside to make room without rising or causing disturbance, displaying the agility of a combat team member. Instinct told her to be on duty, even though there was no indication of danger. Slipping off the bed, the door became her place of sentry, face turned to the small space where light peeked through.

I remained still as Nul moved in. "Have you slept?" I finally asked.

"No. Lanh and I have been to Siena and Rome."

"Why?"

He sat up against the headboard. I did the same, switching on the light. "You look exhausted."

"I'm OK. We have time for a few hours of rest then we need

to go. There is much to be done," he began an explanation of all
that he had learned and arranged, including visit to the riverbank
where the Gypsy camp attack had taken place. Relaxed muscles
of his shoulder provided a cushion for my head as I absorbed his
words.

"You have been busy. Is what you plan possible?"

"It will get done," he answered. "You rest now. I'll go into the
next room. Alice will remain."

"No, you both stay here with me."

He did not resist.

* * *

"There's so much death and sadness here," I said, walking
through the grounds where the Gypsy encampment had been
on the riverbank until the helicopters attacked in the still of that
night. Nothing remained. Shadows of people hovered all around.
Old women and children, dogs and cats, babies in the arms of
their mothers, and working men circling around me. "Why?" they
taunted in menacing chorus.

I bolted upright. Words screaming in my head as I looked
around. It was dark.

What will I do? Who will help me? My fingers touched a body.
It was Nul.

I edged closer. He rolled over on his back, arm across the pillows. I instinctively snuggled into the warm spot. Rise and fall of
his chest was the only movement. The ghosts were gone I discovered upon peeking out of the bedclothes and looking at the ceiling
and around the room in dim illumination from under the door.
His other arm moved across my hip as he turned toward me. It
felt safe. I touched his face, gently tracing around forehead and
cheeks, down a strong arm and hip. He moaned.

"Rest sweet man," I whispered.

* * *

WARMTH ENVELOPED me as my eyes opened. Sunlight surrounded edges of the curtains. I had not moved. Nor had Nul. I lay on his arm with mine draped across his leg touching warm skin.

His eyes shined as they opened. He kissed my hand, squeezing me tightly.

"You're here," I whispered.

"Of course, it is where I should be. Making sure you are safe."

"I had a nightmare." I explained. He nodded pulling me closer.

"What did you see in the dream?" Nul asked.

"On the river, what happened there, Nul?

"The camp seemed to be composed of people and vans full of merchandise, perhaps from the market in Siena. They could have been people we may have seen."

"In my dream, the area was like a freshly plowed field. There were ghosts. They confronted me. I was scared. Nothing else remained. They died because of me, didn't they? Our pursuers want to kill us and leave no trace of me, my children, you, and anybody else involved with me. Just like those poor Gypsies, right? I am responsible for their murder."

"All of what you say is true," he said, sitting up against the headboard, relaxing as he straightened the covers over him. "But your children are safe. I am sure of it."

"Why?"

"Because they pursue us with such intensity," he answered, explaining his discussion with the chief of police.

"So I am to be bait again?" I asked after Nul went over the planned meeting in Repubblica.

"It's the next step."

"I'm ready, just like you and Alice. Dangerous or not is immaterial. This is our crusade," I said, petting our trusty hound who sat on the floor by my side of the bed. I patted the bed clothes, sitting up as well. Alice leapt up to sit between us. I hugged her as my thoughts turned back to other anxieties. Tears ran down my cheeks and into her fur.

"What is it, Jas, what's the matter?"

"I should have been able to protect my children, keep them safe. But I didn't," I said, now sobbing uncontrollably.

"Your guilt overcomes reality," Nul responded, rubbing my arm. "Had you not escaped with Father Michael, they would be dead by now."

"You mean my flight saved their lives?"

"Your absence, and the work of the U.S. Attorney, and now Chief Bearstrike have delayed the stimulus. Had it proceeded, your children would have served no further purpose."

"Our stars are aligned. Does that explain your confidence?"

Nul seemed to agree. "Our success is a function of many elements. Your ability to evolve into a warrior is critical. You may attribute it to your God's plan for you and the children," he consoled. "As your fortitude continues to grow, so too will our success. We are getting closer to your goal."

"I will be whatever it takes. You know that," I agreed, smiling through the tears as Alice lay on my lap. *She is an odd soldier*, I thought massaging her shoulder muscles. "What about yours?"

"My what?"

"Your goal to find or understand your soul. Are you finding what you need?"

Nul moved closer, his hand joining mine in touching our partner with four legs. "I hope so. I need to nurture my ability to open up. To love and be loved," he began in the childlike voice in which he had spoken of himself in the church in Siena before the attack at Paulo's.

"But you love Anloc and her family, your daughter and grandsons. You support your people and orphans. And . . ."

"Anloc told you about us?"

"Yes."

"I wanted to tell you, but I just could not find the time or words. We have been moving so fast since coming to Italy."

"You are correct in that."

"Through you, I now feel there is heart in me. I need for those feelings to be nurtured to grow in the future, just as you need to recover your children for your future."

I leaned forward, placing my hand on top of his. "We have a war to fight," I began, sitting back, as Alice jumped to the floor. "Neither of us may survive I honor what we have accomplished and our commitment to see this through, wherever it takes us."

"And when we are done?" he asked.

"We will both be healed and ready for whatever lies ahead in our lives. I hope we will each experience happiness in our own way."

"Thank you," he said, straightening his shoulders. "I think we're ready. We have a long way to go and will need to depend on each other, as we have, to get through the eye of this needle."

"Let's go," I said, standing, stretching, and smiling. Our comfort with each other augured well for the mission ahead.

"Oh," he said, "I almost forgot. My friend Bearstrike reports another contact step in America. Something about a man named Copper Starr. Chief is at the White House with your president. The next step is London."

"It's all quite amazing," I said when he finished the explanation.

"We are making progress on two fronts. Maybe it's a race," Nul added, making a glider of his hand slicing through the air.

A race? I wondered moments later turning on the shower, letting the steamy water pulsate over every inch of my tired body.

Chapter 40

Repubblica Square, Rome
Two days later

PIAZZA DELLA REPUBBLICA was a spacious traffic semi-circle around the Fountain of the Naiads at the intersection of several prominent streets in north central Rome. Via Nazionale came from the general direction of the Coliseum, the Roman Forum, Palatine Hill, and Circus Maximus. Via Veneto went northwesterly past the U.S. Embassy and into the Borghese Gardens, just past Harry's Bar. There were many areas to relax in the sunshine, a theatre, shops, and restaurants.

People gathered in the spacious area around the Fountain representing the Nymphs of the Lakes (holding a swan), Rivers (stretched out on a monster of the streams), Oceans (riding a horse symbolizing the sea), and Underground Waters (leaning over a mysterious dragon). In the center, Rutelli's Galuco group sculpture symbolized the dominion of man over nature. It was an idyllic setting for lunch, enjoyment of sunshine, shared friendship, or just going about business. A rock band in full swing entertained the mid-afternoon crowd.

Nul and his army arrived late the previous afternoon from Radda to walk through each step of their plan. The van was parked in an empty parking lot about thirty minutes from Rome at Ostia Antica where they slept and hoped to return. They took the train to the Repubblica–Teatro dell' Opera metro station to make final arrangements, wearing clothes of domestic servants, far different than would be the case for show time.

People were occupied with smart phones or messaging devices. The scanner purchased by Lanh at a nearby shop had been installed in the van, together with its power plant overhaul. Lanh operated the equipment, straining to keep track of conversations selected for monitoring. Using the voice of the Siena police chief and numbers of those speaking to him in the interim, Lanh had flagged sounds to be followed. Nul's object for the rendezvous with Madano was to learn the identity of whoever was directing him, the next step up the chain of command. Once he had a list of numbers and voices, the map of the way forward could be clarified, hopefully, in short order. "In a crisis, someone will be in touch," he had explained.

Nul walked along the theatre at the northeast side of the piazza then around the fountain. It was hardly to the standards of Trevi. He chose this location not for its beauty, but for the crowds and traffic in constant motion.

Dressed as a stout Italian woman, Nul moved slowly amidst milling people looking at playbills of the theatre and discussing movie choices. Alice acted as seeing eye-dog. Nul's outfit attracted little attention, yet provided disguise and cover for the armaments he had acquired upon arriving from Radda. He hoped there would be no need for violence, but was ready for whatever occurred. As in each of their steps, there would be surprises. Alice surveyed the scene listening for a specific type of high-pitched signal used to remotely detonate bombs.

Jaspar was in place at the top of the nearby Spanish Steps with about twenty others selected by Anloc, ready to begin their procession down the narrow street that opened into Repubblica.

His face shaded by sunglasses, Nul observed security people listening with earplugs in order to coordinate with their handlers the placement of surveillance devices. He had no illusions about the force that would likely to be arrayed against them. His own earplugs, used to listen to Lanh's recorded data, were concealed by a bandana tied around his head.

A police prison wagon was parked just a block away from Lanh. It hosted an emergency response team. Officers patrolled through the crowd.

Good, Nul thought listening to the coded directions which came from a source other than Madano. *He called in way more resources than needed for a simple exchange. We may have hit pay dirt.*

Watching a pot-bellied man of about fifty walking toward the designated spot just in front of the Nymph of Underground Waters, which he thought to be appropriate for a meeting with Don Navarro, Nul touched the instant message icon notifying Jaspar to proceed. With her troupe dressed in the Philippine habits worn at the Vatican, the plan was for the procession to flow into the crowd upon arrival in the piazza. Like Madano, they would congregate around the spot. When Nul touched a signal, Jaspar was to step forward, remove the hood and pass whatever identity test was demanded. Once the exchange commenced, Nul would hit the signal twice. The sisters would shed their penitent habits to run, like Aphrodite, through the crowd as sirens shrieked and fireworks exploded, which they had stowed in trash containers around Repubblica. It would send the crowd into a frenzy.

Nul envisioned a spectacle of bare breasted women bouncing through the crowd generating chaos. After a short run, the ladies were to cover themselves and disperse, leaving their habits where they fell. In the resultant confusion, Jaspar and Anloc were to descend the stairs into the Repubblica Metro station. Lanh was to return to the van. Nul would have slipped into the crowd, removing the dress and dropping it in a trash can. In jogging shorts, he and Alice would run to whatever exit route was available.

Madano stood close to the spot where Nul had two days earlier made his last call. The man seemed anxious, speaking into an earphone. Nul unhooked Alice's leash, allowing her to cautiously walk among the forest of legs to meet and steer Jaspar and her sisters to the spot, ears always attuned for any signal that would indicate their plan had been invaded.

Lanh picked up conversations involving the voice matrix of Police Chief Madano. The contacts were displayed on a depiction of Repubblica. It revealed a surveillance team closing around the spot to exchange cash for Jaspar. *Check*, Nul thought, as Lanh kept him posted.

They are converging as hoped, but why so many?

As Chief Madano made his way to the spot, Lanh stepped out of the van. Convergence of their adversaries could be followed on his smart phone and ear plugs. Dressed as a young vampire fan, complete with facial piercings, tattoos, and spiked hair with purple-streaks, he blended into the crowd ready to help in case things went awry.

Madano had a red canvas bag in his hand and was walking in a circle. *He's nervous*, Nul thought. *Why doesn't he step to the spot; it's almost time?* The police chief then faced in different directions, almost in a frenzy.

What is he doing? Communicating positions for sharpshooters to measure for Jas?

Nul could see her troupe approaching a little further distant than Madano's team. Suddenly, Alice jumped in the air at a place close to the spot, but away from Jaspar.

What the . . . ? Oh, shit! His instincts screeched, following the dog's point to a backpack lying on the ground then to a woman running through the crowd in the opposite direction. *A bomb to be triggered when the exchange commences? Sacrificing Madano and all these support troops to get Jas? We gotta go, Now!* Nul knew, punching the signal twice to tell Jaspar and the sisters to disrobe and scatter.

SCREE-EE-EE-CH! Violent sounds erupted like security alarms from trash canisters circling the piazza, responding to Nul's next signal. *BOOM! BANG-BAM! KA-BOOM!* Firecrackers exploded from the same sources. The crowd scattered, instinctively running from the noise that echoed around Repubblica as sounds of a war zone were magnified by echoes from the surrounding buildings. Sisters streaked in every direction adding to the confusion.

Even with people scattering in every direction, Madano and his men, as well as Alice, stood in place awaiting their own signal to commence their strategy. Amidst the noise and chaos, the police chief did not hear a different signal sent by Nul. Alice did.

"*A-G-G-H-A!*" Madano screamed as Alice sank sharp teeth into his leg deep enough to hit bone and rip flesh. He fell to the ground holding his damaged leg. Blood flowed freely as the man thrashed about in the chaos of a fearful mob running for safety. Lanh emerged from the scattering crowd to pick up Madano's phone that had fallen as he collapsed. Alice grabbed the red bag on the ground, snarling and racing into the crowd.

Madano's team raced forward with guns drawn looking for their leader.

"Where is he?"

"Where's the woman?"

"What's going on?" they shouted to each other and into their own phones. Fireworks continued to explode as sirens shrieked. Frenzy in the crowd created stampedes in every direction.

Alice ran full steam through the congestion of fearful people. Growling viciously, she shook her head back and forth as violently as possible ripping the bag open until colorful twenty Euro notes spewed into the air. They made a bluish snowfall as swirling air currents swept them away. As the reality of free money dawned on the crowd, chaos took another leap of intensity. Real sirens sounded in the distance.

Adapting to the new reality and seeing that Alice and Lanh were racing to the van. Nul ran into the crowd. "*BOMB! BOMB! BOMB! RUN, RUN! GO!*" he screamed, pushing and pulling people into the streets jammed with cars, people, emergency vehicles, and flooded in utter panic.

KA-BOOM-A-WHAMPA! Fire and shrapnel ripped through people running away in collective fear. The satchel bomb was intended to obliterate Jaspar and anyone within sixty yards. It had been detonated in response to the unexpected turn of events hoping that the conflagration would consume her along with everyone else in a wide radius. Somehow, Alice sensed the signal in the instant before the explosion occurred.

The concussive explosion hurtled chunks of concrete into the air. Incendiary flames ignited shops and cars all around, triggering secondary explosions. Searing shrapnel invaded the bodies of unlucky people closest to the explosion.

Chapter 41

Camp David, Maryland
Next day

"HE APPARENTLY tried to kill himself rather than face the humiliation of betraying his country and triggering his own financial collapse. For a man like Secretary Starr, death would be preferable to having his reputation trashed and serving the rest of his life in prison," Jason Brontus answered the question of President Henrichs about the Copper Starr fiasco.

"He took a gun from a collection on the wall of his study as we were in his vault, which stored valuables and financial records. The FBI agent tried to stop him. They struggled for the gun, but it went off killing the officer. Starr is being held without bail. A variety of charges will be filed. He will live the remainder of his life in disgrace behind bars."

"Copper was always the center of his own universe, never taking adversity into account. He succeeded throughout his life. When confronted as you explained, I am not surprised that he tried to exit the stage. There is nothing any of us can do except let the judicial process run its course," Henrichs responded.

"Yes, but his wife has agreed that there will be a press release advising of his death. The incarceration process will remain confidential until this matter has run its course."

Henrichs nodded, sadly, in agreement.

"What about his records? Are they helpful to your efforts to find out how this mess evolved?"

"They are well organized and complete, including directions to Trevor Moran and a British confidante of the queen," the U.S. Attorney responded. "He certainly directed what was done on these shores."

"Why would he keep such complete records for something he must have known could be a criminal undertaking?" Abram Sanaroff asked.

"I can answer that," Henrichs responded. "I have known the man my whole life. In his mind, his work was the work of America. It would never have occurred to him that he could be used by someone else. Had even I suggested such a thing to him, he would have laughed me out of the room."

"The records are also being compared to my own analysis," Chief Bearstrike added, "which is interesting to me."

"Please bring me up to date on the rest of what is going on," the president asked. "West Mad appears to be transforming from a rumor of the derelictions of Trevor Moran to an effort initiated by him to prevent an attack on our financial health. I hope the day comes when I can explain all of this to our people, including my own failures to discern the true intention of the stimulus suggestions by Copper."

"It appears that Secretary Starr was operating as a silo. Focused on justifying his own theories, he was oblivious to the motivations of those who encouraged and financed his plans. It is obvious that others with huge resources are involved, even to this minute," Brontus concluded. "Our only lead so far is to this man Blair who manages the Queen's Sovereign Trust. We believe it was used as a front. Chief Bearstrike has been trying to establish contact with the man. He is a respected pillar of English government and society."

"Indeed, I left word for several days with no response. Your intelligence agencies have been all over this situation with no cooperation from our British friends," Chief explained. "We have confirmed that the accounts of the Trust were scrupulously cleansed for each reporting period, so nothing amiss would have been observed unless someone got into the depths of the trading records, which this man Blair seems to have kept firmly in his grasp. Returns were excellent. The official board is composed of Royal hangers-on, so it would be unlikely for anyone to look beneath the surface."

"And now?" Henrichs asked feeling more optimism in the Chief's voice than his words would justify. Bearstrike had arrived at Camp David the prior afternoon. Henrichs joined him for dinner. A respectful friendship took hold. "He has the bearing and dignity of a long-reigning prime minister," Henrichs explained to his wife after a long evening of walking and talking. "I feel like the student and he the kind, patient teacher. He seems to exist in a world above partisan politics. He could be a global leader in a time of crisis when reliable, independent inspiration is the order of the day. I would like for him to be my vice president if I get another term."

"The events in Repubblica apparently brought Blair out of his cocoon. I will meet him at five tomorrow morning in Paris at a place to be chosen by him." The horrific videos had been played around the world.

"Because of fear for himself?" Henrichs asked. He had seen the blood bath from many angles, including non-stop media coverage. The death toll was mounting rapidly. "Terrorists Attack Rome" was the headline around the world.

"I am sure it is related, like you, and am anxious to find out," Chief answered, as his mind churned considering the president's question.

"Any word on Mrs. Moran or the aborigine?" the president asked. Bearstrike had explained his understanding of Nul's plan.

"They were both there, right?"

"Yes, they should have been at ground zero. His normal communication channels are mute."

"Dead?"

"In his case, no news is good news."

"Really, why?"

"If he were gone, I would hear from his team. They are as close as family to him. I also have his money and power of attorney."

"I thought he acted alone."

"So he wants the world to think."

"I assume our people on the ground are searching for him?"

"No, they would have no way to know what is going on. In any event, he would want you to stay away. Such operatives would just get in his way. I trust him, and so can you," Chief responded.

"OK. Chief, someday I want you to explain how you came to know this man. I would also like to meet him."

Chief responded with a polite, non-committal nod.

"Do I understand correctly that we have everything we can get on these shores with Starr's records being evaluated?" the president continued.

"So it appears, sir," Brontus answered. "There are no other leads. The action is in Italy and, tomorrow, in Paris."

"Who has the skill and resources to do all of this?" a patient Henrichs asked. "I mean the massive amounts of money that could have bankrupted us had I followed the advice of Starr and the Fed to release that last stimulus. Who outsmarted our best economists? And all the killing in Italy, capped off by the slaughter of innocent people in Rome. It is inconceivable that so much could have been mobilized without any discovery by all of our intelligence agencies, Treasury Departments, and Federal Reserve-type agencies. And the world over to boot. Who?"

"We do not know, sir. In the wake of Repubblica, we at least have the attention of Italian intelligence agencies," Sanaroff responded. "But it looks like their police are part of the problem.

Beyond that, well, even our own Copper Starr was duped. Obviously, the Brits as well. And, frankly, everybody else."

"So, *who* I ask?"

Silence.

"Well then, we can hope that Mrs. Moran and the aborigine survived, and this man Blair is ready to come to our side. He surely knows of Copper and now Repubblica," Henrichs concluded. "You have alerted the French authorities of the meeting in Paris to arrange their protection?"

"No. Mr. Blair insisted it be just me," Chief answered.

"Where will you meet?"

"I do not know. He will send me a message. I will be at the U.S. Embassy."

"Do you have a smart phone, Chief?" Henrichs asked, virtually certain that there was no need for the man to have one in his own world.

"No."

"Then, how will he get a message to you?"

"Beats me."

Henrichs nodded observing the mood of Chief Bearstrike. *He's ready!*

*   *   *

"WHAT IS your advice, Chief?" the president asked as they strolled in the rustic atmosphere of the picturesque enclave. It felt a little more like home to Bearstrike than the city would have after more than thirty years in his own world. Henrichs had offered to come to Oklahoma, perceiving himself the junior head of state. 'I will come to you, sir, as we need to go meet Blair,'" was the response. The helicopter would arrive shortly to commence their journey to Paris.

"Be patient. There is nothing else to be done."

"You seem calm, almost serene."

"No, sir. I am resolute. This thing must be solved."

"You don't mean the kidnapping?"

"Correct. Our system has been attacked. And it is our system. My people are part of your country, as you are part of us. Together, we must discover how this fiasco happened and prevent it from recurring. We also need to punish its perpetrators. This is the style of war of this age."

"It is all quite amazing, Chief. I could not have envisioned this whole situation in a million years. I was certain that our and my policies were the result of the highest level of economic and political analysis. Yet the whole system was tilted by some investment group determined to reap windfalls as we almost destroyed ourselves," the thoughtful president spoke as they walked in early morning peacefulness.

"Nonetheless, I am content that we are in the good hands of an aborigine, a socialite, and a wizened Indian investor all fighting for the good guys."

"Don't forget the dog."

"Indeed," the president responded, enjoying the confidence and humor of the Chief.

He is so unlike any other world leader I have ever met. There is no pretense. Just a friendly, confident, and candid man playing his cards in a world of ambiguity. He would make an excellent president.

"Chief?" Henrichs asked, slowing and turning toward his new friend. "I have positioned search and rescue teams in proximity to the areas where we last heard from your man and Mrs. Moran. They remain offshore and can be deployed at a moment's notice."

"Thank you, Hamilton. It is an appropriate precaution. I will keep that in mind and advise him when we next speak," he answered. "I think this will all come to a head shortly. They may need your help, though it is unlike him to ask for outside assistance of any kind."

"When do you expect to hear from your friend?"

"I have no expectation. He and Mrs. Moran have a plan

and are moving. We need to stay out of their way. Positioning resources is fine, but nothing else. They must be invisible in the world. Agreed?"

"OK. This is all amazing, the stuff of novels," Henrichs responded trying to imagine the solitary life of these commandoes.

They walked in silence enjoying the early morning sounds of the forest, minds framing the work ahead.

"As you proceed, Chief, please know that you have unconditional authority in whatever discussions occur to speak for the United States. I trust your judgment. Your word is mine. Use it as you deem necessary," Henrichs said as they approached the area where a helicopter awaited to take the guests to the military airport.

"Sir," Bearstrike began, turning and stopping Henrichs with hands on the man's shoulders. "Can you do me a huge favor?"

"Of course, name it."

"You want us to announce at the Embassy in Rome that Mrs. Moran was killed in that blast?" the president asked with wonder written all over his face as he thought through the strange request. "Is it true?"

Chief shrugged.

"Then why would we make such an announcement?"

"I understand," he responded to Chief's explanation. "Godspeed to you Chief," the president said clasping the Chief's hands. *I wish that I could be with you.*

"And to you sir," he responded with heartfelt embrace. "Thank you for your confidence."

What awaits him out there? Henrichs wondered as the loud machine lifted off the pad, tilting forward with engines racing.

Solving mysteries? Or being blown up like those poor people in Rome? I should demand that we blanket Paris with security. Of course, that is why the location is kept ambiguous.

Chapter 42

Aix en Provence, France
Next day

"Good work, Mr. Blair. Finally, the Moran woman is out of our hair," Prince Alzjar congratulated his chief of staff. He had asked for a live report of the rapidly evolving events, needing to focus on winning the Grand Prix. He also needed to account to his own benefactors, even more remotely buried from public view than the obscure Prince.

"Indeed, so it seems. Following the blast in Repubblica, there were almost one hundred charred and broken bodies. Roman police quickly took charge working with emergency personnel to get the injured to hospitals. The American Embassy is close and sent their security people to assist. Apparently, they had information that Mrs. Moran was in the area. Examination of the dead revealed that she was present and official confirmation was released a few hours ago," Blair explained, handing his boss a copy of the press release.

"It is understood that an investigation is underway to ascertain if there was any contact with her still missing children. She is reputed to have been traveling with an African friend also killed in the explosion. The incident has filled local hospitals with gravely injured patients," Alzjar read aloud.

"All good," he complimented his subordinate. "My investors will be relieved. Is there any way to confirm whether she had data from her husband?"

"My Sovereign Trust people are in constant communication with the Manhattan U.S. Attorney's office with respect to the West Mad business. I asked them to so inquire as it would be a logical question. The answer was negative."

"I also understand from our Washington lawyers and political consultants that the White House is organizing meetings to reignite the next stimulus injection," Alzjar continued the good news.

"Why do you think the direction has changed once again?"

"I suspect it is because the West Mad scandal is no longer the flavor of the day," Alzjar responded, relaxing and enjoying a rare glass of champagne before his racing of the day. Weather conditions were almost as predicted for the race only two days away. On the last practice day, he would be competing against many of the best drivers in the world.

"Is there any further need for the children?"

"No, dispose of them."

"In the usual manner?" Blair asked. This would be to take living, sedated bodies to sea and drop them in areas of significant shark activity, usually around drilling platforms.

"Whatever. Just get it done. Now, tell me what happened to Mr. Starr. Have you learned anything further since our discussion yesterday?"

"Not really. The family's press release expressed sadness for his rapidly degenerating health, which he decided to address with his own hand rather than await a slow death. 'All who know our father, grandfather, and husband will appreciate his nature of taking control of events,' it said."

"This is all quite strange, I understood him to be in excellent health," the Prince said, sipping slowly. He was vigilant to understand the medical condition of people playing important roles in his empire. Such data was easily recovered by his team of hackers. "I never actually met the man. You made the contacts, though we did invest with him in the CDO mess that created the original American economic crisis," he continued, recalling his admiration for Copper Starr, as well as surprise at how easily the man had been drawn into their plan to destabilize the West.

In growing his personal fortune, Alzjar's ability to slide into roles that suited his purposes served him well. Developing relationships with private wealth, including sovereign resources of royalty and dictators alike, he provided all with stunning returns. Operating outside the reach of securities regulators, he commanded huge resources via his other investors, descended like himself from ancient Lebanese families invisible in the normal world. All external contact and negotiation was conducted through functionaries like Blair. Alzjar never had direct contact outside his own world. With the exception of Blair, his personal staff had been with him for much of his adult life. All were well taken care of financially, harboring not even the concept of disloyalty to their generous benefactor.

Alzjar used the Trust, supervised by the English queen and her Royal Supervisory Board, as a stalking horse for his own activities. He coached Blair in the creation of a series of accounts at Westbury Madison in the name of the Trust to conduct the attack on the Western financial system.

As Trevor Moran began asking questions once he was Treasury secretary and privy to confidential government information, including anxieties about the role that Copper Starr had taken upon leaving the Treasury post, Alzjar directed Blair to eliminate Moran. The West Mad scandal was not intended. It just occurred from media speculation following the mysterious disappearance of Moran's children and then his wife.

Finishing his libation, Alzjar stood and offered his hand to Sir Gordon. "Again, good work. Please attend to these other details. My mind is now clear for the race. Contact me in the normal manner if anything critical arises. Otherwise, please leave me in the world of Henré Tremont."

I wonder what Chief Bearstrike is like? Blair wondered as he departed through the security checkpoints. *I am glad I did not mention his call or our meeting. Alzjar accepts all of these events too easily; he's probably focused on the race. The children can also wait.* Blair got into his car to leave for the quick trip to Paris on an awaiting private jet.

Chapter 43

Siena, Italy

"WHAT THE fuck is going on?" Don Luciano Navarro blubbered flopping around unable to get the night visor off his eyes. Like a whale on its belly, he could not see what invaded his privacy.

He stirred as I lifted the lithe young woman cuddled on the opposite side of the huge bed, subduing her with a quick chop to the neck before a sound could be made. I removed her chemise and twisted it into a rope to secure hands at her rear, looped it through her mouth, around her neck, and secured it to the bed post to prevent any movement. All as Nul had taught me.

He mounted the bed. Placing one foot in the small of the bulbous man's back, the whale struggled as if stranded on a beach. I watched from the shadows.

"Leticia, is that you, honey?" he asked, assuming the woman he often hired for the evening was into to her specialty of bondage and whipping. "Turn me over so I can watch."

The shoe moved up the spine with increasing pressure.

"God damn that hurts!"

A strong hand grasped the Don's hair, lifting his head slowly to the point that Nul could feel tendons straining in neck and back muscles.

"Ah-h-h," the wealthy man whined. "Who did you bring in? You're not this strong."

Nul dropped Navarro's head and removed his foot causing the fat man to collapse face down into the pillows. A quick chop to the neck put him out as well, his bare ass still sticking up in the air.

Oh my God! I thought. It was like the reddish depiction of a fat naked man far up on the wall of paintings in Paulo's studio. Navarro was in almost exactly the same position. Paulo's hideous scene felt sexual.

I dreamed about it, somehow connecting to Theo and Chrissy. I could not see what it meant. My subconscious was telling me it would be on my path.

Nul secured the inert hulk to the bed frame then jumped to the floor to help me get the woman into a closet on the other side of the palatial suite.

* * *

WHEN THE explosion occurred at Repubblica, Anloc and I were already in the train station following the abort plan. The Italian subway system, called the Metro, delivered us to the Colosseo station a few kilometers to the south, across the street from the magnificent Roman Coliseum. We strolled to the next level, as practiced the night before, awaiting the train that would take us to Ostia Antica, the preserved fishing village from Roman times. The path of the Tiber River leading to the Mediterranean had shifted and the village was abandoned, the site never built upon, and ruins preserved as a museum. Nul chose it as a place to hide as we prepared. "No one will look for us there. Tourists barely even know the place."

Lanh reached the van at about the same time as Alice. She had dropped the red bag after releasing the fountain of Euros, scooped up by frenzied hands hoping to find still more money. The van with its powerful engine and drive-train slid into the traffic flow on a side street away from Repubblica. Aftermath of the horrific bomb explosion continued in the distance. Lanh and Alice drove to the RV park where we had spent the prior night, hoping to meet our train if all went according to plan.

In Repubblica, chaos reigned. People were trampled in the stampedes caused by assumed gunshots from trash containers all around the circle, sirens, rabid dog barking, a rain of Euros, and, finally, the satchel that exploded with the force of a full load of incendiary bombs. Nul saved hundreds of people with his heroism. He ran all around until he was blown off his feet by the blast. Recovering, he ran to the main Termini station, purchased the clothes of a street man in the men's room, emerging to wait for his own train. He got to Ostia Antica much later. Anloc and I treated his lacerations from shrapnel using the medical kit he had assembled and stowed in the van as a normal operational preparation.

Once we were together, it took several hours to decompress. On the television that Lanh installed in the van, we watched news coverage of the bombing. It was presumed to be a terrorist act. No group claimed responsibility.

Nul worked with the police chief's phone recovered by Lanh. The call history was instructive. There were many calls from about the time he had first contacted Paulo. The numbers of Madano, Paulo, and some third person predominated. It took some time to identify the last, which was unlisted. Nul and Lanh hacked their way into local phone company records and discovered that its bills were sent to a post office address traced to a company that sounded familiar: Brunello Holdings. Nul had taken care of business for the company in Siena periodically. The assignments were usually the same. Arrange for the disappearance of someone who had become a nuisance or a family member of someone needing a change of attitude. The hits were as easy as the compensation was rewarding. It helped finance the vineyard in Radda and work in the Outback. Wire transfers came from an account in the name of the same company, which Navarro owned.

Connection to our adversary seemed to be at hand. Nul had dealt with subordinates in the company. When each assignment was complete, the Don would personally thank him. After the events in Rome, Nul knew that someone with government, police, and Vatican access was guiding the attacks against us. Escalations in Siena confirmed the assessment. He suspected that it could be Navarro. If not, the Don would likely know who it was in the close-knit Italian mobster world. Accordingly, Nul had to take the steps available to draw their adversary into the open to avoid painful missteps.

When Lanh retrieved data stored in the scanner, the connection was confirmed. The source of the signal was the same one that had detonated the satchel bomb.

* * *

"Let me go!" Navarro demanded when he regained consciousness. He struggled against his bindings. Nul had used satin curtain cords to secure the naked man to the antique platform in the bedchamber. The sleeping eyeshade remained in place.

"I don't think so. However, there is a way for you to be freed, Luciano, my old friend," Nul responded.

The ugly head twisted seeking bearings. He recognized the accent. "Is that you, Nulandi?"

"It is."

"I've been thinking of you."

"Really, why is that?"

"I thought it might be you involved in these events in Siena and Rome," he responded, with a mind clearing from alcohol and events of the evening before he collapsed in exhaustion. "Damn few people could kill so many of my experienced soldiers. And not so many black guys know their way around Tuscany and this area to orchestrate the escapes. Besides, the stories of this Aphrodite and the connection to the American West Mad scandal suggests someone with a lot of money to hire the best. That's you."

"You directed the attacks against us didn't you?" Nul asked, amused at how easily the man revealed his involvement. "Including the bomb in Repubblica."

"Why are you treating me this way? How did you get in here? I am your employer," demanded the Don, assuming his usual attitude of command over servants, ignoring the questions. "What happened to Leticia?"

"Full of questions, aren't you?" Nul responded, in no hurry to get to the point. There was all night to get what we had come to obtain.

K-RACK! reverberated around the room insulated to contain the sounds of the man's sexual fantasies. "Ohhh," spilled out of him as the chop neatly broke his upper arm. Bone ends were twisted against each other. "Jesus, Holy God! What are you doing to me?"

WHACK-A-WHACK-A-WHACK! added to the symphony as Nul slapped the captive's cheeks back and forth.

"Don Navarro, let's get this straight. I want information. If you tell me what I want, you will live. If not, I'll get the information in my own way, and you will never see the sun rise again as I administer the ultimate sadomasochistic experience of your wretched life. Do you understand?"

"What have I done to you to deserve this? I've paid you a lot of damn money. How much do you want?"

"How much did you pay the painter to betray me?"

"I didn't know it was you. There was some woman on the run who had to be caught alive. She had information they wanted. I would never betray you of all people. I know all too well what you could do to me or anybody," he answered, feeling blood dripping from his nose and mouth with no ability to relieve the irritation.

"How much?"

"Nothing. He got himself killed at the same time as my men. You did the killing. You've done all the killing. All I knew was that some black person accompanied the woman to be snatched. They didn't care about the slut, just grab her and whatever information she might possess. Paulo told me she was a good lay. I was looking forward to experiencing it for myself before turning the whore over to collect the bounty. It was a lot of money, even for me. You've probably gotten some yourself, right?" he sputtered through broken teeth and blood.

It was the first time I had ever heard someone use such words to describe me. My efforts had obviously helped move us up the ladder. *If it takes more of the same, well, so be it*, I thought. *Even with this pig. Or worse. I have nothing to lose and everything to gain.*

"Who is that woman?" Nul asked. "Who was so important to sacrifice so many of your men?"

Navarro shook his head.

The room was silent. Nul went to the bathroom and returned, whispering instructions in my ear. Why? I wondered.

Nul pulled a chair in front of Navarro. I stepped forward to cover his chest with the shaving cream as Nul had directed.

"What are you doing?" the prisoner shrieked with escalating fear watching the man he knew to be a deadly assassin sharpen a straight razor on a leather strap.

"Let me go. Please," he said to me.

Nul stepped in front of me. "I'm going to start using this blade. You could use a body shave, you hairy pig. I'll start here at your neck, maybe some blood will flow if I'm awkward in my strokes. Oh, shit! Like that," Nul reacted almost in jest, wiping sticky warm blood across the man's face and under his nose to make sure that, even in soft light, he would have a clear picture of what could lay ahead.

"Please! Don't do any more. What do you want?" he said when the pain subsided.

"Answer my questions. If you don't, I will shave downward until you are a girl. You might even get to eat soft sausage as an early morning snack. Got it?"

The captive nodded.

"Who is the woman you were so anxious to find?"

"I don't know her name exactly. She had apparently escaped from Rome. People were looking for her, like I said. I think it's her," he answered nodding toward me.

"What people? You said 'we didn't care about the slut' a moment ago."

"I can't tell you anything, Nulandi. I can't. You know that."

"*Ow-w-w-w!*" the prisoner screeched, as Nul pulled his left nipple as far as it would stretch, then cut it off cleanly with a healthy slice of blubber.

"Here, taste yourself, Don," Nul said, stuffing the flesh dangling in his hand into the man's mouth. "There is more to come if you don't talk."

The bloody, yellowish flesh was spat upon Nul with the contents of the retching man's stomach. "I cannot betray my contact for any price, you know that."

"Wanna be a girl, eat that piece of salami?" Nul asked, pulling the member in a similar manner, razor ready.

"What about Leticia?" the bleeding man babbled, hoping to change the subject.

"She's in a closet taking a nap."

"Will she awaken?"

"Maybe. Your fingerprints are all over the knife I took from your dressing room, which I will use to cut her throat if I need to."

"Good God!" the Don grimaced, as images of his beautiful plaything slashed to drown in her own blood careened in his mind. "Is that *her* by you?"

He looked me over. The pain in his arm, chest, and face burned to the point that he struggled to focus.

"Yes, it's me, sir—the slut. Kind of hard for you to have your way with me just now," I answered, enjoying the look on his face. "My name is Jaspar Moran."

Suddenly, the events of the day in Repubblica, which had been forgotten during his previous frolic and more recent pain, came to mind. "Wait! You're supposed to be dead. I was told that everyone in that square was dead, which would have included you," he responded in a machine gun-like spew of words. Fright seeped into his soul with the pain. "How could you escape? The police chief and all of his men were consumed, nothing to even bury. And all those other people. Are you ghosts?"

"We are very much alive. It is you who may shortly be a ghost, you asshole," I responded, wanting to use the razor myself. I now understood the ruthlessness of those who held my babies. "You used that bomb to kill everyone, even your own people?"

"It had to be done. I did not push the button."

"Who directed you?" Nul asked. "Who is your contact?"

The Don's eyes closed. *I've said too much already. It's hopeless. If he doesn't kill me, they will.* An image of himself heaped on top of the girl in a spreading pool of blood and entrails played in his mind.

"Just kill me."

"I'd love to, you pig, in a manner so that you suffer pain beyond anything you can imagine," Nul answered. "My favorite way of torture is to skin the target over a period of several hours. I cut an inch or so of skin at a time, maybe splash some cognac on the raw meat. I might even flambé it just for some variation. Sometimes, I even find some hungry fire ants to put in the wounds. How does that sound? Do you want to talk—or do you want to die that way?"

The fat, bleeding man gritted his teeth, determined to be silent.

"While you were unconscious, I searched your space for a computer or smart phone. I found both. I'll bet the memories of those devices will reveal what I want, which is the way we confirmed your involvement. We traced the call to trigger the blast in Repubblica."

The Don looked up, understanding that his secrets could all be revealed, even if he did not speak.

"Do you have my children?" I asked.

"No, *I* don't."

"Are they alive?"

"Yes."

"Where?"

"I do not know."

"You goddam sack of shit, you tell me," I screamed, grabbing his face in both hands and pressing fingers into his eyes.

"*AH-H-H-H!*" he wailed at the new pain.

Nul twisted the chair around. "Answer the question or we begin. Here's the first inch," he said, pushing me aside as the razor made quick slices over his heart. Pinching the skin, drenched in blood, the slice was placed on the man's bound knee for observation. I watched as if seeing tenderloin trimmed for roasting. I had adjusted to the world in which I existed.

"Where are my children? Tell me now or start bleeding to death, you scumbag," I said as Nul departed. He returned in seconds with a bottle of expensive Remy Martin cognac. He poured it into the wound.

Screaming stopped as the bleeding man passed out.

WHACK, WHACK! The blows brought Navarro back to consciousness.

Nul gave him a glass of water as I used a wet towel to clean him up a bit.

The Don looked straight ahead, bracing himself for the worst death he could imagine. *Say no more!*

"I want the information about who you are working with and where this woman's children are. If you want me to proceed, so be it."

"Then, you'll never find out. Maybe you can learn something from my computer or phone. It will not come from my mouth. I am a man of honor," he answered with pride willing the pain into the back of his mind.

We walked into the next room. "He will not say much more,"

Nul advised. There was no danger that the Don could escape. "I can kill him or let him die, but that will get us no further. I'm sure that I can learn more from the devices we have taken, but maybe not enough. He will also have a safe here someplace. What do you think?"

"Can we make a deal of some kind with him?" I asked.

"Maybe, but he has a code that cannot be breached."

When we entered the bedroom again, Navarro was slumped in the chair blood oozing from his many wounds.

"Don," Nul spoke sharply, pulling the man's head up with a clenched fist. "Wake up." He came around with another douse of water and a cold toweling.

"I will ask you one more question. If you answer or confirm it, then we will let you live."

"What?"

"Was your contact a man named Gordon Blair?" Nul asked, having communicated with Bearstrike.

Navarro's eyes glassed over as if he were drowning in slime. "I cannot betray my colleague. I am bound by omertà, my code of silence, as you know Nulandi," he began, stopping after every few words to drink from the glass Nul had gotten for him and then to cough into a wash cloth I had provided from the ornate bathroom.

"You asked about my contacts. There was only one. My original role was to arrange the kidnapping of the children through friends in New York."

Nul restrained me as I reached for the knife. Navarro looked at me with almost blank eyes, as if he did not care if I carried out my rage.

"Then you showed up in Italy," he continued after a drink and some coughing. "My work began again. I see why you were always successful in your missions for me. Your man is the best," he said in halting words nodding toward me. "You are also the famous Aphrodite," he added. Even in his condition, the leer was obvious. "You know that I cannot break my oath."

Nul nodded. "OK then, I want access to all your files. Second, you will tell whomever you deal with, Blair or otherwise, what happened here. If anything happens to those children, I will personally hunt you down and everyone related to you or working with you. If it takes the rest of my life, I will find you. I will devise the most painful manner possible of torturing you to death. Then I'll feed your dumb ass to animals, so that you actually become shit. There will be no moment when you can feel safe for the rest of your life. You will always be looking for me. So will every member of your blood family. Why? Because you know I will do what I say. And I will do the same to those you refuse to identify, them and their families. Every last one of them. I will enjoy making new piles of crap. Do you understand that?"

I held Nul's arms, fearful that he would begin beating the helpless man in his rage. Acknowledgement of Navarro's role in the kidnapping seemed to stoke the fire. The assassin's skin felt like embers ready to burst into flame.

The Don held his hands up, pointing to his throat then coughing and spitting phlegm and blood on the carpet. "*AKH-AG-KUFF-KUFF-KAFOO!*" he choked, apparently trying to speak. The knife Nul had used on him lay in his lap where it had been dropped while Nul stuffed blubber into his mouth. Navarro pointed to the knife and crossed his hands.

After a few breaths, he seemed to regain his composure.

"Nulandi, I honor you. We worked together many times. I even helped you gain confidence of the old man and his family to get the vineyard. Signora, I do not know you at all. I arranged the kidnapping of your children. For that, I humbly apologize. I simply delivered them to the man you mentioned. I wish there was something I could do to get them back for you," he said with simple candor in his eyes.

I did not know how to react. My anger dissipated. I felt somehow like a priest hearing a confession of a sinner.

He took my hand. "I want to do one thing right before I meet

St. Peter," he added, his eyes turning almost kind. Nul looked stunned.

"My safe is over there," Navarro said pointing to an antique bureau. "My records are messy. But you will see tracks to the man in London you mentioned. I have read all the stories speculating about *Aphrodite* and her dead husband. I know nothing beyond what is in my files. There is a button to open the safe on the underside of the top inside the first drawer," he said.

Even with his strength, Nul strained to lift Navarro's body off the chair once the safe was exposed. Navarro stopped him.

"The girl? Is she alive?"

"Yes. We put her in the closet. She should be fine," I answered.

"Before we do anything further, please escort her away from here. I do not want her to see me."

Nul did as requested. I stayed with Navarro. He consumed several glasses of water. I sensed he was composing himself.

"Sorry that I called you those names," he finally said.

"I understand. Nul and I are sorry that we had to do what we did to you. We must . . ."

"No, you do not have to say it. You will do anything to recover your children, as you should. I would do the same if I had children," the Don responded. "Your name is Jaspar, right?"

"Yes."

"Jaspar, I have done everything I can to help you find your children. The details are in the materials in that safe," he said, never letting loose of my hand.

"Will you grant a dying man a request?"

"If I can."

"Are you Catholic?"

"Yes."

"When the safe is open, will you say last rites for me and pray for my eternal soul?" The tough Mafioso had been beaten, lacerated, and humiliated. Tears formed in his eyes. "I should go to the last level of Dante's hell and roast there for eternity. But there is always opportunity for redemption and new birth. This is my only chance."

"I . . . I . . . never . . ." *He is seeking atonement. From me?*

"Yes, I will do that."

"Will you then bless me again by cutting my throat with this knife? I would do it, but I don't think I can," he pleaded, holding out his broken and maimed arms.

"Kill you with my own hands?"

"Yes, which Nulandi would have done in any event. He cannot allow me to live. I understand and respect that."

"I will do it," Nul said stepping into the room. "The girl is on her way home with plenty of money."

"No, not you. The gentle hand of this angel may be some verification of a sliver of goodness in me."

I grasped his hand in my own. "It will be my honor to assist your redemption. It is my duty as a believer."

Nul lifted Navarro and set the chair in front of the bureau, which hid the safe built into the wall.

When the dials were revealed, Nul tipped the chair so Navarro could twist the tumblers. The blood soaked man leaned forward. His fingers trembled, twisting the dials again and again, trying to get the sequence in the right order. Finally, he succeeded. I wrote it down.

The safe held bundles of papers. Navarro pointed to several as Nul lifted them out making some order on the floor. When they were done, the Don turned to me and held out the knife. Nul pulled the chair back into the bedroom. We laid Navarro out on the bed.

I found his rosaries. They were worn from long use.

"They were my mother's and grandmother's," he said. I folded bloody hands on his chest, intertwining the rosaries.

After a lifetime of attending mass and funerals, sitting with friends and relatives in terminal condition, and supporting services of all kinds, my mind was blank. Too much carnage had collapsed on the life that had existed for me. It was as if I felt nothing. No emotion, no forgiveness, no ability to give.

The wounded man looked up at me with the eyes of a penitent clutching my fingers with desperation.

"Luciano Navarro, in the name of the Father, the Son and the Holy Ghost, I anoint you on your way to meet our maker," I began with words that came from a source beyond me. "Do you offer penance for your sins and ask forgiveness of your Father?"

He raised my hands to his bloody lips, trying to nod in affirmation.

"Luciano, my son, I commend your eternal soul into the hands of our Lord and Savior Jesus Christ with the provisions He commended to us." I gave him the tip of my finger. "This is my body,' Jesus said. 'And this is my blood,'" I spoke, lifting a glass of wine that Nul had provided as I spoke. As he swallowed, I kissed the healing man on the forehead and closed his eyes

"Our Father, who art in Heaven . . ."

Chapter 44

Louvre Gardens, Paris
Next day

CHIEF WESTBROOK BEARSTRIKE returned salutes of the U.S. Marine Corps guards at the entranceway to the U.S. Embassy. Located on Avenue Gabriel close to Place de la Concorde, it was an easy walk to the meeting point designated by Gordon Blair. Jason Brontus watched the intrepid investor of the plains stroll with the confidence of a Parisian on his way to a known destination. *I should be with him.*

* * *

UPON ARRIVAL the evening before, the Ambassador personally greeted the Chief. A formal dinner had been planned to honor a guest of President Henrichs. With respectful tact, Brontus suggested that Chief would prefer a local restaurant. At Chez André, the Ambassador's favorite, they enjoyed roasted chicken and fresh vegetables accented by a lovely house Sancerre. Dessert was the chef's famous profiteroles, puff pastry filled with ice cream drenched in dark chocolate sauce. "I must learn to make this," Chief declared digging into a second helping.

Walking the ten blocks or so back to the Embassy, the Ambassador offered security of both U.S. and French secret services continuously blanketing the area. Chief reiterated his insistence to proceed alone. "Besides, I have a tomahawk in my pocket."

* * *

AT 4:30 A.M., there was little traffic. Chief admired the obelisk in the Place de la Concorde adjoining the Embassy grounds, smiled at the Eiffel Tower across the Seine River, and then entered the gates to the Fer á Chavel at the western end of the Louvre Gardens. The sandy path felt like home in the crisp morning air. Rounding the Bassin Octogonal, trees along each side of the Allée Centrale were peaceful. *Blair will be waiting at the gate on the park side of Rue de Rivoli and Allée de Castiglione. It is just ahead. I will be able to see the monument at the Place Vendôme by the Ritz Hotel,* Chief repeated instructions left with the Embassy call desk. The call had been made from a public phone with no name, just "a friend."

Lights from nearby streets and the surrounding park provided just enough illumination to follow the simple tourist map.

How can I find common ground with a stranger from a completely different culture who is guilty of a long list of crimes?

"Chief?" He had not heard a sound or seen a soul walking through the trees.

"Yes?"

Blair asked that no names be used. "Please stand still and do not turn to look at me," the voice said. Bearstrike could feel a scanner traverse him from head to toe.

"I am going to reach around you for a moment," the voice added. The touch shifted to his front side.

"Thank you for being clean. May we go to a different part of town to talk," the voice said, taking his arm to follow Allée de Castiglione and climb up the steps to Rue di Rivoli. A speeding taxi was hailed. It stopped where it would not have been possible during normal traffic conditions. An address was spoken. The taxi sped back around the Place de la Concorde and through the Tracedro with the Eiffel Tower close by. It stopped under a street light. Avenue de Tourville, Bearstrike read having no idea where they actually were. It did not seem so far.

They walked through narrow streets, seemingly in a circle, finally setting on a bench close to a building called Faubourg Saint Germain.

"It is a military facility," the voice said. "I am confident there is no possibility of surveillance here. I already confirmed you have no devices, and my scanner shows none."

"Are you Blair?"

"Yes. You are brave to meet me under these circumstances."

"As are you."

"I want to keep this short and to the point. I know all about the suicide of Copper Starr and death of Luciano Navarro. I was their contact. Whoever on your side connected them is resourceful. You obviously are as well. How did you know to ask for me in your initial call to the Fund?"

"Let's get to the point," Bearstrike answered, not wanting to explain that the name came from Starr's errant e-mail. "I am here to reach an accord and assume you are as well. I have authority to commit the American president."

Blair raised a finger. "My question? Please answer it."

"Let's just say that I discerned the connection from materials I have reviewed."

"What materials?"

"Sir, you asked for this meeting, not me. Let's see if we have common ground."

"This must all be related to West Mad. Correct?"

"Same answer. I called you initially, and then you asked to meet. Let's do my questions, then I will answer yours."

"Fair enough."

"Who directs you? It must be an astute and wealthy person or group to have combined a team of at least Starr, Navarro, Trevor Moran, and yourself with a stupendous amount of money. Your group has undertaken market manipulations that I have traced. Amazingly, that endeavor is not recognized by the governments of the world."

"What did you know to trace?"

"I believed the U.S. and European governments would seek to reverse the global slide into the economic abyss by generating economic growth via massive capital market injections. I placed bets in the rhythm of expansion and contractions, then doubling down for the next stimulus to repeat the process. It began more than two years ago," Bearstrike responded. "I recognized soon enough that a whale of an investor was doing the same. I traced it to the Sovereign Trust. In time, I concluded it was obviously a front for the real parties, though its utilization was clever indeed. I assume that whoever this person or group is, they also had Trevor Moran murdered and his children kidnapped to enforce the silence of his wife. Members of your team as noted were as unlikely as they were interesting. Can you confirm my perception?"

"Let us strike our deal. Then I will address your questions as you do mine."

"What are your terms?"

"When this manipulation, as you call it, is wrapped up, I want a new identity as an Australian living in the Great Barrier Reef on Lizard Island. For public consumption, Sir Gordon Blair died seeking justice," Blair began. "In return, I will provide complete explanation and proof of what has happened and who has been involved."

"And?" Bearstrike asked when silence stretched into minutes.

"I will indicate the location of the children in general terms. They will be delivered in excellent health once my second condition is satisfied, which will seem strange," Blair responded in a voice barely audible even in the quiet setting.

"I am listening."

"You must deliver to me the severed head of the man I work for. I must be assured he is dead," Blair whispered.

"His head? Literally separated from his body?" Bearstrike asked, slowly repeating the condition.

"Yes. Shall I explain?"

"Please."

"The man I work for is invisible to the world. I know him by the name of Prince Anwatol Alzjar. I have never seen a passport. We often meet in exotic places, usually on yachts or in villas. I have often tried to confirm his identity, but there is nothing. Even with the extensive resources of MI5 and British, NATO, and U.S. intelligence files, I could find nothing. His fingerprints have no match," Blair explained, raising his head and looking into Chief's eyes for confirmation.

"I have records of all transactional patterns but nothing of the identity of this man. When we meet, there are security devices and people always in attendance. On the phone, his voice is electronically scrambled through a security screen of some kind. I have never been alone with him."

"What is the object of your work with him? A colleague refers to it as a *dust scenario*."

"That is apt actually. The Prince's hope, and surely that of whoever is behind him providing the vast resources required for this project, is to use the greed of our capitalist culture to destroy it. He has been shrewd pushing markets up or down then parlaying the process when markets reverse, as they inevitably do. The stimulus from your president and Congress magnified the results. To use your friend's term, Alzjer wanted to use the profits to return Western culture to dust. I suppose as in dust-to-dust as written in the Bible."

"What is your role?"

"I run the entire operation. I am the only one in contact with the Prince. I was the contact for Mr. Starr and Don Navarro. I recruited them for specific purposes. Each of them thought the project an element of the Sovereign Trust.

"When Alzjar conceived his planned attack, he needed a team of sophisticated people. In the case of Starr, he could operate at the highest levels of the American and European governments, initially as secretary of the Treasury and then as chairman of EmBank. Starr provided the connection to Trevor Moran.

"During his time in government, Starr observed the pig fest underway in the Western world. 'Our policies are creating a bubble in American home values,' Starr said he counseled the president and Congress in private. 'It cannot inflate forever. When it bursts, there will be a financial disaster of Biblical proportion.'

"The response was that 'these policies are popular. In my administration, our job is to sustain the happy times.' As he contemplated leaving office, Starr was angry about the rejection of his theories, which he believed to be responsible for deteriorating economic conditions."

Chief smiled. *As I thought.*

"The prince knew of his theory and believed it to be correct. He also thought Starr would be flattered to pursue it for the benefit of himself and Her Majesty. Trevor Moran implemented the strategy at his firm. He thought it legitimate until he became secretary of the Treasury and began asking questions."

"You had him killed."

"Not me personally, but he had to be silenced. Even Starr seemed to wonder about some things," Blair answered as they sat undisturbed in the quiet early morning. First rays of sunshine were emerging through openings in the buildings. "But Starr was completely unaware of the actual strategy. He made a fabulous fortune, facilitating growth of his bank."

"What about Navarro?" Bearstrike asked, recording every word in his mind.

Blair smiled. "I have learned in this process that everyone has an aspiration of his own, a fantasy or an insecurity. The Don was descended from families that had financed the German Reich's of the nineteenth and twentieth centuries. Living in Tuscany, he prospered as a senior Mafioso. He could raise huge investible funds from old European families. He also wanted to become legitimate and respected. He had in mind a Japanese Yakuza company, Blessed Moon, which became a global electronics dynamo, named BM Electronics, which rose from similar organized crime origins. He never asked any questions. Finally, in our successful effort to get rid of Mrs. Moran, Navarro even got the Italian police and military into action."

"And you, why did you do this? You obviously understood what was going on."

"I spent my life in public service. When my MI5 career came to an end, my wife died of cancer almost immediately. We had no children. I was devastated. The queen offered the Trust manager post because of my long career in British intelligence, praising my uniquely unblemished record. I was flattered. It seemed perfect. A new post requiring my full time and attention, no time for sadness or despair. Working for the Crown directly, I soon became an element of English society. I quickly spent everything I had and took on lots of debt. The Trust's investments soured. Its advisors were supposedly the cream of British bankers. They were obviously lost in the turmoil of the markets. The prince came along offering an investment strategy, suggesting that I could have a 10 percent override. I was a pig, blinded by my social life and need for money. I became a star, salvaging the fund. In the course of it, I learned that the prince had bet against the Trust's strategy causing it to fail."

"That strategy reflected conventional wisdom, lemmings following each other over the proverbial cliff," Chief agreed. "I bet against it as well, which is when I concluded that someone was throwing fortunes into the process on the same side as me. It does not happen often that my tribe is the minnow in the wake of a whale. Are there participants other than Starr, Navarro, yourself, and this prince?"

"Not that I am aware of, though, as I said, I suspect that the prince is the front for enormous financial strength."

"Where are the Moran children?"

"They are safe. That is enough information for now."

"Let's go back to your demand for the head as the ransom. You mean the head of this prince?"

"Yes."

"How is that possible if he is always protected?" Chief asked "To harvest his head, he would have to be alone. We cannot land an army to fight through a phalanx of guards. In the Don's case, girls were his weakness. Then he was alone. My man followed that trail. Does the prince have any time when he is alone, like working out or running?"

"As I said, this man is almost never alone, probably even when he sleeps and defecates," Blair answered, pausing in thought. "It occurs only in his race cars. He loves to participate in Formula 1, the pinnacle of global auto racing. His main interest just now is the Monte Carlo Grand Prix. It will occur three days from now. Nothing else occupies his mind, even the sharp drop in his investments, which I believe is due to continuing delay of the American stimulus. I also believe that someone has figured out our strategy and is betting against us. With the delay in the stimulus, that bet is rising as ours falls."

"Who could be so prescient?" Chief asked.

"I suspect it is you. Whoever you work with on the ground makes a formidable team, both in the markets and on the street. You have outsmarted the prince on the investment side, and Navarro and his mafia on the ground. To my knowledge, that has never happened before," Blair responded, mind engaged. "Too bad about the Moran woman in the Repubblica disaster.

"With respect to someone who is protected constantly, your team is obviously skilled at that as well. As you say, Navarro was under constant protection. In the case of the prince, you will find a way if that is what has to be done."

"OK, back to racing. How does your prince participate at such a level? Does he have a team?"

"Yes, his own. He is the driver."

"Come on," Chief jeered. "Nobody just competes in such a race. I don't follow racing at all, but even I know that it is the premier event."

"It is true. You also don't know the prince. He could be anyplace and nobody would know the reality. As I have said, he is invisible. An official nobody. He has raced for many years under a pseudonym. He expects to win this year. In fact, he is so serious that he has a complete mock-up of the Monte Carlo Grand Prix race course where he is practicing as we speak."

Chief was silent trying to comprehend what Blair was communicating. It was all too incredible.

"The price for the children is his head. If I am not certain that he is dead, the children will never be seen again," Blair added, speaking slowly and carefully. "I will advise who he is in that context as part of our agreement."

Nulandi will have his hands full on this one, Chief thought. One invisible man after another. "What is the man's taste in women?"

"Why do you ask that?"

"Just curious. Could he be seduced by a mature beauty?"

"I have no idea about that. He could prefer boys for all I know.

The problem would be getting access. As I said, he is almost never in public, and when he is, there is security all around—even with his pit crew during races. Someone procures his women, but it is not me. There is always at least one around. You asked about a mature woman. The only common denominator I see in the women procured for him, as opposed to the stars he sees in public, is mixed race. He must like exotic combinations of race and ethnicity."

"Who gave the order for that bomb in Rome?"

"I did."

"Why?"

"My instruction was to clean the slate. Don and I assumed Mrs. Moran would be present due to a deal he had struck for her. I could take no chance that she and the black people always with her would slip away again," Blair explained. "In Repubblica, I wanted it put to an end, regardless of human cost. Such a bombing could always be blamed on terrorists of some stripe with a grudge against Italy."

"Who did it?"

"I suppose the prince's people, I do not know. I just pushed the button when the exchange seemed to fail for whatever reasons it did."

"Why did you finally return my call?"

"To be honest, the deaths of Starr and Navarro made me realize the magnitude of what I had done. I must also say that I have sympathy for the children and do not want to kill them. I have been blinded by my own ambition, like the others.

"I also knew that Alzjar would likely have me killed as he did Don Navarro. He must be stopped. Somewhere in me, I have Christian blood. It is thoroughly tainted just now, but perhaps I can be forgiven and make something of the remainder of my life."

Amazing, Bearstrike thought, just as Navarro finally gave up with Nulandi.

They rose and walked under the Eiffel Tower and along the

river as the sun rose above Notre Dame in the distance. They talked about Paris in the late springtime while they walked all the way back to where they had met in the Louvre Gardens.

"My question," Blair finally said, "is as to the records that led to all of these conclusions?"

"Does it really matter at this point?"

"Not really, I just want to know."

"Moran copied his records and notes, with an explanation that only his wife understood."

"Did she explain them before her death?"

"Yes."

Alzjar's instincts have been right all along.

"Do we have a deal?" Blair asked.

"Yes, we get you the head, you provide the children and records, and then we give you a new identity when you have guided us through those files."

"And my mother who lives with me?"

"Agreed," Chief responded with an outstretched hand, grasped by Blair.

"The name under which Alzjar races is Henré Tremont. He will be in car red #1 on the pole for the race. Once I have the head, I will advise where you may recover the children who will be with my mother," Blair responded. "Use this number to reach me." He handed Chief a slip of paper. "If I learn that you have failed, I will throw them off a cliff and disappear forever."

"May I use this number for another purpose?"

"What is that?

"Before we can proceed, we must hear the children's voices and ask some questions," Chief responded.

Blair's eyebrows shot up as his eyes widened and mouth dropped. "Who would know their voices? Both parents are dead and there are no surviving relatives. I checked that long ago."

Bearstrike was impassive. "A friend from Connecticut will be on the line with me."

"What is the name?"

"The neighbor and friend of the Moran's, Crystal Jamison."

"I will be traveling, so please contact the Sovereign Fund and leave a message that you are a Thomson Reuters reporter with a question for Mr. Blair and a number for a temporary phone that cannot be traced."

Blair disappeared into the early morning crowds as Bearstrike walked down Rue di Rivoli to the Embassy.

This may stump even Nulandi.

Chapter **45**

Adriatic Sea off the coast of Italy

"How MANY people died yesterday, Nul?" I asked, as our boat rocked in gentle swells of the Adriatic Sea. We were many miles offshore with a group of Vietnamese fishing boats. It was just after sunrise I guessed from the light around the porthole.

"Dozens," he said softly, holding me as he had throughout the night. When we returned to Ostia Antica from Navarro's palace, we boarded a small trawler owned by an extended family member. We joined a commercial flotilla that was to return to port after several days, depending on success of the catch. Alice remained on deck from the time of disengaged mooring lines, loving the smell of the sea and the excitement on board. She could relax. Her masters were safe in their cabin.

Nul smoothed my hair. My emotions were stunned with remorse and pity for the dead and their families.

Innocent people blown up in an effort to kill me.

The grim reality of getting information from Navarro added to the overload. I had never experienced serious pain, much less participated in torturing another human being. His ultimate embrace of Christianity was something I would have to contemplate on another day.

"My children are alive, Nul," I reassured myself after each round of anxiety and tears. Soft caresses of the boat gliding over ocean swells were soothing as strong arms provided a safe place. "We are on our way," he responded. "In a little while, I will contact Chief. Tell him what we learned and see how he did with this Mr. Blair. They should have met by now."

"You will talk to him with your drum beats?" I teased, brightening with memory of the verbalization of their chant that somehow provided a means of communication.

"Mm-hm."

"Nul," I said, kissing him softly on the cheek, "thank you. Thank you for all that you have done for me and my children. I have no way to repay you, whether we succeed or not."

"I'm paid beyond comprehension, Jas. This is my battle as it is yours. We share some demons, and each have our own as well. *I* thank you."

* * *

"THERE IS no answer," Nul responded switching off the radio-transmitter in the Captain's cabin. The seaman was busy on the bridge. Nul tried to reach the Chief several times without response. As my fears rose, Nul squeezed my hand in reassurance.

Fishing activity was underway on deck. While we awaited connection, Nul checked satellite sources for information about Repubblica. Police and counter-terrorism investigations were under way. Immediately following the explosion, a group calling itself the Eritrean Liberation Front claimed responsibility. There was no recent record of any such group. It was active at the time of the Ethiopian wars in the 1970s and early 1980s, but silent in the interim. Italy had no known political problems relating to its former colony. Investigation of the claim was said to be ongoing. "The death toll is approaching one hundred," she continued.

"My God, Nul, it's much worse than we thought."

News broadcasts featured a photo of a fireball rising in the sky taken from a helicopter passenger heading across the city. Airspace over Rome was immediately closed, so there were no further overhead photos, though fuzzy shots from cell phones circulated on the Internet. There was footage of military units from security cameras on rooftops that had survived the explosion and resultant fires. Police interviewed survivors at the scene seeking information to begin tracking the terrorists. Enormous frustration was expressed by all officials and families of the dead and missing.

The computer screen showed crowds congregating at area hospitals seeking information about missing friends or relatives. The only information made public was that a stout black woman had been able to move most of the crowd to safety. "The description is generally similar to that of a woman involved in the gunfight on the Tiber bridge following the riot in the Vatican a few days ago and then the famous Aphrodite shootout in Siena," the anchor reported as scenes of the earlier events scrolled across the screen. I smiled at the picture of myself as the nude Aphrodite that seemed to be everywhere.

I hope to never live this down.

"The woman identified as Aphrodite, Mrs. Jaspar Moran, died in the explosion according to the U.S. Embassy," the announcer commented, as a picture of me then Trevor as Treasury secretary scrolled across the screen. I held onto Nul's arm. He had advised of Chief's request that the president make this public declaration, as well as take other steps that would implement the plan they had developed.

CHIRP—CHIRP! the incoming signal sounded as my guilt for the poor souls punished in an effort to get me collided with anxiety for my children's plight. Nul opened the receiver so I could hear. While I did not understand a word on either end, the emotions were apparent. Nul first smiled, giving me a thumb-up forming the words "Theo and Chrissy" as he concentrated. My heart jumped.

Please, God.

Question and response went back and forth like a tennis match. Nul's eyebrows formed a perplexing knit as tense discussion developed.

What?

"Nul?" I asked as he switched off the set.

"Chief was successful in meeting Mr. Blair in Paris. The children are safe and will be exchanged. That is the . . ."

I leaped upon the man. "My babies! I will get them? Really?"

He hugged me for long moments.

"Jaspar, hold on before you get too excited."

"Why are you so cautious?"

"There is a price for them, a steep and difficult price."

"Pay it!"

"I wish it were that easy. Let me explain," he said, setting me back on the uncomfortable bench.

"Tell me."

When he was done, we stared at each other for long moments. "Cut off some prince's head? Really? During the Monte Carlo Grand Prix with packed stands and a global TV audience, not to mention media crews of all sorts. Everyone has phones that take pictures or movies. It's not possible."

"Sure it is. We just need a plan. Can you picture the race course?"

"I've never been to the race, but Trevor and I walked the course once. I think it goes around the harbor, up into the hills where the museums and government offices are, then back down through sharp turns in the streets, looping around the Casino area and down the hill by the yacht basin to start all over again."

"Good memory. We have this one chance. Chief is confident that Blair will follow through, but only if he is certain that this prince is dead."

"Is this prince the pinnacle of the ladder we have been climbing?" I asked.

"So Chief reports."

"Who is this prince?"

"His name is Anwatol Alzjar. Chief believes it is probably a name used by someone orchestrating all of this on behalf of obviously rich and powerful people. Chief advises to proceed believing this to be the real thing."

"And you trust the Chief to risk our and my children's lives in such a strange undertaking?"

Nul sat beside me on the bench, leaning forward and taking my hand. "Jas you have proven to be a warrior. We have come a long way. We are now at the last rung of the ladder, where we must assume your children await. Do you want them?"

"At any cost."

"Then we must devise and implement our plan, as we have at each step," he responded, eyes riveted on me. He grasped the fingers of my right hand that were twisting imaginary bangles on the other wrist, as I normally did in time of stress or thought.

"Miss them?"

"Not really, just a nervous habit."

"You'll have them back soon enough, like the children," he added with a facial expression that seemed to be far away.

Rolling of the boat in the swells of the ocean had not bothered me. As we spoke and reality of our situation sank in, I felt nauseous. I held his hand with both of my own.

"As luck would have it, driving Formula 1 cars has been a hobby of mine for a long time."

"I remember that from the Outback. You were gone for days at a time. Ismerelda said you were off to the races," I recalled, feeling a little more confident. "And you said just yesterday that a race was in our future. You were prophetic."

"I am not so concerned about the race driving, but have no idea how to get access to a team that will compete. The race is two days from now. Chief says arrangements are being made by your president who is working with us."

My mind went blank. *Amazing*, I thought. I did not even have time to think when Nul mentioned it the first time, almost in passing.

We have come so far. Even President Henrichs is on our side. Maybe we will make it. These remaining steps are daunting, but no worse than where we have come from. No reason to be intimidated now.

"Oh," Nul interrupted himself, sensing confusion. "I forgot to mention that Chief was in Washington meeting with the president. I do not know the details, and frankly don't need to, but Chief says the president is proceeding in the manner we suggested."

"And you learned all of this through those chants?" I asked, a smile crossing my face. In that moment, I remembered reading about the Indian language used by the code talkers during World War II for secrecy of communication. German and Japanese experts could not decipher the Native American languages.

"Yes, and more. In any event, contacts are being made through American racing groups with relationships to Formula 1 teams. Arrangements will somehow be made for me to be in the race if that is what needs to happen."

"How can such a thing be arranged in such a short time?"

"I have no idea. It is the task of the president and his people now."

He seems calm, I thought watching the man I had become dependent upon. I could not take my eyes off of him, comforted in his radiating confidence. It was like Trevor in college and on Wall Street. My emotional connection felt consistent. "If you are in the race, how will you get the man alone to cut his head off?"

Nul did not answer for the longest time.

What's wrong? Did he learn something else on that call he is not telling me?

"The only way would be for me as a racer to somehow force

the man's car into the water where he would be immobile for a short period. As I recall, there are no stands along the downhill course that goes under the hotel and along the yacht basin," he finally said, mind engaged. "But I will need your help, Jas. I cannot do it all by myself. Alice will be no help in this context and I could not trust anybody beyond us, especially in such desperate conditions. We will have to make up a plan and then execute it."

I nodded trying to grasp the image forming in his agile mind. "I will do anything, just tell me what I need to do or be."

"You are a strong swimmer, I recall from watching you in the river in Alice Springs, and again in the river outside Siena."

"I competed at Notre Dame and have taught at the Greenwich Y forever. Trevor and I did that together. Why? What are you thinking?"

"If the plan becomes what I suggested, then you will have to be in the water at the precise place we select."

"You're serious aren't you?" I mumbled. "In the water, awaiting a race car plunging near me, diving to slice off the driver's head then get to the surface with it?"

"Piece of cake, right?" he responded, holding out his hand.

I slapped it with a smile. "Sure, no worse than other things we have done so far. To be honest, cutting this bastard's throat will be a piece of cake compared to doing it to my kangaroo friends. That seems like years ago now."

Our hands rested together.

"What's next?" I asked.

"We will be contacted on this phone by a navy dispatcher. American destroyers are apparently in the vicinity. A helicopter will pick us up," he answered. As he spoke, Nul's gaze seemed to be on the world outside the porthole. After a few long minutes, he released my hands. His eyes seemed to glass over as if he were about to cry. I wanted to take him in my arms.

What is he not telling me?

"Where will the helicopter take us?"

His visage seemed to clear as if some depressing thought had come into focus then departed just as fast. "Somewhere close to Monte Carlo," he answered looking at his watch.

"Chief also said he had arranged for you to speak to your children. Are you ready?" he asked putting both feet on the floor. "He will call back one hour from about now. We will have to make arrangements because Blair understood you to be dead."

Oh my God! My heart gasped as I tried to compose myself. *What will I say? How do I confirm that it is them?*

Anxiety about Nul's momentary distance and emotion was displaced with eager anticipation.

Nul left "to check on something," he said. I was so focused on hearing the voices of Theo and Chrissy that I gave his absence not a second thought.

*   *   *

FOLLOWING THE CALL, Nul leaned forward on the forecastle of the trawler as its bow descended into swells then rose on their successors. Alone, he summoned resources of self-control to counteract conflict in his soul. "You know what to do, Nul-boy," he chanted, "focus on the mission."

I must touch base with Chief to make arrangements.

Chapter 46

Aix en Provence, France
Next day

"WHY WOULD someone torture Navarro?" Anwatol Alzjar asked.

"It could only be punishment or to get information. But who it could be, I have no idea," Gordon Blair responded. The men sat in an arbor of Alzjar's vineyard surrounding the racecourse. The prince planned a heavy day of racing with the Grand Prix just two days away. His competition would be top drivers not qualifying for the actual race. These men and women came and went with elaborate explanations and security precautions, which were accepted as an element of the rich payments they received with special bonuses if their efforts were successful. They did not know the identity of whomever they were racing against. Alzjar's car had no numbers or identifying marks. He could have been any potential champion from a well-financed team.

"When there was no response to their door knocks or calls, Navarro's servants entered his chambers and discovered his body laying in his bed with a knife in his hand. His throat had been cut. It is unlikely he could have done it to himself," Blair explained.

"The servants called the senior security officer, who is our man of course." It was an element of Alzjar's extreme security arrangements. His anxiety had been that Navarro would betray them in some manner if the going got rough, as was likely to be the case at some point. The security detail had orders to eliminate the Don on command of Blair. Loss of the Don was of no concern to Alzjar. There had been no such arrangements for Copper Starr who was deeply compromised by his own double dealing with the U.S. government.

"Our people have contacted no one else and are holding the body awaiting my direction," Blair continued. "I got here as quickly as possible to report in person." It had taken about three hours by the time Blair departed from the Chief. *Elimination of the Don is good for me,* he initially thought. *Simplifies my goal to get out of this mess. I also need to take the children, but to where?* He needed to make logistical arrangements for a potential exchange as agreed with the Chief, or disposal if no head were delivered.

Mother will be perfect.

"Any idea of who would have the motive and skill to get through the Don's security?" Alzjar asked, pensively pondering the possibilities and any danger to himself.

"The obvious candidate would have been the Moran woman and the black person who has been with her. Thankfully, they were blown up in Repubblica," Blair responded, recalling that Chief Bearstrike had in no way contradicted the American Embassy press report that she had perished in the explosion.

I'll bet it was you, yourself, Blair thought looking at the prince, recalling his reaction to the news of Copper Starr. His only concern about Starr had been whether he knew anything that could compromise completion of the planned final stimulus injection.

I think the prince wants to begin eliminating anyone with connections to him. I could be next in line once the stimulus is released, letting the Queen's Trust twist in the spotlight of international fraud scrutiny. Alzjar does not know about Moran's records. I must find refuge before it is too late. An intelligence operative of the first order, Blair understood that Alzjar's demand for unconditional secrecy almost certainly meant that he was also under surveillance. There had been no sign of it in Paris or in the interim.

"It could also have been the Don's own group. They may have been ready for a change. Certainly, they would want no connection to the West Mad mess," Alzjar added.

"If that were the case then they would come after me next," Blair responded. "I was the person in contact with him."

Alzjar acknowledged the point with a smile and tip of his glass. "Fair point, speaking of which is anything missing from the Don's quarters, such as phones or files?"

"Yes, our security people advise that all phone lines were severed. His pagers and phones could not be located. Same with his tablet computer. There was a desktop machine, which is being examined. Files appear to have been downloaded onto a memory stick. There is also a safe. The door was open, files strewn around, so it will take time to decide if anything is missing. Navarro did not handle the details of anything," Blair explained.

"If he used those devices to speak with you, then whoever it is will have you in their sights. I will see to ramping up security around you."

Bloody hell! Blair reacted. "What about the body? Shall I have our team call the police? As you would expect, that office is in chaos from the events of the past few days, including the death of their chief and comrades in Repubblica."

Alzjar refilled his glass of mineral water, cutting slices of lime deliberately. With the citrus making bubbles, he stepped out onto a spacious balcony overlooking vineyards basking in early morning sunshine. He traced the rows with knowledgeable eyes, pleased with the growth of shooting vines.

"Prince, shall I leave you alone?" Sir Gordon asked.

"No, please join me," the reclusive entrepreneur responded. He saw the various aspects of his life that were causing anxiety, as if he were watching a series of videos. His mind moved from one to the other, mentally checking off where there were problems to be addressed. Preparations for the race were coming along as contemplated. *I am ready*, he knew.

The Washington lawyers and lobbyists had advised that the stimulus injection process had been reignited. Briefings from senior Treasury and Federal Reserve officials were positive.

Presidential news conference comments declared that it was time to invest again, and markets were responding in a consistent manner. Alzjar's positions were turning back into positive territory. *I need to continue shutting this thing down*, he thought watching Blair join him. *I will commence that process just after the race. It will not be the first time we have covered our tracks and taken a low profile as crisis defuses with the passage of time.*

"In Siena, the Don's palace is ancient. It is a fire just waiting to happen," Alzjar said, his mind turning to the track where engines could be heard coming to life. "OK?"

Blair nodded. *Clever. One more contagion will be lost in the chaos of Siena*, he thought, cringing at images of the Don's staff being incinerated along with the Don's tortured body.

"As to who could have had motive and access to Navarro, Prince, I have no idea unless it is his own people. What do you think?"

Interesting point, Alzjar thought. *The families behind him are connected in many ways to my own. Maybe something is going on that I am not aware of. Could they have made a decision to shut all of this away? If I were out of the way also, then . . . ? Hmmm. There are some discussions to be had.* His mind focused.

"Have the security team in the Siena palace complete the cleansing process and see if they can discover any hints. Please check in with your former MI5 and CIA colleagues to see if there is any word on the street. We will reconvene after the race," Alzjar directed.

His face turned toward the racecourse over several hills. Telltale noises of engines igniting adrenalin in his own system. *Race time!* Two former Monte Carlo champions were pitted against him for the day. A final set tomorrow. Existence of a replica of Monte Carlo periodically circulated in racing circles, as did rumors of wondrous new engines, turbochargers, or other devices providing competitive edge. Lips of the competitors who competed in these private events were sealed with the best control method possible—a lot of money.

The prince remained pensive, trying to find the way forward. His heart was in the race. His mind was in his responsibility to harvest another windfall of bailout money then proceed with the political agenda to return the civilized world to an appropriate social order, as intended by his ancestors prior to World War I.

Navarro must have used his phones to talk to many people. Someone got them. Maybe there is more here than just that widow? In any event, if they found Navarro they will find Blair. And from there, the path leads to me. There is not much time. The bailout will surely be released. The Washington lawyers seem confident. For what I pay the bastards, there should never have been any doubt. The race will be my crowning glory. First, champion of Monte Carlo. Then architect of the new world with the infidels' own money.

"I will take care of the children today," Blair added, feeling Alzjar drift away.

"The sooner the better."

Should I dump them and get away? Blair wondered on his way to the other side of the compound to wait for the call arranged by the Chief to confirm their existence.

Chapter **47**

Adriatic Sea off the coast of Italy

AT THE PRECISE time agreed upon, the radio phone chimed in the Captain's cabin. Father Michael still in the Outback had connected my friend Crystal Jamison from Greenwich and Chief Bearstrike, explaining that an arrangement may have been made to rescue Theo and Chrissy. Like everyone else in the world, she believed I had been killed. Crystal was delighted to confirm their identity. She also offered to raise Theo and Chrissy as her own children. Alice sat at my side. As if sensing my anxiety, she left her beloved perch by the radar mast atop the steer house where she could watch the fishing in all directions.

"Hello," Chief answered. "As we discussed, here is the friend who can identify the children, Crystal Jamison."

"Hello," Crystal said in a nervous voice. "I was a friend of the children's parents before they died."

"Why did your husband quit playing for the Jets?" Blair asked. Once Bearstrike had identified the friend, a complete background dossier had been assembled by Blair.

"His heart was punctured by broken ribs in a game," she answered. I could sense surprise in her voice at such a specific question.

"Theo, Mrs. Crystal Jamison wants to talk to you," Blair could be heard saying, apparently handing the phone to my son. I tried to imagine it being just another day at home watching Crystal greet Theo and Chrissy walking in the door from school, as she often did when I had other commitments.

"Miss Crystal?" Theo asked.

"Yes, Theo, it's me. How are you?"

"Are my parents with you?"

"No, honey, they are traveling right now. I will be taking care of you."

"Mr. Blair said they were close by, that we had visited," Theo responded, confused by what Blair had explained and the words of Crystal.

"I'm sure he is right, honey," Crystal answered, obviously unaware of Theo's explanation. I had no idea what they were talking about, understanding the only critical element to be the children's health.

"It's always fun with you and Mr. Jamison. Are you going to come get us?"

"I will, honey. Who made the winning hit in your last Wiffle ball game?"

"That's silly," the boy protested, his mind taken off fears of the moment. It was his neighbor's voice. "I hit a home run."

"How many strikes in the count?"

"Two, don't you remember?"

"I do. Who was pitching?"

"My mom, she almost struck me out," he answered in a voice showing the strain of having been awakened from drug-induced sleep. I clutched Alice with the other hand over my mouth. I wanted to grab the phone and jump through the line. *It is my baby!*

"Are you OK, Theo?"

"Yes, but we want to come home."

"Is Chrissy there?"

"Yes, here," he answered. The pause seemed like an eternity. Alice licked the sweat on my hand.

"Hello?"

"Hi, sweetheart. It's Miss Crystal. Your voice sounds wonderful. Where are you?"

"At a resort with a beautiful swimming pool. Are you coming here?" she asked in an eerily calm voice.

"Do you have your teddy bear, Chrissy?"

"No, she is at home."

"What is her name?"

"Scrunchy?"

"Who bought her for you?"

"Mr. Jamison did. He took us to Build-a-Bear with Grandpa. We made him when I was little, at Christmastime."

I nodded to Nul, tears streaming down my face.

"Why did you call him Scrunchy, honey?"

"Because that's what Grandpa called me. He went to Jesus just after that. He loved me. I cried and cried. Don't you remember?" I had to bury my face in Nul's shoulder to silence emotions in me waiting to erupt.

"I do. When did you last see me, honey?"

"We were getting ready for the Native American dancers and

fireworks. Daddy was coming home later. Then we kept waking up in hospital rooms. There's a nice man here taking care of us. He says you're coming to take us home. Is Mommy with you?"

"No, honey, she's traveling with your Dad. I will be there as soon as I can," Crystal answered, obviously not wanting to tell her that Trevor and I were dead.

"Please hurry. We want to go home."

"Can you hand the phone back to the woman?"

Chrissy giggled. "It's a man, Mrs. Jamison, can't you tell?"

"Satisfied?" Blair asked.

They were not fearful, so this man must not be abusing them.

"Yes," Chief answered. "We will proceed as agreed, correct?"

"Affirmative," was the response as connection terminated.

Emotion stifled throughout the call could be contained no more. Nul held me patiently as my dam broke.

"Thank you," I said simply when I was ready, patting his knee and looking into eyes full of care. "I owe you and the Chief all of our lives, and my friend Crystal as well. I hope I will be able to thank them all personally."

"The helicopter will be here within minutes," he answered, pulling away. "There is nothing you need to take. Anloc and Lanh will come with us," he said. Alice trotted across the cabin, pushing the door open.

Tenderness of the night is gone, flickered across my mind, easily lost in the glow from the sounds of their voices ringing in my head. The task ahead seemed insignificant in comparison to the treasure that awaited success.

Chapter 48

Monte Carlo
Next day, night before the race

PRINCE ANWATOL ALZJAR stood patiently behind a public craps table in the elegant Monte Carlo Casino. On this evening, he had no interest in the private rooms above where he was well known or the elegant female escorts awaiting his arrival. There would be no famous movie stars or singers on this night.

He arrived at the sprawling gardens of the casino driving his unique red Ferrari through admiring tourists and race fans. Casino Square's breathtaking beauty was framed by elegant buildings with iconic towers and domes. Originally designed in the nineteenth century, by the designer of the Paris Opera House for Princess Caroline to save the House of Grimaldi from bankruptcy, it felt like his own enclave. Around the circular driveway, past the Hôtel de Paris, then stopping at the sweeping central stairs, he would be greeted by the liveried doorman as Henré Tremont. The world famous grand prix driver paused to greet his public. He enjoyed posing with tourists for pictures and signing photos and autograph books.

His thoughts were far away. Upon return from a victorious practice run at the faux race course late in the afternoon, his investment team had breached his request for solitude to brief him on mounting losses. Investments had been structured to coincide with the anticipated release of stimulus by the Americans, as originally projected by Copper Starr before his suicide and updated by top Washington advisors. Anticipated gains were to be taken as the capitalist system was driven into apocalypse. His end game had been in sight. Losses had started several days earlier and were accelerating.

"Movements against your positions seem to be the mirror of your own strategy," the senior trader advised. A Ph.D. student at Princeton with Alzjar some twenty years earlier, he understood the prince's lives. His service had generated a personal fortune for which he was devoted and grateful. "It is as if someone knows exactly what you are doing and placing bets that there will be no stimulus, even though all public and private signals indicate that the train is on the tracks and headed downhill. These bets are massive. Except for us, markets are still skeptical, due in part to the sudden change of direction in Washington."

"It is just an anomaly and will not persist," Alzjar confidently dismissed the observation.

"Sir, not only have these losses persisted for several days, they are accelerating."

The image of loss forming like an iceberg beneath the ocean surface had occupied his consciousness as the helicopter brought him to his Monaco villa overlooking the yacht basin adjacent to the Grimaldi palace. His plan had been to relax and prepare for the race, his passion since a second place finish a year earlier. Victories in other circuits had only whetted his voracious appetite. Final termination of the Moran threat had cleared a major cloud from his horizon. Others quickly formed. Need to eliminate any connection to Blair and the queen was one. Losses and uncertainty as to their source was another, for which he was accountable to his even more opaque family. An image of a battlefield was framing in his mind. Friendly troops were placed to make a frontal assault on an enemy. On one flank appeared a small unit of attackers. By itself, it was like a mosquito landing on a rampaging elephant, barely an irritant. On the other was a taunting adversary just beyond his reach.

Who is it? First they dispatched Starr, then Navarro. Were the Moran woman and her friend with that adversary? These losses, how can they be happening? What am I missing? Is it my own people, paving the way for a new steward?

Gorgeous women of the evening stood nearby in utter elegance. Bathed in admiration of men crowding around the craps table, their eyes were on Tremont. They were accustomed to taking his arm as he entered. His fame for lavish pay was exceeded only by his capacity to love all night.

A stunning beauty took position with dice at the opposite end of the table. An elegant red dress, embroidered with the distinctive trim colors of his car #1 screamed for attention. Auburn hair bounced around the shoulders of the Asian beauty, whose exotic coloring and features defied easy identification of ancestry as she leaned forward to clasp the dice. Tremont peered through a corset supporting beautiful, alabaster breasts as if for his own consumption. Standing, she kissed the dice and proclaimed the numbers. Winking at Tremont, she threw them toward the velvet wall under his hands. Bouncing true, they came to rest with the proclaimed digits. Shouts erupted around the table, led by the dazzling damsel, who repeated the process as well lubricated celebrants pushed ever larger stacks of chips to the spots she broadcast. On each occasion, a silent pause ensued as the dice made their trek, coming to rest in a cacophony of delirious gamblers raking in their earnings. Tremont became entranced. Soon enough, she was at his side with drinks in hand. He joined in the revelry. Winning accelerated. Hugs and kisses accompanied a steady flow of crystal glasses filled with vodka, ice, and a clear fluid. Cigar smoke added to the ambiance.

Group hysteria and playful fingers had their desired effects. Tactical view of his flanks dissolved in anticipation of a feast. Feverish bettors cheered the Asian beauty on with Tremont at her side, surrounded by beautiful people. "Is she African or Vietnamese?" Bettors and gawkers asked. "Kinda old isn't she for Tremont?"

As the penultimate time arrived, all chips were on the table.

Clasping his hands to her magnificent buttocks and pulling him close, her bulging corset pressing against his chest, she focused on the dice and sweaty hands. "My karma," she whispered in his ear with a quick lick for luck. It worked. Winnings and tips from happy bettors erupted like the cascading fountains in the gardens outside.

At the edge of the crowd, a man moved slowly making sure all evolved smoothly. Had anyone noticed, he would have been dismissed as an element of strict casino security. Anloc's son Tran was on duty, as were a few others performing their own roles. His mother's performance would be saluted in the privacy of La Namviette.

M-m-m-m, Tremont thought, following the sway of the winner's luscious hips to cash in her basket full of chips. In his suite overlooking the race course and yacht basin, he beamed anticipating his triumph the next afternoon as she beckoned from the round bed.

Chapter 49

Race day

THE RACECOURSE for the Grand Prix de Monaco was bathed in bright May sunshine, a perfect day for racing at the pinnacle of the sport. Spectators crowded aprons of the straightaways and steep turns of the circuit laid out on streets of the steep hills of the elegant city. Continuous elevation changes and tight corners, as well as a tunnel, made it one of the most demanding tracks in Formula One. In spite of relatively low average speeds, due to the nature of the circuit, it was easily the most dangerous place to race in the world. It taunted the sleek racing machines and their drivers

to accelerate then brake in hairpin turns, straightaways, picturesque avenues, and around the yacht basin into the hills fighting
for position. Many lives had been lost in the process, each adding
to the glamour and popularity of the event.

Attendance required purchase of extraordinarily expensive
packages for the four days of race festivities plus hotel accommo-
dations. Practice sessions were followed by preliminary races and
qualifying heats. On race day, there had been two prior events and
a parade of drivers. Pageantry and excitement filled the air. Every
seat and even standing room space was filled. Balconies and rooftops with a view of the spectacle were jammed, accompanied by
a global radio and television audience. Bands played and refresh-
ment flowed. Cheering crowds were ready for a spectacle.

Deep-throated bellows of powerful engines reverberated like
earthquake tremors. There would be no place in the principality
where one could escape their bass rumble and treble at maximum
acceleration. Multi-million-dollar rockets on wheels were rolled out
of pit lane. Drivers were primed for the starter's gun. Spectators
streamed from expensive yachts at basin moorings. Others relaxed
with a first-row view of the straightaway along the water. They were
impervious to any sense of danger from flying cars or broken parts.
On two occasions, racers had flown off the track and into the harbor.

Pre-race parties had produced a near universal haze of giddy
feeling. Royalty was nothing special in this milieu, nor were movie
stars and wannabes of all sorts and pedigrees. This was IT! The
Monaco Grand Prix.

On the pole was the custom-built and designed red Ferrari
driven by Henré Tremont bearing #1 on its engine hood and rear
deck. The famous playboy's adoring public was present in force
to cheer his every move. The apparently shy man had, throughout his storied career, declined interviews or personal appearances
of any kind, preferring to allow achievement on the track to speak
for itself. He disappeared after every race, adding to his glamour
and allure. "Why is Henré so distant?" was the common headline

of tabloids following racing and European society events. Pictures of him with bejeweled beautiful ladies, some of royal linage and many of cinematic fame, created the image of a flesh-and-blood James Bond.

KA-WHAMM! the starter's gun exploded when the checkered flag fell from its perch. Engines roared, tires spun with sudden torque, exhaust and pieces of hot rubber filled the air as the pack jockeyed for position in the short space for acceleration before the sharp right hand turn at Virage St. Devote. Red #1 was in second place coming into the most dangerous point in the circuit. As the leader swung a little left to make the turn, its right rear tire was bumped just enough by red #1 to push it into the runoff area and out of the race. The driver lost control hitting a retaining wall. It burst into flames adding to the excitement of a crowd already at fever pitch.

With the initial leader out of the way, Tremont accelerated up the long incline and through gears opened a distance between him and the pack. At Casino Square, he twisted between the Hôtel de Paris and the Casino where he had held court the evening before. He momentarily recalled the sunrise in the morning when he was greeted by his dice-throwing paramour of the night. Ready with champagne and lust, the Vietnamese mixed-race beauty provided a joyful means of awakening for what Tremont anticipated to be the crowning glory of his life. *His energy needs to be injected into me,* she thought, understanding her role.

Heading down the straightaway toward the Hôtel Mirabeau, he geared down to gracefully fly into the hairpin and sharp right turn, then twisting again at the fountains of Virage du Portier and its tunnel. Shrouded in darkness for a few moments, Tremont pushed the throttle full open slamming his head back against its harness for the gentle curve around the marina. Speed approached two hundred miles per hour as the spectacular yachts and beautiful people were lost in full concentration on maximum thrust, as he had practiced at Aix en Provence so often. Anxieties of the evening before had been lost in the arms of the dice throwing friend he planned to meet again for celebration, perhaps even staying in the public eye to celebrate his triumph. Adrenalin merely added fuel to the fire in his spirit. Nothing occupied his consciousness beyond winning.

Slowing down for the sharp, quick turn at the Chicane, Henré hewed to the perfect line to avoid losing any time for unnecessary braking. Such was not the fortune of the two cars just behind, both of which over-braked, slamming into unforgiving barriers in another spectacular crash in a race to be littered with an unusually large series of such disasters. Shrieks of burned spectators and emergency vehicles were lost in the cacophony of the race.

Tremont easily turned through the hairpin at Virage Pascasse, just away from the palace and its historic gardens. Taking the sharp right turn at the Virage Noghes, he saw the signal on the board from his crew that he was in front by a few seconds, a huge amount in this race.

Stay on pace! he coached himself, completing the first lap and beginning the process all over again. He saw the remains of the initial leader beyond the first turn. Any guilt about forcing the wreck was lost, as was the knowledge that he had done it in such a subtle manner that no flags had been raised to slow the race or invoke a penalty.

Millions of Euros were at stake, as prizes and investments. Towering egos of all participants were also on the line. It was the event of the year in Monte Carlo. The Royal family was in place cheering their neighbor and frequent quest. Excitement boiled in the heat of the day as the race progressed.

Red #1 led throughout and stretched the lead continuously heading into the last few laps. Victory was in sight. "Go Henré!" echoed through the racecourse. As the leader flew up the incline to Casino Square, he completed another lap of the field. His lead continued to grow. Like a fighter plane, #1 was ready to transcend the pavement.

"He runs this course as if he practiced here every day," commentators marveled. "There are no signs of brakes even on the steep turns. He must be able to handle everything with gears. He has been the best driver in the world. He deserves this triumph!"

Approaching the Casino Square, red #1 came upon an English racing green Lotus #48 piloted by a British driver lucky enough to qualify for the last spot in the field. Tremont paid it no attention beyond measuring the space on the inside to lap the flunky. So far behind the field was #48 that there had been several car lengths of open space, allowing #1 to accelerate past a few remaining cars with thundering booms assaulting thousands of ears in its wake. As #1 came upon #48, the Englishman seemed to lose control drifting to the right and into the path of #1. Tremont hit his brakes, veering as well, almost hitting a sidewall.

"Damnation!" he screamed, slowing to not lose control as he came into the sharp turns approaching Virage du Portier. Adjusting, he accelerated close to the slow #48 as they approached the tunnel. Once in the open, he could recover time in the gentle curve then straightaway along the yacht basin. Hundreds of rich patrons sitting on every available space of world class boats adorning the water's edge anticipated emergence of the sleek #1 racer from the tunnel flying toward victory. There would be many toasts as he flew by.

"Fucker!" Tremont screamed, as #48 forced him to slow down even more than the hairpin turns would normally require for him to navigate. He could not push against the tire of #48 in that space. Such a touch would be obvious at the slower speed required to navigate the hairpin turns of Virage du Portier. A detected violation would cost a precious time penalty, maybe even disqualification at this point in the race. "Sonofabitch, get outta my way!" he screamed into the microphone in his helmet. There was nothing his pit could do. Tremont anxiously awaited the open space beyond the tunnel.

Exiting the last twist at Virage du Portier, #48 obligingly moved to the right allowing enough space for Tremont to accelerate. Turbochargers throbbed as the mixture of aviation fuel and oxygen surged the light frame of #1 forward on the waterside of #48. Tremont had just this one hurdle to pass, then two more simple laps to victory.

The tunnel acted like a giant amplifier to magnify the sound of the engines in maximum acceleration again. Racers were wheel-to-wheel with just inches separating red-hot rubber of their tires. Nul, who had taken the place of the British driver, guided #48 carefully with the experience of a lifetime playing specific roles on impossible missions. *Just a few more meters*, he thought. His car flew forward as sunshine at the end of the tunnel bathed the road in bright light.

Flying out of the darkness like bullets from guns, the dueling drivers became blinded for a moment by intense light. "#1 = NO STIMULUS!" read signs held aloft on either side of the road by Vietnamese people. The garish red and orange signs distracted Tremont for a moment.

#48 accelerated just enough so its left-front wheel approached the right front of #1. So intent was Tremont on the cars in front and the words on the sign that he did not feel the touch.

"There!" Nul knew twisting his steering to port, lodging his tire inside the wheel of #1. Ready to push left with maximum thrust, Nul looked up to confirm that he had picked the point where spectators on the yachts should be safe.

SCREECH—KABANG! erupted as red #1 slammed into the concrete wall causing its velocity to stall. Pressure from a still accelerating #48 pushed it upward to the point that it crashed through the concrete barriers to soar like an eagle. #48 was just behind. The airborne vehicles rose, then descended quickly to the harbor below. The million-dollar machines began breaking up with fiery parts flying in all directions as high octane fuel ignited.

Incendiary explosions transfixed the global audience awaiting emergence of the leader from the tunnel for triumphant final laps. Helicopter spotters following the race diverted to the explosions as talking heads tried to explain what happened to the leader of the race, the famous recluse Henré Tremont. Cameras had been trained on #1 for his moment of triumph, so the debacle was broadcast live throughout the world.

Emergency teams were activated as the race was stopped. A collective hush settled over the race course as word spread. Media helicopters were diverted to cover the spectacle, but held at a distance as emergency police and medical crews took control.

Fires were extinguished with a sizzle as the parts splashed into the water. Tubs of racer cockpits floated for moments then sank as rushing water expelled oxygen. The protective sheath for drivers was designed for collision, not plunging into water.

Chapter 50

Monaco Yacht Basin

MY HEART pounded hearing sounds of collision far above. I sat on a wave runner well away from the expected point of impact. *Amazing!* I thought, watching the cars soar then fall.

Nul was not sure his plan would work.

I looked for my hero, but could see nothing beyond the falling racers against the background of the concrete pillars under the road beyond the tunnel. We waited, like spectators on other boats and water craft, in a slip between another yacht, hopefully hidden from view.

I moved the sleek craft forward to get within about fifty yards. Other boats arranged by Nul were all around, blending into the collage of spectators for the race in every part of the basin. Our water craft had been rented from a local shop and blended into the crowded harbor. Anloc's sons and I practiced our approach in the days before the race.

I affixed an oxygen device in my mouth and adjusted my goggles as I slid off the seat and over the side. The water was murky. Fortunately, the sizzling steel provided a target to guide my descent. I could only see one chassis. I was confident it was Tremont. Nul would land further forward. Other divers would be attending to him.

Tran and his brother swam at my side as remains of the wreck settled into the muck of the bottom. They held dim lights to provide illumination. I took the heavy knife from my belt. The driver was wearing a red suit not green.

Good, not Nul.

He was struggling to get free from the harness, oxygen bubbles marked the draining of his strength and life in fighting to get free. I grabbed hold of his helmet as Tran smashed in the visor. His fight ceased for moments. Holding onto the back of his headgear, I cut the oxygen and communication lines as I had been coached to do. With gloves on my hands, I was able to hold tightly with no concern about sharp edges of the smashed plastic or jagged steel.

Oxygen escaping from the supply tube created a surreal ambiance. It also seemed to revive the struggling driver. I stood on the steel frame to push him down. The man leaned his head back to look at me through the shattered visor. Bubbles escaped from his mouth as if he were trying to say something with an outstretched hand.

I put the knife in his field of vision. Terror in his eyes felt good all through me. The plan had been to slice his throat to commence the task of cutting through his neck. Instead, I stabbed the blade into his eye socket. *This is for Theo, you asshole!* I twisted it as a trail of blood rose toward me.

I did the same to the other eye. *For Chrissy, whoever you are. I hope you rot in your hell for eternity.*

His hand rose trying to protect himself, but did not get far. I jerked his helmet as far back as possible.

And this is for my Trevor.

I pulled the razor sharp blade across his throat. It cut easily enough until striking spinal bone. I sawed away patiently. Blood in the water became a cloud, obliterating whatever vision had been possible. It was like another explosion. I held my grip. "I must do this," I had said during our training, as Nul and the boys insisted that I stay back and let them do what they assumed would be a job far too gruesome for me.

There! I thought, feeling the head come free in an ever more intense red cloud. I extracted a bag tucked into my waist band and fitted the head with helmet into it, unable to actually see anything for the red haze. We knew that sharks would be attracted. We also knew that we had only moments before emergency crews would descend seeking to recover the drivers. Of course, we could hear nothing underwater.

Anloc's boys took my arms to propel me back in the direction we had come. A diving boat waited a slight distance away with a bay that we could crawl into without having to breach the surface. Cameras were expected to be following every detail of what would become, if we were successful, the sports story of the century: "World Champion Decapitated in the Water."

* * *

"You are Mr. Blair?" I asked the man waiting when we emerged. As soon as we were on board, the yacht slowly began moving. The normally peaceful marina was pure chaos with emergency boats descending from every direction on the crash site. Divers were soon in the water hoping to save the drivers.

Nul was not onboard. He will take care of himself, I thought watching the man who had power to release Theo and Chrissy.

Another man stood nearby. He looked to be in his seventies. Thin and handsome with long grey hair tied in a bun behind his head. He watched passively. Blair took the bag to a table. He extracted the head and placed it on towels. The disgusting site did not even register in me. My only feeling was a little curiosity and a lot of impatience. The helmet was pried off slimy, wet hair.

We all cringed at the site of the severed head, with eyes hanging from their sockets. Blood oozed from each of the wounds, soaking the towel. As we prepared, I had seen pictures of Henré Tremont. The grotesque chunk of gristle and blood looked nothing like the suave hero. Blair wiped the face with a clean towel. Squatting to look the thing straight on, he pushed the hair over the temples back looking for a mark of some kind.

"That's it," he said with his fingers on scars on both sides, which looked like plastic surgery incisions. He stood and turned to me.

"You did this easily enough, madam," he said looking me over.

He does not know who I am.

It had not occurred to me that it was not relevant to him, even if I were not known to be dead. My identity made no difference at that point.

"Is it him?" the grey haired man asked.

"Yes, Chief, it is Alzjar."

Chief Bearstrike! my mind screamed, recognizing the man I had not seen since a college visit with his daughter, Clemenca. I wanted to hold and thank him, knowing that he, like Nul, was responsible for the potential recovery of my children. But I could say nothing.

"The children, where are they?" Chief asked.

Blair explained where they were being held. I looked up into the steep hills over Monaco. "My mother is with them," he said. "When you want them released, just press this button," he said handing Chief what looked like a garage door opener. "She will wait and go with your officers as we agreed."

Our boat crept toward the far end of Monaco, close to the amphitheater where I had attended concerts with Trevor.

After Blair was taken below decks, the man with a pony tail held out his arms. "Jaspar, it is nice to meet you again."

"Oh, Chief Bearstrike, I . . ."

"Go now for your children, we will have time for all this," he said as if there was some future that he had in mind.

Chapter 51

Ezé, France

I RAN WITH every ounce of strength in my soul.

When our escape boat docked, a motorcycle was waiting to take Lanh and me to our destination. Blair's instructions were to go to Ezé, high above the ocean floor. We rode for almost an hour to avoid the normally impassable congestion from streets blocked for the race, as well as the problems created by emergency vehicles trying to reach the crash site. Anxious and animated spectators flooded the entire area.

At the base of the Ezé public area, I pressed the button on the device as Blair had instructed. "They will be at the crescent of a stone path leading up the hill," he said. There was only one path, carefully constructed from what appeared to be flat field stones winding around the steep hillside.

Up the narrow, medieval streets I flew, ignoring burning thighs and pounding heart. "Theo!" Chrissy!" I screamed with hands at my mouth for whatever amplification could occur on the steep hillside surrounded by stone buildings and a weekend touristy crowd on the path. With emotions in overload, I was beyond tears or fear. I would have run through the stone walls.

"Mommy, Mommy," their voices answered in the distance, as the two young souls ran down the path from the famous Château de la Chèvre d'or restaurant. They had watched the race far below, having no idea what was going on, until Sir Gordon Blair's mother pointed them in the direction I was coming.

"Your mother is coming up this path. Go to her now," she said, kissing each on their head as they walked cautiously away from the strange place. When they heard my voice and their names floating upward, they broke into their own run.

We collided in mid-air. Grasping for one another we fell onto the stones of the ancient walkway.

"Oh my God, thank you!" I beseeched the Lord, holding my precious Theo and Chrissy. Bleeding cuts on my knees, like the blood of Alzjar/Tremont, meant nothing. I was home, at last!

Chapter 52

La Namviette, Italy
Ten days later

ANLOC BROUGHT us to the vineyard in the hills of Tuscany. It was a private and peaceful environment to recover from the traumas we had experienced. It had been almost three months, during which our world had changed in unimaginable ways. The children were desperate for affection, as was I.

"Where is Daddy?" they asked and asked. I was so caught up in happiness for their survival and company, I simply said he would be along. When I could postpone the discussion no longer, I explained as patiently as possible. I had buried my own grief at his loss after their kidnapping by escaping from Greenwich, followed by, what I knew to be in hindsight, training and preparation in the

Outback for our mission. Once we got to Rome, the whirlwind of our campaign left no time to experience the loss of my soul mate.

We grieved together. Alice became a pillar. She weathered all the hugs, sitting with each of us for hours at a time. She seemed to understand the needs of people saddened by loss and joyful for reunion.

When alone, my thoughts often turned to Nul. We had become so close in our joint mission. "When he was pulled from the water, Chief Bearstrike had another mission," Anloc explained. "As you went to Ezé, he was taken to Nice, and a private jet whisked him away."

"When will he return?"

"You know that he works in his own way. He will come when he is done, as always."

Hidden away in the lush vineyard, I consciously wanted to know nothing about what was transpiring in the world at large or in the aftermath of the Grand Prix crash. When fleeting thoughts passed through my mind about the investigations surely underway by Monte Carlo and French detectives, I was strong enough to push them away. Not the global media. The headless torso of the famous driver created a firestorm of attention and global media speculation.

"Who could have carried off such an atrocity?"

"Why?"

"Is it some kind of terrorism?"

On the other hand, memories of the grotesque head severed with my hands made me smile. It was a memory that would never leave my consciousness.

I did wonder if anyone would connect it to the West Mad scandal. Or, if the denouement of the quest of Alzjar and Chief Bearstrike's work had as yet improved economic conditions. Those thoughts also passed quickly from my thoughts.

In the peacefulness of being together, I steeled myself to not think about Nul. We had been in near constant company for almost three months. The training, mission, camaraderie, and shared experience drew us close, I believed. My resolve failed. "Does he miss☐or love me?" I asked Alice when alone. She licked my face. Anxiety, gratitude, and affection for him lay unrequited in the joy of being with Theo and Chrissy. I was determined to control my emotions, confident that he must feel the same. A lot had happened in a short period.

It was best that we be apart and let the intensity of our emotions find its natural rhythm.

"Where is he?" I would ask Alice. The calm dog responded with tilted head and contentment on her face.

What does she know that I don't?

Theo and Chrissy enjoyed the sunshine and fresh air of the vineyards. There were many children living in nearby areas. They flocked to the vineyard. We all made as much of the situation as possible.

As the days rolled on, it was not enough. We all needed the familiarity of home and family. Even my thoughts of Nul grew distant.

What do I really feel now that the fear and trauma of our battles recede?

* * *

ANLOC AND I sat on the patio in the late afternoon. The children were playing down the hillside. We discussed what I would do, since the world assumed I was dead and Theo and Chrissy kidnapped. Our rescue was known only to Nul, the Army, Chief Bearstrike, and President Henrichs. "We will decide about the future when the time is right," I told myself. Frankly, I had no idea what to do. It was all so ambiguous and confusing. I often asked Anloc about Nul's current mission, which seemed to be dragging on. I missed his reassuring presence.

"Your friend Crystal asks Chief about the children," Anloc

said. "To see if she needs to come get them. As you know, she offered to raise them."

I nodded. *What will I do?*

Anloc seemed anxious. She often looked down the hillside toward the distant road. I assumed she was watching the children. They were playing hide and seek with a bunch of kids who lived nearby, as Alice, on guard as always, lay under a tree keeping a watchful eye on them.

Anloc had wasted no time integrating us into the community, especially their church. We were welcomed with warmth by the members, reflecting affection for their Vietnamese neighbors. Anloc stood, as well as I, seeing a car wind its way down the long, sandy road leading to the vineyard. I watched the SUV stop just outside the white fence along the road, which turned up the hill, guiding entrance to the compound. A man got out.

It was Nul. He stepped over the fence and began walking through the rows of vines in the opposite direction from us and the children.

"What is he doing," I asked. Anloc just held my arm.

"Go to him," she said, looking over my shoulder. "I will watch the children. Go to the tractor barn."

"Why doesn't he just come here?"

"Just go," she said. "Hurry."

I began running and covered the hundred or so yards in a flash, weaving through gates and around equipment.

My trusty guide and friend stood by a tractor, leaning on a tire of almost equal height.

I slowed, trying to calm a racing heart. He came toward me with open arms. His embrace was comforting. Placing his hands on my shoulders, he pushed me gently back and placed a finger to my lips.

"You look relaxed, Jas. The Italian countryside has been good for you."

I tried to respond. His finger pressed.

"Do not speak, just listen."

I nodded with faith.

"Trevor is alive."

My heart stopped as his words tried to communicate understanding to my brain. Emotional overload made it impossible to comprehend.

"Yes, it is so. I have been in contact with Chief Bearstrike and others responsible for trying to save his life."

He steadied me with strong arms as my knees began to buckle. "Alive?" I finally asked as he sat me on the edge of a workbench. "Yes. It is a long story. I wanted to meet you here because your children must not know just yet. He is in good hands, but may not survive."

"I want to go . . ."

"No. You must stay here," Nul said firmly. "I will keep you advised through Anloc. I must go now. And, God willing, when I return, Trevor will be with me."

I could not respond.

Lifting my hand, Nul slipped something over my wrist, and then lifted it for me to see. A tiny Formula 1 racer atop a silver bangle sparkled in the sunshine. "My gift of thanks," he said gently kissing my forehead.

I bowed my head in prayer trying to speak but words would not come. *Of thanks?* I wondered watching him turn and walk away. *But I owe him.*

Knowing Trevor may survive, my mind shifted back to what the future might hold for our family—and for us. Our lives had been forever transformed. *I am not the wife my husband left behind and never will be again. Will he accept the woman I have become? What will he be like? Can we pick up the pieces of our former life?*

Standing, I must have been transfixed watching the car head back toward Ratta and beyond. My fingers were touched by wet warmth. Then a bite.

"Alice!" I exclaimed, kneeling to hug my friend. Her affection continued on my face. Holding her head in shaking hands, I peered into calm, loving eyes focused on me with only adoration. I felt it in my soul.

Suddenly, anxiety invaded her peacefulness, Alice looked around, as if answering a call from another realm. Then took off.

"Nul?" I asked, returning my gaze to the road. He was gone. Just a whisp of dust rising in the air.

"Dear Lord," I began a prayer, kneeling with a hand on the tractor tire. *He was distant on the boat and in race prep. He must have known of Trevor. He stood back. With love so great as to pave the way for him to return if he survived. Nul loves me that much!*

"Can I survive without you, my Nul?" I asked, looking into the sky.

"You fulfilled his need, child. As he did for you. Let him go, now." I closed my eyes, feeling fulfillment in the words of comfort. I looked up at the sky. The voice was so familiar.

"You became a warrior, you are a hero, Jaspar, now move on."

Huh? My mind froze, familiar images invading the loneliness of Nul's withdrawal. Love still surrounded me. I stood on the tractor with my arms folded imaging what was in front of us. It must have been for many minutes, as I felt peaceful.

"Mom look!"

"Theo has a new pet," Chrissy said, tugging at my jeans.

Turning to release my gaze on the road and thoughts of my assassin, my other world awaited.

Theo held a puppy. Chrissy's hands were with her brother's.

"I . . . I . . . ," emerged from my stammering lips. "What is its name?"

"We named her *A4*," Theo said with pride holding the newborn out to me.

"*WOOOOF*," came from the direction of the barn.

I looked up to see Chief Bearstrike carrying the proud mother. My warrior champion was now a mother. Sunlight reflected in

Alice's eyes. Beacons of pride. As always, she declared the emotion each of us felt in our own ways.

Trevor? I wondered. *Will you be here?*

"Mom?" Theo asked, holding A4 up to me.

I could only look from one of my family to the next. There were no words in me.

My prayers? I thought. *They're all answered.*

Instinct lifted my eyes to the sky to express humbled thanks.

My roo friends from the Outback sat there as if on a cloud. Onur, Yueci, Zeki, and Cari beamed a pride of their own. Ismerelda was with them. The world around me was a haze. The sky looked so real, so vibrant, as had the dreams invading my soul so often in our war, portending the future.

"Mom?"

My thoughts were in that other dimension. He was falling. From the Vatican. A cliff in Tuscany. A burning racer in Monte Carlo. Gunfire and explosions erupted around him. In the Pope's Garden, on the bridge, the streets of Siena, and Repubblica, *Nul? What of you? What of us? Is there room?*

I lifted A4. The newborn puppy nestled in my hands. Touching her to my cheek, she made a faint noise. Lifting her little, sweet face to my ear, it was louder.

"Time will tell all, Jas."

Acknowledgements

JASPAR'S WAR is a community project. Good or bad, it arose from many sources. My son Thomas Lowell offered initial comments and encouragement. Christy and Byron Bright were believers. Christy has become an expert fiction blogger and social media expert in the process. She also led me to the *Buz-z-z* class of best-selling author MJ Rose, who saw something in the early manuscript. In turn, MJ led me to Kristen Weber who offered 26 single-spaced pages of plot suggestions (which she said was a pat on the back). Christy then introduced me to Meryl Moss of Meryl Moss Media Relations, Inc. Meryl has designed a wonderful media campaign. Carole Claps has become collaborator-in-chief. JeriAnn Geller has added final polish.

My friend and best-selling author, Jon Land, encouraged me with his own warrior Caitlin Strong and counsel of patience and persistence to develop my skills as a writer. Childhood friend, Joel Herskowtiz, read earlier work and gave thumbs-up. Roya Sayadi asked many questions about emotion, teaching me the importance of being in tune with what my characters feel. Longtime client and friend Mike Kimps offered critical comment as the final draft evolved. Encouragement of my daughters Whitney Whitehead and Susannah Lowell has been constant. Patricia Hackett has been with me for well over 30 years, providing even more encouragement. Haiyan Zhang makes graphics into art.

ACKNOWLEDGEMENTS

Grandchildren are too young to do more than love me, which is all I need.

My long-gone running dog, Winnifred, taught me what a faithful dog could bring to any situation. She was my Alice.

Finally, Jaspar Moran is in each of us. She became a warrior for her own destiny, as must we all in our own way.

A NOTE ABOUT THE AUTHOR

CYM LOWELL was born in Montana to academics and spent his youth traveling the world. To put it politely, he was an undistinguished student, rewarded with assignment to the U.S. Navy at 18. After two years in Vietnam, college and law school were a challenge. Being a veteran in the political turbulence of the late 1960s and early 1970s taught humility. Raising three children in the Midwest and Texas brought love and responsibility. An international tax practice in the financial crises of the past 40 years provided insight into motivations of actors on the global stage. Friends, clients, adversaries, and colleagues, like victory and defeat, added color and context. The result is a writer with a treasure trove of experience to frame compelling characters enmeshed in heart-thumping challenges.

CPSIA information can be obtained at www.ICGtesting.com
Printed in the USA
LVOW08s1413270514

387421LV00001B/1/P